"What do you want from m

"A kiss. That's all." He shifted to nuzzle her neck. "Just a kiss."

"I don't—"

"Trust me, Callie. I won't ever ask for more than you're willing to give."

Trust? Fane would tell her that she was crazy. That she couldn't trust anyone.

Especially not a norm who all but accused the Mave of being willing to harbor a murderer.

But just for a few minutes she didn't want to be a necromancer who was feared and even hated by others. Or the shy woman who often faded into the shadows.

And more importantly, she wanted to kiss this man.

"Okay."

The word had barely formed before he covered her lips in a kiss that seared her to the tips of her toes . . .

BORN *IN* BLOOD

ALEXANDRA IVY

ZEBRA BOOKS
KENSINGTON PUBLISHING CORP.

http://www.kensingtonbooks.com

ZEBRA BOOKS are published by

Kensington Publishing Corp.
119 West 40th Street
New York, NY 10018

All Kensington titles, imprints, and distributed lines are available at special quantity discounts for bulk purchases for sales promotion, premiums, fund-raising, educational, or institutional use.

Special book excerpts or customized printings can also be created to fit specific needs. For details, write or phone the office of the Kensington Special Sales Manager: Attn. Special Sales Department. Kensington Publishing Corp., 119 West 40th Street, New York, NY 10018. Phone: 1-800-221-2647.

Zebra and the Z logo Reg. U.S. Pat. & TM Off.

ISBN-13: 978-1-4201-2514-6
ISBN-10: 1-4201-2514-1
First Printing: January 2014

eISBN-13: 978-1-4201-3411-7
eISBN-10: 1-4201-3411-6
First Electronic Edition: January 2014

10 9 8 7 6 5 4 3 2 1

Printed in the United States of America

Prologue

Valhalla had always been shrouded in mystery.

The leaders of the sprawling compound, named for the home of the Norse gods, claimed that it was a safe house for those people too unique to live among normal society.

Of course, everyone knew that was just a polite way of saying that it was a home for freaks.

Witches, psychics, necromancers, Sentinels, and god only knew what else roamed the grounds protected by a layer of powerful spells.

For the past century, Valhalla had been a source of fear and fascination throughout the entire world, but most especially for the citizens of the small Midwest town who could see the shimmer of blue reflecting off the protective dome that hid the buildings from view.

Not surprisingly, there were citizens who called for the entire place to be nuked. The freaks were dangerous, they insisted, with powers that none of them truly understood. Who knew what the monsters would do if someone pissed them off?

Then there were others who said they should be locked

away and studied like lab rats. Perhaps their mutations could be used to help normal people.

Most, however, preferred to ignore Valhalla and the high-bloods . . . as they preferred to be called . . . living behind the dome.

Until, of course, they needed them.

Chapter One

Kansas City, Kansas

Sergeant Duncan O'Conner was late to the party.

Nursing a hangover from hell, he took two painkillers with a gallon of hot coffee and steered his POS cop car through the light Sunday traffic and entered the gated community in the Southwest suburbs.

The call had hit his cell phone at three in the afternoon. An hour before, he'd hauled his sorry ass out of bed. It'd taken another half hour under the shower to peel his throbbing eyes open and get rid of the stench of cheap whiskey and even cheaper cigars.

His first thought had been to call in and tell them to find someone else. Wasn't it supposed to be his damned weekend off rotation? Let Caleb deal with the latest stiff.

Then the thought that the entire station would suspect he'd spent the night of his ex-wife's latest wedding getting shit-faced drunk sent him stumbling to his car. Yeah, like his bloodshot eyes and old man shuffle weren't going to give the game away, he acknowledged wryly. But while he could take the razzing, he couldn't take the thought of them feeling sorry for him.

Never that.

He might be a pathetic loser, but he was a pathetic loser who was damned good at his job.

Entering the cul-de-sac, Duncan parked his car and headed into the brick house. He ignored the speculative glances from the neighbors who had gathered in a little clutch across the street. He was accustomed to females checking out his spare, well-honed body shown to advantage in a pair of faded jeans and black tee. Even with his short, pale blond hair damp from the shower and his stubborn jaw shadowed with a golden stubble, he had the look of a man who knew what to do with a woman. Match that with a pair of hazel eyes that sparkled with wicked charm and they were like putty in his hands.

The men tended to be more interested in the gun holstered at his side and the hard expression on his lean face that warned he only needed an excuse to kick someone's ass.

His own attention was focused on the house as he stepped into the small but elegant foyer. Not the sort of house a young woman could afford without some help. From daddy. Or more likely, from sugar daddy.

Not that he was being sexist. He couldn't afford a damned toolshed in this frou-frou neighborhood. Even if his old da chipped in every penny he made driving a cab.

He continued to size up the bold black and white furnishings as a uniformed officer handed him a file with the pertinent details of the case. A beat later another officer arrived to lead him to the back of the house and a sunny kitchen with a perfect view of the pool.

He grimaced as the late spring sunlight sent a stab of agony through his throbbing brain, then lowered his gaze to the female who was lying naked in the middle of the tiled floor.

He wasn't surprised that she was beautiful. Stunningly beautiful with long hair that glistened with chestnut highlights, pretty features, and a slender body that was tight with the muscles of an athlete.

What did surprise him was the lack of any sort of violence. She looked like she'd simply lain down in the middle of the floor and quietly passed away.

In his experience, lovely young women who were killed on Sunday morning were beaten to death by a jealous boyfriend or raped and killed by a passing psycho.

Not . . . what?

His brows jerked together as he took a swift inventory of the kitchen, noting everything was in pristine place, not so much as a coffee mug left in the sink. It could be the female never used the kitchen, preferring to eat out, or at her lover's place. It could be she was OCD and her kitchen was always spotless.

But his gut was telling him that she hadn't lived here long enough to stop caring if the place was a mess.

"Hola, O'Conner. Looking a little rough around the edges," the silver-haired coroner drawled, unfolding a white sheet to drape it over the body. "Heard that Susan found herself a decent man to make an honest woman of her."

Yeah, so decent he was banging her in Duncan's own bed.

Flipping off his companion, Duncan opened the file and glanced through the meager info that had been gathered on the female.

"Who found the body?"

"A silent alarm was tripped."

"Cause of death?"

"She's missing her heart."

Duncan froze, his gaze searching the victim's unmarred skin and the obvious lack of blood.

"How the hell could she be missing her heart?"

"I don't know," Frank Sanchez admitted, the bite in his raspy voice expressing his opinion of "I don't know." "But I ran the portable MRI over her three times to be sure."

The older man could be a pain in the ass to work with, but he knew his shit. Nothing got past his eagle gaze. If he said the female was missing her heart, then she was missing her heart.

Crap. Duncan hated mysteries.

"No DNA?"

"It's clean." Another growl as Frank gathered the tools of his trade to pack them in a black leather bag. "Too clean."

"So a freak?"

"That would be my guess."

Confused, Duncan read through the file.

Leah Meadows.

Twenty-six.

Single, originally from Little Rock.

Current occupation, dancer at the Rabbit Hutch.

That would explain her location, he cynically concluded. Her salary as a dancer wouldn't cover the rent, but the clients who frequented the high-end strip club would easily be able to afford this place to keep a current mistress.

It didn't, however, explain why she was lying naked in her kitchen without her heart.

Lifting his head, he met Frank's troubled gaze. "You made the call?"

The older man grimaced, not needing any further explanation.

When there was a murder that didn't have an eyewitness or a legitimate suspect, it was protocol to call in one of the mutants. And when it might involve another mutant, they were called ASAP.

"Yep. She should be—"

On cue one of the uniforms stepped into the kitchen. "The necro is here."

"Perfect timing," Duncan muttered. "Show her in." For whatever reason, necros were almost always females.

The young man nodded, disappearing back down the hallway while Frank snapped shut his black bag.

"That's my cue for a quick exit."

Duncan grinned. "Scared?"

"Damned straight," the older man said without apology. "Freaks give me the heebie-jeebies. I don't know how you can be in the same room with one."

A bitter smile touched Duncan's lips. *Like draws to like . . .*

No. He grimly crushed the mocking words in the back of his aching head. He wasn't like those mutants from Valhalla.

Lots of people could see the souls of others, couldn't they?

He swallowed his grim urge to laugh, tilting his head toward the sheet on the floor. "You can be in the same room with a corpse, but not a necro?"

Frank shrugged. "I respect the dead. No one should be screwing around with their heads."

"Even if it takes a murderer off the streets?"

"I like getting my criminals the old-fashioned way. Necros should be abolished along with the rest of the—"

"I prefer the term 'diviner' if you don't mind," a soft, compelling voice whispered through the room, turning both men toward the door like a magnet.

Even prepared, Duncan felt the air being jerked from his lungs at the sight of Callie Brown.

It wasn't just that she was a stunning beauty with her short, spiky hair that was so dark red it shimmered like fire in the sunlight. Her pale features were perfectly carved with a sensual invitation for a mouth and a proud nose.

And her body . . . hell, it was slender with just enough curves to make a man think of black silk sheets and long weekends. Today it was displayed to perfection in a pair of black spandex pants and a white stretchy top.

But for Duncan it was the white aura that flickered around her diminutive body that made his blood burn.

So pure. So completely and utterly innocent.

And like any bastard, he ached to be the one who debauched that wholesomeness even as he savored the rare beauty of her soul.

"Shit," Frank muttered, heading for the door leading to the back patio. "Adios, amigo."

His entire body vibrating with an awareness that went way beyond sexual attraction, Duncan barely noticed the hasty departure of the coroner. Not that he wouldn't have Callie flat on her back and her legs wrapped around his waist with the least hint of encouragement.

It was a sensation that should have scared the hell out of him. Instead a wicked smile curved his lips.

"Hello, Callie."

She turned her head, regarding him through the reflective sunglasses that hid her eyes, her expression unreadable.

On the half dozen occasions Duncan had worked with Callie, he'd never seen her be anything but serene. Which, of course, only encouraged him to try and provoke a response from her. Anything to know there was a flesh and blood woman beneath that image of calm.

Why it was so important to find that woman was another one of those things he put on the list of "don't fucking care."

"Sergeant O'Conner," she said, moving with an unearthly grace to stand beside the sheet.

"Duncan," he insisted, shifting to stand across the body, his gaze never leaving Callie's pale face.

"Has the body been processed?"

"As much as can be done in the field. You're free to do your thing."

"Time of death?"

"At least an hour ago."

"Then I should have time." She knelt down, reaching for the edge of the sheet. "The spark—"

"Yeah, no need explain." He held up a restraining hand. He might not share the prejudices of most of society against the freaks, but that didn't mean he wanted an insider's guide to necromancy. Christ. The mere thought made his stomach clench. "Just see what you can do."

"Fine." Cool, indifferent. Then her body tensed. "So young," she murmured softly.

"Twenty-six." He crouched down, studying her silken skin unmarred by wrinkles. "Older than you?"

"A woman never shares that information."

"You share nothing."

"Do you blame me?"

His lips twisted at the smooth thrust. Most people went out of their way to avoid freaks, but there were others who thought the only good freak was a dead freak. There were even a handful of cults where people trained to kill them. Mostly simpleminded idiots who needed someone to tell them what to think and angry outcasts who had nowhere else to go, but that didn't make them any less dangerous.

"No, not really."

"What was her name?"

His jaw tightened. Okay, he was vain. He'd spent most of his life knowing women found him irresistible. The fact he wasn't certain if Callie had even noticed he was a male annoyed the hell out of him.

Then with a silent curse he shoved aside his ego and concentrated on the only thing important at the moment. Finding the son of a bitch who'd killed this woman.

"Leah Meadows."

"Is that her real name?"

He shrugged. "That's all I got for now."

She paused before giving a slow nod. "It should do."

"Why do you need her name?" He asked the question that he'd wondered about more than once.

By law they couldn't give details of the death in the fear that the necro might be swayed into naming a murderer even if the victim couldn't reveal the truth.

But a necro always asked for a name.

"It helps me to connect with her mind."

He shuddered. "Christ."

"You asked," she reminded him in a low voice. "Do you need any other details?"

"I need to touch her."

"There." He pointed toward the forearm where Frank would have prepped the victim. "It's been sanitized."

She at last lifted her head. "Would you make sure—"

"That no one enters?" he finished for her.

"Yes."

He abruptly frowned. "Where's your Sentinel?"

A necro never left the compound without a guardian Sentinel. Not only were they capable of opening portals to travel from place to place (a mysterious talent that was never discussed among the mundane mortals), but they were also trained warriors who were covered in intricate tattoos. From what little Duncan had been able to learn, the ceremonial markings protected the warriors from magic as well as any attempt at mind control.

And, oh yeah, they were capable of killing with their bare hands.

There were also rumors that there were other Sentinels— hunters who weren't marked and could travel among the humans unnoticed. But info on them was kept top secret.

"I asked him to wait outside."

He lifted a brow. "Why?"

"Because you take such pleasure in tormenting him and he's too well trained to fight back."

"Are you saying I'm not well trained?"

She ignored the open invitation to point out that he was barely civilized and instead returned her attention to the victim.

"The door, please."

He slowly straightened, swallowing his groan as his head

gave another protesting throb. Whiskey was the devil's brew, just as his ma had always claimed.

"No one's coming in," he muttered, "but I'll keep guard at the door if it makes you feel better."

"Thank you, Sergeant."

"Duncan." His headache forgotten, he flashed a smile of pure challenge. "One day you'll say it. Hell, one day you might even scream it."

No response. With a low growl, Duncan made his way to the door, leaning on the doorjamb to make sure no one could enter, while keeping his attention on the woman kneeling beside the corpse.

She ignored his unwavering attention, lifting a hand to remove her sunglasses and setting them aside. At the same time the slanting sunlight spilled over her, catching in the sapphire blue of her eyes.

Duncan's heart forgot how to beat.

He'd seen them before. At a distance. At the time he'd thought they looked like expensive gems, perfectly faceted and shimmering with an inner light. Up close they were even more magnificent.

Christ.

The beauty of those eyes was hypnotizing.

Priceless jewels that revealed this was no ordinary woman.

Duncan would be pleased to know that it was only her years of training that allowed Callie to ignore his raw sexual magnetism.

He was the sort of primitive male that should have infuriated her, not tantalized her deepest fantasies.

Of course, the Mave would tell her that fantasies were meant to be filled with unsuitable desires. Why not lust after a bad boy cop? It wasn't as if she was going to do anything about it. She didn't know if his flirtations were a way to taunt her or if he was one of those groupies who got off on sleeping with "freaks," but either way, it had nothing to do with her as a person.

Still, it was only with an effort that she managed to crush the tiny tingles of excitement fluttering in the pit of her stomach and the dampness of her palms.

Now wasn't the time or place.

Tonight in her dreams . . . well, that was a different story.

Clearing her thoughts, she laid her hands on the victim's arm and closed her eyes.

It took a second to slip from her own mind and into the female stretched on the floor. There was always a strange sense of . . . floating. As if her consciousness was hovering between one body and the next. Then, focusing on the feel of the female's arm beneath her fingers, she murmured her name.

"Leah."

The soft word was enough.

With a hair-raising jolt, she was sucked from her body and into Leah's mind.

She could easily sense the female soul, just as she could sense she was fading.

Fast.

Despite the ridiculous myths, a necromancer couldn't control or raise the dead. Her only ability was to tap into the mind of the murdered victim to see the last few minutes of their life.

And only within a very short time frame.

Once the . . . spark, for lack of a better word . . . was extinguished and the soul moved on, the memories were lost.

A meaningless talent for the most part. But on rare occasion it could mean the opportunity for justice.

With a well-honed skill, Callie touched on the female's memory center. Just being born a diviner didn't automatically mean that a person would be capable of reading memories. There were many necromancers who were never able to do more than enter the body and hopefully catch a stray thought.

Callie, however, was one of the most talented.

Which was why she was always sent when there was a suspicion the death might have been caused by a high-blood, as the freaks preferred to call themselves.

Finding the spot she was searching for, she delicately slipped into the fading memories and allowed them to flow through her.

Suddenly she was no longer kneeling on the hard floor. Instead she was in the attached garage, stepping out of her sleek black Jag. She sensed a pleasant weariness in her limbs, as if she'd just finished a vigorous workout at the gym, a suspicion confirmed when she glanced down to see she was wearing a pair of stretchy pants and a matching sports bra.

Rounding the car, she moved to unlock the door that led to the house. She stepped into the small laundry room and stripped off her sweaty clothes to toss them in the washing machine. Now naked, she moved into the sun-drenched kitchen.

As she headed for the stainless steel refrigerator to pull out a bottle of water there was an ease in her steps that hinted this was a routine morning for her, and a comfort with her surroundings that said she had lived in the house for at least a few weeks.

Callie, however, could sense a faint surge of pride as she turned to study the large kitchen that looked like a picture out of a fancy magazine.

Leah had recently moved up in the world.

And she was fully enjoying her elevation.

Callie had barely managed to grasp the knowledge when Leah was stiffening, her head turning toward the French doors.

Was there a shadow lurking by the trimmed hedges that lined the patio?

She gave a strained laugh, lifting the bottle to drink the last of the water before tossing it into the recycle bin next to the fridge.

The neighborhood was the safest in the city. Besides, the house was guarded by a security system.

If there was a creep out there trying to sneak a peek through the windows, then he'd set off a hundred bells and whistles the minute he stepped on the patio.

Brave thoughts, but a tiny shiver inched down the female's spine as the shadow moved, stepping away from the hedges to reveal—

Without warning the image was snatched away.

Just like that.

Callie blinked, expecting to have been returned to her body. When the spark left, it destroyed any connection that Callie had to the dead.

But instead she found she remained in Leah's body, standing in the center of the kitchen as if she were still in the memory . . . without Leah.

What the hell?

"I'm afraid I can't allow you to see any more," an unexpected male voice drawled.

Callie turned in shock to watch the tall man with silver hair pulled from his lean, darkly bronzed face stroll through the door leading into the dining room.

She pressed a hand to her racing heart.

No one should be here.

No one but her and the soul she'd connected to in the physical world.

Unfortunately, no one had given the stranger the handbook on necromancy. Instead of disappearing, he continued forward, the muted light revealing his painfully beautiful features. His brow was high and intelligent, his nose a thin blade, and his lips carved along full lines. And his eyes . . .

They were gemstone like hers, only instead of blue they

were perfectly clear, like diamonds glittering with a cold light.

A male necromancer? Of the few she'd met, none had those color eyes. And certainly they didn't have the sort of bone-chilling strength she could feel swirling through the air around him.

His muscular body was covered by a thick gray robe that covered him from neck to feet, although she caught a glimpse of slender fingers the same bronze shade as his face.

More terrified than she'd ever been in her life, Callie struggled to speak. "Are you the one who killed Leah?"

He halted a mere foot from her, studying her as if she were a rare bug beneath a microscope.

"A diviner," he at last said, his words edged with a faint accent. "And one of astonishing power."

"How is this possible? Are you in Leah's mind?"

He seemed to pause, his eyes widening before he suddenly tilted back his head to laugh with a cold amusement.

"Callie Brown. How very ironic." The diamond eyes glittered with a blinding light. "It must be fate that brought us here together."

He knew who she was? The thought disturbed her on a cellular level.

"Who are you?" she rasped.

A slow, mysterious smile curved his sensuous lips. "That's not the right question."

Did he think this was a game?

"Okay." She forced herself to hold the diamond gaze. "What are you?"

"That's not right, either," he warned, lifting a hand toward her face.

Callie leaped backward, her heart slamming against her ribs with the force of a steam hammer.

"Don't touch me."

His low chuckle seemed to wrap around her like sinful

magic. "The question, my beautiful Callie, is"—he deliberately paused—"who are you?"

Her pulsing fear was disturbed by the unexpected sensation of Fane tugging her back to reality.

"No." She tried to fight against her Sentinel's ruthless pull, knowing that there was more at risk than the death of one young female. "Wait. Damn you."

Her last sight was of the stranger blowing her a taunting kiss.

Chapter Two

Callie opened her eyes, puzzled to discover she was sprawled on the hard floor, her head cradled in Fane's lap.

As always the Sentinel looked like he'd been carved from granite. At six-foot-three he had the chiseled muscles of a warrior and the strength of an ox. Not surprising considering he'd been honed from the cradle to become a weapon.

He was also covered from the top of his shaved head to the tips of his toes in intricate tattoos that protected him from all magic.

There were two sects of Sentinels.

The first sect contained warriors who were born with superior senses and reflexes as well as innate strength but no magic. They were made into hunters since they were easily able to "pass" as human and were often used by the Mave to track down renegade high-bloods who had committed a crime or were a danger to themselves or others.

Those few born with superior physical abilities as well as a claim to magic were taken by the monks and trained to become guardian Sentinels. They were Sentinels that guarded high-bloods who were incapable of protecting themselves.

The monks did everything in their power to make them

the most proficient, most feared killers ever to walk the earth.

And they surpassed all expectations with Fane.

He was death walking to his enemies.

And his enemies included anyone who threatened Callie.

She frowned, focusing on the bleak face of her guardian. The dark eyes were harder than usual and the stark features that were savagely beautiful beneath the swirls of black tattoos were set in a fierce expression.

"Fane, what are you doing?" she demanded, startled when her voice came out as a croak.

"The cop came for me," the Sentinel said, his voice a low rumble. "He said you were in trouble."

"Why?"

"Why?" Duncan's lean, annoyingly handsome face swam into focus as he moved to stand over her, the hazel eyes snapping with a combination of combustible emotions. "Are you fucking kidding me? You fell backward and started flopping like a damned fish out of water. I thought you were having a seizure."

Abruptly she recalled what had happened during her last seconds inside Leah's mind. "Oh," she breathed.

The hazel eyes narrowed. "You can say thank you now."

"Thank you," she forced herself to mutter as she sat upright.

A part of her was furious at having been pulled away from the stranger before she could determine what the hell he was. But a larger part realized that she'd been in grave danger. Perhaps more danger than she wanted to imagine, if her throbbing head was anything to go by.

Duncan snorted. "Your gratitude overwhelms me."

She reached to slide her glasses on. Usually, they were her personal armor against a world that considered her a freak.

Now, she used them to conceal the raw fear pulsing through her.

"I need to speak to Fane."

Duncan's features sharpened to his cop face. Hard. Unyielding. Pain-in-the-ass. "No one's stopping you."

"In private."

"No."

She met his glare with a lift of her brow, allowing Fane to help her to her feet. Her knees briefly protested, threatening to crumble, but with a ruthless resolve she willed them to hold steady. She'd survived being tossed in a Dumpster when she was less than a week old. She'd survived thirty years of being hated, feared, and even hunted by crazy-ass norms.

She would survive this.

"That wasn't a request, Sergeant."

"This is my crime scene, Ms. Brown," he growled. "And anything you saw in Leah's mind is evidence."

She paused. Legally he was right. Anything she discovered during her investigation went into an official transcript that could be used in court.

But technically Leah had already passed on when the stranger had popped into her mind. So that left jurisdiction . . . fuzzy.

At least as far as she was concerned.

"This has nothing to do with your case."

"Oh yeah?" He stepped closer. "I'll decide what does or doesn't have to do with my case," he retorted, reaching to grab her arm. As if he thought she was intending to disappear in a puff of smoke.

Not an unreasonable fear.

Most people didn't understand how a Sentinel was capable of traveling. They simply assumed they popped place to place with some mysterious magic.

The cop, however, had forgotten an important rule when working with a diviner.

His hand was still inches away from her when Fane reached out to grasp his wrist in a punishing grip.

"Don't. Touch. Her."

Duncan hissed, his gaze never shifting from Callie as he used his free hand to grasp the butt of the handgun that was holstered at his side.

"Call off your dog," he commanded through clenched teeth.

Fane kept his grip as he stepped forward to stand at Callie's side. "I'm her Sentinel, not her servant. If I decide someone is a threat I'll do whatever necessary to protect her." Although casually dressed in a pair of combat pants and white muscle shirt, no one, absolutely no one, could mistake Fane as anything less than lethal. "That badge doesn't scare me."

"Fane." She laid a light hand on his arm. This went beyond Fane protecting her. The air was choking with male testosterone. One wrong word and things could get very, very messy. "Please."

"Someday we're going to settle this," Fane snarled before grudgingly releasing his hold.

Duncan made a show of releasing his gun. "Sooner rather than later."

Callie rolled her eyes.

Men.

"Perhaps the sergeant should hear this," she said, accepting that Duncan was going to dig and prod and generally make a nuisance of himself until he had what he wanted.

Or until Fane snapped and killed him.

As if to prove her point, Fane wrapped an arm around her shoulders, his touch as much a warning to Duncan as a support for her shaky balance. "You need to rest," he said.

She shook her head. "There's no time."

Fane frowned, not missing the edge of fear in her voice. "What happened?"

"I'm not entirely sure."

"Did you—" Duncan tried to hide his grimace.

She completed his sentence. "I was able to locate her memories."

"Then you know what happened to her?" Duncan asked.

"Not exactly."

Duncan frowned. "Not exactly?"

"I'm not sure."

"How can you not be sure?"

"Her soul left before I could access her final memory."

"Dammit," Duncan muttered, frustration smoldering in his hazel eyes. As annoying as he might be, his dedication to his job was never in doubt. He was as tenacious as a bulldog when it came to solving a case. "Then you didn't see her murderer?"

She shivered, vividly recalling the diamond-bright eyes.

"Actually . . . he was still there."

Duncan stepped forward, his lean face tight with shock. "What the hell are you talking about?"

"Back off." Fane lifted a warning hand before turning to study her with a searching gaze. "Callie?"

"A man appeared. I think it was the same man who killed Leah."

Fane hissed, turning her so he could run an assessing gaze over her. "Did he hurt you?" he rasped. "Is that why you were having a seizure?"

She lifted an unconscious hand to her head. It was beginning to throb with an uncomfortable persistence. "It must have been, but I didn't feel his attack while we were speaking."

"You need to see a healer."

"Later." She placed a hand on his wide neck. It was a gesture of intimacy without being sexual. Trust between partners. "I promise."

"How is this possible?" Duncan sharply intruded, his voice filled with annoyance. "Was he a necro?"

She turned back to meet his narrowed gaze, inanely noticing

the bruises beneath the hazel eyes and the unusual pallor of his tanned face. Sick? Or just a late night?

Not that either was her business.

"He must have some powers of necromancy, but he was more than that," she said, wrapping her arms around her waist as she returned her attention to Fane. "Much more," she emphasized. "I must speak with the Mave. She may know who, or at least what, he might be."

Fane didn't hesitate, moving toward the door. On the point of following him, Callie was halted as Duncan moved to stand in her way.

"I'm going with you," he said, stubbornly holding his ground, although he was smart enough not to touch her.

Fane was on edge. One wrong move and he would explode.

She shook her head. "It's not possible."

He leaned forward, wrapping her in the scent of warm male and . . . was that whiskey?

Ah. So not sick, but hungover.

"Then make it possible."

In the blink of an eye Fane's huge body was between them, his muscles primed for violence. "A man with a death wish," he drawled.

"What I am is a cop with a victim who's missing her heart with no visible wounds," Duncan countered.

Callie gave a soft gasp, stepping around Fane to regard the cop in horror. She never asked how a victim died. It might influence her when she was reliving their memories.

"She's missing her heart?"

"Gone, just like magic." He held her gaze, his expression grim. "That means the killer is a freak. I'm not letting you out of my sight until I know what's going on."

It took a minute for her to realize she'd just been insulted. Odd considering it happened with tedious regularity.

"Are you implying I would try and hide the identity of a murderer?"

He ignored the bristling Fane as he moved to stand directly in front of her.

"I'm implying that you're stuck with me, Callie Brown."

Fane growled, but before he could give in to his desire to smash his fist into Duncan's face, Callie turned to distract his attention.

"Would you contact the Mave and tell her we'll be bringing a visitor?"

Fane's lips tightened, but he gave a ready nod of his head.

When it came to her safety, Fane was in charge. But when she was making decisions as a diviner, she was boss.

Pulling the phone from his pocket, he moved toward the door. Calls to Valhalla were always made in private.

Of course, the Sentinel couldn't leave without halting long enough to offer Duncan a warning. "You're going to be on my territory, cop," he murmured.

"Can't wait," Duncan assured him, turning to watch the dangerous warrior exit the room.

"Is that really necessary?" Callie demanded in exasperation.

Duncan turned his head back with a snap. "Is he your lover?"

She blinked at the abrupt question. "That's none of your business."

He boldly reached to grasp her chin in his hand. "Since you're going to be sharing my bed, I'd say it's very much my business."

She scowled, pretending that her stomach wasn't fluttering with excitement. "Fane was right."

His gaze lowered to her lips, the heat smoldering in the hazel eyes promising all sorts of wicked pleasure.

"Right about what?"

"You are a menace."

* * *

Duncan paced the long room that was painted in soothing shades of blue and filled with sleek furniture built of steel and upholstered with black leather.

It looked more like a reception room for an upscale plastic surgeon than the Funny Farm. No, not the Funny Farm. Valhalla, he grimly corrected himself.

He doubted the residents would appreciate the nickname the norms used to reference the strange compound hidden beneath the shimmering dome. And since more than a few of them could read his thoughts, he would be an idiot to deliberately provoke them.

His lips twisted as he came to the end of the room where images were being projected onto the smooth wall. It looked like the local news program, although he didn't bother to try and read the lips of the pretty anchorwoman. Instead he turned on his heels and continued his pacing.

He had to keep moving. If he stopped then he might remember being taken to a small monastery on the outskirts of Kansas City where he'd stepped into a hidden chamber with Callie and her guard dog, Fane. At first he'd assumed he was going to have to endure a few prayers to whatever gods the freaks worshipped. After all, Sentinels were raised by monks and while they never seemed overly pious, it had to have some effect on them.

But there'd been no praying when Fane demanded they all touch the strange copper post set in the middle of the barren room.

In fact there'd been nothing but silence before the world abruptly melted.

There were no other words to explain what'd happened.

One minute Duncan was standing close to Callie, breathing in her delicate scent and thinking thoughts that could get him arrested, and the next there was . . . nothing.

A vast emptiness that made his stomach fall to his feet and his mouth dry.

For a frantic few minutes he feared that he'd been tossed into an endless oblivion. Which was strange. His ma had always assured him that he was destined for the fiery pits of hell.

But the blackness lasted only seconds before the world flickered back into focus and he found himself in a room so similar to the one that they'd just left that he wondered if it'd been no more than an elaborate joke to scare the stupid human.

Then he'd been led out of the room and through a labyrinth of hallways that could only mean they were at the infamous Valhalla. A knowledge that had done nothing to soothe his raw nerves.

Neither had Fane's gruff command to stay in the room and not touch anything before he'd left with Callie to speak with the elusive Mave.

"Walk here, O'Conner. Wait there, O'Conner," Duncan mocked beneath his breath. "Lie down and play dead like a good doggie, O'Conner."

"And you call *us* freaks?" a female voice drawled from behind him. "At least we don't talk to ourselves."

Pulling his gun, he whirled to watch a stranger stroll into the room from a hidden door, his fingers instinctively tightening on the trigger.

Not that she looked like someone who needed to be shot. Hell, she looked like she'd been created to fulfill a man's deepest fantasy.

Statuesque, with lush curves that were shown to jaw-dropping perfection by a pair of black leather pants and red bustier, she had a long mane of raven hair that contrasted with her pale skin.

But there was a dangerous glint in the light green eyes that warned that this was no harmless sex kitten. This woman had claws she wouldn't hesitate to use.

Especially on him, if her slow smile of anticipation was any indication.

"Who are you?" he demanded.

She halted in the center of the room, her legs spread wide and looking impossibly long in her knee-high boots with three-inch heels.

"Serra," she offered, a hint of a Russian accent edging her voice.

He studied her. Not as a male interested in a woman. He'd already chosen his next lover, even if Callie hadn't accepted the inevitable.

But as a cop assessing a loaded weapon.

"You're not a necro."

"No, my power isn't necromancy. And no"—her lips curled in a taunting smile—"I'm not a witch."

He hissed. That hadn't been a lucky guess.

"A reader."

"Ding, ding. Give the dog a Milk-Bone."

He didn't try to hide his unease. Why bother? A reader was capable of rummaging around in people's minds. Or at least, that was the word on the streets.

But that didn't mean he was going to roll over and let the bitch intimidate him.

"Let me go out on a limb and guess you don't like me," he said, his smile designed for maximum annoyance. "Is it because I'm not a—"

"Watch it," she murmured, her eyes crystallizing with a dangerous power.

"High-blood?" he finished.

She sashayed forward, her every move a wicked invitation. "You upset my friend."

He frowned. Okay. That wasn't what he was expecting. "You mean Callie?"

"That would be the one."

"Obviously you didn't get the memo." He shoved the gun back in his holster. No sense asking for trouble. He couldn't shoot the female just because she pissed him off. Besides, it was more likely she would force him to put a bullet in his own head before he could squeeze off a round in her direction. "I wasn't the one who upset her."

"You aren't the one who scared the hell out of her, but you upset her every time she's forced to work with you."

Upset her? How the hell could he . . . ah. This time his smile was genuine.

So the lovely, frustratingly aloof diviner wasn't completely indifferent to him.

Thank god.

"Because I remind her that she's a woman?" He shrugged. "How can that be a bad thing?"

"Are you a 'freak' groupie?"

"Hell no."

"Hmmm." She narrowed her gaze. "What do you want from her?"

He arched a brow. "You don't have to read my mind to guess what I want."

"Callie might not be a virgin, but she's an innocent."

"I know."

There was a startled pause before the female strolled forward, circling him like a predator sizing up her prey.

"Well, well," she at last drawled. "What secrets are you hiding, Sergeant O'Conner?"

Duncan went rigid with fury. "Get the fuck out of my mind."

She chuckled, but before she could continue her tormenting there was a prickle in the air and a misty shape began to form in the center of the room.

"Serra," a soft voice chastised.

Astonishingly, the Queen Bitch was hastily stepping forward to perform a deep bow.

"Forgive me, Inhera."

Duncan frowned. The figure remained misty, making him assume that it was some sort of projected image. Like the TV on the far wall.

Technology or magic?

Impossible to say.

"Please see that a room is prepared for our guest," Inhera commanded, the misty vision hinting at a female, although it was impossible to determine her features. "Then return to me so we can continue your studies."

"At once," Serra instantly agreed, her tone deeply reverent. Then, the second the image flickered she turned to send Duncan a glare. "O'Conner?"

He kicked his chin up a notch. "What?"

"You hurt Callie in any way, shape, or form and I'll give you nightmares that will make you scream." She smiled with an evil intent. "Literally."

She left the room with the fluid grace that most freaks seemed to possess, her heels clicking on the polished wood floor.

Once again alone, Duncan heaved a shaky sigh. Teleportation with tattooed Sentinels, mind-reading chicks in SMBD leather, projections of females that could appear and disappear, and a necro who made his blood run hot even when she was treating him as if she were cold as ice.

"My da warned me to stay away from the freaks," he muttered.

Chapter Three

The office of the Mave was designed for maximum impact.

Done in shades of black and white, it was lined with floor-to-ceiling bookshelves and low leather chairs set opposite the heavy ebony desk. The floor was covered by a white carpet with a black geometric pattern. And the far wall was made entirely of glass to provide a stunning view of the formal rose gardens.

Not that the female currently seated behind the desk needed the traditional trappings to prove her authority.

The leader of the high-bloods barely looked thirty and was a stunning beauty with her smooth curtain of black hair and pale, oval face. But there was a thunderous power that shimmered in her storm gray eyes and a dignified calm that was oddly intimidating. And while the more daring men might covertly lust after the tall, slender body that was casually displayed in a pair of faded jeans and a cashmere sweater, it only took one glance at the birthmark on the upper curve of her breast that she deliberately exposed to make them treat her with respect.

The small mark in the shape of an eye proved that she was

a born witch, and the brilliance of the shimmering emerald color revealed that her powers were off the charts. The darker the color, the greater her magic.

The fact she was also one of the most talented telepaths ever recorded only added to her considerable arsenal.

And her reputation.

Being called to the Mave's office had been known to make the most bad-ass Sentinels piss their pants.

Thankfully Callie had already had all the piss terrified out of her by her unexpected powwow with the stranger in the mind of a dead woman. Now she was just desperate for answers.

The Mave sat perfectly still, her classically beautiful face unreadable as she considered Callie's bizarre story.

"You say his eyes were clear?" she at last asked, her slender fingers drumming a steady beat on the glossy desktop.

"Yes." Callie shivered as she recalled the cold brilliance of the stranger's eyes. "They were faceted and shimmered like diamonds."

"And his hair was gray?"

"More silver, I think," she clarified, not entirely sure what might be relevant.

"From age?"

"I'm not certain." Callie felt Fane's hand gently land on her shoulder. The warrior stood behind her chair, offering a silent support that she desperately needed. "His face looked mature, but it's impossible for me to guess his age."

"Unusual." Tap, tap, tap went the finger.

Callie didn't know if that meant the Mave was troubled by what she was saying, or simply bored.

And she didn't care.

She wasn't leaving until she had some answers.

"And his power . . ." She gave another shiver. "I've never felt anything like it."

Fane gave her shoulder a squeeze, his growing disapproval

heating the air. Sentinels' body temperature naturally ran higher than others'. And the heat spiked with their mood.

It gave a whole new meaning to a man being smoking hot in bed. Not that Callie knew from personal experience, but she'd heard the rumors.

"She's been over this a dozen times," he growled, his tone respectful—barely. "She needs to rest."

Callie reached up to pat her guardian's hand, worried he was going to get himself tossed in the dungeons. And yes, there were dungeons.

"I'm fine, Fane."

"No, he's right. You're weary and I need to do some research." She sent them both a warning gaze. "For now I want this kept strictly between us. Until I know more there's no point in allowing the gossips to get ahold of the story and cause an uproar."

Callie nodded. "Of course."

The Mave smoothly rose to her feet. "Rest for an hour or so and we'll speak again."

Callie was out of the chair before she even realized she was moving.

"What about Sergeant O'Conner?" Callie demanded.

A wry amusement shimmered in the smoke eyes. "A very stubborn man."

"I can get rid of him if you want," Fane promptly offered.

"No, we must work with the authorities. Our"—the Mave hesitated as she searched for the proper word—"relationship is difficult enough without humans worrying that we're trying to hide a murderer. Besides, I have a few questions I must ask him." She headed toward the door leading to her private quarters, pausing long enough to glance over her shoulder, a mysterious smile on her lips as she looked directly at Callie. "I've had him taken to the guest quarters if you're interested."

"Pity," Fane muttered as the Mave left the office and closed the door.

Callie frowned. "What's a pity?"

"I was hoping for the opportunity to kick his ass out of here."

"Why do you dislike him?"

"Don't ask foolish questions, Callie." He moved to stand directly in front of her, capturing her chin between his fingers as he studied the faint bruises beneath her eyes. "What did the healer say?"

Fane had insisted on carrying her directly to the healers, growling at anyone who came close to her. Including Duncan, who'd been led off before she could say a word to him.

"There was evidence of pressure on my frontal lobe, but no damage." She wrinkled her nose. "They suspect the stranger was searching my mind."

The dark eyes glittered with the promise of revenge. "Bastard."

She bit her bottom lip, disturbed by the mere thought of Fane coming up against the stranger who'd stolen a young female's heart without leaving a trace. "I'm worried."

"A premonition?"

"No, I don't have any talent for seeing the future, but I do know that whoever, or whatever, I encountered isn't done." A chill crawled down her spine. "There's going to be more deaths."

His expression was as hard as granite. "We should go to the Tabuk."

The monastery that was tucked in the Himalayas was a safe house for high-bloods who needed a time-out from civilization. It was not only hidden from the norms, it was so off the grid that it couldn't be found by the usual technology.

She gently tugged free of his hold. If it was up to Fane she would be locked away for the rest of her life.

"I told you I'm fine."

"You're in danger." The magnificent swirls and arcs of his tattoos appeared even more vivid against his skin as his muscles clenched with frustration. "This creature knows you. He's been inside your head. I won't allow you to be the next victim."

She lifted a brow. "Allow?"

"I am your protector."

"And I appreciate your dedication, Fane," she said softly. "But if he had wanted me dead he could already have killed me."

Fane wasn't impressed with her logic. "Maybe he likes the hunt."

She couldn't argue. She sensed the predatory nature of the stranger. But who or what it was hunting remained a mystery.

"It doesn't matter. I can't leave. I'm the only one who can identify the man."

The Sentinel scowled. "You won't be able to identify him if you're dead."

She reached to brush her fingers down the rigid muscles of his forearm. "Fane, with this man's power there's nowhere I would be safe."

"I won't lose you."

She felt a familiar tide of affection for this man who'd committed his life to keeping her safe. "I'm not going anywhere," she assured him, then dropped her hand when his cell phone beeped. It didn't take a genius to know who was trying to contact him. Fane lacked the sort of friends who would call him just to chat. "Wolfe?" she asked as he pulled the phone from his pocket with a soft curse.

"He's waiting for me to report."

Callie grimaced. Wolfe was the Tagos, the current leader of the Sentinels, and the only man scarier than Fane.

An amazing accomplishment.

"He's going to cause a riot," she muttered. "You know how he hates to be kept out of the loop."

"I'll deal with the Tagos." He sent her a warning glare. "You . . . be careful."

She flashed a teasing smile, drawing her finger over the middle of her chest. "Cross my heart."

With a shake of his head, he left the office.

Callie waited. No point in leaving until she was certain Fane was out of sight. If he knew she didn't intend to return directly to her apartment, he would throw her over his shoulder and carry her there.

At last she slipped from the room and headed down the white corridor, which was painted pink by the encroaching dusk. The overhead skylights offered a perfect view of the sky, despite the magical dome that surrounded the compound. From the outside the spell hid Valhalla from prying eyes, but from the inside it was invisible.

She turned the corner, ignoring the gleaming silver elevators that would take her to her apartment.

Valhalla was a vast complex that sprawled over several thousand acres, with a number of workshops, garages, barns, a school, and a fully equipped hospital. The central building was constructed in the shape of a pentagon with a large inner courtyard.

Most people never saw beyond the official offices on the main floor or the formal reception rooms, although a small number were allowed the rare honor of being given guest rooms if their visit was expected to last more than a few hours. Certainly no one was allowed to explore the nine levels of private quarters and secret labs that were dug deep into the earth.

Ignoring the speculative glances from the occasional high-blood she passed, she followed the corridor until she took another turn. This one into the guest quarters.

Her steps slowed as she suddenly realized that she didn't know what the hell she was doing.

Well, she knew that she didn't want to return to her empty apartment.

And that she had an odd compulsion to speak with the aggravating, sinfully sexy human cop.

But beyond that . . . what was the plan?

It wasn't like she intended to march up to Duncan O'Conner's door and start pounding. And she could hardly spend hours walking up and down the hallway, could she?

Busy mulling the wisdom of turning around and heading to her apartment, fate took the choice out of her hands as the door just down the corridor was yanked open and the man who'd been gnawing at the edge of her thoughts since they'd arrived at Valhalla stepped out of his rooms.

She came to a halt, her brows arching as he wandered in an absent pattern, his arm lifted over his head and his head tilted back.

"Duncan?" She cleared her throat. "What are you doing?"

His head snapped down as he realized he wasn't alone, his hand shifting to reveal the cell phone tucked in his palm.

"Trying to find a damned signal."

"Oh." She pointed toward the skylight that offered a view of the darkening sky, reminding him of the invisible spell that was wrapped around the area. "Cell phones don't work at Valhalla."

"Of course not," he muttered, shoving the phone into the front pocket of his jeans even as he prowled toward her, his hazel eyes studying her with an unnerving intensity.

"There should be a landline in your rooms," she said, barely resisting the urge to back away. She didn't know what it was with this man. He fascinated her even as he made her as twitchy as a deer caught in headlights. "Or if it's an emergency the Mave can send a telepathic message."

"It can wait."

His husky growl brushed over her skin like a physical caress. She shivered. Oh god. This was crazy.

She licked her dry lips. "I should go."

"No." His hand lifted to cup her cheek, his brows drawing together as his piercing gaze seared over her face. Belatedly she remembered that she'd left her glasses in the Mave's office. "Stay," he husked.

She stilled, wondering what he saw. "Is something wrong?"

"You have shadows." His finger brushed the fragile skin below her eyes. His expression was grim, but his touch was gentle. "Are you in pain?"

"No. The healers took care of the damage."

His expression only hardened. "Do you know who . . . or what . . . it was?"

"Not yet," she admitted. "The Mave will want to speak with you. She has some questions."

His finger stroked down her cheek to trace the lower curve of her mouth.

"So do I."

Her eyes abruptly narrowed at the reminder. "Yes, you've made your suspicions of our intent to protect a killer very clear."

He didn't apologize. She doubted he knew how.

"At least tell me that your Mave has some way to make sure the bastard can't get inside your head."

Her skin tingled beneath his light caress, as if every nerve ending was being set on fire.

"No one can say for sure, but I suspect his powers are similar to a diviner's, not a telepath's."

"Which means?"

She hesitated. The golden rule of every high-blood was never to discuss mutant powers with the norms. Not only did it give them another reason to fear the freaks, but talking about a person's talent was like talking about sex.

Way too intimate to be shared with just anyone.

But Duncan's position as a cop meant he had greater access to the secrets of Valhalla than most.

And more importantly, she suspected that he had a few secrets of his own.

"I doubt he'll be able to touch my mind unless I'm using my powers to enter the memories of the dead."

"Then you're officially off duty."

Briefly lost in the gold-flecked hazel of his eyes, it took a beat for Callie to realize she'd just been given an order.

Big mistake.

Pulling away from his lingering touch, she planted her hands on her hips. "Not your call, Sergeant."

"Duncan," he insisted, the muscle in his jaw bulging with frustration. "And I can make it my call. All it takes is one word whispered into the ear of the Head of Justice."

Oh, he didn't just go there, did he?

"I don't need your protection."

"It's not just about you," he shot back. "If word gets out there was some sort of interference during your divining, then any info you manage to get will be tossed out of court."

She stiffened. What the hell had she been thinking? She should have gone straight to her apartment. She could have been relaxing in a hot bubble bath with a nice glass of Chardonnay. Instead she was fighting the urge to kick this aggravating man in the nuts.

"Fine. I'm off duty." She turned on her heel, marching back down the hallway. "Which means that we have nothing left to discuss."

With a speed worthy of a Sentinel, Duncan had moved to block her path.

"Where's your guard dog?"

She blinked at the unexpected question. "If you're referring to Fane, he's also off duty."

A sinful smile curved his lips as he reached forward to grasp her wrist and tugged her back down the hall.

"Good."

Duncan had never been a Zen sort of guy.

His temper ran hot, his foot was perpetually stuck in his mouth, and he had all the charm of a pissed-off badger. But he was smart enough to know when he was being a jackass.

There'd been no need to bark out orders like he was at the station house dealing with the usual dregs of society. Callie was an intelligent, reasonable female who would already have realized that she couldn't be called in on police cases. Not when there was some stranger lurking in the minds of the dead.

Unfortunately a dark fear that he'd never felt before had roared through him with enough force to knock his brain off-line, leaving him at the mercy of his most primitive male instincts.

Never a good thing.

Now it was time for damage control.

And if he hadn't truly screwed this up . . . maybe a chance to catch a glimpse of the woman beneath the diviner.

Reaching the door to his rooms, he pushed it open and pulled Callie over the threshold, getting her far enough inside to close the door before she was whirling to send him a wary scowl.

"What are you doing?"

"We need to speak in private."

Duncan watched as her gaze shifted to the small but tidy living room that was furnished with a pale green couch and matching chairs. There was a large window that offered a view of the surrounding countryside and a built-in kitchen painted a cheery yellow. He assumed the connecting door led to a bedroom, but he hadn't had time to check it out.

"We have no need for privacy," she at last muttered.

He deliberately leaned against the door, folding his arms over his chest. "Afraid, Callie?"

"Should I be?"

"My morals might be questionable, my manners are often compared to a rabid pit bull, but I would never hurt you, Callie Brown." He held her wary gaze, his expression somber. "And I'll kill anyone who tries."

She blinked, clearly caught off guard by the lethal edge in his voice. And she wasn't alone, he wryly acknowledged. This female brought out a side of him he didn't recognize.

"Do you have a thing for freaks?" she demanded.

"Only one."

Blink, blink. "Why?"

His lungs tightened at the sight of the gemstone eyes glittering in the overhead light. Oh man. With those eyes and her flame-kissed hair she reminded him of the birds his ma used to take him to see in the zoo.

Brilliant. Exotic. And so fucking fragile.

"Why what?" he asked in a distracted voice.

"You barely know me."

"Something I intend to correct." He straightened, catching a whiff of her sweet, feminine scent. Instantly he was hard. As if the enticing aroma had a direct connection to his cock. "Do I need to lock the door?"

She took a step backward. "Only if you intend to hold me prisoner."

"My charm is all I need to hold you prisoner," he said with a smug smile. "I'm more concerned with Fane charging in here to rip off my balls."

"If he decides to rip off your balls a locked door isn't

going to stop him," she informed him, not appearing particularly worried at the fate of his dangly bits.

"Not comforting."

She shrugged. "He's only my guardian when I'm traveling away from Valhalla."

"Have you told him that?"

"There's no need." A mysterious smile curved her lips. The sort of smile that should make a sane man run in the opposite direction. "I'm confident that someone else will soon convince him."

Hmm. He strolled forward, pleased by the thought of Fane being distracted by someone other than Callie.

"Should I ask?"

"No." A nervous color touched her cheeks as she abruptly turned to pace toward the window. "Are you satisfied with your rooms?"

With a snort he followed in her wake, careful not to crowd her. He might enjoy poking at her shell of composure, but he never wanted her to feel threatened.

Not by him.

"You wouldn't ask that question if you'd ever seen my apartment," he told her.

She glanced over her shoulder. "I don't understand."

"My ex-wife was smart enough to hire a barracuda for a lawyer. She ended up with the house, the larger chunk of my paycheck, and the dog." His lips twisted. "Oh, and the delivery man, who she married yesterday."

She tilted her head, the gemstone gaze studying him with open curiosity. "And you?"

He shoved his hands into the pockets of his jeans. "A shitty apartment and a case of perfectly aged whiskey that I polished off last night."

"I'm sorry."

"Don't be," he said gruffly.

He never discussed his ex-wife. And he sure the hell didn't talk about the wracking guilt he felt at the painful demise of his marriage. But he needed Callie to understand that he wasn't living in the past. That he might have regrets, but deep inside he was relieved that Susan had moved on. Which, of course, made him a true ass.

Why was it important that she know? A question to be considered . . . never.

Yeah, never seemed perfect.

"Duncan?" she softly prompted.

"Susan was a decent woman who got tired of waiting for me to be a husband instead of a cop," he confessed. "I couldn't give her what she needed so she found someone who could."

She nodded, her expression thankfully free of censure. "So you're one of those men who live for their jobs?"

"Being a cop is who I am." Truer words had never been spoken. "I can't leave it at the office."

"I don't suppose you can."

He risked moving closer, laying a hand on her shoulder so he could gently turn her to face him. "What about you?"

"Me?"

"You spend a lot of time in very bad places. It can't be easy."

He felt her stiffen at his question, as if no one had ever considered the cost of her gift. Strange considering she spent the last hideous moments in the mind of a victim watching a murder unfold in Technicolor.

"No," she whispered, a shadow dimming the brilliance of her eyes. "It isn't easy."

His gaze swept over the pale perfection of her face. "Do you have nightmares?"

She frowned. "How did you know?"

"Because a man who's had as many sleepless nights as I have recognizes the symptoms."

"What symptoms?"

His hand trailed down the line of her arm until he could circle her tiny wrist with his fingers.

"For all your pretense of serenity you're all hard angles and fragile edges." He lifted her hand to his lips, pressing a kiss to the center of her palm. "One day I'm afraid you're going to shatter."

Chapter Four

Nightmares . . .

Callie forgot to breathe as she allowed his words to seep through her fierce barriers.

He understood.

He truly, truly understood.

How odd.

She was surrounded by high-bloods, including three fellow diviners, and they all knew precisely what she did. But not one had ever asked her if she had nightmares.

Oh, it wasn't that they didn't care. The people of Valhalla were her family and they loved her. Not to mention the fact they would fight to the death for her.

But high-bloods were excessively protective of each other's privacy. A much needed rule considering that many of them were psychics, telepaths, and a rare few empaths. They would never press her to share more than she was willing.

But this man . . . this supposed norm . . . had peered deep in her eyes and seen far too much.

Not only seen, but understood.

She ignored the warnings in the back of her mind. She already knew that his ability to pierce through her walls of protection was dangerous. Almost as dangerous as the jolts of excitement from the press of his lips to her palm.

Instead, she squarely met his knowing gaze. "How do you deal with the nightmares?"

"Whiskey." His lips drifted to her inner wrist. "Work." His tongue pressed against her thundering pulse. "Sex."

She shivered, trying to pretend his touch wasn't setting her on fire.

"Predictable."

"Well, I'm a norm," he murmured, a teasing hint of gold in his hazel eyes. "What did you expect?"

"Are you?"

If she hadn't been watching him so closely she would never have noticed his sudden tension.

"Am I what?"

"A norm?"

He nipped the pad of her thumb, his gaze watchful. "What are you asking?"

"You . . . see more than most humans."

"I'm a cop," he smoothly retorted. Too smoothly. "It's my job to see what other people don't."

"Hmm." She didn't try to hide her disbelief. "I suspect there's more."

Without warning his arms were wrapped around her waist and she was tugged against his hard frame. He lowered his head until they were nose to nose.

"Become my lover and I'll tell you."

Logically, she knew he was trying to distract her. Physically, she didn't give a shit.

White-hot excitement curled through the pit of her stomach, searing away her usual discomfort with allowing anyone to touch her beyond her most intimate friends.

It was . . . terrifying, exhilarating. Glorious.

"Blackmail?"

"Incentive."

She lifted a teasing brow. "Not so certain of those O'Conner charms you claimed would imprison me, are you?"

"It hasn't just been my nightmares that are keeping me up at night, sweet Callie." He placed her hand flat against the rapid beat of his heart, his breath brushing her cheek. "You share part of the blame."

She quivered even as she tried to pretend that his touch wasn't magic.

"Does that line actually work?"

He traced a line of kisses to the corner of her mouth. "For once it isn't a line."

She sucked in a shallow breath. "Yeah, right."

He splayed his hands at her lower back, pressing her against his hardening cock.

"I don't know why, but I can't get you out of my head."

"Because you want sex?"

His sharp laugh ricocheted off the walls. "That would be the preferable explanation."

She tilted back her head to meet his brooding survey. "As opposed to what?"

"Yet another question I don't intend to consider," he muttered, his hand lifting to lightly cup her cheek. "Were your eyes this color when you were born?"

Wow. She struggled to follow his conversational leapfrog. Duncan O'Conner clearly had a narrow list of subjects he was willing to discuss.

"Yes." She shrugged. "I assume they were the reason my parents abandoned me."

"You were abandoned?"

She shrugged. "It's not that uncommon. People expect to have a child who's exactly like them. They don't know how to handle a mutant."

His expression tightened, as if he were angered by her answer.

"People can be shitty."

"True."

"I suppose I shouldn't feel sorry for your parents, but I do."

She frowned, wondering if she'd heard him right. Few among the high-bloods felt sympathy for the families who abandoned their own children. No matter how hard it might be to accept a freak.

"Feel sorry for them?"

His thumb stroked her cheek, as if fascinated by the texture of her skin.

"They have a beautiful, intelligent, outrageously sexy daughter who uses her gifts to make the world a better place." He lowered his head to speak directly into her ear. "But they'll never know you and that's their very great loss."

Desire, along with a far more dangerous sensation, spread through her until she feared she might melt into a puddle of need at his feet. Instinctively she lifted her arms to wrap them around his neck.

"Maybe you do have a small smidgeon of charm," she grudgingly admitted.

The hazel eyes smoldered with pure sin. "There's nothing small about me, Callie." He tilted his hips forward, as if she'd somehow missed the rigid length of his arousal pressing against her lower stomach. "Let me prove it."

She breathed in his warm, sexy scent. She'd never noticed the smell of a man before.

Of course, there were a lot of things about Duncan she noticed. The way his ass perfectly filled out his jeans. The stubborn line of his jaw that was usually shadowed by a hint of golden beard. The utter focus on his goal. Whether it was finding the bad guy, or making her tremble in anticipation.

"A friend warned me that if a man has to brag about his

size it's because he knows it's going to be a disappointment," she murmured, her fingers teasing the hair at his nape.

"Let me take a stab in the dark," he said wryly. "Was this friend named Serra?"

Callie made a sound of astonishment. "You know her?"

"Our paths have crossed." His lips found an exquisitely tender spot just below her ear. "Unfortunately."

She arched against the welcome hardness of his body, strangely pleased he didn't have the usual male reaction to her dearest friend.

"Most men find her irresistible."

He kissed down the curve of her throat, the rasp of his whiskers making her tremble in pleasure.

"She's a man-eater."

It was growing difficult to think. "What does that mean?"

"It doesn't matter," he assured her, his hand gripping the back of her neck, his tongue doing wicked things as it traced the bodice of her stretchy top. "The only opinion I care about is yours."

Her head fell back, offering Duncan greater access. He seemed to know what he was doing. Why interfere?

"Hmm."

"I've never touched such soft skin," he rasped, his lips lingering on the gentle swell of her breast. "It's like heated satin."

Her nipples tightened, the tingles of excitement becoming a sharp-edged hunger that made her hesitate.

Okay. This was spiraling out of control way too fast.

And one of the first things all high-bloods learned was that bad things happened when they let themselves be out of control.

"What do you want from me?" she abruptly demanded.

"A kiss. That's all." He shifted to nibble her bottom lip. "Just a kiss."

"I don't—"

"Trust me, Callie. I won't ever ask for more than you're willing to give."

Trust? Fane would tell her that she was crazy. That she couldn't trust anyone.

Especially not a norm who all but accused the Mave of being willing to harbor a murderer.

But just for a few minutes she didn't want to be a necromancer who was feared and even hated by others. Or the shy woman who often faded into the shadows.

And more importantly, she wanted to kiss this man.

"Okay."

The word had barely formed before he covered her lips in a kiss that seared her to the tips of her toes.

Oh . . . baby.

Serra's three-inch heels clicked against the floor of the hallway as she walked past the wide doors to the dining hall and then the art center.

As always the two floors directly beneath the main structure were crowded with high-bloods. The shared area was a place to relax and mingle. Or, for those who were of a more solitary nature, there was a vast library and a Japanese rock garden.

And for the elusive Sentinels, there was a fully equipped gym and attached firing range that allowed them to hone their skills to a lethal edge, while releasing the aggression that was so much a part of their nature.

And that's where she was headed.

Indifferent to the male, and a few female, gazes that followed her elegant body, shown to lush advantage in the black leather pants and red bustier, she gave a toss of her long, raven hair.

She was far more interested in the tall, lean man storming away from the gym with a thunderous scowl.

Even at a distance, Wolfe, the current Tagos and leader of all Sentinels, looked like a dangerous predator.

He was a hunter rather than a guardian like Fane, which meant he had no magic and no tattoos, but anyone stupid enough to think he'd earned his position by being a slick politician was quickly taught the error of their ways.

He was faster, stronger, and more ruthless than any other warrior. He was also a cunning bastard who could charm the birds from the trees when it suited his purpose. And of course, he wasn't above using his potent sexual appeal to manipulate others.

With copper skin and eyes that were as black as ebony, he resembled an ancient Egyptian deity. He had a proud, hawkish nose and prominent cheekbones. His dark brows were heavy and his lips carved along generous lines. It was a striking face rather than handsome and so fiercely masculine that some women found it intimidating.

Just as striking was the glossy dark hair that brushed his shoulders with a startling streak of silver that started at his right temple. It was rumored that he'd been touched by the devil when he was in the cradle. Something he never bothered to deny.

Hanging back until he'd continued his ill-tempered stomping in the opposite direction, Serra headed into the gym. She might be fearless, but no one crossed paths with a rabid Wolfe.

Bypassing the mats and the boxing ring, she entered the weight room, honing in on her prey with practiced skill.

Too practiced, she wryly conceded, catching sight of Fane bench-pressing enough weight to crush most men.

How long had she been stalking this stoic, aloof Sentinel? It seemed like an eternity.

Halting next to the stack of weights, she admired the ripple of muscle as Fane seamlessly lifted the massive weights in a smooth rhythm.

God Almighty. He was a masterpiece.

From the top of his bald head to the tip of his bare toes he was hard, chiseled perfection. As if he'd been created by the hand of Michelangelo. Was it any wonder he'd managed to capture her jaded interest?

And there was the added bonus of his sacred tattooing. The powerful spells made it impossible for her to read his mind, even by accident.

A necessary barrier for any psychic. Nothing like being in the moment and realizing your partner was fantasizing about another woman.

Yeah . . . real turn-off.

Of course, the whole lack of high-def peekaboos into his mind wasn't all good.

The man kept his emotions locked down as if they were some precious commodity that could only be doled out in sparse measure.

His conversations were just as meager. A yes. A no. And an occasional grunt if she was lucky.

There'd been times when she would have given her favorite Fendi boots just for a glimpse of what was going on behind the grim visage.

"I just saw Wolfe stomping off," she said as Fane continued with his self-imposed task, ignoring her arrival despite the fact he would have sensed her presence the minute she entered the gym.

Aggravating asshole.

Good thing he was so edible.

"He's not happy that I've been forbidden to answer his questions," Fane said, at least speaking to her.

Sometimes he went into a deep trance that allowed him to block out everything but what he wanted to concentrate on.

A trick he was taught by the monks. As well as how to kill a man in three seconds flat.

"I'm hoping he doesn't plan on confronting the Mave in

his current mood," she murmured. The only person not afraid of Wolfe when he was on the warpath was the Mave.

She might turn him into a toad if he went charging into her office half cocked.

"Wolfe doesn't always choose the path of wisdom," Fane pointed out.

She grimaced. "Few of us do." No answer. Okay, new subject. "How's Callie?"

"Wouldn't it be easier to ask her that question?"

"I went by her apartment but she wasn't there."

Clank. The weights were slammed onto the rack behind his head. Flowing to his feet, Fane grabbed a towel to wipe his bare chest, clearly determined to go in search of his missing chick. "Dammit."

Serra felt the familiar irritation scour through her body. She adored Callie. They were, in fact, as close as sisters.

But the knowledge that this man was bound to the beautiful diviner on a level so deep it could never be broken was a constant source of frustration.

"You aren't her babysitter, Fane," she said in sour tones. "She's allowed to travel around Valhalla without asking your permission."

The dark eyes held an unspoken censor. "She's mine to protect."

"Yours to protect or just yours?"

"Now isn't the time for this conversation."

She shouldn't press. She didn't need to be a psychic to know something was going on. Something bad. And that Fane would be hypercrazy—well, even more hypercrazy than usual—with his need to keep Callie safe.

But she was a female. Which meant she was allowed to be completely illogical when it came to the man she wanted.

Hell, it was her duty.

"When will be the time?"

His forbidding expression never altered. "I don't know."

"And if I decide not to wait?"

"I've never lied to you, Serra."

The soft, unyielding response stole her thunder.

Dammit. Why couldn't he at least get mad like any normal man? A good shouting match was just what she needed to release the resentment that had reached a boiling level.

Instead she ran face first into a wall of truth. Never fun.

"No, you've always been brutally honest," she admitted, her lips twisting in a self-derisive smile.

He frowned, tossing aside the towel. "You can have any man you desire."

Her gaze compulsively slid over the broad chest, then down to the six-pack that begged to be licked.

"Obviously not any man," she muttered.

"Serra—"

"Don't." She held up a pleading hand. "It's so . . . fucking tragic." Taking a step back, she folded her arms over her stomach in an unconsciously defensive gesture. "At least tell me that Callie is okay."

Fane hesitated, as if wrestling with some inner demon. Then, at last, he gave a dip of his head. "For now."

"Can you tell me what happened?"

"No."

She shrugged. She didn't expect him to share. Even routine duties the Sentinels performed were kept top secret. But her curiosity was making her nuts. She was desperate to know what was going on.

"It must have something to do with Callie's trip into the memories of the dead woman," she reasoned out loud. "Otherwise the cop would never have been allowed into Valhalla."

With a speed that was always unnerving, Fane was standing directly in front of her, the sudden heat in the air warning that she was at last provoking a reaction.

Even if it wasn't the one she wanted.

"This isn't a game, Serra. The Mave has taken personal

command of the . . . situation," he growled. "She won't be forgiving if she discovers you're poking your nose into her business."

She shrugged. It wouldn't be the first time she'd pissed off the higher powers.

"But it's such a cute nose."

"Not cute," he denied in gruff tones, his finger lightly tracing the line of her nose. "Forceful. Proud. Unique. I wouldn't want to see it hurt."

Silence. And shock. And a whole lot of *what-the-hell* as Fane belatedly jerked his hand back.

It was a toss-up which of them was more astonished by his display of affection, but it was Serra who spoke first.

"Don't tell me you care?" she tried to tease, although the words came out as a croak.

"I've always cared," he said, crawling back behind his emotional no-go zone as he reached to pull on a cammo tee. "Which is why I've told you to find a man who can offer you the relationship that you deserve."

Fury burned through her. "Damn you, Fane, you're not my guardian," she hissed.

He didn't meet her glare. "I'm aware of that."

"Then stop trying to protect me."

Afraid she might do something like punch him—or worse . . . kiss him—Serra turned on her heel and stomped away.

She was going to find out what Callie had gotten herself into.

One way or another.

Chapter Five

Rocking a Hogwarts vibe, the lakefront house on the outskirts of Kansas City had over twenty rooms built among the sprawling wings and towering turrets.

Most people assumed that a reclusive rock star lived behind the high gates and armed security that patrolled the massive grounds. That or a gunrunner.

The last thing they would have expected was a professor.

Well, at least he called himself a professor.

Dr. Zakary had appeared in Kansas City eight months before, moving into the secluded mansion in the middle of the night. No one in the neighborhood had seen him, although if they'd been looking they might have caught sight of the stretch limo that pulled between the heavy gates before disappearing into the five-car garage.

Which meant, of course, they were eaten up with curiosity.

Not that Zak gave a shit. The nosy neighbors were the least of his concern.

Sitting in the library that was surrounded by shelves that towered two stories beneath the alcove ceiling, he studied the ancient scroll that was carefully stretched on the cherrywood desk.

Light from the overhead chandelier spilled over his silver hair, which he'd left loose to frame his lean, darkly bronzed face, and shimmered in his diamond eyes.

Eyes that marked him as different despite his deliberate choice of a black turtleneck sweater and silk slacks.

Of course, even if he kept his eyes covered he would never pass as a norm.

Not when his powers filled the air with a constant chill.

Few people could remain in the same room with him without being battered by the urge to flee. Not if they had a functioning brain.

In the middle of trying to decipher a particularly difficult passage, Zak reached for the Baccarat crystal glass that was filled with a priceless cognac.

He basked in the warm glow that slid down his throat, setting it aside as a knock on the door interrupted his blessed silence.

"Enter," he called, resting back in his leather chair as the young, burly man hesitantly stepped into the room.

Stanley York had been released from jail less than a year before and anxious for a quick influx of cash. Which meant he was willing to do anything with no questions asked.

Wearing faded jeans and a sleeveless tee, his features were blunt with dark, cunning eyes and his hair buzzed to his skull. He had several tattoos, but none of them were magical. A ridiculous waste of ink.

Always edgy in Zak's presence, the ex-con lingered near the open door, his gaze darting around the room as if sensing unseen eyes. "Forgive me."

"You have news?" Zak asked in a soft, accented voice.

"Yes." The henchman glanced toward Zak without meeting his gaze. For all his tough-guy attitude, he was as spineless as everyone else beneath Zak's diamond stare. "Tony retrieved the . . . bundle."

Zak tapped a slender finger on the edge of the desk, his

flawless features impossible to read. "He packed it precisely as I told him to?"

The man grimaced. "I promise he followed your directions as if his life depended on it."

"A wise choice," Zak murmured.

It was amazing how eager his servants were to please him after witnessing him remove the heart of a fellow servant who was unfortunate enough to have returned to the house without their latest package.

"Yeah." Stanley cleared his throat. "He should be here in two hours. Maybe less, depending on the traffic."

"Make sure he doesn't do anything that would attract the attention of the authorities." His voice remained soft. Only a bully needed to shout and bluster. Zak led with pure, unrelenting fear. Far more efficient. "I will be excessively displeased if my name appears in a police report."

"He's a pro at avoiding the authorities. Everything's under control."

"You'd better pray that's true."

Stanley paled to an interesting shade of gray. "Yes, professor." His hands twitched, as if he didn't know quite what to do with them. "Will there be anything else?"

"I want to know the minute Tony arrives."

"Of course."

Shuffling backward, Stanley shut the door before beating a hasty retreat back to the servants' quarters.

Zak reached for his glass, draining the cognac as he waited for the shadow to detach from the far bookshelf, revealing a female form.

He'd sensed Anya's presence for the past half hour, but he'd been in no mood to deal with her.

Now he accepted that she wasn't going to leave him in peace until she'd had her say.

"Thugs," she muttered in disgust.

He set aside his glass, his gaze indifferently flicking over the tight black dress that revealed more than it concealed. With her long red hair flowing down her back in a shimmering river of fire, the witch was a fantasy come to life.

Not that he was in the mood to appreciate her beauty. Unlike most men he wasn't controlled by his cock.

Not ever.

"True, but every general needs a few expendable soldiers to do the grunt work," he reminded his companion.

"A pity they have to be so stupid." She halted next to the desk, the scent of herbs and blood clinging to her. A sure indication she'd been in her rooms brewing up some concoction or another. "It's entirely their fault the body was found by the authorities."

Zak steepled his fingers beneath his chin. He didn't need the reminder.

He'd been furious when his servant had returned to the house without the female that Zak had personally selected. That didn't mean, however, he was prepared to accept defeat.

"Charles paid for his mistakes."

"Perhaps, but—"

Zak narrowed his eyes as the words deliberately trailed away. "Say what you have to say, Anya."

"You should have chosen another female." She was the only creature in the world with the nerve to lecture him, although her tone was carefully devoid of censure. "It's too risky to take the body from the police morgue."

"It took us twenty years to track down Calso and another six months trying to find a way past his security." He curled his lips in disgust. "Did you want to throw it all away because you have cold feet?"

"Not cold feet," she denied in petulant tones. "But I'm not going to be happy if we're forced to move again."

With a deliberate motion, Zak pushed himself out of the

chair, the swirl of his power tugging on Anya's hair in icy warning.

The witch had saved his life when he'd been burning on the stake. She was also the one who'd managed to stumble across the means for his ultimate triumph.

But he'd been born during a time when only the strong survived and he didn't believe in democracies.

He was in charge.

Which meant he didn't confess just whom he'd encountered while he was in Leah's mind. Or that he'd all but thrown down the gauntlet to those fools who cowered behind the walls of Valhalla.

He was done waiting for his unjust rewards.

"There will be no more running."

Belatedly realizing she'd crossed a dangerous line, Anya took a step backward. "No, of course not," she hastily purred, lacing her words with a spell of soothing. As if her magic could actually sway a man with his powers. "Soon you will have endless followers who will be worthy of your greatness."

"So you have promised for the past—" He deliberately paused. "How long has it been, Anya?"

Her lips tightened. "Nearly three hundred years."

Zak grimaced. He had a vivid memory of the night he'd been captured by the local villagers and burned at the stake. Hard not to. It played and replayed every night. Like his nightmares were stuck on one channel.

The next hundred years had been spent in a protective cocoon of magic Anya had wrapped around his burnt body that had barely clung to life, followed by another tedious century of regenerating his physical form. Time that was fuzzy in his memories.

Thank the gods.

The past hundred years had been devoted to restoring his

former powers. And more importantly, to locating the key to unlocking the ancient secrets to his ultimate destiny.

"My patience is at an end," he informed the witch.

"I understand, I truly do, but our enemies are searching for you," Anya attempted to soothe. "It's too dangerous to draw such attention to yourself."

Zak stepped forward, the overhead light catching in his faceted eyes until they shimmered with blinding glitter that filled the room.

"Is there a reason you want me to wait?"

"I don't want you taking unnecessary risks." Her chin tilted. "I have devoted my life to you."

"You have devoted your life to the hope that I will make you a queen."

He watched her shrug. "So what? I'm a woman with ambition."

"Just make certain you're a woman who is prepared to travel to the temple."

"I will be prepared," she promised with an arrogance that could rival his own. "So long as you don't get both of us killed before you can get your hands on the coin."

"Careful, Anya. You aren't the only means of taking me where I need to go." He smiled. "Understood?"

The very gentleness of his threat made Anya grasp the small amulet hung around her neck even as she hurried toward the door.

"Bastard."

"So they say," he murmured toward her retreating back.

Duncan had done some stupid things in his life.

Hell, he'd done stupid on a spectacular level.

There was the time he'd emptied his savings account to buy a piece of shit sports car that died before he got it out of the driveway.

The night he'd chased a perp into gang territory and had the crap beaten out of him.

The day he decided to swing by home to surprise Susan only to find her enjoying a little afternoon delight in their bed.

And ten minutes ago when he'd promised Callie all he wanted was a kiss.

Anyone who knew him realized that he had impulse control problems.

Like a five-year-old, he never believed in deferring pleasure when he could have immediate satisfaction.

But Callie had naively accepted his promise, melting into his arms with such trust he couldn't possibly take advantage of her.

Dammit.

Grimly shackling his desire that thundered through his rigid body, Duncan concentrated on the intoxicating taste of Callie's lips. Until this minute he'd considered kissing a necessary step to getting a woman naked beneath him. It might be enjoyable, but only because it led to the ultimate destination.

He'd never truly appreciated the pleasure in simply . . . smooching.

Now he savored every slow brush of their mouths. The wet heat when he dipped his tongue between her lips. Her shudder when he spread tiny caresses over her upturned face.

Cupping her nape with one hand, he allowed the other to stroke through the silken strands of her hair. It was perfect for this woman. Soft, yet with a spunky fire that would always keep a man in place.

At least any man fortunate enough to earn a place in her secluded world.

The reminder that he would soon be returning to his life of murders, sleepless nights, and empty apartments while this extraordinary woman remained hidden behind the magic of Valhalla had him fusing their lips with a kiss that bordered on desperation.

She returned the heat and fury for a blissful second, then with a faint frown she pulled back to study his brooding expression.

"Duncan?"

"I've wondered for so long what you taste like," he rasped.

Her tongue peeked out to touch her swollen lips in an unconscious gesture that made him groan in agony.

He might have developed a sudden addiction to sweet Callie-kisses, but that didn't mean his cock was happy to be all revved up with no place to go.

"And what's the verdict?" she asked.

"Danger."

She blinked, the stunning gemstone eyes shimmering with an inner glow.

God . . . they were glorious.

Mesmerizing.

"I taste of danger?"

"Yes."

"I'm not sure what that means."

His lips twisted. If she'd been any other woman he would never have offered her such a powerful weapon. History had taught him that women, even good women, enjoyed holding the whip if a man was foolish enough to put it in her hand.

And knowing that a man was willing to give anything, pay any price, to have a female in his bed was one hell of a whip.

"Good."

She shook her head. "Do you always speak in riddles?"

His eyes lowered to her lips. "I'd rather not be speaking at all."

A blush stained her cheeks, but even as his gut clenched with anticipation there was a sharp rap on the door.

"Go away," he snapped, his gaze never shifting from the invitation of her lips.

"You have a call." A male voice floated through the wooden barrier.

"Take a message."

"Duncan, it could be important," Callie chided.

"I'll call back later."

"It's your chief," the voice said with an unmistakable hint of satisfaction at the untimely interruption. A friend of Fane's or just another male anxious to be with Callie? "She says it's important."

"Shit."

Reluctantly, Duncan dropped his arms and stepped back. If Molinari was calling then it had to be important.

Which meant his brief time with Callie was well and truly over.

Obviously coming to the same conclusion, Callie moved to pull open the door just far enough to speak to the handsome young man standing in the hall. "Has the call been transferred?"

The man nodded, his gaze shifting over her shoulder to stab Duncan with a glare of open dislike. "Yes, line two."

"Thank you, Mel."

"No problem."

The man sent one last glare through the doorway before turning to stalk down the hallway, but Duncan was already crossing the room to punch the extension number as he pressed the receiver to his ear.

"O'Conner."

"We have a problem." As always Molinari was blunt to the point of rudeness.

The five-foot-five middle-aged woman didn't weigh a hundred pounds soaking wet, but she ruled the station house with an iron fist.

"Another one?"

"The body's missing."

He sucked in a sharp breath. He didn't know what he'd been expecting, but it sure the hell wasn't that.

"Leah?"

"Yep."

"What the fuck happened to it?"

"No one knows."

Distantly he was aware of Callie politely stepping away, giving him the illusion of privacy despite the fact she couldn't help but overhear the conversation. It wasn't as if he or Molinari were bothering to keep their voices lowered.

"A body doesn't just disappear," he growled.

"You think I don't know that?"

"You checked the tapes?"

"Clean."

"And no one saw anyone enter or leave the morgue?"

"No one."

"What about—"

"You wanna come do my job?" the chief interrupted, her tone warning he'd trespassed on her last nerve. "Maybe wipe my ass while you're at it?"

Duncan grimaced. "I want to know what the hell is going on."

"Then find out."

Rubbing his forefinger against the pain beginning to shoot through his temple, he tried to think.

Something that would have been a hell of a lot easier if freaky shit didn't keep happening.

"The usual chop shops wouldn't risk stealing a body from the police morgue," he muttered, referring to the gangs that occasionally made a grab for bodies in the hospital. If they could get them fresh enough the organs went for a fortune on the black market. "Unless there's a new player in town."

"I have Caleb checking out the usual suspects," Molinari said.

"What do you want from me?"

"Find out if the freaks have an extra body hanging around."

Duncan rolled his eyes. "Great."

Callie leaned against the bar that separated the small kitchen from the living room.

Despite the rumors, all high-bloods were taught proper manners. She knew that she should leave the room so that Duncan could speak to his chief in privacy.

But she couldn't deny an irresistible curiosity to discover if the human police had learned any information on the dead female. If they could determine why she'd been chosen as the victim, they would surely be one step closer to finding the murderer, right?

And more importantly, she simply wanted to remain close to Duncan. At least for a little while longer.

Unconsciously her fingers lifted to touch her lips, still swollen from his kisses. She'd half expected to be disappointed. After all, the sexy cop had filled more than one fantasy over the years. How could he possibly live up to her obscenely high expectations?

But he'd not only lived up to them, he'd blown past them as he'd tutored her in the vast array of kisses from tender sweet to raw, bone-melting perfection.

She'd been lost in the sensations that seared through her. The pounding of her heart. The squeeze of her lungs as she struggled to breathe. The aching need that twisted her stomach.

And all from a kiss . . .

She wasn't sure she could survive a full-out assault.

Not that she wasn't willing to give it a try, she acknowledged with a shiver.

Realizing that Duncan was slamming down the phone, Callie fiercely squashed her renegade thoughts. A dead girl was missing. Now wasn't the time to be wishing that they'd ignored the knock on the door.

They would have time later to explore the heat that sizzled between them. She intended to make damned sure of that.

Pushing away from the bar, she watched as he turned to meet her steady gaze, a surprising hint of color on his cheekbones.

Because his chief had called them freaks? Or because they were still considered suspects?

Probably both.

"You heard?" he demanded.

She nodded. "I wasn't trying to eavesdrop."

"It doesn't matter." He shoved his fingers through the pale gold of his hair, making her breath hitch at the desire to smooth the short satin strands. "We need to find out what happened to the body."

Damn. With an abrupt jerk, she was heading across the room. She couldn't concentrate when she was alone with this man.

"We need to share this information with the Mave."

She opened the door before he managed to capture her arm and tug her back to meet his hooded gaze.

"Callie."

A shiver of anticipation crept down her spine. "Yes?"

He leaned down until they were nose to nose. "This isn't done."

"You said a kiss," she reminded him, not about to admit that she'd already made the decision to lock him in her apartment until he proved whether the rest of his skills lived up to her fantasies.

His ego was big enough, thank you very much.

"A kiss for now," he corrected, his voice gruff.

"And later?"

He pressed his lips to the edge of her mouth before lifting his head.

"I want . . . everything," he whispered in warning.

They were standing there, staring at one another in emotion-charged silence when the sound of approaching footsteps had them both turning to the door.

Once again it was Mel. The healer had clearly broken some rule that demanded community service. Not unusual for a young, impetuous man who'd barely left his teens. And he wasn't a bit pleased with his duty of carrying messages.

Especially when that duty included playing servant in front of an aggressive male norm.

He glared toward Duncan. "The Mave wants to see you in her office."

"Good news travels fast," Duncan muttered.

Callie grimaced. Nothing happened in Valhalla that escaped the Mave's attention. And a call from the human police chief would have hit her radar at record speed.

"Would you rather speak to her alone?" she asked.

"Hell no."

There was a snicker from Mel, as if he'd never wet his pants when the Mave called him to her office.

"I'll show our visitor to the Mave," she informed the young man.

He sent Duncan another glare. "Should I alert the dungeons they're about to have a guest?"

"Enough," Callie said in dismissal, waiting until Mel turned to stroll down the hallway before leading Duncan in the opposite direction.

She kept the pace brisk, but there was no missing the cold, suspicious glances that followed their path.

"Friendly bunch."

"As friendly as your fellow cops would be if I strolled into the station house," she pointed out in low tones.

"Touché," he muttered.

"This way." Callie turned the corner, headed directly for the Mave's office. It wasn't until they were standing in the small alcove directly in front of her door that she realized Duncan was dragging his feet. Halting, she glanced over her shoulder in confusion. "What's wrong?"

"I've heard a lot of rumors about your leader," he confessed.

"Which rumors would those be, Sergeant O'Conner?" the Mave asked as she pulled open the door to offer Duncan a serene smile. "The one that claims I have actual horns and a tail? Or my personal favorite, the one that suggests I'm nothing more than a myth? Like the Wizard of Oz?"

Chapter Six

Duncan was accustomed to shoving his size twelve foot into his mouth.

It was one of his few talents.

But he wasn't used to being struck speechless.

Holy shit. He felt like he'd been kicked by a mule as he caught his first glimpse of the mysterious Mave of Valhalla.

It wasn't just that she was drop dead gorgeous. He had a distinct preference for flame-haired pixies with eyes of sapphires. Or that she displayed her witch's mark with obvious pride. It was dark enough to warn even a thick-skulled norm that she had enough magic to turn them into something nasty if they didn't keep their prejudices to themselves.

No, it was simply the power of her presence.

It was etched onto the pale, perfect oval of a face. In the storm gray eyes. And flickered in the aura only his gaze could detect.

Even if he didn't know a damned thing about this woman, he would realize she was a force of nature.

"Good god," he breathed.

"Not quite, Sergeant O'Conner," she murmured as she stepped back and waved an arm toward the black and white room behind her. "Will you come in?"

Awkwardly moving past her slender form, he headed toward the nearest chair. "I'm sorry," he muttered.

"Trust me, I've heard worse." The Mave crossed to stand beside the large desk where a fully loaded tea tray was waiting. "Refreshment?"

"No." Callie stepped next to him, elbowing him in the ribs to remind him of his manners. "Thank you," he tagged on lamely, dropping into the leather seat.

Callie took the one next to him while the Mave slid into her seat behind the desk, her gaze on the young diviner.

"Callie, how are you feeling?"

"Fine."

"No headaches?"

"None."

"Good." The gray eyes shifted toward Duncan. "I heard that you had a telephone call from your chief?"

Refusing to answer wasn't an option. Not beneath that unnerving gaze.

"Leah's body is missing."

Something darkened the gray eyes. Not the shock he'd been expecting, but . . . unease?

"Missing?"

"Yes."

"Negligence or theft?"

He shrugged, wise enough not to take offense at the blunt question. "No one knows for sure."

"But your chief suspects that a high-blood was involved?"

He swallowed a groan. Why had he insisted on traveling to Valhalla? It should be Molinari sitting in this chair being grilled by the Mave.

Talk about a clash of the Titans.

Now he was forced to choose his words with care. "She's just covering all the bases."

A wry smile twisted her lips. "Very diplomatic, Sergeant."

"I'm not often accused of diplomacy."

"No kidding," Callie muttered beside him.

He flashed her an unrepentant grin before returning his attention to the powerful woman behind the desk.

"The chief has another officer checking out the usual suspects."

"But?" she prompted.

"There was nothing on the cameras and no eye witnesses," Duncan confessed. "So either it was an inside job or magic."

The Mave leaned back in her seat, her expression troubled. "A pity."

"What do you mean?"

"I was hoping it was a common body snatching."

A ball of dread settled in the pit of his stomach.

If this woman was bothered by something then it had to be bad.

Bad on an epic scale.

"You know something," he breathed.

Taking a file from the top drawer, she handed it across the desk. "Here."

His dread deepened as he opened the file to discover newspaper clippings, police reports, and faded photos.

"Paris. Vienna. Johannesburg." He glanced up in surprise. "How did you get these?"

"I called in a few favors after I spoke with Callie. I thought it important to know if the strange death of Leah was an isolated incident or something"—she considered a beat—"larger."

Duncan read through the police reports, some that dated back fifty years, before moving to the newspaper clippings that were even older.

He suddenly understood the Mave's concern.

"Shit."

Callie reached to lightly touch his arm. "What is it?"

"Leah wasn't the first murder victim to be missing their heart," he rasped.

The young diviner frowned, glancing at the file in his hands. "How could you not hear of them? I thought police shared that sort of information?"

"They've all happened several years apart and on different continents. The first was nearly a hundred years ago." He returned his attention to the grainy photos. There was nothing to connect the victims. An aging priest. A rugged explorer. An artist. "Can I share these with the chief?"

"Of course," the Mave readily agreed.

He lifted his head to meet her steady gaze. "Do these murders have any meaning?"

"Not to me."

His cop's instincts picked up on what she wasn't saying. "But it might to someone else?"

"Most old tales have some kernel of truth at the heart of them," she murmured.

"Are you speaking of a specific old tale?"

"The ones that claim a necromancer can truly control the dead."

He shot a startled glance toward Callie, who held up her hands in denial.

"Don't look at me."

He turned back to the Mave. "Is it possible?"

"Yesterday I would have said no. Today . . ." She shrugged.

Great. Just fucking fantastic.

He could already feel the panic that would spread through the human population if word got out there was a necromancer out there killing young females and stealing their bodies. They would load their guns, ready to shoot every freak they could find, regardless of their innocence.

"Tell me more about what these necromancers could do," he abruptly demanded. He needed a way to halt the killer.

Fast.

"My knowledge is no more than bedside stories." The

gray eyes held a grim understanding of the looming tragedy. "The same ones I'm sure you've heard."

He hissed in frustration. "So I'm looking for a creature from a fairy tale?"

"I'm afraid so."

"Do you have any suggestions where I might start?"

She lifted a dark brow, regarding him as if he were disappointingly dense. "Where else would you start but the Keeper of Tales?"

There was a choked sound before Callie was surging to her feet. "You can't be serious."

Duncan slowly rose, astonished by Callie's fierce reaction. "Who is the Keeper of Tales?" he demanded, almost afraid to ask.

"Boggs. He's—" The Mave struggled for the right word.

Callie had it. "Crazy," she said. "Stark raving mad."

"Eccentric, as are many scholars," the older woman smoothly corrected. "But he's managed to collect and preserve our folk tales."

Duncan frowned. "So he's a . . . librarian?"

"Of sorts," the Mave hedged.

"Fine, I'll talk to him." Duncan shrugged. At this point he'd make a lunch date with Beelzebub if necessary. "If he has information I don't care if he's crazy or not."

The two women exchanged a look that spoke of secrets.

"He isn't here," the Mave at last admitted.

"How long will he be gone?"

"Actually, you'll have to go to him," the witch informed him.

"If he'll let you," Callie added in disgusted tones.

Okay. There were enough undercurrents in the room to drown an elephant. Or a very suspicious cop.

"What am I missing?"

The Mave rose to cross toward the window, moving with a regal grace. "Boggs is unusual even among high-bloods."

A freakish freak?

Not comforting.

"How unusual?"

"He was born blind, but he insists that people and even objects whisper to him." Sympathy softened her grim expression. "That's why he lives in absolute isolation."

Well . . . that didn't seem so bad. He half expected a lunatic who ate babies for breakfast.

"Whisper what to him?"

"It's never the same. Sometimes the future . . . or at least, a possible future," the Mave said. "More often it's the past or the present."

"It's nonsense," Callie muttered.

Duncan studied her flushed face with a lift of his brows. "Do I sense a history?"

She wrapped her arms around her waist. "He demanded to see me on the day that Fane became my guardian."

Duncan's hands clenched at the thought of this woman being bonded to another. Platonic or not, the relationship made Fane far too possessive.

"Was there significance in the date?" he growled.

"Who knows?" Callie gave a wave of her hand. "The man is a whack job."

Duncan stilled, studying her growing agitation with a curious gaze. This was not the cool and composed Callie he knew.

"What did he tell you?"

"It doesn't matter. As I said, he's nuts."

Accepting that now wasn't the time to demand a full confession, Duncan glanced toward the Mave, who was regarding Callie with a worried expression.

"What do you think I can learn from Boggs?" he asked, barely leashing his instinctive urge to tug the fragile diviner into the protection of his arms.

The witch smoothed her features into an unreadable mask

as she turned toward Duncan. "His gifts have allowed him to amass a vast amount of knowledge."

"Yeah, but is it trustworthy?" He grimaced. "We have witnesses coming into the station on a daily basis claiming to have seen murders and kidnappings and even Elvis Presley in a spaceship."

She held his gaze for a long, unnerving minute. "That's for you to decide."

Holy shit. Did she suspect that he had a few unusual talents of his own? He'd never considered the possibility that so many freaks would sense he wasn't normal when he insisted on traveling to Valhalla.

Stupid of him.

He cleared his throat. Time for a diversion.

"So how do I find him?"

"You can't," the Mave informed him. "Not unless he wants to be found."

So the one person who could potentially give them a clue to the murders was impossible to find. Duncan rolled his eyes. "Perfect."

"I'll try to contact him," the Mave promised, returning to her seat behind the desk. "If he's willing to speak with you then Fane will be able to locate him."

"Christ, I thought the day started off bad." Duncan shuddered, not happy with the thought of being yanked through space with the Sentinel. He didn't trust the bastard not to deliberately scramble his molecules. "Now I have to spend more time with Lurch?"

Callie snorted. "I doubt Fane will be any happier."

The Mave glanced toward the young diviner. "I fear he'll be even less pleased when he discovers you are to accompany them."

"Ah." Duncan smiled even as Callie turned a sickly shade of gray. "The day is looking up."

"Crap," Callie muttered.

Chapter Seven

Callie hadn't expected to eat.

The choice of taking Duncan to the dining hall and settling at a table next to the windows overlooking the inner courtyard had been more a case of self-preservation than a desire for food.

She wasn't sure what would happen if they were alone together in a room, but she did know it would include heated kisses and missing clothes . . .

A tempting way to spend the night, but not when they were destined to be interrupted.

When she finally had this man in her bed she intended to devote several hours to exploring his naked body.

But once the plates of salad, lasagna, and garlic bread arrived, she found herself polishing her plate and even indulging in a serving of tiramisu.

The chefs of Valhalla could work at any five-star hotel. Thank god her metabolism burned at an accelerated rate.

At last pushing back her empty plates, she looked up to discover Duncan glancing around the crowded room with a wary expression.

"Are they glaring at me because I'm a norm or because I'm with you?" he demanded sourly.

She shrugged. When this was all over with she was going to have her friends lining up for an explanation of why she'd looked so cozy with Duncan O'Conner, but for now she didn't care what they thought.

"Probably because you're a cop."

He sent her a disgruntled frown. "What's wrong with cops?"

"Many high-bloods have had unpleasant encounters with authority figures."

He reached for his chilled bottle of beer. "Haven't we all?"

She narrowed her gaze at his casual disregard for what her people had suffered over the years. "It's not the same. Most police assume we're evil by nature."

"You shouldn't take it personal," he denied. "Cops are always suspicious."

"Yeah right."

Perhaps recalling his coroner's reaction to her presence only hours ago, he took a deep swig of the beer.

"Change takes time."

"So they say."

He leaned back in his seat, setting aside the beer bottle. In the overhead lights his pale hair had the smooth sheen of polished gold and his lean features were more starkly beautiful than ever.

It made her regret her decision to choose the public dining room instead of her apartment.

At least until the next words fell from his lips. "Tell me what happened with Boggs."

It was the question she'd been expecting since they'd left the Mave's office, but it still managed to catch her off guard.

"That's none of your business."

He focused on her with that stubborn concentration that made him such a good cop.

And an annoying dinner companion.

"And what if I want it to be my business?"

She shifted to make sure her back was to the rest of the room. If any of her friends caught sight of her scowl they'd be charging over in a heartbeat to rescue her.

"Are you willing to let me pry into your privacy?"

He lifted one shoulder. "What do you want to know?"

"Did you love your wife?"

He sucked in a deep breath, his hand clenched on top of the table. "Straight for the jugular, eh, Callie?"

"Not so eager to play now?" she taunted.

There was a short, explosive pause before he folded his arms over his chest. "I knew Susan from the first day of kindergarten," he said in clipped tones, his expression screwed down tight. "She was a good Catholic girl from the neighborhood who seemed exactly the sort of woman I should marry. My parents were delighted."

She knew she should back off. It was obviously still difficult for him to discuss his wife.

Ex-wife.

And she had no right to press. But a part of her had to know. It was like a thorn beneath her skin that was becoming unbearable.

"That didn't answer my question," she said, her gaze never leaving his hard expression.

There was another long, painful pause.

"I was truly fond of Susan, but I didn't crave her like a man should crave his wife," he abruptly admitted.

"Crave?" She blinked in surprise. "That's an interesting choice of words."

He surged forward, grabbing her hand and pressing her inner wrist to his lips.

"A relationship shouldn't be a comfortable arrangement," he growled against her racing pulse. "It should be heat and passion and raw emotions."

An electric jolt of excitement arrowed straight through her, making her squirm in her seat.

Yow. Talk about heat. She felt singed.

"I get the picture," she breathed.

Lowering her hand, he kept his fingers wrapped around her wrist, his thumb teasing the spot he'd just kissed.

"Tell me about Boggs."

She sighed, but she made no move to pull away from his light grasp. If she were to be honest, she needed the comforting warmth of his touch. The memory of her visit to Boggs wasn't something she wanted to dredge up.

Not ever.

"He sent word to the Mave that he'd come across an artifact that spoke about a coming threat," she said in low tones.

"The usual mumbo jumbo of supposed prophets?"

"Exactly," she said, her skin growing clammy as she remembered the dark cave that had been filled with stale air and piles of strange objects that looked like they'd come from a Hollywood set. It'd been creepy as hell. Especially for a girl who'd rarely left Valhalla. "He insisted that he needed to speak with the *'young diviner with the eyes like sapphires.'*"

"He did get the eyes right," Duncan murmured. "Are they unusual?"

"Most diviners have green or brown eyes."

"How many diviners are there? Or is that a secret?"

"There are less than twenty spread around the world."

He seemed startled by her confession. "A rare gift."

She shrugged. "Yes, but not the most rare."

He frowned, as if wanting to know exactly what else might be out there that was even more rare than a necro, but then he gave a sharp shake of his head.

"So Boggs demanded to see you?" he asked, clearly refusing to be distracted.

"Yes."

"And what did he say?"

She shuddered. Even after twelve years she could still

recall the sight of Boggs when he shed his robe and revealed his hidden power.

"That the dead rest uneasy in their graves."

He studied her carefully bland expression. "You weren't impressed?"

Her lips stretched in a humorless smile. "I'd have been more impressed if he hadn't kept me waiting in a damp cave for ten hours only to tell me the exact same thing I'd heard from a carnival fortune-teller when I was twelve."

"The fortune-teller told you the same thing?"

Damn. She wished she hadn't let that slip.

It made the coincidence seem far more important than it was.

Or at least, more important than she'd always hoped it was.

Now . . . well, she wasn't so sure.

"It's no secret I'm a diviner," she said in what she hoped was dismissive tones. "What else would they say?"

"Oh, I don't know." The hint of gold was suddenly more pronounced in the hazel eyes. A sure sign he was imagining her naked. "Maybe that you were destined to meet a handsome cop who was going to rock your world."

The tight bands closing around her chest eased at his deliberate teasing. "You really have the most god-awful pickup lines," she said with a shake of her head.

"Good thing I'm gorgeous."

"And so modest."

His brief smile faded, his expression somber. "Are you sure it wasn't more than just a fluke that you received the same warning from two different sources?"

She wrinkled her nose. It'd been a question that had haunted her more than once over the years. And always, she came to the same conclusion.

"What if it was?" she asked with growing impatience. "What am I supposed to do about restless corpses?"

He couldn't disguise his shudder of horror. "I'm the wrong person to ask."

"You're the wrong person for a lot of things," Fane mocked as he came to a halt beside their table.

Duncan was instantly bristling with an overdose of male aggression. "You know I still have my gun?"

"I could kill you before you ever got it out of the holster," the guardian promised, laying his hands flat on the table as he smiled with lethal promise.

Callie heaved a sigh as the entire room went eerily silent. Just like a Wild West movie when there was a looming gunfight.

Idiots.

She pulled her hand away from Duncan. No need to throw gasoline on a smoldering fire.

"Did you need something, Fane?"

"The Mave contacted me. We leave in an hour." His dark gaze shifted to study her pale face. "You should rest."

"I will." She offered a reassuring smile. "I promise."

"We'll meet at the chapel."

"Okay." She held his gaze, allowing him to see that she was strong enough to face the upcoming ordeal. "It's going to be okay."

"I intend to make sure of that," he swore, shooting a scowl toward Duncan. "Watch yourself."

With his warning delivered, Fane turned to stroll out of the dining hall, impervious to the avid gazes that followed his exit.

Fane really and truly didn't give a shit what people thought.

Knowing the attention was bound to shift back to them the minute the Sentinel disappeared from view, Callie surged to her feet.

"Let's get out of here."

* * *

Duncan breathed a sigh of relief as they left the dining hall by a side door and entered the moon-drenched gardens.

He'd always assumed that he knew how the freaks must feel when they were out and about in the world. The covert (and not so covert) stares. The bristling fear of those around them. The active dislike that could fill the atmosphere with a dark threat.

Now he had to accept that he hadn't had a clue. Logically understanding the basic concept of bigotry and actually enduring it in action were two separate things.

For several minutes they walked in silence, Duncan trying to shake off the lingering feel of suspicious gazes, and Callie clearly worrying over the upcoming encounter with Boggs.

At last he sucked in a deep breath and glanced around the rose beds that were already in full bloom despite the fact that it was only April. Velvet petals from deep burgundy to purest white perfumed the air while a marble fountain sent water dancing in a sparkling display. There were beautifully carved benches and birdbaths, and along the edge of the gardens were low hedges so perfectly trimmed they didn't seem real.

His lips twitched as he recalled his enthusiastic attempts to trim the hedges when he'd owned a house. They'd not only ended up as barren stumps, but he'd accidentally taken out a few of the neighbors'. Needless to say he hadn't been invited to the block party.

One upside to living in a shitty apartment building . . . no yard work.

"I didn't realize it would be so beautiful," he murmured, allowing his hand to brush hers as they walked along the flagstone path.

A strained smile curved her lips. "Mother Nature is always spectacular, but it doesn't hurt to have a witch as a gardener."

"True." He studied her upturned face, his cock twitching at the sight of her in the moonlight. She looked lovely. As always. But she didn't belong in this garden. She wasn't a hothouse rose. She was too rare, too exotic. Like a flower plucked from a distant, tropical island. "Were you happy growing up here?"

"I was." Her smile lost its tension, pleasant memories replacing her looming fear. "Children who are brought to Valhalla are given to foster families, but everyone is involved in raising them. I had a dozen mothers fussing over me."

"You never considered tracking down your birth parents?"

"They stopped being my parents when they dumped me in the trash," she said with blunt dismissal. "I've never had any urge to know anything about them."

He nodded. She had obviously been given all the love and protection she needed. Why would she want to know the bastards who'd tossed her away like garbage? "Fair enough."

She tilted her head to the side. "What about your childhood?"

He instinctively slowed his pace as they neared a shadowed corner of the garden conveniently hidden by a trellis covered in climbing roses.

"Loud, messy." He shot her a grin. "Occasionally painful."

She came to a startled halt. "Painful?"

"I had two older brothers who threw me out our bedroom window, hog-tied me and left me in the back shed until my da found me. They also dared me to kiss my fourth-grade teacher, who promptly kicked me out of school for a week."

She arched a brow, not a hint of sympathy to be found.

"Any sisters?"

"Three."

"Older?"

"Yep."

"That explains it."

He pressed his lips together to hide his smile. He was about to be insulted. Amusement would only ruin her fun.

"Explains what?" he dutifully demanded.

"Your assumption that women should adore you."

"Of course they should. I'm adorable."

She snorted. "What you are is spoiled."

He couldn't deny the accusation. Along with being a true pain in his ass, his sisters had shamelessly indulged him.

"There might have been a little spoiling," he agreed.

She reached to pluck a rose bloom from the trellis, her fingers caressing the peach petals.

"Does your family live in Kansas City?"

"Yes." He cleared his throat. Damn, but the sight of those delicate fingers brushing over the flower made him hard. He wanted her hands on him. Stroking, exploring, maybe doing a little squeezing. "My ma would be devastated if any of her chicks flew too far from the nest."

She smiled. "You were fortunate."

"It didn't always feel like it. A big family can smother a young man trying to spread his wings." Nothing like two parents and five older siblings prying into his business. Privacy was more precious than gold when he was an oversexed, hormone-charged teenager. "Now I've learned to appreciate the O'Conner clan." He paused, struck by a sudden inspiration. "Maybe I'll take you to Sunday dinner."

She blinked. Then blinked again. "Me?"

"Why not you?"

"I think that's obvious."

"Clearly it's not."

"Fine." She tilted her chin to a defensive angle. "I doubt I would be welcome."

Duncan sucked in a sharp breath. It was frighteningly easy to picture Callie in his childhood home. The O'Conners were loud and boisterous and rough around the edges, but they all possessed the same overriding urge to be protectors. One look at this fragile beauty with her jewel eyes and they'd be tripping over each other to play mother hen.

"You're wrong. My ma is a remarkable woman. She

would never turn anyone away from her table," he assured
her. Then he gave a short laugh as he thought of his da's reaction to Callie Brown. "Of course, it might be dangerous."

"Why? She might stick me with a carving knife?"

"Worse, she might start sizing you up for a wedding
gown."

More blinking. "You can't be serious?"

"My ma is old school." He shrugged. "She believes a man
is incapable of happiness unless he's under the rule of a wife."

Her expression was wary, as if she feared he might be
playing a cruel game. "I can't imagine she would ever be desperate enough to think of me as a potential daughter-in-law."

He reached to sweep his hand over her spiky hair, his
touch gentle despite the violent anger that surged through
him. Man, he wanted to punch every ignorant jackass who'd
made this remarkable female feel she was anything but extraordinary.

Or maybe he'd just shoot them.

Yeah. Shooting them sounded much more satisfying.

"Why wouldn't she want you?" he demanded. "You're
young, beautiful, and I presume you're capable of producing
the mandatory grandchildren?"

She licked her lips, sending another jolt of heat through
his body. Okay. No more thinking of kids. Or how a man
went about acquiring them.

"I'm a freak who can see into the minds of the dead,"
she said.

He tugged a fiery strand of her hair. "Darling, it's not exactly a secret. I've seen you in action."

"Mothers don't invite people like me to Sunday dinner."

"So you're special," he said. "All the better."

She studied him in puzzlement for a long minute. Then
abruptly she narrowed her eyes. "Ah. I know what you're
doing."

She did?

"I'm glad one of us does," he muttered.

"You're trying to distract me from our upcoming meeting with Boggs."

True. He'd certainly started out trying to tease a smile to those full, delectable lips, but somehow he'd lost track of his goal.

And worse, he knew he wasn't going to easily dismiss the image of Callie surrounded by his family at his mother's kitchen table.

A dangerous fantasy.

Far better to concentrate on the simple lust that hummed through his body like a live current.

That was the kind of danger he could handle.

Skimming his fingers over the curve of her ear, he shifted to make sure he was blocking her from sight of anyone entering the garden.

"I have better ways to distract you," he murmured, lowering his head to nip her bottom lip.

"Really?" she breathed, her hands lifting to grasp his shoulders.

He shuddered at her ready response. "Oh yeah."

Cupping her face in his hands, he tilted her head to the exact angle for him to claim her mouth in a kiss that was a blatant sexual demand.

They had mere minutes before they would be forced to leave Valhalla. Not nearly long enough to do what he wanted to do with this woman.

But he intended to take advantage of every second.

Slipping his tongue into the silken heat of her mouth, he lost himself in the sweet addiction of Callie Brown.

Chapter Eight

Below the sweeping mansion the rooms weren't elegantly furnished or designed to impress.

In fact, it looked exactly like a morgue.

Probably because that's what it was.

The long, open room had white tiled floors and built-in stainless steel freezers along the walls, which filled the air with a soft hum. Overhead the rows of lights blazed as bright as the sun.

And in the very center of the room was a steel gurney where a young female was laid out, her skin as white as the blanket that covered her naked body and her chestnut hair spilling over the edges.

Zak crossed to the gurney, the hem of his gray robe brushing the floor. He peered down at her delicate features, clinically comprehending why a man would make a fool of himself over such a creature although his passions had been purged in the flames of his enemies.

"Ah." He tilted her face to the side, examining for any defects. "She's exquisite."

The man standing beside him shifted in unease.

Tony was exactly what Anya had called him.

A genuine thug.

Short, with a barrel-chest, he was as strong as an ox and about as smart as one. His dark hair was slicked from a square face that had a crooked nose and small, beady eyes.

His personality was as pleasant as a pit bull, but he did have several relatives who always knew someone who knew someone who knew someone—which meant he had a cousin who worked in the police station who was willing to switch off the surveillance tapes long enough for Tony to get in and out without setting off the alarms.

"Whatever you say," the thug muttered, unconsciously wiping his beefy hands on his jeans.

Not everyone was as comfortable as Zak with the dead.

Strange. The man had reputedly killed over a dozen people, including women and children. How could you be squeamish about death when you were so good at dealing it?

Besides, corpses were far better company than the living.

"You may go," Zak dismissed.

"Thank god." The man bolted toward the door.

"Tony," Zak halted his retreat.

He glanced over his shoulder. "Yes?"

"I don't need to remind you that it would be extremely unhealthy to discuss anything connected to your job."

His voice was a gentle whisper, but Tony was suddenly as pale as the dead female. "I swear, my lips are sealed."

"Go."

Tony didn't need to be told twice. Moving with a surprising speed considering his bulk, he disappeared out of the lab and up the stairs.

Dismissing the servant from his mind, Zak continued his inspection of the female. It wasn't for pleasure. He had to be certain that the coroner hadn't started his autopsy.

"Are you satisfied?" Anya purred as she entered the lab

attired in yet another dress, this one a deep shade of green to contrast with her rich curtain of hair.

Unimpressed, Zak returned his attention to the pretty corpse.

"We retrieved her before any damage could be done."

"Then you can complete the ritual?"

Assured that the female was still viable to complete her part of his plan, he straightened the blanket and moved to a counter that ran between two of the freezers.

"Are you in a hurry now?" he demanded, washing his slender hands in a sink before drying them on a towel. "Before you were urging me to wait."

"I haven't seen any news of her death, but it's only a matter of time," Anya snapped. "The risk you took to get the female won't do us any good if Calso learns that she's dead."

He reached beneath the counter to pull out two candles and a shallow bowl made of ivory. From a drawer, he pulled out a large ceremonial knife.

"Some things can't be hurried."

"Fine."

A blessed silence filled the lab (yet another reason to prefer the dead over the living) as he sliced a razor-thin cut in his palm and allowed several drops of blood to fill the bottom of the bowl.

Then, wrapping a linen cloth around his hand to halt the bleeding, he lit the candles and softly chanted the familiar incantation.

Over and over, he repeated the chant, his hands passing over the pool of blood in the bowl.

It wasn't the words or the candles that mattered.

They were merely the focus to call upon his latent talents.

Slowly, almost imperceptibly, a cold wind began to swirl

through the lab, bringing with it the moist scent of earth and something else.

Something foreign.

He opened himself to the encroaching chill, allowing it to fill his body with a power greater than his own.

He didn't know when he'd discovered the ability to go beyond glimpsing into the minds of the dead. He'd been too young to be frightened when the power had risen to consume him and yet old enough to realize that he needed to keep it a secret.

Living on a remote estate in Russia, it had been a simple matter to practice his growing skills away from prying eyes. And if he'd been caught once or twice by a serf, well they were easy enough to dispose of.

In time his powers had become more than a source of fascination.

He'd used them to climb his way from a minor nobleman to a favorite among the czar's court, surrounded by the wealth and luxury his weak, feebleminded father could never have imagined.

Of course, he was no longer a man who would be satisfied by such shallow desires.

His blessings weren't given to him for pleasure.

They were given to him to rule.

And that's exactly what he intended to do.

"Bring me the urn," he said, his body numb from the cold power thundering through him.

"As you command," the witch grumbled, moving to pull the ceramic urn from the nearest freezer.

"If you wish to act like a child, you may leave."

She muttered beneath her breath, but she was wise enough to handle the urn with care as she set it on the counter next to him. "Here."

Zak ignored his petulant companion, reaching into the

urn to pull out a frozen heart. He returned to his chanting as he set the delicate organ in the bowl and covered it with his hands.

He ignored the witch, who fidgeted with growing impatience, and even the heavy tread of Tony walking upstairs, no doubt heading to the kitchen to raid the fridge. The man ate on a continuous basis.

Nothing was allowed to distract him from the biting power. Not when it was hammering through him with a growingly painful force.

The ability to wrench a person from the jaws of death wasn't a gift for the weak. Not like those ridiculous diviners who hid behind the walls of Valhalla and barely scratched the surface of what was possible.

With every second he risked being consumed by the icy darkness that pulsed through him.

He battled with the grim reaper, never certain he would win.

At last the force that churned inside him burst through his hands and arrowed into the heart beneath his palms.

The heart shuddered, the ice abruptly melting as it was filled with a magic as old as time.

Sucking in a deep breath, Zak turned to make his way back to the gurney. He kept his steps steady despite the weariness seeping through his body.

He never revealed weakness.

Especially not in front of Anya.

The witch might have pledged her loyalty, but she was a treacherous bitch who'd turn on him in the blink of an eye.

Halting next to the gurney, Zak placed his hand on the female's forehead. "Leah, wake," he commanded, watching as her lashes fluttered upward.

The light brown eyes were devoid of emotion, but they held an awareness that was all he needed.

* * *

Duncan squeezed his eyes shut, desperately clinging to the copper post while trying not to scream like a wussy.

Had it only been a quarter of an hour ago that he'd been in the rose-scented darkness with Callie in his arms?

He'd been lost in the intoxicating pleasure of her kiss, trying to ignore the world around them, when Fane had made his untimely arrival.

From there things had only gone downhill.

The tattooed pain-in-the-ass had arrived in silence, filling the air with a bristling antagonism that had Callie awkwardly pulling from Duncan's grasp, a stain of color on her cheeks.

For a crazed minute, Duncan had curled his hands into fists. As if he was going to slug the bastard.

It was only the knowledge that the Sentinel had devoted his entire life to protecting Callie, and that she might very well need his considerable powers before this was all said and done, that kept him from breaking his knuckles on Fane's arrogant jaw.

A choice he regretted as the Sentinel led them to the small chapel. Duncan was barely allowed to glance around his barren surroundings when Fane roughly grasped his hand to shove it against the post in the center of the room and the world melted to nothingness.

A punch wouldn't actually damage the bastard, and broken hand or not, it would have been satisfying to have landed a blow.

The sense of emptiness abruptly vanished as the world once again coalesced around him. Briefly disoriented, Duncan clutched the post, his head whirling.

"Shit."

"Troubles, cop?"

Duncan scowled at the Sentinel, who was watching his discomfort with a smug smile. "Nothing that couldn't be solved with a well-placed bullet."

"Keep telling yourself that if it makes you feel better."

Ignoring their squabble, Callie walked across the stone floor to study the strange etchings on the wall.

"This is a different place."

Duncan moved to join her. "What?"

"This isn't where Boggs was when I met him last time," she explained, glancing toward Fane. "Where are we?"

"Germany."

Without another word, the warrior turned to leave the cramped room, clearly expecting them to follow.

For once Duncan didn't mind the man's arrogance.

Not only was he still trying to find his balance, but his mind was reeling from the casual announcement he'd just been zipped halfway around the world.

Holy shit.

The furthest he'd ever been from KC was his honeymoon in Key West.

And that'd taken him two days to drive.

In the process of wondering if Sentinels kept passports and foreign money stashed around the world, Duncan realized that Callie was moving.

With a shake of his head he was following her, stepping out of the circular chapel into the refectory.

The long room was what he'd expected of an ancient abbey. Made of plain stone and lined with towering arches that opened to side passages, it had several tables shoved at the back, as if the monks gathered in the space to eat. Or maybe pray.

The ceiling was vaulted to give the impression of a vast space and painted with the same hieroglyphs that were tattooed on Fane.

Protection against magic.

And god only knew what else.

Callie came to a halt as they caught sight of Fane at the far end of the room, quietly speaking with a hooded monk. Clearly it was bad manners to interrupt.

"What's going on?" Duncan instead demanded.

"I assume that we'll need transportation to travel to Boggs," she said, her arms wrapping around her body in an unconsciously defensive motion.

He stepped behind her, gently massaging the taut muscles of her shoulders. "I'm not going to let anything happen to you," he swore.

She glanced back, her eyes catching and reflecting the lights of the candelabras. "Haven't you heard that the days of damsels in distress are over?"

His breath caught. How could he be constantly caught off guard by her beauty? His hands skimmed up and down her arms, driven by a compulsive need to touch her.

"I don't doubt you can take care of yourself, Callie, but we all need someone to watch our backs," he said in a husky voice.

"Even macho cops?"

"Especially macho cops."

Silence. The sort filled with potent fascination, licks of treacherous heat, and a mutual wariness of the bonds forming between them.

This hadn't been in the cards.

For either of them.

"Come on," Fane intruded, his heightened temper heating the air as he glared at Duncan. "We have to hurry."

"What's the rush?" Duncan snarled, promising himself that as soon as he was certain Callie was safe he was whisking her far away from her guard dog. *Intrusive, pushy bastard.*

He didn't care if he had to chain the warrior to the wall and throw away the keys.

As if sensing his dark promise, Fane sent him a last searing glare before leading them through one of the arches.

"Boggs refuses to speak once the sun rises."

Falling into step, Duncan grimaced. "He's not a vampire, is he?"

Fane shrugged. "You'll see."

Duncan glanced toward the silent Callie. "I'm not going to like this, am I?"

"As the Mave said . . . he's eccentric."

He shook his head. There was no use speculating what might be waiting for him.

They walked through the narrow hallways of the abbey, the occasional flicker of candlelight the only thing to hold back the thick gloom.

Although for him it was seven or eight in the evening (he never wore a watch), the abbey was shrouded in sleep with only an occasional glimpse of robed figures who were unfortunate enough to have the night shift.

They passed through an empty workroom filled with wooden tables piled high with rolls of parchment and bottles filled with a dark liquid he assumed was ink. There were even feathered quills piled on a far bench.

Scribes? In this day and age?

That seemed . . . redundant.

Fane kept his pace brisk as they left the abbey and crossed a paved courtyard to stand next to a large building that looked like it had once been the stables. Within minutes a black SUV with tinted windows appeared from around the corner of the building and Fane pulled open the back door to help Callie into the backseat.

Duncan was quick to slide in after her, sinking into the buttery leather seat so that the Sentinel was forced to climb into the front seat with the hooded monk.

Childish?

Hell, yeah.

But it was common knowledge that most men stopped maturing about the age of five.

Closing the door, he'd barely managed to click his seat belt in place when the monk shoved his foot down on the accelerator and they were hurtling away from the abbey at a speed that had to be illegal.

Silence filled the interior of the expensive vehicle as Callie retreated inside her thoughts. Fane appeared to be in some Zen-like zone. The monk presumably had made some sort of vow of silence, or maybe he was just enjoying his pretense they were racing the Grand Prix.

And Duncan . . . well, his jaws were clenched too tight to utter more than a squeak.

Duncan caught a glimpse of a wide river that he assumed was the Rhine following the narrow road that wound through a dense forest. They raced through a tiny village so fast he barely made out the quaint shops with their wooden signs and polished front windows that were filled with hand-carved cuckoo clocks, squishy teddy bears, and the inevitable beer steins.

His ma would be enchanted, he acknowledged, making a mental note to have his siblings chip in to send his parents on a well-deserved vacation. His da would insist on visiting Ireland, but would make sure his ma had a say in the plans.

They'd been traveling less than a quarter of an hour when the SUV made a sharp turn onto an overgrown path. He instinctively reached to tuck Callie against him as they jolted over the uneven path, wondering who taught the damned monk how to drive.

Thankfully the bone-jarring journey at last came to an end at the top of a hill, and with a low groan, Duncan shoved open the door and climbed out of the vehicle. He turned to help Callie out, not surprised that she'd barely stepped onto the path when Fane was smoothly taking his place at her side.

Duncan clenched his teeth and concentrated on his surroundings. Now wasn't the time to play caveman. The only thing that mattered was getting the answers they needed without putting Callie at risk.

It took a moment of peering through the gloom to realize

that the mound that was rising from the trees wasn't another hill, but a stone structure that was being slowly consumed by the forest.

"He lives in a castle?" he muttered in surprise.

"I doubt he has an actual home," Fane said, pulling a clear crystal that was hung on a leather strap from his pocket. "He's more of a squatter."

Duncan grimaced, taking in the crumbling curtain wall that had once surrounded the grounds. "He couldn't have squatted at the Ritz?"

Fane spoke a soft word and the crystal began to glow. "Be on guard, cop," he warned, urging Callie toward the bridge that crossed the long-forgotten moat.

Bringing up the rear, Duncan pulled his gun and searched the shadows for something to shoot. "You expect trouble?"

Fane passed beneath the barbican and entered what must have been the lower bailey. Now it was just a rough patch of weeds and bramble. "Don't you?" he growled.

"Yeah." Duncan felt a chill trickle over his skin, as if he was being watched by unseen eyes.

They crossed the open ground, Fane neatly leading them past the gaping hole where there'd once been a drinking well and around the nearly hidden cannon.

Before them the inner keep loomed three stories high with empty windows and the appearance of a hollow shell. No doubt it was a treasure trove for the local historians, but it was making Duncan twitch.

He was a cop who'd mastered the urban landscape.

He could spot a suspicious perp in the middle of a crowd. He could tail a car for days without being noticed. He could enter a room and instantly tell you the number of exits, the placement of obstructions if he needed to move in a hurry, and if anyone in the room was carrying a concealed weapon.

But suddenly surrounded by the untamed wildness of nature, he felt like a fish out of water.

It wasn't the thick foliage that was a constant threat to trip him, or the clinging shadows that could hide anything. Or even the silence that made it impossible to sneak up without giving away his position.

It was the strange pulse of power that brushed the very edge of his awareness.

He'd heard rumors of norms who could *feel* magic. As if it was a tangible force. He suspected they were recruited by the government to keep track of the high-bloods.

Until now, he'd never thought it was a talent he possessed. He still didn't. No. If he had to guess he would say that everyone had some ability to sense when there was a disturbance in the air. It was simply the degree of sensitivity to that disturbance. And when it was as strong as it was in the lower bailey even the most oblivious person could feel it.

Fane led them up the steps of the keep, kicking open the heavy wooden door and continuing forward without missing a step.

"No knocking?" Duncan mocked, glancing up at the open-beamed ceiling that was swathed in cobwebs.

Fane held his crystal over his head, bathing the open space in a soft light.

There wasn't much to see.

Stone walls. Stone floor. Stone fireplace.

At one time the room was no doubt made homey by a blazing fire that danced light over the ornate tapestries that had been draped on the walls and the air had been filled with the scent of fresh straw spread over the floor.

Now it was just . . . stone.

And dust.

A damned tidal wave of dust.

"If he didn't want us to enter he would have put up wards," Fane was saying, his pace cautious as he walked toward the steps that led to the floor above. "Of course, that doesn't mean he didn't create a few traps for the unwary. Hermits have an odd sense of humor."

Duncan rolled his eyes. Of course they did.

They climbed the stairs, finding yet another empty room that matched the one below. Except the floor was rotting wood, not stone.

Fane halted, his body coiled for attack. "He's above us."

Duncan clicked off the safety on his gun. "You can sense him?"

The Sentinel flashed Duncan a mocking smile. "I don't have the same talent as a hunter Sentinel, but I can sense a high-blood when they have Boggs's level of power."

Duncan grimaced. Just fucking perfect. Another freak who obviously suspected that he wasn't entirely normal.

Not that this was the time to worry about his little secret. "Do you sense anything else?"

"No. He's alone." Fane stepped to the side, his gaze in constant movement. "I'll keep guard here."

The dark gaze briefly rested on Duncan, silently warning him that the Sentinel was trusting him to keep Callie safe. And that if he failed there would be hell to pay.

Duncan resisted the urge to flip him off as he wrapped his arm around Callie and started up the next flight of stairs. He might logically appreciate Fane's fierce loyalty to Callie, but he didn't need the bastard telling him to keep this woman safe.

Reaching the top floor, he forgot the aggravating Sentinel and even the constant pulse of magic that was wearing on his nerves.

A lone candle was set in the center of the grimy floor, casting flickers of light over the piles of rubbish that consumed half the room.

And it was rubbish.

Broken chairs, tarnished silver teapots, a mound of clothing, ice skates, a framed mirror, ratty books, and hundreds of other items that he didn't recognize.

It was like *Hoarders* on steroids.

"Good . . . god," he muttered. "What is all this crap?"

"History, Duncan O'Conner." A hooded form stepped from behind the piles, his voice oddly melodic. "As well as a promise of the future."

Just for a second Duncan thought it was one of the monks who'd followed them from the monastery. Then the candlelight caught in the folds of the robe and he realized it was black, not the brown of the monks.

He pointed his gun at the center of the deep hood. "That's close enough."

"I have no intention of harming the diviner," the stranger assured him. "No more than you would."

With a flamboyant motion, the man whipped off the robe and tossed it aside.

Even braced to expect the unexpected, Duncan nearly went to his knees in shock.

"Son of a bitch," he breathed, struggling to comprehend the fact that he was looking at an exact replica of himself. No, not exact, his stunned mind accepted. The pale hair and lean face with a shadow of golden whiskers might be a mirror image. As well as his lean form dressed in jeans and casual shirt. But the eyes were all wrong. They were a pure, unnerving white. Not pale, not clear. Just . . . white.

"What's going on?"

Callie lightly touched his arm, urging him to lower his gun. Smart female. His nerves were on a hair trigger.

He didn't want any accidents.

"Boggs is a doppelganger."

Duncan frowned. "A what?"

The . . . creature smiled. "I can take the appearance of those who are close to me."

Holy shit.

A cop to his bones, Duncan was instantly on high alert. A creature who could alter its appearance to look like anyone?

The possibilities for disaster were endless.

He could become a guard and rob a bank. He could go on a murder spree and create a new persona for each killing. Hell, he could turn into the president and start a war.

And worse, his aura flickered with a hint of darkness that revealed he had more than once dipped his toes in the evil pool.

"Why haven't I ever heard of doppelgangers?"

Boggs laughed with creepy delight, throwing his arms wide. "'There are more things in heaven and earth, Duncan O'Conner, than are dreamt of in your philosophy.'"

"Stop that," Duncan commanded.

The white eyes were lit with a sudden inner glow. "Perhaps you prefer this form?"

In the blink of an eye the doppelganger had become Callie, with spiky crimson hair and a slender body displayed in spandex pants and stretchy top.

"No, I damned well . . . wait." His furious words were bit off as he recalled Callie's words. "I thought you said he was blind."

Chapter Nine

Callie shivered. Even knowing what was coming, she still found it impossible not to be flipped out.

"He is," she said, trying to keep the distaste out of her voice.

She was a high-blood. She understood exactly what it meant to be treated as if she were an outcast. Still . . . Boggs took strange to a whole new level.

"Then how does he know what we look like?" Duncan rasped.

"I sense your essence," Boggs admitted, releasing his magic to reveal his true form. Duncan hissed at the sight of the pale, hairless creature that looked disturbingly like a larva. His features were indistinct and his eyes glowed with power. The robe had returned, but it was open to reveal a body that was lacking genitalia. "And before your policeman's imagination begins to run wild, let me assure you that I have to be standing within a few feet of those I duplicate and that I can only hold the image for a few minutes. I'm no danger to society."

Callie felt Duncan stiffen, as if Boggs had managed to strike a nerve, but as usual the cop tilted his chin and held his ground.

Foolish courage.

It was going to get him killed.

"Can you read minds?" he growled.

"I don't need to be a psychic to know what you're think-ing. I'm tediously familiar with the prejudices of men with badges. They instantly assume that freaks have no morals."

"The Mave sent us to ask you questions," Callie inter-rupted. Men. Did they always have to have a pissing match? "Are you willing to answer them?"

A cunning expression flickered over Boggs's alien fea-tures as he subtly shifted closer, closing the robe to hide his body. "I suppose it depends on the questions."

Duncan moved to make sure he could step between her and Boggs if he sensed a threat, his gun still in his hand.

"There have been bodies found without their hearts." Duncan took the lead. Of course. He was such a cop. "But there are no wounds. It's as if the heart just disappeared from their bodies."

Boggs made a sound deep in his throat. Not shock. But . . . resignation?

"A bokor," he muttered.

Duncan frowned. "A what?"

"One of the living dead."

Not surprising, the cop paled at the blunt explanation. "Like a zombie?"

Callie wasn't quite as stunned as Duncan. Since she'd left the cradle she'd heard stories of the walking dead and the necromancers who could raise them.

Of course, she'd never believed them.

Not until now.

"I thought they were a myth," she said.

Boggs stroked a too-thin finger down the line of his jaw. "There has been only one necromancer capable of control-ling the dead."

"Who?" she asked.

"He's been known by many names."

Duncan snorted. "I don't suppose you know his current one?"

Boggs shook his head. "No, but he was once Lord Zakhar."

Callie licked her dry lips. A true necromancer. It didn't seem possible. Like discovering Santa Claus was real.

Only scarier.

"What can you tell us about him?"

"Very little. He was a nobleman in the Russian court. From what I could learn he was growing in power when he was accused of being a sorcerer."

"Not uncommon," Duncan surprisingly answered. "Russian politics were always dangerous and social climbers often accused their rivals of foul deeds."

Boggs tapped the tip of his finger on his chin. "True or not, he was burned at the stake three hundred years ago."

"Christ," Duncan growled. "Necromancers can raise themselves from the dead?"

He took the words straight from Callie's mouth.

"I didn't say he died," Boggs pointed out in sly tones.

Callie arched a brow. Many high-bloods had extended lives. Something not commonly known among norms. But not many could survive being burned at the stake.

"Then what happened to him?"

"No one knows." There was an edge in his voice that spoke of his annoyance at the lack of information. Boggs clearly understood that knowledge was power. "The locals assumed he died in the flames, but there were rumors a dark power swooped in to rescue him. Some say the devil rose up to claim him."

Callie wrapped her arms around her waist, suddenly chilled to the bone.

Could it be him?

Was it possible that the man she'd encountered in Leah's mind was a three-hundred-year-old necromancer with the ability to raise the dead?

"Do you know what he looked like?"

"The stories claimed that he had eyes of diamond."

"Shit," Duncan muttered as he watched the color drain from her face.

Boggs released his breath with a low hiss. "You've seen him?"

"Not in the flesh." Callie shuddered. "He was in the mind of a dead woman."

"What did he say?"

"Aren't you the one who's supposed to be answering the questions?" Duncan snapped.

Boggs waved a thin hand. "It's an exchange of information."

"He said that the question is—" She was forced to halt and clear her throat. "The question is . . . *Who are you?*"

The white eyes widened. "Interesting."

Callie frowned. It wasn't interesting. It was ominous. And threatening. And spooky as hell.

"What did you see when you demanded that we meet the first time?" she abruptly demanded.

The doppelganger froze, as if caught off guard by her question. Then, with a twitch of his robe, he was turning to head toward his pile of junk.

"A minute," he murmured, delicately shifting through the strange collection. Duncan muttered something about lunatics, but she remained focused on Boggs as he made a sound of satisfaction. "Ah, here it is."

He returned to stand in front of her, holding up a tangled mound of pink yarn.

"A baby blanket?" she guessed.

Boggs held it to his face, his features becoming even more indistinct as he rubbed the material over his cheek.

"It speaks of you."

Eek.

She ignored the way he seemed to savor the tactile feel of the cashmere against his skin. Or maybe it was the silent communication between him and the blanket.

"Why would a blanket speak of me?"

He shrugged. "Perhaps it was once yours."

Highly doubtful, but she was willing to play along. "What does it say?"

"You're walking through a graveyard."

"That's it?"

"The dead are stirring beneath your feet."

A far too vivid image of hands reaching from the grave to touch her seared through her mind. It was a dream she'd been having all too frequently.

"Are they trying to warn me?"

"No, Callie Brown."

A cold ball of premonition formed in the pit of her stomach.

"Then what?"

"They're trying to follow you."

The words hit Callie with the force of a tsunami, the stunned tidal wave of horror sweeping her under before she knew what was happening.

Falling forward, she was vaguely aware of Duncan racing to catch her in his arms before the darkness swallowed her whole.

Duncan muttered a string of curses, shifting Callie's limp body against his side, and pointed his gun at the bastard who was surging forward.

"I'm sorry. I didn't mean—"

Duncan fired a warning shot close enough to the doppelganger's head to make him duck in fear. "Stay back," he warned.

"Duncan, I'm fine," Callie murmured, managing to regain her balance although he kept a stubborn arm wrapped around her waist.

He turned to study her too-pale face with a scowl. "People who are fine don't faint."

"I didn't faint," she ridiculously protested. "I was just . . . surprised."

"Yeah, that's one way of putting it."

She turned toward Boggs, her expression defiant despite the tiny tremors that Duncan could feel still racing through her body.

"I don't know what you saw, Boggs, but I can't raise the dead."

He lifted his thin hands in a pretense of innocence. "I'm just the messenger."

Yeah, right. Duncan's finger twitched as he tried to leash the urge to fire off another round. A bullet or two in Boggs's spongy flesh might teach him that not everyone enjoyed his mysterious mumbo jumbo.

"Did you see anything else?" Callie asked, her voice unsteady.

"Yes."

"Are you going to share?" Duncan snapped.

Boggs gave another lift of his hands. "I did."

Callie shook her head. "I don't understand."

"He spoke to me," Fane said, his voice coming from directly behind them.

Duncan didn't allow his attention to stray from the doppelganger as the Sentinel moved to stand beside a puzzled Callie.

"Fane?" she muttered in disbelief.

Duncan made a sound of disgust. "I presume there was a reason you didn't offer a full disclosure."

"After our first visit to Boggs I took Callie back to Valhalla before returning to the cave."

"Why?"

Boggs answered. "He threatened to kill me."

"I don't like men who give little girls nightmares," Fane growled, earning Duncan's complete approval.

Boggs, however, gave a click of his tongue. "The whispers were driving me nuts. Besides, I waited until she turned eighteen."

Duncan shot a brief glance toward Fane, but it was Callie who asked the burning question.

"What did he say to you?"

"He warned me that a shadow was growing," the Sentinel said, his gaze trained on the doppelganger. "And that if I failed in my duty to you, I would fail all high-bloods."

He heard Callie's breath catch at the reluctant confession. "Why didn't you say anything?"

Fane shrugged. "You had enough to worry about."

"It's no wonder you've been uberprotective," Callie muttered.

Duncan frowned. The warning might be vague, but unless the creature was a complete fraud then they were in some deep shit.

Corpses without hearts who disappeared from the morgue.

A crazy necro who could actually raise the dead.

And now some ominous shadow.

"So what is this shadow?" he asked Boggs, not at all surprised when the thing shook his head.

"I don't know. All I see is a darkness creeping over the high-bloods with Callie standing in the center." A genuine fear glowed in the white eyes. "If the darkness covers her then all is lost."

Duncan's fingers tightened on the gun. The thought that

Callie was at the center of the brewing danger made him want to shoot something.

"You're a master of melodrama with very few actual details that would help," he snapped, glaring at the doppelganger.

Boggs stiffened, clearly offended by Duncan's sharp accusation. "I have offered all I have to give."

Callie sent him a chiding glance before stepping toward the creature. "Can you tell us anything more about the necromancer?" she asked, her voice pleading. "How do we find him?"

A dense power filled the air as Boggs seemed to swell in size, his presence an overwhelming force.

"Sometimes to see into the future you must look into the past," he said in a voice that echoed through the room.

Duncan flinched. Oh man. He'd been treating Boggs as if he were some harmless whack-job, not a magical high-blood that could quite possibly squash him like a bug.

It was a wonder he was still standing.

Then just to emphasize the point, Boggs spread his arms wide and with a shock wave of energy, he abruptly disappeared.

Poof.

Gone.

"Fuck," Duncan rasped in shock.

Fane snorted. "That just about sums it up, cop."

Chapter Ten

Callie was exhausted by the time they reported their encounter with Boggs to the Mave. Even by a high-blood's standard it'd been one hell of a day and all she wanted was to crawl into her bed and tumble into oblivion.

So why had she followed Duncan to his rooms instead of simply going to her apartment?

He was a big boy. She was fairly certain he could make the short distance without an escort. But even as she told herself to turn around and walk away, her feet were carrying her through his doorway and straight to the window that offered a view of the surrounding countryside bathed in moonlight.

"Doppelganger," Duncan muttered as he shut the door. "What other creatures don't I know about?"

She didn't bother to turn; she could see his reflection in the window. The lean, hard body. The stark features that were shadowed with weariness. The hazel gaze that was checking out her ass.

He might be tired, but he was all male.

"You know I won't answer that question," she said.

He strolled to halt beside her. "You don't think I have a right to know?"

"It's not my place to make those decisions." She shrugged. "You're welcomed to return to the Mave and ask her if you want."

He snorted at her helpful suggestion. "Yeah, thanks but no thanks."

She turned to study him with a lift of her brows. "Does it matter?"

"Only if they're dangerous."

"We have our own method of dealing with dangerous high-bloods."

"Hunters?"

She nodded at the mention of the Sentinels who chased down renegades. Even now they were on the trail of a murderous high-blood who was creating chaos through Texas.

"Sometimes."

"And other times?"

"Psychics. Witches." She grimaced. "And Wolfe."

"Wolfe?"

"The head of the Sentinels. No one wants to piss him off," she said before giving a sudden shake of her head. "Well, except the Mave. She does it on a regular basis."

"I'm not remotely surprised."

"Sometimes I think—" She bit off her words, startled to discover she'd come close to confessing her suspicion that there were more than control issues that set off sparks between the Tagos and the Mave.

What was it about Duncan that made her feel as if she could share her most private thoughts and feelings?

It was . . . unnerving.

His brow furrowed. "Callie?"

"I should let you get some rest," she abruptly said, turning to head for the door. "You can use the phone if you need to call your chief."

"Wait."

With a swift motion he was blocking her path, his hands lightly grasping her upper arms.

"It's late," she protested, her heart fluttering at his gentle touch. "We can talk in the morning."

His gaze slid over her face, lingering on her lips before returning to meet her wary eyes. "You're right."

"I am?"

"I don't want to talk."

She shivered. The heat of his fingers seared her skin, sending jolts of sensual electricity darting through her body. "Duncan," she breathed.

His hooded gaze sparked with gold in the dim overhead light. "Can I hold you?"

She licked her dry lips. "What?"

His fingers stroked up and down the back of her arm. "We're both tired and more than a little freaked out."

"True."

"I don't want to be alone tonight."

"Is that another cheesy line?"

"Not this time." His expression was oddly somber. "I just want to feel you in my arms while I sleep."

Her heart missed a beat at the simple words. She'd never had a man who just wanted to hold her. Actually, most men who were willing to have sex with her would have been horrified by the thought of sharing her bed.

She did, after all, peer into the minds of the dead.

The fact that Duncan genuinely seemed to want to hold her touched her in a deep, vulnerable place.

"Oh."

He wrinkled his nose. "Too cheesy?"

Cheesy? It was . . . perilously perfect.

Dammit.

"No," she husked.

His jaw tightened, as if preparing to be rejected. "But?"

There was a tense pause as Callie silently weighed her options.

Logic warned that she should walk out the door and never look back.

She didn't understand what was happening between her and Duncan O'Conner, though she did know that it was more than the usual lust for a prime stud-muffin.

But she didn't want to be logical.

Not tonight.

She might be accustomed to her lonely bed, she might even have convinced herself she preferred to be on her own, but as Duncan had pointed out, it had been a long, freaky day. No doubt the first of many.

Why shouldn't she enjoy a few hours wrapped in the arms of this gorgeous, drop-dead sexy cop?

A small smile curved her lips. "I don't have my nightie."

An undefinable emotion flared through the hazel eyes as Duncan moved with a speed that would have rivaled a Sentinel to scoop her off her feet.

"That's okay," he rasped, headed toward the bedroom. "Neither do I."

She allowed herself to relax against the hard muscles of his chest, her gaze caught by the golden stubble that shadowed the line of his jaw.

He was so . . . male.

Uncompromisingly, ruthlessly male.

And yet, he held her with a gentle care that was oddly reassuring.

He might be aggressive and even violent when necessary, but he would never, ever harm her.

"I don't believe you wear a nightie."

"Some night soon I'll show you just what I do or don't wear," he promised with a wicked grin. "Tonight there are a couple robes hanging in the bathroom." Entering the comfortable, if impersonal bedroom done in shades of black and silver, he lowered her until her feet were touching the carpet. "You can use the bathroom first."

With a nod she hurried into the attached bathroom and closed the door.

It wasn't that she was shy. Or scared.

Or at least not exactly.

But on the day of her eighteenth birthday she'd moved into her own apartment. She wasn't used to sharing a private space with anyone.

Stripping off her clothes, she stepped into the shower and turned it on hot enough to turn her skin rosy. Steam billowed around her as she soaped herself from head to toe before squeezing her favorite apple shampoo into her palm and quickly washing her hair.

She admired women like Serra who could keep their long hair perfectly coiffed (whatever the hell that meant). She, however, ended up looking like a porcupine by the end of the day. Besides, the unique color attracted the sort of attention she didn't want.

Hopping out of the shower, she quickly dried herself and pulled on one of the thick terry cloth robes. Then, leaving the bathroom, she returned to the bedroom, keeping her gaze locked on her bare toes.

"Your turn."

She felt him hesitate, as if he wanted to say something. Then she heard the steady tread of his footsteps as he headed into the bathroom, shutting the door behind him.

Callie released the breath she'd been unconsciously holding.

This was what she wanted.

It truly was.

But she felt as awkward as a teenager about to go on her first date.

No. This was worse. Her first date had been with a boy she'd known for years. He'd been warned by her foster mother, who happened to be a witch, that if he did anything more than hold her hand he would be turned into a slimy slug.

Certainly she hadn't been pacing the floor with the sensation of demented butterflies filling her belly.

And what was the deal with the temperature?

She was hot then cold then hot then . . .

"Hey, relax, sweetheart," a male voice whispered in her ear, those strong arms again sweeping her off her feet to carry her to the nearby bed. "I just want you close."

With care he settled her on the mattress and shucked off his robe to reveal his lean, surprisingly bronzed body covered by a pair of green boxers. She barely had the opportunity to appreciate the broad shoulders, the well-defined six-pack, and powerful thighs before he was sliding in the bed behind her, tugging the blanket over both of them.

"Are you all right?" he asked.

"I'm fine." She sucked in a deep breath, forcing her tense muscles to relax as the heat of his body seeped through her skin. He smelled of soap and toothpaste and an enticing scent that was uniquely Duncan O'Conner. "I've never slept with anyone before . . . I mean . . . not for the whole night."

Cautiously he scooted closer, wrapping his arms around her waist.

"Do all high-bloods keep themselves so isolated?"

She settled her head on the pillow, her gaze absently studying the oil painting depicting a field of daffodils that hung on the wall.

"It does seem to be a common trait."

"Is it because you're afraid of trusting anyone?"

She struggled to concentrate. She told herself her jitters were because she'd never cuddled in bed with a man and tried to have a conversation. Her few sexual encounters had been brief with little in the way of actual chitchat.

It was bound to be awkward the first time, wasn't it?

Certainly it had nothing to do with the intrusive images of what would happen if she shimmied out of her robe and turned to face him.

"For some." She was forced to clear her throat. She wasn't going to imagine rubbing herself against all that male hardness. Or her sensitive nipples being tickled by his golden chest hair as he nuzzled kisses down the curve of her neck. Nope. Not gonna do it. "Most have special abilities that mean they have to maintain constant control when they're around others," she managed to continue. "They need time and space just to relax."

"I get that." His warm breath puffed against her nape, sending arrows of pleasure down her spine. "Cops don't have special powers, but after a day spent in the gutters they need some serious decompression. Not all spouses understand why we want to go to a bar and toss back a few shots or lay on the couch and try to pretend that we can forget the sight of a young woman found dead on her kitchen floor."

She stilled. For once they were completely alone with no danger of being overheard.

"That's not entirely true, is it?" she asked softly.

"What isn't true?"

"That you don't have special powers."

He tensed, remaining silent for a long minute. Callie bit her bottom lip, regretting her impulsive question. It was beyond intrusive to prod into a person's private gifts. Even the youngest high-blood knew that.

If Duncan wanted her to know about his powers he would have told her.

The apology was on the tip of her tongue when Duncan abruptly broke the silence.

"How long have you known?"

"I don't know anything for certain," she assured him. "You work very hard to keep them hidden." She hesitated, torn between curiosity and the manners that had been drilled into her from the cradle. Curiosity won. "Are you ashamed?"

"Not ashamed," he clarified, his voice pensive but thankfully not angry. "But when I was very young my ma warned me never to speak about my . . . gift."

A typical response. Mothers around the world did what they could to protect their children.

Well, except for hers. Her loving parents dropped her in the nearest trash can.

"Did she think it was a curse?"

"No, she was worried I might be taken from her."

"Ah." She kept her gaze trained on the daffodil painting even as she was vividly aware of his lean body pressed against her back. It was somehow easier to share confidences without being face to face. "Will you tell me?"

Another pause before he answered in a voice so low she barely heard him.

"I see auras."

She sucked in a startled breath. "A soul-gazer."

"Soul-gazer." Duncan allowed the words to rattle around his brain. He'd never heard the term, but it seemed oddly right.

"You can see the souls of people, right?" Callie asked, the very casualness of her tone easing the raw knot of discomfort in the pit of his stomach.

Revealing his darkest secret was like stripping in a crowd and allowing a bunch of strangers to measure his dick. The fact that she treated his "big-reveal" like it was an everyday occurrence made him feel less . . . exposed.

"Yeah, I guess that's what I do."

"A rare gift," she murmured. "No wonder you're such a good cop."

He frowned at her soft words. He'd worked his ass off over the years to reach his position of sergeant.

"Hey, it takes more than a flash of color around a perp to make me a good cop."

"But it doesn't hurt."

His lips twitched with a grudging humor. Okay. Maybe he'd used his abilities to sense the guilt or innocence of a perp.

"No, it doesn't hurt," he agreed, his fingers absently toying with the belt of her robe.

When he'd first climbed into bed with Callie he'd barely been able to think beyond the fierce desire that had pounded through him. He wasn't an animal. Or at least most of the time he wasn't an animal. But being in bed with the female who'd haunted his dreams for more nights than he wanted to admit was doing wicked things to his libido.

He wanted her with a compulsive need that was becoming downright painful.

Only the memory of her trembling unease when he'd come out of the bathroom kept him from sliding his hands beneath the robe to explore the ivory silk of her skin.

When he became her lover it would be when she was soft and melting in his arms.

Not skittish with nerves.

"No one but your mother knows?" she asked, thankfully unaware of his struggles.

"No." He was struck by a sudden thought. "Are you going to tell anyone?"

"Not unless you want me to."

That sounded waaaay too easy.

"It isn't some sort of duty to report high-bloods?"

"Not for me."

Ah. Now the catch.

"But?" he prompted.

She hesitated, as if considering her words. "I'm sure Fane would have sensed your powers."

He'd suspected as much, but that didn't stop his stab of annoyance. The last thing he wanted was the pain-in-the-ass Sentinel to have something to hold over his head.

"And he said nothing?" he growled. "I find that hard to believe."

"Nothing to you," she corrected, snuggling deeper into the mattress, the short strands of her damp hair glistening like licks of flame against the white pillow. "But he would have reported to the Master of Gifts."

"Master of Gifts?" He made a sound of disbelief. It sounded like a character from a video game. "Is that a joke?"

"No. Calder and his order search for high-bloods around the world."

Great. There was an entire order searching for high-bloods.

"Should I expect to be hauled to his office?"

"The truth?"

He actually considered her question.

He'd been going along just fine by pretending his abilities were nothing more than a quirk of nature. Like being double jointed or color blind.

Why rock the boat?

Then the realization that if Fane knew he had powers, the boat was not only rocked but in danger of capsizing. He heaved a sigh of resignation.

"Hit me with it."

"They would already have checked you out and determined you aren't a threat to yourself or others."

Oh. He wasn't dancing for freaking joy that he'd been secretly checked out, but really was it that much different from Internal Affairs?

Besides, if it meant he was going to be left in peace, he'd take it.

"So they're not going to try and keep me here?" he asked, not about to take anything for granted.

You know, assumptions making asses out of gullible cops.

"Valhalla isn't a prison." She paused, clearly realizing she wasn't being completely honest. "At least it's not a prison unless you've committed some sort of crime."

He wasn't going to dig into the justice system set up by the high-bloods. Cops who poked their noses where they didn't belong soon had them chopped off.

"And they won't say anything? My chief— "

"Your secret is safe, cop," she assured him, abruptly yawning as the stressful day caught up with her. "Now can we go to sleep?"

"We can," he murmured, pressing a kiss to the nape of her neck.

Closing his eyes, Duncan allowed himself to appreciate the simple joy of having Callie in his arms.

It didn't matter that he was hard and aching with a desire to consume her. Or that her robe rubbed roughly against his bare skin.

The creepy Boggs had warned that Callie was the center of a coming darkness, and whether the doppelganger was the real deal or just a nut-bar, Duncan sensed that this moment of peace was going to be a rare commodity in the future.

He intended to savor every second of holding her close.

Unfortunately, as much as he was enjoying the feel and scent of his beautiful companion, he couldn't shut off his mind as it shuffled and reshuffled through the implications of his secret no longer being so secret.

Assuming that Callie had fallen asleep, he was caught off guard when her hand lightly brushed over his fingers, still clutching the belt of her robe.

"Duncan?"

He squeezed his eyes shut as a jolt of heat speared through him at her light touch.

"Hmm?" he managed from between clenched teeth.

"What's bothering you?"

His eyes popped open with surprise. How the hell had she known something was bothering him?

"Are you psychic?"

"Female intuition."

"Yow." He grimaced. "Now that I'm all too familiar with. My ma and sisters could sniff out a lie a mile away."

"Then you know it's a waste of time to deny that something's wrong."

"Not wrong," he denied.

She squeezed his fingers. "Talk to me, cop."

Wild horses couldn't have dragged the question from him if it had come from anyone but this woman.

But Callie was different.

She . . . understood. In every way.

"Are there other people like me?" He asked the question that had been gnawing at him.

"Soul-gazers?" She seemed startled by his interest. "Of course."

"Here?"

"Yes." A short pause. "Do you want to meet them?"

Did he? There was no denying a tiny temptation to actually speak with someone who shared his talents. Perhaps even to discover how to hone it so it would be a more effective tool.

But was he truly prepared to come out of the closet?

"I don't know," he said, his voice tight. "Not yet."

"There's no need to hurry," she assured him, her tone distracted, as if she were troubled by a sudden thought. "In fact, it might be better that your gift doesn't become common knowledge."

"Why?"

She paused. "It's just a theory."

"Tell me."

"If the necromancer we're searching for can truly raise the dead then we need to be able to spot them."

Yeesh. Walking dead? They belonged in B-rated movies. Not shuffling along the streets of Kansas City.

"I would think walking corpses would be a little obvious in a crowd."

"Not if the magic gives them the appearance of life."

"Damn." Duncan scowled. Like the thought of rotting zombies wasn't bad enough without the possibility that dead people could be waltzing around without anyone knowing. "I suppose I can't just start shooting people to see if they're alive or dead."

"I would prefer you didn't." Slowly she turned her head to glance over her shoulder. "There's an easier way you could help."

He braced for her answer, already sensing he wasn't going to like it. "How?"

"A dead person has no soul."

He studied her pale face in confusion, wondering if she were teasing him.

Then he sucked in a sharp breath.

Of course. He could see the auras that flickered around people.

Which meant if there was no aura, he was seeing a corpse.

"You want me to be a zombie-hunter," he muttered.

"Who better?"

"Shit."

Chapter Eleven

Callie wasn't entirely shocked that she managed to sleep through the night. She'd been on the verge of utter exhaustion, both mentally and physically.

And there was something to be said for having her own private heater to keep her toasty warm.

But she'd been so tense when he'd snuggled in behind her that it seemed difficult to imagine that she could actually relax enough to fall asleep.

Slowly coming awake, she managed to pry open her heavy eyes, surprised to discover the room still shrouded in shadows. Usually she had to set her alarm clock if she wanted to wake up before noon.

So why was she awake at such an ungodly hour?

It took several minutes to realize what had pulled her out of her dreams. Probably because the feel of warm, male lips stroking over the sensitive skin of her neck was precisely what she'd been dreaming about.

Clearly sensing she was awake, Duncan buried his face in the curve of her neck. "Mmm."

She shivered, but it wasn't with nerves. After an entire night of erotic dreams, she was no longer tense at the thought of spending a few hours in the arms of this man.

Actually, she felt all melty as he spooned close enough for her to feel the hard length of his arousal pressing against her lower back.

"You woke me," she murmured, her voice husky.

"Did I?" His tongue traced up the back of her neck, pausing at the tiny dip just below her ear. "You smell like apples."

She trembled at the rasp of his morning beard, instinctively pressing her head deeper into the pillow as she invited him to continue his sensual exploration.

"What time is it?"

"Early," he breathed in her ear, giving her lobe a sharp nip.

She jerked in pleasure, her heart picking up speed. "Then why aren't you sleeping?"

He trailed his lips along her jaw, his touch seeming to sear her skin.

"I'm a morning person."

Of course he was. She wrinkled her nose.

"Ugh."

"Hey." His arms tightened around her, surrounding her in delicious heat. "'Ugh' isn't a word a man likes to hear from the woman waking in his arms."

Callie swallowed her moan as he pressed his cheek to hers, his breath brushing her lips with the promise of a kiss.

"Then you shouldn't have woken me up in the middle of the night."

He chuckled. "Haven't you heard that the early bird gets the worm?"

"Fine, you go hunt your worms and I'll . . ." She forgot how to speak as his hand slid beneath her robe to cup one aching breast. "Duncan."

With a skill that made her eyes slide shut in feminine bliss, he circled her nipple with the tip of his finger.

"You told me to go hunting," he reminded her. "You're the only prey I'm interested in."

Her hand clutched his arm as he tormented the sensitive bud with light, teasing strokes.

"I don't think I like being called prey."

"Okay." With a speed that caught her off guard, Duncan had her robe pulled open and was yanking it off her body. "You be the bird and I'll be the worm." He pressed his fully engorged cock against the bare skin of her ass. "I have better equipment for the role."

She gave a husky chuckle as he pressed a line of kisses down her shoulder.

"You're such a man."

"I try." He growled low in his throat, one hand continuing to pleasure her breast while the other slid down the flat plane of her stomach. "My god, you feel so good in my arms."

She arched her back, shocked by her sizzling reaction to his every touch. It was as if she were perfectly tuned to his seduction.

Or maybe he was so practiced in pleasing a female he knew just how to elicit the response he wanted.

The thought was oddly troublesome.

"Do you do this often?"

His lips explored down her shoulder blade, his hand skimming along her hip and over her thigh to slip between her legs.

"Hold you in my arms?" he teased. "Not nearly often enough."

She pulled in a shaky breath, barely capable of thinking as he gently tugged her leg up and over his hip, leaving her exposed to the caress of his searching fingers.

"Wake up in strange beds," she managed in a strangled voice.

"I haven't been with a woman since my divorce," he confessed, his lips settling at a tender point on her nape as his fingers drew absent patterns on her inner thigh.

She groaned, a damp heat forming between her legs as his fingers strayed ever higher.

Oh . . . baby.

It was almost more than she could stand. The tingles of electric pleasure darted from the tips of his fingers straight to the aching void in the pit of her stomach. The gentle tug on her hardened nipple. And the brush of warm lips up and down her nape.

No man had taken such care to ensure she was so fully aroused.

"Why me?" she demanded.

His fingers traveled another inch higher. "There's the obvious reason."

She grasped his forearm. Not to stop him. Hell, she might strangle him if he tried to halt.

But it was becoming increasingly difficult to remain still beneath his bold caresses and she had to do something to keep from squirming right off the bed.

"And what's that?"

"I can't be in the same room with you without imagining you stripped naked and spread across the nearest bed."

"That's . . ." She squeaked as his fingers at last found the tender cleft, his touch so feather-light it only added to her rising frustration.

"Dangerous," he whispered in her ear. "But not as dangerous as the less obvious reasons."

Oh lord, it was hard to follow his words.

Her nails dug into his arm, her hips angling forward in a silent plea for satisfaction.

"Should I ask?"

His fingers gave a tug on her nipple, sending a blast of heat through her taut body.

"You fascinate me."

Trembling beneath the onslaught of sensations, Callie

lightly raked her nails up his hair-roughened arm, ridiculously pleased when he gave a low hiss of pleasure.

Hey, what was good for the gander was good for the goose.

Or something like that.

"Because I'm a freak?" she asked, her heart missing a beat as one finger slid into the slick heat of her body.

"Because you're clever." He stroked deeper. "And strong." Another mind-destroying stroke. "And aggravatingly elusive." Stroke, stroke. She bit her bottom lip, straining to contain her building explosion. "Your talents are just the icing on the cake."

How did he always know exactly what to say?

"I've never thought of them as icing," she teased.

"Callie, you're sweet goodness from the top of your head to the tips of your toes." With a swift motion he had her turned flat on her back. Before she could even catch her breath, he was poised above her, offering her a wicked grin. "Let me demonstrate."

An exquisite shudder shook her body. Oh lord, she was more than eager for a demonstration.

In this moment, she no longer cared that there was a powerful necromancer out there potentially raising an army of the walking dead. Or that Boggs had more or less implied she was supposed to stop them.

Or even that Duncan would soon be returning to his world of norms while she was destined to remain at Valhalla.

There were times when a woman had to grab at happiness, no matter how fleeting it might prove to be.

As if sensing her capitulation, Duncan growled low in his throat, his hands skimming restlessly over her bare skin as he lowered his head to scatter tiny kisses over her face.

"I've wanted this for so long," he muttered, his tongue outlining her lips. "Too long."

Callie gave a welcoming groan as one roaming hand

returned between her thighs to stroke through her growing dampness.

"No one's stopping you," she pointed out, breathless.

He crushed her lips in a searing kiss. "I want to worship you," he husked as his finger slid into her tight flesh. "Slowly."

Callie instinctively dug her heels into the mattress as she arched her hips upward.

"Slow is fine. But, this is . . . is . . ." Oh man, his finger was creating the most delicious sensations as he dipped it in and out of her. "Torture."

His lips cruised over her cheek, then down the line of her jaw. "No, sweetheart, this is torture." He pressed a kiss to the pulse racing at the base of her throat. "And this." His mouth trailed down until he could latch onto the tip of her breast. "And this." He used his tongue to lash the delicate nipple until she was panting with need.

The aggravating man. He wasn't playing fair.

Lifting her hands, she shoved her fingers in his golden hair and wrapped her legs around his hips.

"You're going to pay for this, cop."

Pulling back, he regarded her with a faint smile, the flecks of gold shimmering in the hazel eyes.

"Do you promise?"

She deliberately rubbed herself against the granite-hard length of his erection.

"Oh, I promise."

He started to lower his head, only to pause as his gaze caught sight of the tiny tattoo hidden behind her ear. His finger brushed the delicate black hieroglyph.

"What's this?"

"A spell of protection against common diseases."

"You can't get sick?"

"Not by any human illness."

His eyes narrowed as a blush stained her cheeks. "What else?"

"It keeps me from becoming pregnant until I'm ready to have children." She shifted beneath him. "Of course I have to have sex before I need to worry about that possibility."

His breath caught. "Callie." Bracing himself on his elbow, he shifted until the tip of his cock pressed against her entrance. "Are you sure?"

She tugged his hair, meeting his oddly watchful gaze. "I'm a big girl. I know what I want."

"I just don't want any regrets."

"Duncan, if you don't get on with it, I'm going to—"

Not giving her time to complete her empty threat, Duncan tilted his hips forward, sliding into her with a slow, relentless thrust.

Hissing softly, Callie clutched at Duncan's shoulders, her nails digging into his skin. Yes, yes, yes. It felt . . . perfect.

Achingly perfect.

Already prepared for his entry, her body readily accommodated his erection. Still, there was a delicious sense of fullness, and a startling connection, that she hadn't been expecting.

In this moment she was joined to Duncan. Joined in a way that seemed far more poignant than two bodies simply having sex.

It was . . .

Her mind instantly veered from examining the powerful feelings that sizzled through her. Dammit. This wasn't supposed to be more than a fleeting pleasure.

"Callie," he whispered close to her ear. "Are you okay?"

"I'm fine, just don't stop," she moaned, burying her face in the curve of his neck.

"Stop? Not even if there was a gun pointed to my head," he muttered, pulling from her body before pushing back in with an increasing urgency. "I've never felt anything so good."

Callie agreed as he was once again withdrawing and thrusting forward with a rhythm that stole her breath. Mmmm. This was what she'd wanted from the minute she'd laid eyes on Duncan O'Conner.

Squeezing her eyes shut, Callie scored her nails down his back, pleased when he hissed in pleasure. She dug her nails deeper, rewarded as his lips found hers in a wild, demanding kiss.

His hips rocked faster, his hands scooping beneath her hips to angle them upward to meet his deep, steady thrusts.

"Duncan . . . hurry," she muttered against his lips, her body clenched so tightly she felt as if she might shatter.

"Just let it happen, sweetheart." Angling his head downward, he tormented her tender nipple, his hips pumping faster and faster as she arched off the bed to meet him.

Callie's breath rasped through the shadows, her concentration narrowing to the precise point where Duncan's body surged in and out of her.

She was racing toward a critical goal.

And she was close.

So close.

And then . . . it happened.

With one last surge he catapulted her over the finish line, sending her into a convulsion of exquisite bliss.

He muffled her scream of pleasure with a fierce kiss, continuing to pump into her shuddering body until he stiffened with his own release.

Dropping his head into the curve of her neck, Duncan struggled to catch his breath.

"My god."

Chapter Twelve

Dawn was barely creeping over the horizon when Zak entered the panic room built in the basement.

The six-by-six cement room was built for protection, not comfort. There were no windows, the door was six-inch steel, and there was no furniture beyond a narrow bed.

Certain the door was locked and Anya standing guard outside, Zak settled on the bed and closed his eyes. Slowing his breath, then the beat of his heart, he delved into the place inside himself that contained his power.

It was dark and cold. A bottomless pit that had nearly swallowed him whole the first time he tapped it.

Now he grimly braced himself as he touched the icy depths, battling not to be sucked in even as he forced the darkness to pulse through his veins, the frigid power searing through him with a pain few others would be able to tolerate.

For him, it was a reminder of the cost of failure.

One slip and the darkness would destroy him.

Submerged in his power, Zak reached for the small bowl on the mattress next to him. Once it was settled in his lap, he placed his hands over Leah's heart, releasing the magic into the beating organ.

There was a brief, disorienting moment as he slid from

his corporal body and winged his way south of town to a neighborhood even more exclusive than the one he'd chosen.

He entered Leah's body, hissing as the darkness abruptly swelled up, trying to claim him.

No. He clenched his teeth, his muscles rigid with strain. He was the master. Death would bow to him.

Sweat beaded his brow, but with clenched jaw he leashed the power and carefully allowed it to trickle into Leah's corpse.

Slowly, slowly he filled her, lodging his consciousness in her mind.

Only when he was certain he had full control did he open the eyes of his vessel and glance around.

Not surprising, he was lying in the back of a parked car. Tony had once again been pressed into service, driving Leah's corpse to the chichi neighborhood, close enough to the house he wanted without being noticeable.

As Zak sat up in Leah's body, he caught sight of Tony slumped against the door, lazily surfing the net on his phone. Then, perhaps sensing he was being watched, he turned to cast a bored glance over his shoulder.

At the sight of Leah the vicious killer released a scream that would have rivaled a teenage girl, emptying his bladder all over his fine chino slacks.

Ignoring the servant, Zak awkwardly pushed open the door of the car and stepped onto the shadowed street.

He (or rather Leah) swayed as he struggled to keep his balance. For all his skill it always took a few minutes to gain command over the body. Glancing down, he vaguely noticed he was dressed in a new pair of stretchy workout pants and a sports bra. Anya had chosen the clothing, claiming that Leah liked to go to the gym in the mornings. He didn't care what was covering the body so long as it didn't attract unwanted attention.

His focus was on the amulet that was strung around his

neck by a thin gold chain. A lethal spell was etched into the soft metal, just waiting to be released.

Assured he had his weapon, Zak gave a swift glance around the sleeping neighborhood before crossing the tree-lined street. His movements grew progressively more fluid as he followed the curved driveway leading to a three-storied home built of a pale red stone.

The roof was sharply slanted and shingled with dark tiles. The large windows were framed by white shutters and to one side was a four-car garage.

At the front was a wide veranda with stately columns and double doors that were an invitation for the enemy to enter.

A sneer curved Zak's lips, an odd sensation as he realized Leah had recently had them plumped with a noxious silicone. He'd spent decades tracking down the relic demanded by Anya's gods. And years more, to discover who was hiding the object.

The last six months had been devoted to monitoring Calso's every movement.

He knew when the bastard woke up, when he went to work, when he went to bed, when he shit. He'd also done an equally thorough investigation on the man's servants. He knew their routine better than they did.

Unfortunately, the constant surveillance on Calso hadn't revealed the location of the coin, and with no guarantee he could pluck the knowledge from his mind once he was dead, Zak had been forced to come up with a plan that would give him the opportunity to search the house without alerting his prey.

Which was how he'd chosen Leah.

As Calso's lover she'd been put into his security system. Which meant she was the only person besides Calso who could enter and leave without disturbing the security guard who patrolled the grounds.

And more importantly she remained human despite his

magic that filled her corpse. The paranoid Calso had paid a fortune to have a powerful spell wrapped around his property to detect high-bloods. If he or Anya had gotten within a hundred feet of the house they would have set off a dozen alarms.

Halting in front of the door, Zak pressed his hand to the electronic reader. There was a low buzzing sound as the scanner read his fingerprints, then with a soft click the doors swung inward.

Zak didn't hesitate as he entered the marble foyer that towered two stories, with arched windows that gave ample light for the tangle of plants that grew along the edge of the black and white marble tiled floor.

He ignored the double staircase that swept in a graceful arch toward the second floor, walking directly between them to the sunken living room at the back of the house.

He was equally indifferent to the white sectional couch that was arranged around the glass cylinder aquarium that was built from floor to ceiling. And the beautifully carved white marble fireplace where two black vases offered a stark contrast to the acres of white.

His only interest was reaching the office that he'd seen in Leah's memories.

From what he could determine before Callie had so rudely intruded into his search of the young female's mind, the office was the one place in the mansion that Calso refused to allow her to enter.

It seemed the feasible place to start his search.

Crossing the white carpet, he was just steps away from the closed door on the far side of the room when a faint sound had him spinning around.

He swallowed a curse at the sight of the short, nearly bald man with a round face and black, beady eyes. Around sixty years old, he was wearing nothing but a pair of boxers with his rotund belly sticking out like a hairy basketball.

Zak barely suppressed his sneer. It seemed impossible to

believe that this pathetic norm could actually hold a piece of the gods.

"Leah?" Calso frowned, his expression wary even as his gaze slid a compulsive glance down Leah's slender body. "What are you doing here?"

Zak clinically debated his option.

The easiest path would be to kill the fool and continue with his search.

On the downside, there were servants who would soon be waking. They were bound to eventually stumble over their dead employer.

Besides, he could use Calso's pathetic obsession with the young female to help narrow down the exact location of his prize.

Forcing his feet to take a step forward, he gave a toss of his head, feeling his hair brushing the bare skin of his arms. It might have been centuries since he'd allowed himself to be led by his dick, but he remembered what had once excited him.

"I'm sorry." He licked his lips. "I didn't mean to wake you."

The dark gaze compulsively lowered to Leah's breasts, barely concealed by the sports bra, but his frown remained.

"I asked you a question."

"I lost my phone." Zak shrugged. "I thought I might have left it here."

"And you decided to search for it at this hour?"

"I couldn't sleep."

There was a pause as the man struggled between suspicion and his libido.

Not surprisingly his libido won.

"A lucky coincidence," he growled, strolling forward.

Zak covertly turned his head away from the windows that were beginning to lighten with the coming dawn.

His motor skills were improving, but only the shadows hid Leah's lack of facial expression.

"And why's that?"

"I couldn't sleep either."

"Ah. What do you suppose we should do about it?"

The man trailed his fingers along the neckline of Leah's sports bra before slipping his fingers beneath the stretchy material and giving the breast a squeeze. Miles away, Zak grimaced, fiercely thankful he didn't have to feel the pudgy fingers groping him.

"I have a few ideas," Calso purred.

"I bet you do."

A flush stained the man's round face. "Upstairs. Now."

Zak made what he hoped sounded like a giggle. "I have a better idea."

He arched a brow. "Games?"

"Catch me."

Without giving the fool a chance to react, Zak turned and hurried the short distance to the end of the room.

"Dammit, Leah, what are you doing?" the man growled, in instant pursuit.

"Playing." Zak opened the door and darted into the office, taking a quick inventory of the room.

A leather sofa and wing chairs surrounding a lacquer table. Several tall bookcases that were stuffed with aged leather books. A heavy walnut desk set by the marble fireplace with a wide mantel that held a number of bronze statues.

At last he turned back to watch Calso storm into the room.

"What the hell are you doing?" he rasped.

"You don't like my game?" Zak prodded, carefully monitoring Calso's gaze, which instinctively shifted toward the area of the desk.

"You know you're not allowed in here."

Zak backed toward the desk, his gaze never leaving Calso's revealing eyes.

"Why not?"

"It's my private office."

"It's not business hours. Don't you want me naked on your desk?"

Zak reached the corner of the desk, lifting a hand to shove back his thick curtain of hair. How did females tolerate the itchy stuff?

Calso hesitated, the dark eyes narrowing in speculation. Was he debating the pleasure of banging her on the glossy surface?

Clearly, Zak hadn't found the sweet spot.

Before Calso could try and pin him to the desk, Zak was sliding to the side, heading directly for the fireplace.

"Or maybe you would rather I—"

"Enough," Calso snapped as he lurched forward. "Get away from there."

Zak followed the man's worried gaze. Ah. How tediously predictable. A wall safe hidden behind the Picasso.

"As you command," he drawled, moving to stand directly in front of Calso.

The man started to relax until he caught sight of the amulet that was beginning to glow in the clinging darkness.

"What's this?"

Zak managed to stretch the rigid lips into a smile. "Death."

Calso stumbled back, fear and confusion twisting the pudgy face. But it was far too late. He'd barely taken a step backward when the amulet released its magic, slamming into him with a lethal force.

Zak watched Calso drop to his knees, the skin ripping like tissue paper as the magic inside him began to swell and expand.

Magic was never a pleasant way to die.

And this was a particularly nasty spell.

But effective, he had to concede, stepping back as the dead man fell face first onto the rare Persian carpet, swiftly turning into nothing but charred ashes.

Anya was nothing if not efficient.

Assured the man was dead, Zak turned away, crossing to the fireplace.

It took less than five minutes to find the trigger on the Picasso that allowed it to swing forward, revealing the safe set in the wall. Reaching up, he pressed his hand against the scanner, not at all surprised when he heard the lock click.

The arrogant bastard never considered his own lover might betray him.

Hubris.

The weakness of every wealthy man.

Reaching for the small handle on the safe, he tugged it open.

Anticipation hummed through him as he reached inside and shoved aside the papers to find the pale stone vessel that was shaped like a small vase with an odd winged creature etched on the front. With care he pried out the cotton that blocked the opening at the top of the vessel and turned it upside down to shake out the coin inside.

A mile to the north, his heart in his real body gave a sudden leap.

Soon . . .

Soon he would have the just rewards he so richly deserved.

Still struggling to catch his breath, Duncan shifted to lie on his side, studying Callie's delicate profile outlined by the rosy promise of dawn.

Christ.

That hadn't been good sex.

It had been . . . cataclysmic sex.

Shattering.

But why?

Holding her close, he tried on a few excuses.

He'd been celibate for too long. A man wasn't meant to be without a woman in his bed, right?

He'd been fantasizing about this woman for longer than he wanted to admit.

He was under a shitload of stress. Everyone knew that adrenaline made everything seem to be in Technicolor. Including sex.

Unfortunately he couldn't make any of the lame-ass excuses fit.

What had just happened between them defied explanation.

A fact that should have scared the hell out of him.

Instead, it just juiced him up with the need to have her again.

And again.

And again . . .

Already hardening with anticipation, Duncan abruptly frowned as he realized that while he'd been reveling in the image of round two, Callie was lost in thoughts that had nothing to do with him or hot, sweaty sex.

"Hey." He brushed his finger down the thin blade of her nose. "Where did you go?"

She blinked, as if coming back from a long distance. Then slowly she turned her head to meet his narrowed gaze. "I was just thinking."

"And it brought a frown to that lovely face?" His finger moved to trace the furrow that marred her brow. "You promised you weren't going to regret what happened in this bed."

"I wasn't thinking about"—a lovely blush stained her cheeks—"that."

"That's even worse," he chided, captivated by the sight of her gemstone eyes catching and reflecting the first strands of light. Man. Had there ever been anything more beautiful? "I'm already a distant memory." Using his free hand, he stroked down the curve of her back, pressing her against his stirring arousal. "Maybe I should remind you the kind of fireworks we strike off each other."

Her breath caught. "Trust me, I'm never going to forget."

He smiled at her husky tone, his gaze lingering on her lips, which were still red and swollen from his kisses.

"That's what I want to hear."

She rolled her eyes. "Arrogant."

His smile faded as he sensed her lingering distraction. As much as he longed to drown in the silken pleasure of her body, Duncan wanted her full and complete attention when he was seducing her.

"Okay, Callie," he murmured. "Tell me what's on your mind."

She wrinkled her nose. "I was just thinking about what Boggs said."

"Before breakfast?" He gave a dramatic shudder. "No wonder you're not a morning person."

She ignored his teasing. "He said that 'to see into the future you must look into the past.'"

Duncan snorted. Boggs had unnerved him more than he wanted to admit, but he didn't want Callie taking risks just because some crazy doppelganger implied that he'd seen her in some psychic vision.

"He said a lot of ridiculous things."

"Maybe." She chewed her bottom lip. "Maybe not."

His spidey-senses jangled. He knew that look. And it was never good.

"So what are you scheming?"

She didn't even blink at his impressive ability to read her expression. Why would she? She'd been raised among people who could peer into her every thought.

"There has to be some way we can discover more about Lord Zakhar."

He stiffened, desperately battling against the primitive male urge to inform her that there was no way in hell she was going to put herself in danger. His sisters had taught him that the swiftest way to get a woman to do something was to tell her she couldn't. Sexist? Maybe. But the knowledge had come in handy on more than one occasion.

"Internet?" he instead suggested. "I know a computer whiz at the station who could locate any information you need."

"I prefer to find original journals if possible. They tend to be a little more reliable."

Of course she preferred the originals. It couldn't have been that simple.

"Will you travel to Russia?"

"Yes. Fane can take me."

"Great," he muttered.

She arched a brow. "It's his job."

It was. That didn't mean Duncan had to like it.

"Fine. Then I'll do my job and start a search for a strange Russian who has recently come to town." His mind was already shifting through his various contacts. "If there's word in the streets I'll hear it."

She reached up to touch the whiskers that shadowed his jaw. "You sound like a cop."

"I don't feel like a cop."

"No?"

He turned his head to press his lips to the center of her palm. "No, I feel like a man who wants to lock away his lover to keep her safe."

She jerked her hand away, her lips thinning in silent warning. "Duncan."

"Don't worry, sweetheart," he hastily assured her. "I might occasionally act like a caveman, but I'm well aware I can't drag you off to my cave."

"Not if you want to keep your family jewels."

He flinched. "Point made." He smoothed his fingers through the rumpled crimson silk of her hair. "Besides, I understand better than anyone how important your gifts are to the world. It would be a sin against nature not to share them."

She frowned. "You don't have to mock me."

"Is that what you think I'm doing?" He shifted his hand to cup her cheek as she tried to turn away. "Callie, look at me."

Grudgingly she turned back to meet his somber gaze. "What?"

"I know what you've done."

"Done?"

"Every time you take a murderer off the street you save lives." He brushed her bottom lip with his thumb. "I can't even imagine how many people owe you their future."

She blushed, clearly uncomfortable at being praised for her gifts. "Hopefully a few."

"A few?" He made a sound of disbelief. "Smithfield alone was on a pace to kill at least one child a week. He would have slaughtered hundreds of innocents." He leaned forward to steal a kiss. "You saved them."

"Not just me," she protested, her voice breathless as he traced her mouth with the tip of his tongue. "He wouldn't be off the street unless you tracked him down."

"We make a good team."

"A team?"

"Why not?" He pulled back to study her startled expression. "We'd be perfect together."

Her eyes darkened with an emotion she was swiftly hiding behind a pretense of indifference. "You barely know me."

He smiled with sinful enjoyment. "I'd say I know you better than most. Although I'm not opposed to further exploration."

She punched his chest. "That's not what I meant."

His smile faded. "I know you, Callie Brown. At least what you're willing to share. Which isn't much."

"What do you mean?"

"Like me you're forced to wade through the muck to accomplish your job."

She grimaced. "True."

"Which means you never celebrate when a killer is arrested because you remember the death and destruction that you weren't able to prevent." His fingers lightly traced the stubborn line of her jaw. "Am I right?"

A hint of need softened her expression. "Yes."

"And, like me, you keep others at a distance because you know they don't see the world with the same eyes."

She studied him for a long minute. Wary. Or maybe cautious. "You think we're the same?"

He paused. It would be easy to make a flippant comment. A teasing remark that would deflect her attention without revealing his growing vulnerability.

But meeting the sapphire gaze, he knew this was important.

"I think we connect on a level that goes way beyond the physical, don't you?"

"It's—"

"Scary as hell?" He filled in the blanks. "Yeah, I know."

Her eyes narrowed as his hand smoothed down the curve of her ass, urging her onto her side so they were face to face.

"You don't seem particularly scared," she accused.

He lost a heartbeat as she pressed against the thrust of his erection.

He was so hard the mere brush of her hot skin was nearly enough to send him over the edge.

"I have other things on my mind," he muttered.

She wiggled against him, a small smile curving her lips. "Not just on your mind."

His teeth clenched at her teasing. Oh . . . hell. When did she become so bold?

"No, it's kind of an all-over thing," he managed to rasp, his fingers digging into the softness of her backside as he tried to leash his hunger, which was swiftly spiraling out of control. "So if you want me to stop, tell me now."

Without warning, she pressed her hands to his chest, exploring his rigid muscles with a light, devastating touch.

"Is that what you want?"

"Hell no," he groaned, brushing his mouth over her parted lips. "But you're a temptation I can't resist, and if you don't say no then I'm going to take everything you're willing to give."

She nipped his bottom lip, her hands skimming downward. Duncan hissed, his stomach muscles clenching in anticipation.

Oh . . . hell.

Did she even know her soft touch was setting him on fire?

"You're many things, Duncan O'Conner, but weak isn't one of them," she murmured.

He squeezed his eyes shut, desperately wanting to roll her onto her back and unleash his most primal desires.

"I am when it comes to you, Callie Brown," he admitted in thick tones.

He felt her lips plant butterfly kisses along the rough edge of his jaw before following the line of his throat.

"I'm glad."

"That I find you irresistible?"

She licked the pulse that pounded at the base of his neck. "Yep."

"You like me in your power?"

"Oh yeah. I want you begging for me."

His cock jerked, as if trying to prove to the tormenting female just how much he wanted her.

His hands slid up her back with an impatient caress. "Shit, Callie, you shouldn't say that when we're in bed."

She chuckled, nibbling along the prominent line of his collarbone.

"Where would you prefer I say it?"

He buried his nose in her apple-scented hair, struggling to suck air into his lungs, which felt oddly tight.

"I'm hanging on by a thread here, sweetheart."

"Let go, cop," she whispered, wriggling downward to lick one flat nipple before softly blowing on it until it pebbled in arousal.

"Callie?" he gasped, his eyes wrenched open in shocked pleasure.

"Hmm?" She found his other nipple, giving soft licks as he shuddered in helpless response.

"What are you doing?" he croaked.

She tilted back her head to regard him with eyes that were far more rare and beautiful than any sapphires.

"I promised revenge, didn't I?" she said, smiling with wicked intent as she returned to her slow, intimate exploration.

He nearly leapt off the mattress as she kissed a path down his stomach, at last taking the tender tip of his cock into the silken heat of her mouth.

Oh . . . hell yeah.

She could have all the revenge she wanted.

Chapter Thirteen

Morning had fully arrived by the time they at last crawled out of bed, and then spent another half hour in the shower.

Callie felt deliciously sated as she pulled on the terry cloth robe and dried her hair with a towel.

And something else.

Something thrilling and dangerous and completely unfamiliar.

Something she wasn't ready to examine.

Sensing Duncan pull on his jeans and tee behind her, Callie wandered into the living room, not sure what etiquette covered the "morning after wild monkey sex" procedure.

Did she suggest they go to breakfast? They'd used a lot of energy—a massive amount of energy—and Duncan had to be starving. But what if he didn't want to spend more time with her? Would she feel obligated?

Maybe she should just go back to her apartment and—

The abrupt knock on the door interrupted her idiotic musings, making her stiffen in surprise.

"Can I hope that's room service with our breakfast?" Duncan drawled, moving to stand beside her.

She snuck a peek to the side, admiring the way the tee clung with loving perfection to the hard muscles of his chest, before lifting her head to meet his amused gaze. She wrinkled her nose at him. So smug.

"You can always hope."

"That doesn't sound promising."

There was another pounding on the door. "Neither does that." Accepting her time with Duncan was at an end regardless of what she wanted, she moved forward to pull open the door. She blinked in confusion at the sight of her guardian. Sentinels were never used as messengers. Which meant his arrival couldn't be good. "Fane. Is something wrong?"

His tattooed face remained stoic, although the heat from his body warned he wasn't pleased by her presence in Duncan's rooms.

"The Mave wants you in her office." His dark gaze never strayed from her flushed face. "Bring the cop."

With his message delivered, Fane turned on his heel and swiftly disappeared.

Yeah. Not happy.

Not happy at all.

Swallowing a sigh, Callie briefly rued ever leaving Duncan's bed. Tucked against him, she'd felt warm and secure and almost normal. Like any other woman who'd spent the night in the arms of her lover.

Now reality had intruded. With a vengeance.

"I need to go to my apartment and change," she murmured, still standing in the doorway gazing down the empty hallway. "I'll meet you at the Mave's office."

With surprising speed, Duncan snapped out his hand to grasp her upper arm. "Callie."

She kept her gaze averted. "We should hurry."

He muttered something beneath his breath before slowly dropping his hand.

"Fine. But don't think for a minute that I'm going to let you lock me out," he warned, his voice cop-hard. "We're way beyond those games."

"I need to go."

Dashing away like a naughty child, Callie ignored the feel of his glare burning a hole in the back of her head.

I am a coward.

A genuine, Grade A coward.

But it wasn't entirely her fault. She'd made the decision to have sex with Duncan. She was a grown, unattached woman who was free to share the bed of an equally grown, unattached man.

And the sex had been magnificent. The stuff of fantasies.

Unfortunately, it wasn't quite the uncomplicated night of fun she'd been hoping for.

Taking the elevator to the private quarters, she'd actually managed to reach her door when she at last realized someone was calling her name.

"Callie."

Glancing over her shoulder, she caught sight of the tall woman with long raven hair and light green eyes. As always Serra looked ravishing, with her lush curves shown to advantage in a pair of black satin pants and halter top. She was sex walking in Manolo Blahnik boots.

She was also intelligent, witty, loyal, and one of the most powerful psychics ever recorded.

If Callie didn't love her like a sister she would have been obligated to shove her off a high, high ledge.

"Oh, Serra." She offered an apologetic smile as she placed her thumb on the tiny screen that released the door lock. "I'm sorry but I have to meet with the Mave. Maybe we can get together later."

Callie entered the small but tidy living room painted a soft cream with lavender accents. Her sofa and chairs were the same cream with glass coffee tables in the center of the floor and a plasma TV on the wall. The floors were a polished hardwood with hand-woven rugs tossed in a casual pattern.

There was nothing fancy about it, but it was comfortable. More importantly, it was home.

She headed directly for the back bedroom, which was decorated in the same cream tones, but with peach accents, not at all surprised when Serra followed in her wake.

The two had been raised by the same foster parents. Which meant she knew that nothing was going to make Serra leave until she'd dug out whatever information she wanted.

"Does that mean you won't be spending more quality time with your cop?"

Ah. She'd heard that she'd spent the night with Duncan. Predictable.

Gossip traveled with hyperspeed through Valhalla.

"He's not mine," she denied, trying to ignore the tiny pang at the truth of her words.

What would she do with him if he was hers?

Serra moved to sit on the edge of the bed, leaning back on her elbows as she studied Callie with a knowing gaze. "But you're not denying the quality time you spent with him?"

Callie tugged off the robe, heat jolting through her body at the memory of Duncan's demanding touch.

Her previous experiences had been with callow youths.

The cop had been all man.

"It was top-notch quality."

"You go, girl."

In the process of pulling on a clean pair of panties and matching bra, Callie regarded her visitor in confusion.

"I thought you didn't trust him."

Serra's lips curled. "I don't trust any man. They're all bastards."

Callie carefully considered her response. Despite their unbreakable bond, they had learned never to discuss Serra's fierce attraction toward Fane. It wasn't that Serra was jealous. But she was frustrated by the Sentinel's refusal to think of anything beyond his duty to Callie.

"Not all," Callie protested, pulling on a pair of faded jeans. "What about Arel?"

Arel was a hunter Sentinel who was sinfully beautiful with honey brown hair and eyes of pure gold. Serra had dated him the previous year.

"Charming. Beautiful. And a thorough bastard." Serra paused, studying Callic with a searching gaze. "Still, I haven't seen that pretty flush on your cheeks for a long time. And if he hurts you I can always kick his ass."

Callie chose a stretchy top in a bright yellow, pulling it over her head and tucking it into her jeans.

"I can do my own ass-kicking, thank you very much."

"You could, but you're far too softhearted," Serra pointed out. The lovely psychic was three years older than Callie and had appointed herself Callic's ass-kicker from the day she'd been brought as a baby to Valhalla. "How long is the cop going to be hanging around?"

Callie moved to the attached bathroom to run a comb through the short strands of her hair, pretending she didn't notice the lingering glow that blushed her cheeks and shimmered in her eyes.

"I don't know."

"What do you know?"

She returned to the bedroom, slipping on a pair of running shoes before turning to meet her friend's curious gaze.

"He scares me," she admitted with blunt honesty.

Without warning Serra was on her feet, her eyes narrowed to dangerous slits. "Okay, that's it. I'm going to chop off his dick."

Oh hell. Callie dashed to block the dangerous psychic from leaving the room. "No, Serra."

"What?"

"What I meant was that he makes me feel things that scare me."

Serra blinked, startled. Callie was the sensible one. The

one who never took risks. Who never tumbled in and out of lust with every cute guy who crossed her path. Who preferred an evening spent with a good book to hitting the nightclubs.

"Are you falling in love with him?"

Callie bit her lower lip. "That's what concerns me."

Seeming to wrap her brain around Callie's startling confession, Serra gave a slow shake of her head. "Why are you concerned?" she asked. "I was only with him for a few minutes, but I can promise that he's obsessed with you."

"Obsessed?"

"You're constantly on his mind." Serra's lips twisted in a self-derisive smile. "Something most women would envy."

Callie reached to lightly touch her friend's arm, offering an unspoken comfort.

"Whether I'm on his mind or not, we live in two different worlds." She wrinkled her nose. "And that's not a cliché. We literally live in two different worlds."

Serra arched a brow. "Are you so sure?"

"What do . . ." Callie made a sound of disapproval. Clearly her friend had used her powers to peek into Duncan's thoughts. It was the only way she could know that the cop wasn't entirely normal. "Serra, you know you're not supposed to be rummaging through the minds of our guests."

Serra shrugged. "I wanted to make sure he was no threat to you."

Callie gave her companion's arm a squeeze. "I love you, too."

Serra shifted her feet, as always embarrassed by Callie's open display of affection. She was far more comfortable in her role as bad-ass.

"So he confessed his secret powers to you?"

"After a little prompting."

"Then you realize you're not from separate worlds. He's one of us."

Callie shook her head. Duncan had been painfully clear.

"Not so long as he chooses to keep his gift secret," she said. "For now he prefers his life with the norms."

Serra snorted. "Why?"

"He loves his job as a cop, which he'd never be allowed to keep if it was discovered he is a soul-gazer. Plus, he's very close to his family." She heaved a faint sigh. "Both potent reasons to keep the status quo."

Serra slowly smiled. "Then I suppose you'll have to give him a more potent reason to switch teams."

Could she?

More importantly, did she *want* to?

She hastily shoved aside the question. She wasn't ready to open that particular can of worms.

Not until she had the time to deal with the consequences.

"Something to consider," she murmured vaguely. "First, however, I have to survive whatever latest disaster is waiting for me."

Duncan wasn't overly fussy.

He had only a handful of items on his "never want to do" list:

Wrestle a gator.

Eat a turnip.

See his wife banging the delivery man.

And share a private tête-à-tête with Fane the pain-in-his-ass Sentinel.

A damned shame that he'd been forced to endure every single item on his list.

Pacing the hall, he did his best to ignore the tattooed bastard who leaned against the wall, standing so still he could have passed as a statue. Well, if a statue had obsidian eyes that held the promise of death and could pump enough heat into the air to make any man sweat.

"You seem nervous, cop," the Sentinel drawled, folding his arms across his bare, tattooed chest, which was broad enough to put an ox to shame.

Steroids? It'd be nice to think so.

"I doubt we were called here because of good news," Duncan growled. "Unless you know something I don't."

Fane snorted. "What I know that you don't could fill libraries."

Duncan ignored the taunt, studying the man's face. It looked like it had been carved from stone, giving it an ageless quality.

"Just how old are you?" Duncan felt the temperature in the hall amp up another degree.

"That's not a question you ask a high-blood."

Yeah, like I give a shit. "There are rumors that the Sentinels are immortal."

"There are a lot of rumors about Sentinels."

"At least one of them is true."

"Oh yeah?"

"You're all pricks."

The door to the office opened, revealing the impressive form of the Mave dressed in a white cashmere sweater that was scooped low enough to reveal the shimmering emerald of her witch mark and a black pencil skirt with black pumps. Her hair was pulled into a tidy bun at the nape of her neck to enhance the pale perfection of her face and the slender length of her neck.

"You two done playing?" she murmured with a lift of her brow.

Fane shoved away from the wall, his gaze never leaving Duncan. "For now."

She stepped back. "You may come in."

Duncan frowned. "Callie—"

"I'm here," Callie announced, rounding the corner on cue. Well, maybe not on cue. The Mave no doubt had seen her approach on a security monitor. Or perhaps she had witchy powers that warned who was in the vicinity.

Either way, Duncan was far more concerned about the pale strain he could easily detect on Callie's pretty face.

What the hell had happened? When she'd left his rooms she'd been flushed and sated and delightfully flustered.

Now she could barely meet his gaze.

He reached out, intending to halt her and demand an explanation of what had caused her sudden discomfort with him only to let his hand drop as the Mave sent him a curious glance and Fane gave a low growl, deep in his throat.

Shit.

Any private chat was going to have to wait.

In silence they shuffled into the elegant office, Fane taking his familiar position in the corner so he could keep an eye on the door and window, his large body leaning against the wall even as his muscles remained coiled to attack.

Did the man ever relax?

The Mave settled behind her desk, waving a hand to the two chairs opposite her. "Have a seat."

A command despite the polite tone. Duncan waited for Callie to perch on the nearest chair before taking his own seat, bracing himself for the latest disaster.

"Has something happened?" he asked, already knowing the answer.

The Mave wasn't the type to invite people into her office for chitchat.

"I received a message from your chief this morning," the powerful witch said in tones that revealed nothing.

Duncan frowned. Why hadn't Molinari contacted him directly?

"What did she say?"

"I think you should view it for yourself." The Mave reached to pick up a remote lying on her desk and pressed a button.

Immediately the light dimmed and flickering images appeared on the far wall.

At first there was nothing to see but the dim shadows that filled an empty house.

No, not a house.

A mansion.

One of those cold, sprawling places that looked beautiful in photographs, but had to be as uncomfortable as hell to try and live in.

So what was the deal? A big house with a lot of fancy artwork wasn't that uncommon, even in Kansas City.

About to demand an explanation, he was halted when the security system shifted to a camera displaying the front yard, obviously set on motion detectors.

Duncan sucked in a sharp breath as he watched a woman with long chestnut hair and a slender build boldly striding onto the porch.

She was no longer naked and she was standing upright instead of being sprawled on her kitchen floor, but there was no mistaking that it was Leah Meadows.

"Is that . . ." He shuddered, the name sticking in his throat. He'd heard a hundred victims tell him that their blood ran cold. Until this minute he'd never actually experienced it for himself. "Holy shit."

"Leah," Callie breathed for him, her hands clutching the arms of her chair.

He resisted the urge to reach out and lay his hand over her clenched fingers. "Where is she?" he instead demanded.

"Mission Hills."

That explained the McMansion. The upscale neighborhood was south of the city and populated with the swankiest of the swanky.

Callie leaned forward, her eyes narrowing as she studied Leah placing her hand on a small screen.

"What's she doing?"

"Disarming the security system," Duncan absently responded, almost missing the significance as she turned to push open the door and stepped inside the house. Through a fog of horror he watched as the young, beautiful girl walked around as if she didn't have a care in the world. Christ. Was it possible she was an empty shell being used as a puppet by some psycho necromancer? "That's it."

The Mave sent him a small frown. "What?"

"That's the reason the . . ." He struggled for the right word. The bastard wasn't a diviner like Callie. He was the bogeyman the norms feared. "Necromancer chose Leah."

"Of course," Callie gasped as she easily followed his logic. "She could pass through security."

The Mave nodded, her expression unreadable as they all turned back to the images flickering on the wall. The camera angle shifted to follow Leah as she moved through the house, her movements chillingly fluid considering she was a corpse. She was walking across a long living room when another form, this one a male, entered the room.

"Busted." Duncan unconsciously leaned forward, taking a swift inventory of the newest player. An aging white male who moved toward Leah like a peacock. Puffed out chest, strutting walk. All he was missing was tail feathers to spread. Pompous dick. "This should be interesting."

They watched in silence as there was an exchange. There was no sound, but they didn't need to hear the conversation to know that the man wasn't happy. At least not at first. There was a short tête-à-tête, then clearly reassured, the man was shoving his hand under Leah's stretchy little top.

"A little too interesting," Callie said with a grimace.

"Keep watching," the Mave coolly commanded.

The zombie-Leah flirted with a disturbing ease before she turned to dash into what looked like an office. There was more flirting. But, even as Duncan felt a burning fury at the thought the mysterious necromancer was going to allow the ultimate defamation of Leah's body, the young female was moving to stand directly in front of her lover, her necklace beginning to glow.

"What is that?" he muttered.

The words had barely left his mouth when the man jerked backward in shock, his skin ripping open like it was being torn from the inside.

"An amulet with a powerful spell," the Mave answered.

"This is . . ." Duncan shoved his hand through his hair, his stomach threatening revolt as the man turned gray and began to flake away like a smoked cigar. "Fucking crazy," he breathed. "Men don't turn into ash. And dead women aren't supposed to be walking around town."

"No, they're not," the Mave said, her voice crystal hard with an anger she kept hidden behind her mask of smooth composure. "Which is why we're going to put a halt to whoever is responsible."

Yes. Yes he was.

Being a stubborn ass who refused to admit he was in over his head was actually a bonus in his job.

"Who's the decomposed corpse?"

"A Mr. Calso."

Duncan frowned. The name was vaguely familiar.

"A high-blood?"

"What's left of him is being brought to our medical facility," the Mave said. "We'll soon know."

Duncan glanced toward the witch in surprise. "The chief signed off on you taking the remains?"

The Mave shrugged. "Mr. Calso is a prominent figure in the norms' financial world. She didn't want to risk the PR disaster of having what's left of his body disappearing from her morgue."

Duncan snorted. "Yeah, not to mention the hysteria if a man who is supposed to be dead is seen at the country club."

"I don't think he'll be walking anywhere, but yes, that was a concern," the woman smoothly agreed.

"What is she stealing?"

Callie's abrupt question had Duncan returning his attention to watch as Leah turned a stone vessel upside down and allowed a small metal object to fall into her open palm. Copper? Bronze? Impossible to say at a distance.

"A good question," he muttered. "It looks like a coin."

"It was locked in a hidden safe so it must be rare," Callie pointed out.

"Maybe," Duncan agreed. "But so is the Picasso hiding the safe and the Matisse statue on the mantel." He pointed toward the small bronzed statue of a woman, belatedly realizing that three sets of eyes were regarding him with varying degrees of astonishment. "What? I'm not a complete barbarian. I like art."

"What's your point, Sergeant O'Conner?" the Mave prodded.

"The robbery wasn't about money. Could the coin have powers?"

"Any item can be a focus for magic," the Mave answered. "But if you desired true power it surely makes more sense to steal a witch."

Duncan blinked. "Can a witch be stolen?"

"Can the dead walk?" the Mave smoothly countered.

"Touché." Duncan's lips twitched. The Mave had a subtle sense of humor. Unexpected and no doubt lethal to the poor fool who ever thought he could claim this woman. "And speaking of the dead, did anyone notice Leah after she left the house?"

"That's your territory," she informed him without hesitation.

"I suppose it is." He pulled out his phone to start making

notes. What made him a good cop were his instincts and his hidden talent. What made him a great cop was his acceptance that ninety percent of his job was dull, old-fashioned legwork. "We'll need to canvas the neighborhood to see if anyone noticed how she arrived or left. We also need to find out more about Calso and his mysterious coin."

"Your chief said to tell you she would meet you at Mr. Calso's house," the Mave said, pressing a button to allow the early morning sunlight to return to the room.

Duncan turned to glance toward Callie. "Are you going to join me?"

"Not yet." She furrowed her brow, clearly debating how she could best use her talents to help. "I think I should try to discover the identity of the necromancer."

His lips parted in denial only to snap shut as he met the glittering sapphire gaze.

She was clearly waiting for him to make a jackass out of himself and try to forbid her to put herself at risk. Maybe she even wanted him to annoy her so she'd have a legitimate reason to keep him at a distance.

Thankfully, he hadn't been plagued by a gaggle of older sisters for nothing.

Swallowing his impulsive words, he managed a tight smile. "Where will you start your search?"

"Russia," Fane announced from the corner.

Chapter Fourteen

Zak had time to shower and return to the main part of the house when Tony returned with Leah's body and the coin.

Not surprising, the henchman was barely functioning, his human brain unable to process what he'd witnessed. That, of course, didn't keep Zak from sending him off to dispose of Leah's body. What did it matter where he took the corpse, just so long as it was far enough that it couldn't be traced back to this house?

Now he sat in his office and studied the tiny object that he'd waited three hundred years to hold in his hand.

It didn't look like it could offer him the power he'd been promised. Less than two inches in diameter, it was paper thin and tarnished to a blue green. It might have been mistaken for a piece of trash if not for the odd, winged bird etched into the metal.

Rubbing his finger over the ancient artifact, Zak felt the gnawing sensation in the dark pit of his heart.

It was a familiar ache.

It had started when he was barely five and he'd realized that his brothers were destined to become his father's heirs while he was doomed to a suffocating existence in the middle of fucking nowhere, surrounded by superstitious serfs who'd taken one glance at his peculiar eyes and claimed his mother had slept with a demon.

Ignorant peasants.

Boris and Viktor had been easy enough to get rid of. The two had been ruthless bullies to Zak, but they'd also been as dumb as a box of rocks. And once Zak had started to come into his powers, it'd only been a matter of time before he could put them in their graves.

Boris had been disposed of by the simple process of having his dead lover make an appearance in the woods. The fool had tumbled from his horse in shock and broke his own neck. Viktor had been a little more difficult, but eventually Zak had stumbled across the body of a recently shot poacher whom he used to pull Viktor from the stables and snap his neck.

It had never occurred to him that his father would refuse to make him his heir. He was, after all, the only remaining son.

But the bastard had coldly informed Zak that he'd never allow a deformed brat to claim his title.

This time Zak had taken matters into his own hands, quite literally, strangling his father and hiding his body. Hours later he'd used his powers to ensure his father appeared long enough to formally proclaim Zak as his heir before he allowed his father's dead body to tumble to the floor.

From there he'd traveled to Saint Petersburg, confident he'd at last satisfy that sense of emptiness.

Instead he'd been consumed with fury as the nobles had treated him with the same contempt as his father. He'd managed to forge a place for himself at court with sheer cunning, but it hadn't been enough.

And then he'd met Anya, who'd revealed to him the power to make certain he'd never again be treated as anything less than a king.

As if the thought of Anya had conjured the witch, she stepped into the office and crossed to where he sat behind his desk. "You have the coin?"

"At last," he confirmed, his fingers continuing to stroke over the copper coin.

Anya leaned against the edge of the desk, her slender form barely covered by the microdress that was a brilliant shade of yellow.

Why she bothered to play the role of sex kitten defied logic. He never wasted his time or energy on a project unless it promised reward.

And any reward he'd gain by taking the witch to his bed had already been reaped.

"The female?" she demanded, placing her hand flat on the desk and leaning sideways to study the artifact in his fingers.

Zak shrugged. "Tony's disposing the body."

Anya wrinkled her nose. "The servant has seen more than is good for him."

"He still has his uses."

She reached a hand toward the coin. "May I?"

Zak smoothly rose to his feet and stepped away. "No."

Her face flushed at his uncompromising rejection. "You can't be afraid that I might try to steal it?" She gave a short, humorless laugh. "We need one another."

"Certainly you need me."

She muttered something beneath her breath as she pushed away from the desk and headed for the door. "Fine."

"Where are you going?"

She halted, glancing over her shoulder. "It's time for my pedicure."

"It will have to wait."

Her eyes narrowed. "Why?"

"I want you to take me to the temple."

The witch froze, her expression wary. "Now?"

"Yes."

"But . . ." She shook her head, licking her dry lips. "I haven't prepared the sacrifice."

He held up the coin. "Then get prepared."

She slowly turned back to face him, her movements wary, as if she feared his response.

Smart witch.

"And what about you? Are you fully prepared?"

"What do you mean?"

"You have convinced yourself that you're destined to succeed, but have you considered the consequences of failure?" she muttered in defensive tones. "We can't be sure that using a surrogate will protect you."

He smiled with a cold arrogance. "Don't worry about me, witch. Take me to the temple and I'll become nothing less than a god."

Her eyes flashed with fear. "You should at least consider the danger."

"I would be flattered if I truly thought you cared, Anya," he mocked. "But we both know your only concern is losing your luxurious lifestyle." He carefully plucked a bit of lint off the sleeve of his white satin shirt before lifting his gaze to stab her with a lethal glare. "Or at least that had better be the only reason you hesitate."

Anya wrapped her arms around her waist. "Sometimes you frightened me."

He arched a brow. "Only sometimes?"

After being returned to Kansas City by Fane and his magical portal, Duncan made a brief stop by his apartment for clean clothes before heading to the station house to speak with the techy who was dissecting Calso's security tapes. He forced the poor bastard to go frame by tedious frame until Duncan had the information he needed.

Only then did he head south of town to the mansion that was now a crime scene.

Parking a block away, Duncan blatantly trespassed through private yards to enter through the back terrace doors. A death in this neighborhood would bring out the vultures in hordes. He didn't want to have to shoot paparazzi. No matter how satisfying it might be.

Entering the kitchen, he was met by a rookie who looked impossibly young with his face flushed and his pale eyes shimmering with excitement.

Christ. Had he ever been that wide eyed and fresh faced?

Probably not. By the time he was four his special little talent had revealed just how often a face of an angel could disguise a soul as black as the pits of hell.

"You had the entire neighborhood canvassed?"

The young man squared his shoulders, his uniform perfectly pressed and his shoes shining.

"Yes, Sergeant."

"And?"

"And nothing was seen except a silver Taurus parked a block south of here," a female voice answered as Molinari stepped into the kitchen.

A small woman in her early fifties, the chief of police didn't have the muscles or the bluster to intimidate others, but there wasn't a cop in the city who didn't quake beneath the dark gaze.

There was something in that glare that reminded him of the day he was busted by his ma for hiding a stash of *Playboy*s beneath his mattress.

"Any one jot down the plates?"

Molinari shook her head, the dark hair that was dyed, sprayed, and pinned into a bun at her nape not moving an inch. Her tailored jacket and matching skirt were equally rigid as she stood in the doorway. "No."

"Of course not." Duncan rolled his eyes. "I can't sneeze

in my apartment without old lady Rogers asking if I'm coming down with a cold. Where are the nosy neighbors when you need them?"

"Nosy neighbors aren't allowed in the communities where power brokers live," the chief said, her dark gaze flicking toward the backyard, which was as large as a football field. "They have too many secrets."

"So what were Mr. Calso's secrets?"

Molinari lifted a slender hand. "Follow me, O'Conner." She glanced toward the silent rookie. "Blackwell."

The cop audibly swallowed the lump in his throat. "Chief?"

"Make sure we're not interrupted."

"Yes, ma'am."

Duncan followed Molinari through the house to the office where Calso had died. He smiled as he caught a glimpse through the windows at the dozen cops who surrounded the house, keeping the gathering jackals at bay.

"Trying to keep a lid on things?"

The woman moved toward the desk, making a wide path around the spot where Calso had . . . disintegrated.

Duncan didn't blame her. The memory of watching the body turn to ash was something that was going to haunt him for a long time.

"When it gets out that one of the richest men in Kansas City was killed by magic all hell's going to break loose," Molinari muttered, reaching to pluck a manila file off the desk.

"You left out the fact that the person casting the spell was a zombie who escaped from our own morgue."

That dark glare swiveled in his direction. "I've already named my first ulcer Mayor Stanford. Do you want me to name the next one O'Conner?"

"I'll pass."

"This whole damned thing is a nightmare just waiting to happen."

Just waiting to happen?

Duncan was fairly certain they were knee-deep in the nightmare.

"You can't keep this from the press for long," he said, waving a hand toward the window that revealed the line of news vans already blocking the street. "Not with such a high profile victim."

"Instead of stating the obvious, why don't you make your-self useful and assure me the freaks know who's doing this."

Duncan moved, studying the open safe, effectively hiding his expression. He was loyal to his job and to his chief, but he'd go to the grave protecting Callie and her connection to the case.

"Like us, they're following leads," he said, absently noting the stack of crisp thousand-dollar bills just begging to be taken.

Whatever the reason for Calso's death, it had nothing to do with money.

"And?" Molinari prompted.

"And that's all I know."

"You wouldn't be keeping anything from me, would you, O'Conner?"

He turned to meet her suspicious frown. "The Mave has her people trying to track down info on a necromancer capa-ble of truly raising the dead. I assume they'll contact us when they discover anything."

The suspicion remained. "Hmm."

"Tell me about Calso."

The chief's lips parted to cross-examine him, then clearly deciding it wasn't worth the battle, she instead turned her at-tention to the file folder in her hand. Flicking it open, she read from the top page.

"Sixty-two-year-old Caucasian male, in decent health, who made a fortune in the financial world."

"Anyone want him dead?"

"Two ex-wives who were stupid enough to sign prenups

and a dozen employees with pending lawsuits that accuse him of everything from sexual harassment to insider trading."

Typical. What was it with rich guys having to be dickheads?

"So not the most popular guy."

"I have Caleb running down the more obvious suspects. But—"

"But this murder was anything but obvious," Duncan finished for her.

"Exactly."

He strolled toward the desk, allowing his gaze to wander aimlessly over the room. He'd discovered over the years that clues rarely came attached with labels or blinking neon lights. Instead it was almost always something subtle.

A chair moved for no apparent reason.

A drawer not fully closed.

A recently repaired window.

Anything out of place that was inexplicably easier to notice with a casual glance instead of a focused search.

"Do you know anything about the coin that was stolen?"

Molinari shrugged. "I have the research department enlarging a picture of it. They haven't found anything yet."

"Yeah. I picked up a copy." Not that it helped. Even with the details of the coin brought into focus it meant nothing to Duncan. He needed an expert. "Was it listed on his homeowners policy?"

"No."

"So, black market."

"That would be my guess."

"What about the other artwork?"

Molinari shuffled through the papers in her file. "It looks like most of the pieces have legitimate paperwork, but I'll have it double checked."

Duncan grimaced. No one would be stupid enough to

display such famous pieces if they were off the black market. Unless they were forgeries.

His hand reached to pick up the stone vase that was safely wrapped in an evidence bag.

"What about the container?"

"What about it?"

"What is it?"

"I don't have a damned clue. It looks old."

It looked older than old. It looked ancient.

Holding it to the light, he studied the strange symbols etched into the stone.

"Can I keep it?"

Molinari frowned at the unexpected request. "It's evidence."

"I won't let anything happen to it."

There was a long silence as the chief weighed the need for information against protocol.

At last the shouts from the growing crowd of gawkers across the street made her heave a sigh of resignation.

"I suppose it couldn't hurt. It's already been dusted for prints," she muttered. "What do you want it for?"

"Callie and her pet Sentinel are searching for the history of the necromancer in an effort to locate him. I want to start at the other end." He glanced toward the black mark on the carpet where Calso had died. "The present."

"You lost me."

He lifted his head to meet his companion's puzzled gaze. "If we find out where Calso got the coin and what makes it worth killing for, we might be able to use the information to discover who else was interested in the coin," he explained, his mind already shifting through his various contacts. "There can't be that many numismatists willing to dabble in black markets. This vessel can hopefully lead me to a specific dealer."

Molinari gave a slow nod. "Clever, but we don't know for sure that the vessel and the coin are actually connected."

"It's a place to start."

The chief abruptly tossed the file back on the desk, her expression tight with frustration.

"Shit, I hate this."

Duncan grimaced. "I think we're going to hate what's coming even more."

Chapter Fifteen

The journey from Kansas City to Saint Petersburg might have been made in the blink of an eye, but it was as disconcerting as hell. It seemed no matter how great the power, you couldn't jerk a body halfway around the world and nine hours into the future without it making a girl feel dizzy.

Moving to lean against the wall that was covered in delicately painted hieroglyphs, Callie sucked in a deep breath, waiting for her head to stop spinning.

Across the small room Fane stood in silence, unaffected by the teleportation.

Not that he was entirely happy.

Callie grimaced as her gaze skimmed over his large tattooed body, which was covered by a pair of casual khakis, heavy black boots, and a tight muscle shirt. There was no missing the rigid tension of his shoulders and the tightness of his starkly male features.

For all his stoic calm, Fane was royally pissed.

At her.

"Why don't you spit out what you have to say before your head explodes?" she murmured.

He turned to study her with a steady gaze. "Would it do any good?"

She briefly considered the pleasure she'd found in Duncan's arms. Had it been a mistake? Maybe. Did she give a damn? No.

"Doubtful," she admitted with a rueful smile.

"Then there's no point."

"It might make you less grumpy."

"Doubtful."

She rolled her eyes as he turned on his heels and headed out of the portal room. Fane had never tried to interfere in her intimate affairs. Usually because she had no affairs, intimate or otherwise.

But they both understood that Duncan O'Conner threatened to become more than a passing distraction.

They entered the main section of the monastery, and Callie forced herself to ignore Fane's foul mood as a heavily cloaked monk moved toward her.

Her guardian was like an older brother. No matter how much they might fuss and fight, nothing could break their bond of trust.

She would never, ever doubt he had her back.

"Welcome to our humble abbey." The monk offered a bow before he straightened and pulled back his hood to reveal a long, deeply wrinkled face that was made beautiful by his kind blue eyes and sweet smile. "I am Brandon."

Beside her, Fane returned the bow, his hand pressed over his heart in a gesture of respect.

"We are honored to be your guests. I'm Fane and this is Callie Brown."

"Fane. Ms. Brown." He sent them both a piercing glance. "A pleasure."

"Please call me Callie."

"Thank you." Another sweet smile before Brandon waved a hand toward a nearby archway. "We have prepared for your arrival. If you'll follow me."

They traveled through the reception room, which was built of stark gray stones with narrow slits that offered a mere glimpse of the fading sunlight. She didn't allow herself to think that it was still late morning at Valhalla. Her stomach was just settling from the journey.

There was a long, narrow hallway that ended in a heavy wooden door with an old-fashioned iron lock. Brandon pulled an equally old-fashioned key from the pocket of his robe and used it to tumble the lock. Then, with a strange air of ceremony he pushed open the door and stepped aside so Callie could enter first.

She wasn't sure what to expect.

Although she'd been surrounded by Sentinels all her life, not to mention traveled by portal with Fane from one monastery to another, she'd never been beyond the public rooms that were always stark and uninviting. The monks were OCD when it came to the privacy of the students and their training.

Now she sucked in a startled breath as she glanced around the vast library.

The place was . . . stunning.

Unlike the sleek, high-tech library at Valhalla, this room spoke of Russia's past, with an onion-domed ceiling that was richly painted with Orthodox icons and edged with gilt. The floor was a white marble inset with pieces of jade and gold that shimmered in the light from the candelabras. The walls were lined with towering bookshelves that were ornately carved and separated by fluted columns. The rosewood furniture was clearly the work of master craftsmen and so highly polished it seemed to glow.

"Oh." Callie twirled in a circle, absorbing the sheer beauty of the room. "This is exquisite."

The monk chuckled. "I will share your appreciation with our students."

Callie widened her eyes. "Sentinels did this?"

"We train all our Sentinels with some craft."

Callie shot a glance toward the silent Fane. "So that's how you learned to carve such beautiful figurines."

Fane shrugged, but his features eased as he studied her dazzled expression. He would have his tongue cut out before he admitted he took pride in his small carvings that filled the nurseries at Valhalla.

Tiny ballerinas, trees with squirrels perched on leafy branches, intricate castles, and mind-twisting puzzles. Bewitching creations that the children adored.

"It teaches that anything worthy comes from patience and dedication to detail," Brandon explained.

Callie smiled. "We should all learn that particular lesson."

Brandon moved to a fireplace set behind a large desk, brushing his hand over a jade vase. Without warning a panel beside the fireplace slid open to reveal a hidden staircase.

"This way," the monk urged, leading them down the dark stairs.

Callie followed behind him with Fane bringing up the rear.

"Where are we going?" she asked in confusion, skimming her hand down the cement wall as the darkness thickened to the point she was nearly blind. Her own skills didn't include seeing in the dark.

"This is where we keep items that are too fragile to be put on display," Brandon answered, opening the door at the bottom of the stairs to reveal a brilliantly lit room that was built in the shape of an octagon and lined with steel. Eight doors were set in the steel. "These vaults are specially designed to maintain the proper temperature and humidity." Brandon headed to the nearest door, pressing his thumb against a digital scanner. If the library upstairs had been a vision of old-world elegance, this was a glimpse into the future. "And, of course, the scribes are trained to handle even the most ancient artifacts."

Callie frowned, wondering if there had been a miscommunication. "The information we seek isn't particularly ancient."

Brandon nodded toward the door that silently slid open. "This particular vault contains various books and journals and even letters that refer to . . ." He paused to consider his words. "Let us say sensitive issues dealing with our people."

"Secret histories?" Callie asked.

"Not secret." Brandon smiled his sweet, sweet smile. "Regulated on a need-to-know basis."

Ah. Callie got it.

No need to creep out the norms with doppelgangers that could change shape or necromancers who could control the dead.

They entered a long room that was lined with glass cases. The ceiling was curved and crisscrossed with bright lights, the floor was grated metal that allowed a cool breeze to flow through the air.

Callie managed to catch a glimpse of books and rolled parchments and pretty feminine diaries that were wrapped with ribbons.

There were also strange objects that she'd never seen before and never wanted to see again. She grimaced at the sight of a large crystal ball with what looked like a human eye staring directly at her and the strange hammer that violently smashed into the glass as they passed by.

Yeesh.

At the end of the room was an open space with a large metal table that was cluttered with several leather-bound books, maps, as well as a pile of letters that were yellowed from age.

As they approached the table, a slender girl rose to her feet, brushing her hands down the long black robe she wore. "Brandon," the girl murmured, giving a low bow before glancing toward Callie and Fane.

The overhead light revealed she wasn't as young as Callie had first thought. Maybe midtwenties instead of early teens, but there remained an air of fragility about her pale, perfect face that was dominated by a large pair of velvet brown eyes. Her hair was pulled into a long braid that fell to her waist, the silvery-blond color so pale it didn't look real.

She looked like a fairy princess.

Until the brown gaze turned in Callie's direction. There was an age-old wisdom in those eyes. As if she'd seen more in her twenty or so years of life than most people did in their entire existence.

"This is Myst," Brandon introduced the girl. Myst. It suited her. "She'll be here to assist you."

"Thank you," Fane murmured, moving to stand guard at the door as the monk left.

Callie moved forward, joining the scribe at the table.

Myst pulled a pair of white, protective gloves from a box and held them toward Callie. "I believe I have all the relative material gathered here."

Callie wrinkled her nose at the daunting stack of books, letters, and what looked to be official reports.

It would take her hours, if not days, to search through the pile. Always assuming she happened to read Russian, French, and what she could only guess was Latin.

Which she could not.

"Have you read them all?" she asked the scribe.

"Of course."

"Then maybe you can give us the Cliffs Notes."

Myst blinked. "Cliffs Notes?"

"A condensed version," Fane explained from the door.

"Oh, I see. Very well." The girl gave a nod, her accent light, but definitely not Russian. Scandinavian? Perhaps. "The church records reveal that Lord Zakhar was born the youngest son of a minor nobleman in Kokorino. It was a small, remote village in what is now Siberia. He had two older brothers who both died before they reached the age of eighteen."

"Cause?" Fane demanded.

"Both were found in the woods with their necks broken." Myst absently put on the gloves in her hands, pulling one of the books toward her. "It was assumed that they were thrown from their horses."

"At the same time?" Callie asked.

Myst checked her book. "No, five years apart."

Callie lifted her brows. Okay, there might not have been a CSI team back then, but they weren't stupid.

"And no one was suspicious?"

"Very suspicious, especially when there were claims of seeing the dead walking just before they took their falls." Myst shrugged. "Of course, no one paid any attention to the gossip of mere serfs, not even the Shaman."

Callie shivered. Zakhar had been able to raise the dead when he'd been so young?

She'd somehow thought that it was a power he'd honed over the centuries.

Which begged the question . . . If he could raise the dead when he was a mere teenager, what could he do now?

The possibilities were terrifying.

"What about the parents?" she at last asked.

"The mother is never mentioned. The father, however, was found dead of what was called 'a failure of the heart' only minutes after he officially named Lord Zakhar his heir."

Fane snorted. "Convenient."

Myst turned to another book. "After a few months of mourning he traveled to Saint Petersburg to become a member of the royal court."

"He wasn't married?" Callie abruptly asked, struck by the sudden horror the necromancer had created offspring.

One necromancer raising the dead was bad enough, thank you very much.

"No." Myst pointed toward the stack of papers. "In fact the letters I've found mention several times he was loathed and feared by society."

Callie resisted the urge to touch the crumbling letters. "Do they say why?"

"His eyes, for one thing."

"What about them?"

"They were described as diamonds."

Callie shot a glance toward Fane, her heart missing a beat at the memory of those cold, ruthless eyes.

"That's him," she breathed.

He gave a slow nod. "It seems so, but I don't think we should jump to conclusions."

Not nearly as cautious as her guardian, Callie turned back toward the scribe. "Were there any paintings or photos of him?"

Myst shook her head. "Not that I could find."

Callie sighed. Of course not.

Before revealing themselves to the norms the high-bloods had learned to avoid having their images captured.

"What happened to him?"

"He gained power over the years."

"How?"

Myst ran her fingers lightly over the gold-edged page of the book in front of her, seeming to take comfort in the feel of the aged paper.

It had to be a scribe thing.

"It's not clear," she admitted. "But I would guess that he gathered information for the czar."

"A spy?" Callie asked.

"Yes." Myst nodded. "He knew things that made people believe he could read their minds."

Callie blinked in confusion. "A psychic?"

Myst glanced down, suddenly looking uncomfortable. "Actually—"

"What is it?" Callie prodded.

"One powerful aristocrat swore that his valet had helped him dress for dinner only to learn when he arrived downstairs that the man had been found dead in the stables with a knife in his heart that afternoon."

Fane gave a grunt of disgust. "He was using the dead to uncover secrets."

"Oh." Callie grimaced. The scribe's discomfort was a sharp warning of what would happen if it became common knowledge there was a necromancer who could raise the dead. Diviners were already feared. Even by other high-bloods. Dealing with the dead, no matter how respectfully done, tended to creep people out. If they thought that diviners were secretly abusing the corpses of their loved ones . . . it truly was going to be a nightmare. "Did they realize that Lord Zakhar was responsible?"

"There were rumors, but it wasn't until he formed an alliance with the czarina's mystic that the whispers became open accusations of sorcery," Myst said.

He had an accomplice?

Callie was somehow surprised.

Surely a crazy necromancer should work alone?

"What do you know about the mystic?"

"Very little." The scribe reached to flip open one of the leather-bound diaries. On one page was a charcoal etching of a narrow female face. It was too faded to make out more than a slender nose and high cheekbones with sensually lush lips, but Callie detected an arrogance in her faintly slanted eyes and tilted chin. "There's no record of her until she arrives in Saint Petersburg to act as an advisor."

"A high-blood?" Fane asked.

Myst nodded. "Yes."

So it was possible she was still alive.

Callie shifted her gaze back to the scribe. "Can you tell what her talent was?"

"There's no proof—"

"Your best guess," Callie urged. Myst hesitated. No doubt she was trained to offer facts, not theories. Callie, however, trusted the young woman's instincts. "Please."

"A witch," the young woman at last muttered.

Callie nodded. That would be her guess as well.

"Do you say that because she claimed to be a mystic?"

"That and the fact that there are mentions of the strange jewelry she wore on a bracelet."

"Amulets," Fane said.

Witches used amulets to hold spells, curses, and charms. Unlike Sentinels, who occasionally used crystals to focus their magic.

"There were also rumors that she had the ability to heal," Myst added.

Callie frowned. Healers had abilities that had nothing to do with magic.

"Really?"

"She would foresee outbreaks of illness."

Fane again made a sound of disgust. "Illness that she no doubt caused."

"Yes, and then she would cure the sick." Myst snapped the diary shut, something in her eyes speaking of wounds that hadn't yet healed. "Or at least those who could afford her exorbitant prices."

"A clever racket," Fane muttered.

Callie studied her companion's pale face. She wondered what pain was keeping the young woman hidden down in these vaults, but it wasn't the time or place to pry.

Once she was back at Valhalla she would mention Myst to the Mave. The powerful witch had the ability to get answers far more discreetly than Callie could.

"So what happened to the mystic?" she asked instead.

As if sensing she'd revealed more than she intended, Myst lowered her head and carefully opened yet another book. This one had neat columns of handwritten script, as if it were an official record book.

"She, along with Lord Zakhar, was discovered in her private rooms with the missing child of a servant. His throat was slit and he was lying on a wooden altar."

"Human sacrifice?" Fane's voice was edged with shock.

Murder of innocents was as rare among high-bloods as among norms.

Myst nodded. "So it would seem."

"Why?" Callie gave a puzzled shake of her head. "Witches have no need for blood."

"There are forbidden spells that demand the blood of innocents," Myst revealed with a grimace.

There was a short silence as Callie and Fane shared a startled glance.

It wasn't bad enough that there was a necromancer out there who could raise the dead? Now they had to worry about a psycho witch who was willing to sacrifice children?

Callie shuddered in horror.

Fane glanced back at the scribe. "Was Lord Zakhar condemned along with her?"

"Yes, but they managed to escape from Saint Petersburg." Myst turned the page of the book, skimming her finger down to the bottom of the text. "Eventually they were tracked to his family estate. The records become fuzzy but it seems that Lord Zakhar was handed over to the villagers who were eager to burn their lord and master at the stake."

"The woman?" Callie pressed. If the witch was still alive they had to stop her.

"There's no mention of her except in a footnote that claims she disappeared along with Lord Zakhar's charred body."

Fane abruptly moved forward, halting at the edge of the table as if sensing Myst wasn't entirely comfortable having him so close.

Of course, Fane tended to make a lot of people uncomfortable.

"Was there any mention of a coin?" he demanded.

"Coin?" Myst frowned at the unexpected question. "What kind of coin?"

Fane pulled out his phone, turning the screen to show the image of the coin that had been taken from Calso's security tape.

The IT wizards hadn't had time to clean up the grainy image, but astonishingly Myst widened her eyes in surprise.

"Come with me." She was darting to the back of the room, pulling open a door that led to another vault. This one was lined with wide wooden drawers from floor to ceiling.

Callie and Fane stood near the door watching the scribe scanning the small plaques on the front of the drawers, her lips moving as she muttered beneath her breath.

"Etruscan . . . no." She moved to another drawer. "Minoan. Byzantine. Oh." She pulled open a drawer and removed a small stone tablet that was etched with faded hieroglyphs. "This is it."

She moved back to Callie and Fane, her finger brushing over the strange symbol of a bird that matched the one on the coin.

Callie lifted her brows, impressed by the young woman's ability to recall the symbol among all the endless information stored in the vaults.

Did she have an eidetic memory?

Or was it a high-blood power?

Fane leaned to study the tablet, his finger lightly tracing the bird that was carved in the upper left corner. "What is it?" he muttered.

"It comes from a secret sect of ancient Sumerians," Myst answered, her expression troubled.

Callie felt a chill inch down her spine. "What was it intended to do?"

Myst lifted her head, genuine fear shimmering in her eyes. "It opens a doorway to forbidden knowledge."

Fane frowned. "What does that mean?"

"I don't know."

Chapter Sixteen

While Duncan was growing up his da had a no-frills routine. During the week he worked his ass off driving a taxi to support his family. The weekends were spent mowing their small patch of grass or working in the attached garage on the latest POS car they were driving that month.

Duncan occasionally hung out in the garage. It was the one certain place to avoid the constant squabbling of his sisters. And while he'd never developed his da's talent for tinkering with engines, he did learn that the best way to get a job done was by using the proper tool.

You want to catch a drug dealer? Hang out in a crack house.

You want to find a car thief? Set up a bait car in a high theft neighborhood.

You want to find a dealer in black-market art, you go to a pawnshop.

A very exclusive one.

Stepping out of his car, he studied the building, made entirely of glass and steel.

It didn't look like a pawnshop.

In fact, the main building was used as a perfectly legit art gallery that provided a much needed connection between local artists and the public.

The basement, however, was notorious for hosting "private" auctions to move artwork and antiques that didn't always have the paperwork necessary for a legal sale.

Duncan didn't bother trying to shut down the auctions. What was the point? They would pack up and move to a new location before he could get a warrant.

Besides, having an inside informant who understood that Duncan could disrupt his very profitable business meant that he could get the facts he needed with the minimum of fuss.

Entering the building, he ignored the beautiful brunette who sashayed toward him in a silver dress that cost more than his car. Instead he weaved his way past the artwork hung from the open girders that passed as a ceiling, not bothering to glance at the bold spatters of paint on the canvases.

Unlike many, he appreciated modern art, but today he was focused on getting in and out.

The quicker the better.

Shoving open the small door at the back of the main show-room, Duncan stepped into the office and shut it behind him.

At his entrance Jacques Girard rose to his feet. A small, slender man, he was wearing a black designer suit and red silk tie, his black hair peppered with silver brushed away from his severely handsome face.

He flashed a smooth smile to reveal his perfectly capped teeth. "Sergeant O'Conner, what a delightful surprise." The accent was French, but Duncan would bet his right nut the man had never stepped foot outside Kansas City. "Have a seat, *s'il vous plaît*."

Duncan waved aside the invitation, crossing the sparse office that was the same mixture of glass and steel as the gallery. Reaching the desk, he placed the stone vessel wrapped in plastic directly in front of the man.

"I need your expertise."

Jacques leaned down, studying the object with sudden interest. He might be a fraud as a sophisticated Frenchman, but he knew his shit when it came to art.

"Nice," he murmured. "Where did you get this?"

"Not your concern," Duncan said. Jacques was too smart not to eventually realize the vessel was a part of Calso's murder investigation, but Duncan wasn't about to share confidential police info. "Do you recognize the symbol?"

The dealer continued to study the vessel, his expression oddly tense. "I'm not an expert on antiquities, but my guess would be Sumerian."

Sumerian?

That seemed . . . random.

"Who deals with this sort of item?"

The man straightened. "None locally."

Duncan frowned. "Don't jerk me around, Girard."

"I'm not." Jacques held up his hands. "This is museum quality. Very rare."

"So give me a name."

The man shrugged. "I'm going to have to do some digging."

Duncan tossed the picture he'd grabbed at the station onto the desk. "What about this?"

Jacques picked up the twelve-by-twelve glossy picture of the coin that had been taken from the security tape. It had been blown up as large as possible without turning it into a fuzzy blob, but with a sharp motion, Jacques reached for a magnifying glass lying on his desk to study it in grim silence.

"Did it come with the vessel?" he at last demanded.

"Yes."

"Hmm." Another long silence. "Not currency. Maybe a symbol of authority."

"How much would it be worth?"

"I can't say for certain."

Jacques made a sound of shock as Duncan smoothly

pulled his gun and aimed it at his head. "*Mon Dieu.* I truly don't know. Were they found together?"

Duncan kept his gun pointed at his companion. He didn't intend to shoot the con man. But he sensed Jacques knew more about the coin than he was willing to admit. Obviously, he needed . . . inspiration to share his full range of knowledge.

"How did you know they were found together?"

Jacques licked his lips, using the magnifying glass to point toward the vessel on his desk. "The symbols along the top of the vase."

"What about them?"

"I'm no expert, but I suspect that they describe the purpose of the coin."

Duncan furrowed his brow, considering his words. "Like an instruction manual?"

"Exactly. And here . . ." The magnifying glass lowered to point toward the odd bird sketched into the stone. "It matches the hieroglyph etched on the coin. It can't be a coincidence. Together the pair would be almost priceless."

Duncan stiffened, abruptly realizing what had been nagging at him since he'd walked into Calso's office and caught sight of the ancient vessel.

"A pair," he breathed softly.

Jacques shrugged. "That's what I just said."

"So why would somebody take the coin and leave behind the vessel it came in?"

"No collector would," Jacques instantly denied. "Apart they're extremely valuable. Together . . ." He set the picture next to the vase, emphasizing their matching symbols. "As I said. Priceless."

Duncan had already ruled out robbery as a reason for the murder. A thief didn't leave behind millions in artwork, let alone a stack of untraceable bills.

Now he had to rule out an obsessed antiquities collector.

Which left . . .

More goddamn questions than answers.

The realization had just struck when he felt the vibration of his phone in his pocket. Stepping back, he holstered his gun before pulling out the phone and pressing it to his ear.

It would be a pity to shoot one of his best informants just because he didn't like the latest news.

And he didn't doubt for a minute he wasn't going to like it.

"O'Conner," he snapped, stiffening as he heard the dispatcher's unsteady voice telling him that Leah's body had been found. Again. "Where?" He made a mental note of the directions. "I'll be there. Contact Valhalla."

Replacing the phone in his pocket, Duncan reached to grasp the vessel and picture from the desk.

Jacques had turned a peculiar shade of ash, his suave French facade shattered by a surge of genuine fear.

"What the hell? You didn't tell me that this has something to do with the freaks."

Duncan turned and headed for the door. "I need the names of dealers who could move these items and I need them fast."

"I don't want to get involved with high-bloods," the con man protested, his voice approaching a screech. "They're nothing but trouble."

Duncan spared a glance over his shoulder. "Not nearly as much trouble as disappointing me."

Confident the man understood the cost of failure, Duncan headed across the showroom, his expression dark enough to keep the hovering assistant at a safe distance.

Then, getting into his car, he raced out of town at a speed that would make his ma faint.

He had to do something to vent his simmering frustration.

Okay, maybe the morning hadn't been a complete waste. He'd discovered the vessel and coin were unmistakably connected and that they had been crafted by the ancient Sumerians.

But the information didn't give him a direct path to Zakhar, which he needed if he was going to help Callie.

And now he was headed to collect the body of a young female who should have been protected by the police, if not while she was alive, then most certainly after she was dead.

Was it any wonder his foot was a little heavy on the accelerator?

Arriving at the remote location east of town, he parked his car on the bluff and made his way cautiously down to the muddy bank of the Missouri River.

He was immediately hit by the stench of brackish water and green slime that had collected in a small pool that was blocked from the river by a pile of rotting logs. His grimace, however, was for the young woman who was stretched on the mud. She'd clearly been dumped in the river in the hopes her body would float far enough away that she wouldn't be connected to Kansas City.

Instead she'd gotten caught on the logs.

Another surge of frustration flared through him. Dammit. Leah should be shopping with her friends. Or attending college. Or hell, dancing at the Rabbit Hutch, making old men pop little blue pills in the hope they might get lucky.

Anything but lying in the mud with her eyes staring blindly at the cloudless sky.

Turning his attention from the body, Duncan frowned at the sight of Frank with a crowd of uniformed police standing several feet away. Why the hell wasn't the silver-haired coroner processing the body? Were they waiting on something? Or someone?

At his approach Frank stepped away from the other cops, his expression hard. "O'Conner. About damned time you got here."

Duncan sighed. Knowing the older man as well as he did, he had no doubt Frank took the theft and abuse of Leah's body personally.

"Who found her?"

Frank jerked a thumb toward the large man standing at the top of the bluff, his beefy face flushed with adrenaline.

"A local farmer. He was searching for a missing cow."

"He's been warned not to speak to anyone?" Duncan demanded.

"Yeah." Frank rolled his eyes. "For all the good it will do."

Duncan shrugged. It wasn't like the farmer found a dead girl every day. Thank god. Who could blame him if he made the most of the rare event?

"Have you been able to examine her?"

Frank muttered a curse. "I just started when I was told to stop."

"By who?"

"The chief."

Duncan frowned. "Did she say why?"

The coroner's expression went from hard to bleak. "The freaks are coming to collect her."

If Frank had said those words just yesterday, Duncan would have gone ballistic. This was his case and he'd be damned if any freak was going to interfere.

Now, he squashed his territorial urges. Whatever was happening was way beyond his comfort zone. The more help the better. And speaking of help . . .

"Did you learn anything?" he asked his companion.

Frank scowled. "Are you deaf? I just said I was told not to touch her."

"I'm not deaf and I'm not stupid," Duncan drawled. "The day you do what you're told is the day I sprout wings and a halo."

A rueful smile replaced the scowl. "Fine," Frank muttered. "Her heart is still missing."

"No surprise. What else?"

Frank stepped closer, pitching his voice so it wouldn't carry. Word would eventually leak through the police department that their missing corpse had been caught on video surveillance killing one of Kansas City's most powerful citizens. But the longer they could keep it quiet, the longer they could avoid outright panic.

"Her body's not in bad shape considering she's been walking around the city," Frank admitted, his voice edged with a soul-deep anger.

Duncan glanced toward the slender female who lay like a broken flower in the mud. He understood his companion's fury.

It was wrong. Obscene.

"No obvious wounds?"

"Nada."

"Anything to indicate where she's been?"

Frank hesitated before giving a small shrug. "One thing."

Hah. Duncan knew he could count on Frank. The man might be a norm, but nothing got past his eagle eye. "What?"

"The tags in her clothing."

Duncan glanced back to Leah, skimming a puzzled gaze over the stretchy pants and top.

"What about them?"

"The clothes we found in her house were all from the local mall."

Duncan whipped his gaze back to his companion. "How do you know?"

Frank flashed a droll smile. "Are you fucking kidding me? I have three teenage daughters. There's not a store in that mall I haven't been dragged through a thousand times."

"I guess that would do it," Duncan admitted, startled by the tiny pang of envy. He'd always known he wanted children. It was imprinted into the O'Conner DNA. So why was he suddenly feeling that he wanted those children *now*?

Christ. Did men have biological clocks? Shaking his head at his moronic thoughts, he returned his attention to what Frank was trying to explain. "Is there something different about the clothes she's wearing now?"

"Your Sung."

"My Sung?"

"Your Sung. A local designer," Frank said. "Very high end."

Weird. Why would the necro go to the expense of designer clothes for a corpse he was going to toss in the river?

"Thanks, amigo," he said, making a mental note to check with the more exclusive salons.

Frank stiffened, his glance shooting over Duncan's shoulder. "The cavalry has arrived."

Duncan turned, prepared for the uniformed medics who were swiftly moving to wrap Leah in a protective bag that would hide her from prying eyes as well as preserve any evidence on her body.

What he wasn't prepared for was the sight of Callie and Fane, who followed closely behind the medics.

Had they already traveled to Russia and back? The thought would have boggled his mind if he hadn't been even more boggled by the lightning strike of awareness that sizzled through him.

Dressed in casual jeans with a white tee and her stunning eyes covered by sunglasses, she should have been easily overlooked. She was certainly tiny enough to be lost in the crowd.

But there wasn't a male gaze that didn't linger on the exotic crimson of her spiky hair and the grace of her movements as she halted several feet away while Fane moved to place himself directly between the medics and the gathered human police.

Like a rabid guard dog.

"So it would seem," he murmured to Frank in absent tones.

"I heard you stayed at Valhalla." Frank cleared his throat. "And not alone."

Duncan sent his companion a warning glare. "You have a problem?"

"Don't get your panties in a twist." Frank lifted his hands. "I was just wondering what's going on with you."

With a snort Duncan began walking toward Callie. "Tell you what, Frank. When I figure it out you'll be the first to know."

"You're playing a dangerous game, amigo," the coroner called behind him.

Callie stood, stiff and uncomfortable as Duncan casually strolled in her direction.

It wasn't that she wasn't pleased to see him.

She snorted softly. Not pleased? Why not just admit it?

She was tingling from head to toe.

Just catching sight of him with his golden hair shimmering in the sunlight and his lean body shown to advantage in the faded jeans and black tee made her heart leap and her mouth go as dry as the Sahara.

She wanted to cross the rough ground and wrap her arms around him. Not just because she remembered the pleasure of being pressed against those hard muscles; delving into the dark history of Lord Zakhar had left her feeling edgy. As if a shadow was looming over her. She could definitely use a hug.

Instead, she wrapped her arms around herself, acutely aware of the suspicious glances from Duncan's human friends. They'd clearly heard rumors of Duncan staying at Valhalla and were keeping watch to make sure he hadn't been "contaminated" by the freaks.

And, besides, she hadn't yet decided if seeking comfort from this particular male was really a wise choice.

Had she?

The disturbing question whirled through her mind as Duncan halted in front of her, making her even more edgy.

"Hello, Sergeant O'Conner," she murmured in a tight voice.

"Sergeant O'Conner?" He blinked. "Is that a joke?"

"I didn't expect you to be here. We just returned to Valhalla when the Mave asked that we bring the medics to collect the body," she found herself babbling, taking a step backward. "She hopes that an autopsy of Leah might reveal the precise magic the necromancer used to animate her."

Duncan frowned as he studied her wary expression. "What the hell is going on?"

She licked her lips at his impatient question. "I just told you."

"You told me why you're here," he growled. "You haven't told me why you're acting like I didn't spend the morning kissing every satin inch of you."

Heat stained her cheeks. "Shh."

"Answer the question or I'm going to get a hell of a lot louder."

"It's . . . I didn't know—"

"Know what?"

"If you wanted people to realize that we'd been together," she said, giving a startled grunt when he grasped her arm and tugged her toward a trail leading back up the bluff. Far enough away to make sure no one could overhear them, although they remained in full view of the gawking cops. "Duncan. What are you doing?"

"I want to make sure I have this right." The hazel eyes sparked with gold, warning his temper was roused. "Are you implying that you thought I might be ashamed of sleeping with you?"

Put that way it sounded . . . bad.

She shot a glance toward the crowd, shifting her feet. She

hated being the center of attention. Especially when she was surrounded by norms. "Can we discuss this later?"

His jaw hardened. He was well and truly pissed.

"No, we damned well can't discuss this later. We discuss this now."

"People are staring."

"I don't give a shit." He leaned close enough to whisper directly in her ear, his scent teasing her nose and making her blood heat. Man. She loved the smell of him. Blood rushed to her cheeks as she realized her nipples had hardened and excitement was buzzing through her lower stomach. She wanted to shove her fingers into his hair and trail a line of kisses over his stubborn jaw. Or bury her face in the curve of his neck and savor his intoxicating scent. "Just like I don't give a damn if they know I've taken you as my lover," he continued, placing an intimate kiss just below her ear before he pulled back to study her with a brooding gaze. "Unless that's not the problem?"

She blinked, struggling to concentrate on his words.

Dammit. She was the Queen of Composure. Nothing rattled her. Especially not a mere man.

But Duncan O'Conner possessed an aggravating ability to slip beneath her defenses.

"What do you mean?"

"Maybe you're ashamed that people might suspect that you've lowered your standards to allow a barely civilized cop into your bed?"

She made a sound of disbelief at the idiotic suggestion. There wasn't a woman alive who wouldn't be proud to claim this man as her lover.

"If that was the case then I would never have spent the night with you." She pointed out the obvious. "There isn't anyone in Valhalla who doesn't know we were together."

His eyes narrowed, his cop face on full display. "Then why did you act like I was the enemy?"

She bit her lip, shifting to hide her expression from the onlookers. The man might be gorgeous, sexy, and unexpectedly tender beneath his macho facade, but he was as stubborn as a Missouri mule.

"It's difficult."

He hooked a finger beneath her chin, tilting back her head to regard her with open concern. "Talk to me, sweetheart."

Okay. Fine. Maybe it was better if he knew.

"I've never been a couple," she grudgingly admitted.

He stilled, his eyes focusing on her with laser intensity. Like a hunter catching sight of unexpected prey.

"Never?"

She shivered. Not with fear. But . . . anticipation.

"No. I've only dated a few times and they were always casual."

His thumb brushed her lower lip, the light caress sending a jolt of sweet pleasure to the pit of her stomach.

"So I embarrassed you with my public display of affection?"

"Not exactly."

"Callie?"

She wrinkled her nose, recalling her awkwardness this morning and then again when she'd first seen Duncan this afternoon.

"It's more the fact I don't understand the rules of the game."

His expression softened, the wicked sensuality warming his hazel eyes.

"Between us there are no rules. We'll work our way through this . . ." He leaned down to brush her lips in a light kiss. "Together."

Another delectable shiver raced through her body and she lifted her hands to rest them against the hard contours of his chest.

"I don't think your friends are going to approve."

He nibbled the corner of her mouth. "Then they're not my friends."

An unexpected warmth spread through her heart at his simple words. Strange. Was it really that important to her that he wasn't the least hesitant to claim her in public?

Obviously, it was.

"And your family?"

"I already promised I was taking you to Sunday dinner."

It was once again the perfect answer, so naturally Callie panicked.

"No. I mean . . . not this Sunday."

A wry smile tugged at his lips. "Why the cold feet?"

It was a legitimate question. And one she had no answer for.

Everything had turned upside down in the past two days.

Her belief that there were rigid laws of physics that controlled the powers of high-bloods.

The assumption that she had her peaceful, if somewhat isolated, future all planned out.

The unspoken rule that norms and freaks didn't mix.

Was it any wonder she was torn between the intense desire to haul this man into the bushes and rip off his clothes and the urge to return to Valhalla and hide beneath her covers? Unfortunately, neither option was viable.

Not until they'd tracked down Lord Zakhar and put a stop to his gruesome abuse of the dead.

"I don't think I'm ready."

"Okay." He dropped a light kiss on her nose before he pulled back and studied her with a resigned smile. "We'll wait until you don't hyperventilate at the mere mention of family."

Her missing sense of humor returned at his gentle teasing. "So generous."

"And when we're working the case I'll be professional," he promised, a sinful heat melting the gold in his eyes until they shimmered in the afternoon sunlight. "Even if I'm counting the seconds until I can get you naked and lick you from top to bottom."

Her heart slammed against her ribs in instant hunger. Suddenly the option of pushing him into the bushes and stripping off his clothes was much more viable.

Too viable.

"You are—"

"Yeah, I know. Barely civilized." With a wicked grin he glanced over her shoulder. "We'd better go before Fane terrifies the entire KC police department into early retirement."

Chapter Seventeen

With swift efficiency the medics had Leah's body wrapped in a protective bag while Callie gave Duncan a condensed version of what they'd learned in Russia. With an equally condensed version, Duncan had shared his trip to the art expert, revealing the man had spoken of the coin being Sumerian in origin.

It was a step forward, but not nearly far enough or fast enough.

Deep inside her was a growing pulse of anxiety.

As if something was warning her that time was running out.

There was a faint stir from the cops still grouped together and, turning her head, Callie realized that Fane was coming to demand that they leave.

Squaring her shoulders, she crossed the short distance to speak with the Sentinel in private.

He wasn't going to like what she had to say, but for once she was determined. It was time to put on her big girl panties. She was done hiding behind her loyal guardian and the protective walls of Valhalla.

"I'm going to stay here and work on the investigation with Duncan," she said, barely waiting for Fane to come to a halt.

His face was devoid of expression, his dark eyes hard. "No."

"Fane, listen to me."

"You know the rules."

She did. A diviner was never to travel outside Valhalla without protection. There were far too many loonies who thought that the only good diviner was a dead one.

And that was before the news started to spread that there was a necromancer out there toying with young, female corpses.

She deliberately glanced toward Duncan, who watched them with a narrowed gaze. "I won't be alone."

"Are you deliberately trying to piss me off?"

"No. I'm trying to be logical." She ignored his muttered opinion of her logic. "Only you can return Leah and the medics to Valhalla. It makes sense for me to remain here and continue the investigation."

"What does this investigation include?"

She turned back, her gaze ricocheting off his granite-hard expression. "Duncan mentioned that Leah was wearing clothing from an exclusive salon," she said. "He wants to see if he can find the specific store and interview the owner."

He folded his arms over his chest. "That's all?"

"He's searching for a lead on the coin." She shrugged. "I suggested we stop by the Rabbit Hutch to see if any of Leah's friends—"

"Absolutely not."

Callie sighed at his immediate rejection of a perfectly sound proposal. As if that would stop her if she was truly determined to visit the strip joint.

"Yeah, that's the same answer I got from Duncan." She rolled her eyes. "Men."

He studied her for a long, silent minute. Intimidation at its finest.

"You could wait for my return so I could go with you."

It was her turn to nip the suggestion in the bud. She might be used to the Sentinel, but to most people he was a scary-ass MOFO.

"Fane, I love you, but you terrify the norms," she pointed out gently. "There's no way they would talk if they caught a glimpse of you."

A dangerous smile curled his lips. "I could make them talk."

She snorted. Fane had made hardened warriors weep in fear. "I don't doubt that for a minute, but I think we should try it Duncan's way first," she said, reaching in to place her fingers against the side of his throat. "If that doesn't work we'll call in the big guns."

His dark eyes remained flat, unrelenting. "He can't protect you from the witch. Or any other high-blood."

Callie couldn't argue. Duncan might be a hell of a cop, but he wasn't a Sentinel.

Although, with his special powers he could always . . . She squashed the unexpected thought.

Duncan loved being a cop. Being human. And wishing for him to join her world was the sort of thing that could break a woman's heart.

Or maybe just break her.

"I won't take any risks," she assured her companion. "I swear."

As if sensing her growing vulnerability, Fane narrowed his dark gaze. "This is bigger than you, Callie."

She flinched at the unwelcomed reminder of Boggs's warning. "We don't know I'm actually involved."

"You're no longer a child," he chided. "You can't stick your head in the sand and pretend that you don't sense the growing danger."

"You're right," she abruptly admitted. "I'm sorry."

He gave an exaggerated blink. "Do you have a fever?"

She shook her head, not about to admit the nightmares

that plagued her or the looming sense of doom. She'd be locked in her apartment before she could say "Jack Robinson." Whatever the hell that meant.

"I can't ignore the warnings," she said, keeping it vague. "If there's a darkness that threatens us then we have to stop it. The sooner, the better." She lowered her hand to poke Fane in the center of his steel-hard chest. "Which means accepting whatever assistance we can get."

He arched a brow. "And this isn't just about being alone with the cop?"

She hesitated. She might not always fully confess to her guardian, but she never deliberately lied.

Their relationship was built on having complete faith in one another and she would never do anything to jeopardize it.

"Maybe a small part, but I won't be distracted. Trust me."

"You, I trust." He sent a burning glare toward Duncan. "Him—never."

Only a few feet away Duncan stiffened, his hands curling at his sides as he met Fane glare for glare.

"I'll call you with any information we get," she said, giving him another poke to distract him from his silent stare-off with Duncan.

Christ. Testosterone was a pain in the ass.

Grudgingly Fane turned back to meet her annoyed gaze. "I'm going to see if I can find information on the coin."

His words caught Callie off guard. "You're going back to see Myst?" she demanded, recalling the fragile beauty of the scribe.

Was it possible that the stoic Sentinel had been smitten?

She wouldn't begrudge him an opportunity for a bit of happiness. He'd sacrificed far too much for her. But she couldn't deny a sense of disappointment for Serra.

The beautiful psychic would be devastated if Fane chose another.

"No." He tapped her nose—a silent warning to keep it out of his personal business. "I know a monk who has studied the Sumerians."

Ah. She grinned in relief. "He isn't Sumerian, is he?" she demanded. Monks were rumored to live as long as any high-blood.

Another tap. "It's not polite to ask."

She stepped back, her smile fading. "Be careful, Fane. You're not as invincible as you think."

"Yes, I am." He held her gaze. "I'll come for you first thing in the morning."

"But—"

"Don't push me."

He took off, moving with a fluid grace as he led the medics up the bluff and away from the humans who gaped at him like he was a wild animal who might very well ravage them if he slipped his leash.

They weren't wrong.

Zak was seated at his desk in his private library when the scent of blood had him lifting his head to watch as Anya stepped into the room.

For once she'd put aside her designer clothing and was covered from neck to toe in a black satin robe with her hair pulled into a tight braid that fell down her back. Zak was similarly attired, although his robe was made of a silver silk that would be disposed of once they were done.

Blood and death were a messy business.

"You have prepared the spell?"

She shrugged. "The blood has opened a pathway to our destination."

He rose to his feet, unconcerned by the knowledge she'd had to sacrifice a young child to create the magic necessary to create a gateway.

It was, after all, the reason he'd first been attracted to Anya.

There were any number of witches and mystics among the Russian court, some of them even real. But Anya was special. Long before high-bloods had become known by the norms, she'd trained with a clandestine coven that had taught her magic that was long since banned. Including the ability to travel that was similar to a Sentinel, although she was drawn to objects with magical power instead of using well-established portals from monastery to monastery.

Which was how she first stumbled across the ancient ziggurat covered in hieroglyphics that was nearly buried in the deserts of Iran.

"Good," he said, grim satisfaction edging his voice. "Then let's go before my destiny can be once again snatched away."

"Snatched away?" Her eyes narrowed. "What are you talking about?"

"A traitor."

"A traitor?"

He arched a brow. "Did I stutter?"

"No, but—" Anya frowned. "I don't understand."

"Really? I should think it was obvious. Someone has betrayed me." A chill swirled through the air. "Someone very close to me."

"You can't possibly suspect me? It would be ridiculous."

"Don't pretend moral outrage, Anya," he warned in cold tones. "It doesn't suit you."

The witch clenched her bloodstained hands. "I have as much invested as you, Zak. Why would I devote my life to you only to become a traitor?"

He was far from impressed by her fierce response. Only an idiot would trust a woman who would willingly sell her soul to the highest bidder.

"And what do you have invested?" he drawled.

She sucked in an outraged breath. "I saved your life."

"Maybe."

"What do you mean? I pulled you from the flames." Temper abruptly snapped in her emerald eyes. "It was my magic that kept your heart beating while your body healed."

His own expression remained glacial. "You also promised a dozen times we were about to get your hands on the coin, only to discover that it had once again slipped from our grasp."

She muttered a foul curse. "It was your bokors that failed, not my magic."

His fingers stroked over the coin hidden in the pocket of his robe. Over the years he'd meticulously reviewed his failures to acquire the coin. He'd wasted enormous resources and risked exposure each time he raised the dead. The fact that they'd missed carrying out their mission by mere hours, sometimes minutes, had been enough to stir his suspicions.

"Hmm."

Anya narrowed her gaze. "What?"

"The more simple explanation was that someone was warning the owners of the coin that I was on their trail."

She appeared genuinely outraged by his words. "If you suspected I was a traitor then why did you allow me to stay with you?"

He shrugged. "I've always believed in the theory that it's best to keep your enemies close."

"This is insanity," she hissed. "If it was me, then why wouldn't I have warned Calso?"

"Perhaps you're actually innocent. Or perhaps this is a cleverly constructed trap." He shrugged. "Until I know which it is, I can assure you I will be on constant guard." He offered a cold smile. "Now, are we traveling to the temple or not?"

"Fine." With a swirl of satin robes, the witch was heading out the door. "Follow me."

In silence they made their way to Anya's private rooms on the upper floor. The stench of blood became almost overwhelming as she pushed open the door to reveal her sitting room, which had been converted into a basic chapel.

With a grimace, Zak glanced over the scrolled chairs with pretty pastel cushions that were arranged in a semicircle around the rough wooden altar. The expensive artwork that had once hung on the ivory walls had been piled in one corner and replaced with shelves of murky bottles that held an assortment of nasty ingredients used by Anya when she was cooking up her potions or casting her spells.

The curtains had been pulled across the window, shrouding the room in shadows. The only light was a lone candle that sat on the altar next to the wooden bowl filled with blood.

The blood of an innocent.

Moving forward, Anya waved a hand toward the altar. "Stand beside me," she commanded.

Zak joined her, reaching to grasp her wrist in a grip tight enough to hurt.

"Anya," he murmured in silken tones, "make very certain there are no mistakes."

Duncan was damned proud of himself.

He hadn't pulled his gun when Fane had stood protectively close to Callie, his expression hard as he clearly tried to convince the young diviner to return to Valhalla with him.

Or when Callie had lifted her hand to touch the Sentinel with an intimacy that made him growl like a fucking dog.

Or even when Fane had sent Duncan a glare that warned

all sorts of bad, bad repercussions if Callie was hurt on his watch.

Yeah, so kudos to him.

Still, he couldn't resist wrapping a possessive arm around her shoulders when she at last returned to his side and the hulking guardian jogged up the steep path, pausing at the top to send Duncan one last glare.

And if that made him a caveman . . . then so be it.

"He doesn't look happy," he muttered, tugging her even closer to his side.

At least he hadn't pounded his chest, right?

"He's not." She heaved a faint sigh before turning to study him with a determined expression. "Where do we go first?"

His gaze slid over her pale, perfect features, barely resisting the urge to pluck off her reflective glasses so he could drown in the sapphire beauty of her eyes.

"I know where I'd like to go," he murmured softly.

She lifted a brow. "Should I ask?"

His hands lightly skimmed up and down the back of her arms. "My apartment is only a few miles away."

He felt her revealing shiver of pleasure, but she shook her head in warning.

"I thought you genuinely wanted me to help in your investigation."

He grinned. "I do, but I'm a man."

"And?"

With a chuckle he stepped back, reaching in his front pocket to remove his cell phone.

As much as he preferred the idea of luring her to his apartment, he understood that their relationship had become physical at supersonic speed. Not that he was complaining. Hell, no. But the lack of traditional wooing meant Callie couldn't be certain that he valued her as much for her swift intelligence and quiet courage as he did for her beauty.

Something he intended to prove beyond a shadow of a doubt.

"And I'm about to call the station so we can get on with the investigation," he assured her.

She smirked at his overly innocent smile, but reached out to grab his arm. "Why do you have to call the station? I thought we were going to investigate the designer shops?"

"We are, but I'm hoping to narrow down the search by finding out which salons carry a local designer." He struggled to remember what Frank had told him. "Sung something or other."

"Let me." She pulled out her own phone and scrolled through her contacts.

"Who are you calling?"

"Serra." She lifted the phone to her ear. "She's intimately familiar with every store in a hundred-mile radius."

Duncan had a searing memory of Serra's skin-tight clothing and kick-ass boots. He didn't have his coroner's personal experience with female attire, but he did have a butt-load of sisters. He'd learned to recognize a fashionista.

His da had nearly strangled his youngest sister when he discovered she'd used his credit card to buy a six-hundred-dollar designer purse. He shuddered to think what the psychic had spent on her boots.

"Somehow that doesn't surprise me."

She pretended she didn't hear his muttered words as she spoke into the phone. "Serra, do you know a designer named Sung? Great, where can you buy the label?" She listened, nodding her head. "Thanks, you're a doll." She paused, a faint smile curling her lips. "Fane? Actually he's on his way back to Valhalla, although it's going to be a touch and go landing, so if you want to catch him you need to be prepared. Good luck."

She returned her phone to her pocket, then sent him a curious smile as she felt his lingering gaze. "What?"

"I thought you liked your guardian?"

"Of course I do."

"Then why would you leave him at the mercy of that man-eater?"

"Hey." She punched him in the shoulder, the blow surprisingly strong despite her lack of bulk. Were all high-bloods more powerful than norms? It would explain why his bench press record at the police academy was still unbeaten. And deflate a small piece of his ego. "Serra's my dearest friend."

"She's terrifying," he countered, giving an exaggerated shudder.

"You think I can't be terrifying?" she asked, only partially teasing. "You haven't seen me mad yet."

Hmm. His gaze briefly flicked to the crimson flames of her hair. He'd already discovered the passionate nature beneath her facade of calm. He didn't doubt for a second that included a temper that could flay him alive.

"And I don't intend to," he warned, brushing his thumb over the lush curve of her lower lip. "I am, after all, completely adorable."

"What you are is full of shit," she corrected dryly.

His bark of laughter echoed around the secluded alcove. "Possibly." Ignoring the gazes from his fellow cops, which ranged from disgust to blatant envy, he steered Callie toward the path leading up the bluff. "Did she give you the name of a store?"

"Two. Victoria's Boutique at the Plaza and the Paris Gallery in Independence."

She easily jogged up the steep incline, the sway of her ass encased in the tight jeans sending a sizzling heat through Duncan's body. Oh, he wanted his hands on the rounded derriere, preferably as she was riding him to oblivion. Or maybe while she was on her hands and knees as he took her from behind.

"Duncan? Is something wrong?"

Callie's question intruded into his sinful fantasy, forcing him to realize that they'd reached the top of the bluff.

Damn.

He hadn't responded to a woman with this sort of mindless lust since . . .

Since never, he was forced to concede.

Not even during his crazed, hormonal teen years.

Clearing his throat, he tapped the name of the salons into his phone's GPS, feeling a heat crawl up the back of his neck. Thank god, Callie was a diviner and not a psychic.

She'd push him back down the bluff.

Head first.

"All set," he muttered, lifting his gaze to meet her puzzled frown. "Let's go."

She followed in silence, allowing him to settle her in the front seat of his car and take off at a speed considerably less reckless than when he'd arrived. She wasn't obeying his order, merely trying to figure out why he was blushing like an idiot.

Thankfully her lingering scrutiny was distracted as he turned onto Broadway and made his way to the Plaza.

Pressing her nose to the window, she appeared fascinated by the Spanish-inspired buildings and exquisite fountains that were a trademark of the area. At night the neighborhood was bathed in stunning lights and the air was filled with soft jazz, but during the day it was the domain of the upscale shoppers.

With a low laugh, Duncan pulled into an underground parking lot and turned off the motor.

Callie turned to meet his smile with a frown. "What's so funny?"

He slid out of the car, not surprised that Callie was already standing near the hood by the time he'd shut the door. She might be forced to travel with a guardian, but that didn't mean she meekly depended on a man.

If anything, she fought for every inch of independence she could claim.

"You look like my five-year-old niece, Tabby, when I take her to the carnival," he answered her question, placing a gentle hand on her elbow as he strolled toward the nearby stairs.

"And how's that?"

"All wide-eyed wonder."

A faint smile tugged at her lips. "I don't often leave Valhalla and when I do it's rarely for pleasure."

A deep, aching regret clutched at his heart. Her words were simple, spoken without bitterness. But to a man who'd grown up surrounded by loving family and a community who'd easily accepted him, it made him want to hit something.

What kind of world forced a little girl to remain hidden behind protective walls or risk being attacked by small-minded vigilantes?

He had an easy answer.

It was the same world that would happily demand her help when her "curse" could help solve a murder.

With an effort, he squashed his surge of anger. He couldn't change Callie's past. All he could do was try to show her that there were good and beautiful things to be discovered beyond Valhalla.

They stepped onto the sun-drenched street just a block from their destination.

"You've never been to the Plaza?" he asked as they strolled along the sidewalk.

"No."

"We have time if you want to look around." He nodded

toward an exclusive jewelry store across the road. "Maybe do a little shopping."

The sun glinted off her reflective glasses as she turned in his direction. "You assume because I'm a woman I must love to shop?"

He leaned down to steal an all too brief kiss. "Absolutely, sweetheart."

Chapter Eighteen

Callie did her best to hide her smile as she planted her hands on her hips.

Deep inside she had to admit that she was enchanted by Duncan's teasing. She'd never spent her days indulging in light flirtations like other young girls. Not because she didn't want to, but people treated diviners differently, even among high-bloods. It might not always be suspicion, but at the very least . . . wariness. And Callie was by nature more serious than many of her friends.

Now she couldn't deny a giddy enjoyment at being treated like a pretty woman who'd caught the attention of a virile, drop-dead sexy man.

Of course, she might be naive, but she wasn't stupid. Duncan was a man who expected to have his way, either with charm or sheer arrogance. If she didn't keep him in line, he'd trample all over her.

"I think we should find the boutique before I punch you in the nose," she threatened.

"All right."

He held his hands up in mock surrender before turning to stroll down the street. Well, stroll wasn't exactly what he did. Like Fane, he was on constant guard, his eyes searching for potential enemies among the passing pedestrians and his body angled to make sure any approaching danger had to go through him first. A panther on the prowl. She smiled wryly. The Sentinel would be proud of her companion. Even if he'd rather have his tongue cut out than admit it.

And she wasn't the only one to notice the potent appeal of his dangerous appearance.

A dozen female gazes were laser-focused on the hard muscles beneath his tight tee and faded jeans, while another dozen were lingering on the chiseled perfection of his face, which was kept from being pretty by the golden stubble on his stubborn jaw and the lethal shimmer in his hazel eyes. Even with the pale, satin smooth hair tumbled onto his brow there was no mistaking he was all male.

Ruthless, unattainable.

Perhaps sensing her growing annoyance at the female ogling, Duncan flashed her a wicked smile. "If you don't shop, what do you like to do?"

She shrugged, forcing away her ridiculous stab of jealousy. Okay. Women liked to stare at Duncan O'Conner. Who could blame them? It certainly wasn't worth ruining this rare opportunity to enjoy the city.

And, despite her grim duty to locate the dangerous necromancer, she intended to appreciate her time away from Valhalla.

"Different stuff," she said with a shrug.

The hazel eyes studied her with open curiosity. "You don't have a hobby?"

"Do you?"

"I work too many hours, but if I did have the time I've always wanted to coach Little League," he answered with an easy frankness that she envied.

She was too used to keeping her thoughts and feelings to herself.

"Little League?" She lifted a surprised brow. "Really?"

"I love kids and I love baseball." He shrugged. "It seems the perfect choice."

Suddenly she had an image of him surrounded by rambunctious boys, his expression stern while his eyes twinkled with indulgent merriment.

"Yes," she abruptly admitted. "It does."

His gaze narrowed. "Are you mocking me?"

"No, not at all. I think you would make a great coach."

His expression remained wary, as if not sure whether she was insulting him or not. "Because I still act like I'm five?"

"There's that," she teased.

"Thanks," he muttered. "Anything else?"

A rare chuckle escaped her lips. He even sounded like a petulant five-year-old.

"Yes," she murmured, deciding to put him out of his misery. "You're also a natural leader without being overbearing. Your fellow cops obviously respect you. And you have a certain amount of charm when you aren't being an ass." She elbowed him in the side. "The kids would adore you."

He reached to brush his fingers through her short, spiky hair. A silent thank-you for her belief in him.

"What about you, Callie?" he asked in a husky voice. "What makes you happy?"

She paused, truly considering his question. There were a lot of things she enjoyed. Being with her friends. Working in the garden. A quiet night in her apartment reading a good book.

"Spending time in the nursery," she at last said, for the first time realizing just how much she depended on the pleasure she found surrounded by children.

"Ah." He grinned in appreciation. "A sucker for the babies, are you?"

"Not just babies," she corrected. "At Valhalla all children under the age of five spend at least a few hours every day in the nursery."

He seemed fascinated by the glimpse into a world that was shrouded in mystery for most people. "Is there a particular reason?"

"To make sure they become accustomed to being with kids who aren't like them. In such a confined space we can't afford prejudices," she explained without hesitation. It wasn't a state secret. And besides, Duncan wasn't just another norm. "It also helps them to learn to control their powers when they're in public."

"That's what you meant when you said you had a lot of mothers?"

"Yes." Warmth flowed through her at the memory of being surrounded by love. After seeing the trauma of children brought into Valhalla who'd been neglected and even abused, she understood what a gift her childhood had been. "High-bloods aren't like most people."

He ran his fingers down the center of her back, the light caress making her toes curl in her shoes.

"Actually, I pretty much worked that out for myself."

"I mean that ninety-nine percent of the time they aren't born to high-blood parents," she said, relieved when her voice was steady. No need feeding his outrageous ego with the fact he could make her melt with one careless touch. "So they're brought to us as abandoned babies or as children who can no longer live with their biological families. They need the reassurance they're wanted and valued by their new community."

He came to an abrupt halt, swinging her until they were face to face. "My ma is going to love you."

Her heart missed a beat at his unexpected words. "Because I enjoy children?"

"Because she was forever taking in stray chicks despite our constant protests the house was about ready to bust at the seams." His gaze swept over her upturned face with a piercing intensity. "She'll be delighted to meet a fellow mother hen."

His mother . . . The woman who no doubt thought no one was good enough for her baby.

Certainly not a freak from Valhalla.

Aaaaand cue panic.

She pulled away, waving an unsteady hand toward the door on the corner that was shaded by an elegant ivory canopy. "I think that's the place."

With a heavy sigh, he reached down to brush her lips in a brief kiss.

"Someday," he murmured against her lips.

Duncan leashed his impatience. *Baby steps,* he silently told himself. *If I rush her, I might lose her.* And he wasn't prepared to risk that.

Instead he led her into the chichi store, surprised when she pulled away to wander through the racks of clothing that cost more than he made in a year.

Maybe she liked shopping more than she was willing to admit. With a shrug, he turned to watch the silver-haired woman wearing a discreet black dress cross the plush ivory carpet, her thin face pinched as if she'd caught a foul odor.

Duncan hid a wry smile. He wasn't the sort of cop who got off on busting the balls of perps. He did what had to be done, no extracurricular activity included.

But he couldn't deny a very human anticipation in pissing off this sour-faced female. There were few things that peeved him as much as someone thinking a few bucks in the bank made them better than others.

"May I help you?" she asked in tones that indicated he needed to return to the gutter he crawled out of ASAP.

Reaching into his back pocket, he pulled out his badge to

flash it with a feral smile. "KCPD. I'm here to ask you a few questions."

The woman gave a small gasp, her hard blue eyes shooting around the empty store as if afraid someone might overhear them. "I can't imagine what questions you could have for me."

Duncan replaced the badge with his phone, flipping through the images until he found one of Leah he'd pulled from the Rabbit Hutch's Web site.

"I need you to tell me if you've seen this woman in your shop."

She glanced at the picture, her lip curling in disdain at Leah's flashy makeup and revealing outfit. "Certainly not."

A cold anger sliced through him. The bitch. Whatever Leah's career choice, she'd been a young woman who deserved a far better fate than she'd been given.

"How many employees do you have?" he growled.

"I have two assistants, but I'm Victoria, the owner of this boutique, and if the store is open, then I'm here." Her lips thinned until they were nearly invisible. "If the woman was a customer I would recognize her."

"You know every customer?"

"Naturally."

Duncan snorted, skimming his thumb over the screen of his phone to bring up Calso's image.

"What about this man?"

Her pencil thin brows arched in surprise. "Mr. Calso?"

"He's a customer?"

"Unfortunately no."

"But you know him?"

"Our paths have crossed at various charity functions," she said in haughty tones. Translated . . . this woman hung on the fringes of Kansas City society in the hopes of luring them into her shop. "He's a prominent businessman who has always been very generous in giving to those less fortunate."

"Yeah, I bet," he muttered. Nothing like tossing a few dollars at a charity to gain the goodwill of a city.

"I don't understand," she snapped. "Why are you here?"

"Duncan." Callie's voice floated from the corner of the showroom. "This looks similar."

Turning his head, he watched as the diviner held up a pair of stretchy pants and tiny top that looked remarkably close to what Leah had been wearing.

"Smart girl," he breathed in low tones before turning back to carefully monitor the older woman's expression. He didn't think she was involved, but he treated everyone as a suspect until they were proved innocent. He was a cop, not a judge. "How many of those have you sold?"

Victoria gave an impatient wave of her hand, the diamonds that were crammed onto her knobby fingers nearly blinding as they caught the overhead light. "I don't discuss my customers—"

"You can discuss your customers or I can get a warrant and start hauling them down to the station," he warned, his expression grim. "Your call."

She paled, her spine so stiff it was a wonder it didn't snap beneath the strain. "It's impossible to answer your question," Victoria at last managed to respond, her teeth clenched. "Each Your Sung piece is individually designed. No two are alike."

Without hesitation, he pulled up yet another image on his phone. If she wanted to play rough, he would play rough. "What about this one?" he demanded, showing her the picture of Leah lying on the bank of the Missouri River.

For the first time the woman's icy composure cracked, her hand lifting to press against her lips.

"Oh my god. Is she—"

"Dead," Duncan supplied.

"I need a . . ." She bit off her hasty words, looking with obvious longing toward the counter at the back of the store.

No doubt she had a stash of prescription feel-good-pills hidden in her purse. "Water."

"You can pop your Prozac after you've told me who bought this particular outfit, Victoria," he informed her, his flat tone revealing he didn't give a shit about her rattled nerves.

Her fingers fluttered to toy with the pearls hung around her neck. "I don't know."

That was it. That was the straw that broke the camel's back.

"Lady, I've tried to be polite, but you've pissed on my last nerve," he snarled. "Tell me what you know or I'll haul you out of here in handcuffs."

"Please." She took a hasty step backward. "I truly can't."

"Maybe you should just tell us what you know," Callie suggested in soothing tones, sending him a chiding glare as she moved to stand at his side.

"I . . ." The woman licked her lips. "She started coming in six months ago. Maybe a little longer."

She.

Duncan wasn't entirely shocked. It would have been too much to hope that the mysterious necromancer had waltzed into the shop and used his credit card to buy clothing for his macabre marionette.

And Callie had mentioned that she'd discovered rumors of a witch who'd been his accomplice.

Ignoring Callie's disapproval, he allowed her to take the role of the good cop. He always sucked at it anyway. Bad cop? That was easy.

"Her name?" he barked out.

"She never told me."

"It had to be on her credit card."

Victoria shook her head until the starched silver-hair threatened to move. "She always paid in cash."

Cash? Who carried around the sort of cash necessary for designer clothes?

"You didn't think that was strange?"

"It's not unheard of." The woman shrugged. "There are occasions when a woman needs to keep her liaison . . . discreet."

Ah.

Callie looked confused. Duncan, however, instantly understood.

Unfortunately, he had friends who enjoyed the benefits of marriage while pursuing other women. The first rule of cheating was never, ever to leave a paper trail.

"A mistress to a married man?" he asked.

Victoria continued to tug at her pearls, discomfort etched into every line of her thin body. "I don't ask uncomfortable questions."

Duncan believed her. A woman who peddled overpriced clothes to the lovers of the rich and powerful would learn to turn a blind eye to a lot of things.

"Did she come in alone?"

"Always." The woman paused, and Duncan assumed she was frowning. Or would be if the Botox hadn't frozen her brow. "Of course, she had a driver who waited for her outside."

"Make and model of the car?" he pounced.

"It was silver, I think." She shrugged. "I really didn't pay attention."

Duncan glanced toward the ceiling. "Surveillance tapes?"

"They aren't saved unless there's a reason to keep them." She doused Duncan's last hope. "As I said, this boutique promises discretion."

He swallowed his opinion about people who needed to hide their dirty laundry. He had a few secrets of his own.

"What about the woman?" he instead demanded "Can you describe her?"

Another wave of her hand, another blinding flash of

diamonds. "She was average height, a size four, with an autumn skin tone."

Duncan blinked. "Autumn?"

"Pale skin. Green eyes."

Duncan made the notes on his phone. "Her hair?"

"She always wore it hidden beneath a hat."

"Of course she did." He grimaced. "Not that it matters. Women change hair color more often than most men change their underwear." The older woman looked shocked while Callie rolled her eyes.

"Anything else?" he continued.

"No . . ." Victoria appeared to be struck by a sudden thought. "Wait."

"What?"

"She wore a strange bracelet."

"Describe it."

"It had a collection of small metal disks with strange symbols scratched on them." Victoria gave a curl of her lip. "Not at all the sort of thing a true lady would wear."

Duncan turned his head to meet Callie's wide gaze. "Witch," he mouthed.

"Anya," she breathed.

He squashed the urge to jump to conclusions. It, along with day old calamari, was dangerous.

"Perhaps." He reached into his back pocket to pull out a small business card. "This has the numbers of the station as well as my cell phone. Call me if she returns."

From a distance the ziggurat was nothing more than a crumbling ruin that had been left to the ravages of the desert. Constructed of sunbaked bricks, it had once been a part of a temple complex for the Sumerians. Now, there was nothing left but a brittle shell of four receding tiers with two sharply angled stone staircases. Even the shrine that had once been a magnificent crown on top of the temple had been swept away by the relentless blast of sand.

It was a place of shattered dreams.

Not even a ghost remained to speak for those long departed.

Standing in the shifting landscape less than a mile from the temple, Zak sought to regain his balance. The witch's trip to the Middle East hadn't been nearly as pleasant as traveling with a Sentinel.

In truth, it had been more like being jerked inside out by a raging vortex than a smooth transition from one place to another.

Which was why he so rarely consented to enter a witch's spell. It was almost always more trouble than it was worth.

At last confident that he'd regained his equilibrium, Zak smoothed his hands down his robe, covertly ensuring the coin, along with a small pistol, was still in his pocket.

In the other pocket was a tiny amulet that held a lethal spell.

If this was a trap, he wouldn't go down easily.

Glancing toward the witch at his side, he waved a hand toward the ruin. "Get rid of the illusion, Anya."

Anya was on her knees, her pale face tight with exhaustion in the pool of moonlight. Unlike the Sentinels who used the established pathways that were held open by the monks, Anya was forced to use her own magic to travel. It left her on the brink of collapse.

"I have to be closer," she panted.

Zak made a sound of impatience. He had no sympathy for his companion. Not when a thick layer of magic concealed the true temple, and anyone who might be hiding inside.

"I'm not taking a step closer until the illusion is gone," he warned, the chilled breeze tugging at his silver hair and stirring the sand beneath his feet.

Anya cursed, but lifting an unsteady hand, she spoke the words that would temporarily lower the illusion.

"There," she croaked.

There was a rippling shimmer, like a passing mirage, then the full splendor of the temple was revealed.

The tiers were no longer crumbling shells, but complete walls made of blue glazed bricks that once had been the pride of the surrounding city. The windows were covered with delicate bronze lattices and at the top was an oval shrine that had been reserved for the priests who'd offered sacrifices to the gods.

"Remain here," he commanded, his eyes searching the shadows as he began walking toward the nearest staircase.

"You're just going to leave me?" Anya protested.

"So it would seem."

Ignoring her demand for him to wait, Zak continued forward, the darkness that lived inside him pulsing with an intoxicating recognition.

He'd been here once before. It had been shortly after Anya had appeared in Saint Petersburg and she'd convinced him that she'd seen his future etched on a wall in the middle of a desert.

Naturally he'd demanded to see for himself.

A grim smile touched his lips as he climbed the stairs and entered the narrow door that led into the first chamber of the temple. He crossed directly to the wall bathed in moonlight, his fingers reaching to trace the hieroglyphs that spoke of a man with eyes of diamonds who whispered to the dead. There was even a carved figurine on a nearby pedestal that possessed an eerie resemblance to him.

He moved to the next wall, once again stroking his fingers over the hieroglyphics. These were centered on the same diamond-eyed man; this time he held a coin in his hand. The same coin that was now tucked in his pocket.

The odd symbols continued over the smooth stone,

displaying the man placing the coin in a shallow notch that had been carved at the base of the wall. From there the meaning became less clear.

From his hours of studying the glyphs he'd concluded that the coin opened a doorway. Maybe a physical doorway, maybe a metaphysical doorway. It didn't matter. What was important was the next image revealed the man holding a chalice over his head with an army of the dead walking behind him.

His army.

To rule the world.

His gaze briefly rested on the marks that were etched onto the arms of the man. Long gouges with what appeared to be blood dripping from his elbows to pool at his feet.

He understood that blood would be demanded.

Power was never without cost.

But, that didn't mean he intended to die for a few brief moments of glory.

Reaching the end of the glyphs, Zak lowered himself to his knees and pulled the coin from his pocket.

A strange hush filled the air, an electric buzz racing over his skin.

It was as if the world held its breath, waiting for him to complete his destiny.

Barely aware he was moving, Zak leaned forward to place the coin in the shallow indention.

He wasn't sure what he expected.

A burst of heavenly light.

A chorus of angels.

A lightning strike that would turn him to ash.

Instead the ground shook beneath his knees and a rock dislodged from the ceiling to smack him on top of the head.

Pain blasted through his skull, blood dripping down his neck as he toppled face first onto the stone floor.

So much for his moment of glory.

Chapter Nineteen

Callie settled into the front seat of Duncan's car, her mind shifting through what they'd discovered.

It wasn't much. They didn't have an address. No phone number. Not even a name.

But she was convinced that the clothing that Leah had been wearing had been bought by Anya. Which meant that the witch was still with Lord Zakhar. And that they were in the Kansas City area.

It was a start.

"Are you hungry?"

Duncan's question jerked her out of her thoughts and she turned her head to study his chiseled profile.

Out of nowhere she was struck by a jolt of intense awareness.

God Almighty.

She struggled to breathe as she took in the stark beauty of his face. How many times over the past few years had she covertly snuck glances at the golden-haired cop with the grim expression? How many nights had her dreams been filled with ripping off his tight tee and faded jeans?

And now that she actually knew just how it felt to spend

the night in his arms, his lips kissing paths of destruction down her throat as he slid deep into her body . . .

It was enough to make even nice girls think about handcuffing a man to her bed and having her wicked way with him.

Obviously puzzled by her sudden silence, Duncan sent her a searching glance. "Callie?"

A blush stained her cheeks as she cleared her throat. "Actually, I'm starving."

"Good." Returning his attention to the growingly narrow streets, he weaved his way through the traffic with the ease of a native. "I know a little joint that has BBQ to die for."

Her gaze slid down to the broad chest outlined in magnificent detail by the T-shirt. Was the temperature rising? Suddenly it felt way too hot in the car.

"Do they deliver?"

"Of course." He gave a lift of his shoulder. "It's a beautiful day. We can go to the park or—"

"Your apartment?"

His knuckles turned white as he gripped the steering wheel. "That's an option."

Callie lifted her brows at his carefully bland response. "But?"

"But I thought I was supposed to behave myself."

She gave a relieved laugh. For a second she'd wondered if he'd lost interest.

"You can't behave yourself at your apartment?" she teased.

The hazel eyes flashed in her direction, a searing desire turning the gold flecks into molten need. "No."

Her mouth went dry. "You're at least honest."

"Not always, although my ma tried her best." His lopsided grin was strained. Callie felt her shirt stick to her damp skin. "She was convinced washing out my mouth with soap would cure me of my tendency to bend the truth."

"She has my sympathy." Callie tried to match his casual

tone even as they both shivered beneath the sensual tension pulsing in the air. "My guess is that you were a precocious brat growing up."

"And you weren't?" he challenged.

"Not really. I was usually the shy kid sitting in the corner."

"Serra never talked you into breaking the rules?"

She wrinkled her nose. Serra had been a vivacious child and a natural leader who'd taken huge pleasure in causing chaos. Of course, unlike Callie, she also had loving biological parents who often collected her from Valhalla when her teachers and foster family needed a break.

She never had to fear she might lose her only home.

"Maybe once or twice," she conceded.

Without warning, Duncan pulled into an empty parking lot, turning to study her with a somber expression.

"Look, sweetheart, we can go anywhere you want, and I promise to try and keep my hands to myself." His fingers brushed her cheek in a gentle caress. "But I want you in the worst way and I'm not entirely sure it wouldn't be better to stay in public."

She stilled at the fierce edge in his voice and the tight knot of muscles that throbbed in his jaw.

"Are you saying—"

His finger moved to stroke her lower lip. "What?"

"That you crave me?"

Their gazes clashed at her deliberate choice of words. No doubt a more experienced woman would have kept the question to herself.

Most men didn't like to confess vulnerability. Not even with their lovers.

And she'd all but demanded to know if he desired her more than he'd desired his own wife.

Yeah, not too pushy. Yeesh.

But even as she was desperately trying to find a way to

laugh off the question, he was surging forward to claim her lips in a kiss that was all raw male possession.

"Hell, yes," he admitted without hesitation.

Oh. Her heart melted.

Tangling her fingers in the short strands of his hair, she determinedly ignored the warmth that spread like honey through her body.

She wasn't about to ruin the moment with silly emotions.

"I want to be alone with you," she murmured against his lips.

"You're sure?"

"Absolutely, positively."

He pulled back, studying her for a long minute. Then clearly satisfied she was as ready as he was, he flashed a smile filled with sinful anticipation.

"Hold on, baby."

Turning to face front, he shoved the car into gear, then with a flick of his finger he had the siren blaring.

Callie's lips parted, but before she could speak he was pulling out of the parking lot and hurtling across town with speed that made her grip the dashboard.

She had brief glimpses of redbrick factories that gave way to warehouses. Then small, family-owned stores that were situated between shabby houses and squat apartment buildings.

They squealed to a halt in a narrow parking lot. Duncan shut off the engine and the siren with a twist of the key, leaving them in a strangely thick silence.

Callie swallowed the sudden lump in her throat. "Are you allowed to do that?"

An astonishing hint of color lined his narrow cheekbones. Was he embarrassed? "I'd rather you didn't mention this to Molinari."

She hid her burst of amusement. He looked like a kid caught with his hand in the cookie jar.

Well, maybe not a kid, she conceded as a white-hot lick of excitement curled through the pit of her stomach.

More like a sexy beast who wasn't entirely tamed.

Clicking the lock to release her seat belt, Callie closed the small distance between them and pressed a kiss to the hollow just below his ear.

She'd already learned it was a particularly sensitive spot. "My lips are sealed," she promised softly.

"Shit," he groaned, fumbling with his own seat belt. "You're killing me."

Lingering just long enough to suck in the intoxicating scent of his warm, male skin, Callie scooted back across the seat and out the door.

She had time to glance at the faded brick structure that matched the connecting buildings to form a bland wall of depressing architecture before Duncan was scooping her off her feet and they were entering the nearest doorway.

He was forced to set her down so he could unlock his apartment, but he kept one arm wrapped around her, as if he thought she might bolt.

Poor sap. There wasn't a chance in hell he was getting rid of her.

Hustling her inside, he closed and locked the door. Then, still keeping a tight grip on her, he led her into the kitchen-slash-dining room, pausing to toss his keys on the square Formica table.

"Do you want me to call for lunch now or—"

"Later," she interrupted.

"Later is great," he admitted with a groan of relief, leaning down to kiss her with a frustrated hunger that had nothing to do with BBQ. "Much later would be fantastic."

He glanced toward the table, obviously debating the pleasure of immediate satisfaction against the comfort of a bed and a soft mattress.

She didn't know what tilted the balance, but one minute

she was glancing at the pictures set on the china cabinet of various men and women who looked enough like Duncan to be family, and the next she was abruptly being tugged through a tidy living room with furniture that was worn but surprisingly homey, with more pictures on the wall.

A few steps later and she found herself in a bedroom that was decorated in shades of tan and chocolate. Her brows lifted as she studied the comforter that was neatly spread across the double bed and the lack of clothes on the carpet.

"I'm surprised," she murmured.

He carefully removed his holstered gun as he nuzzled a trail of kisses down her neck, the feel of his whiskers against her sensitive skin making her shiver with pleasure.

"I warned you it's a shithole," he husked.

"No, I meant . . ." She lost her train of thought as his hands skimmed beneath her top, his fingers moving like the brush of a butterfly wing over her ribs to rest just below the swell of her breasts.

"You meant?" he prompted with a hint of amusement.

Not about to let him have complete control, she grabbed the hem of his tee and yanked it over his head, exposing a delectable expanse of bronzed skin stretched taut over chiseled muscles.

Oh . . . yum.

It was like a feast for her senses.

"It's cleaner than I expected," she explained, her hands lifting to explore the triangle of golden hair on his upper chest.

He gave a low growl, his hands cupping her breasts as his hot breath seared over her ear.

"My sisters love to do drop-by inspections," he said in a husky voice. "If the place isn't up to their code then I'm stuck with them until they get it cleaned to their satisfaction."

His words sliced through her sensual haze. She was already terrified at the thought of meeting Duncan's family—

the last thing she needed was to worry that the meeting might take place while she was naked in his bed.

"They won't be stopping by today, will they?"

His thumbs found the tight peaks of her breasts, sending darts of scorching excitement through her body.

"Not unless they want to get shot," he muttered.

She pulled back to stab him with a worried frown. "Duncan."

"They know if I'm home during the day I pulled an all-nighter and I'm in bed." He leaned forward to kiss her with a slow, lingering thoroughness. "We won't be disturbed."

Melting beneath the heat of his kiss, Callie forgot his sisters and the missing necromancer and all the reasons this was a terrible idea.

Stolen moments might very well be all she had with this man.

She intended to savor each and every one of them.

Perhaps sensing her urgency, Duncan pulled her shirt over her head and tossed it aside. Her bra followed.

She kicked off her shoes, enjoying the sheer male possession in his touch as he unsnapped her jeans and tugged them downward.

"You're very good at this," she breathed.

He dropped to his knees; his lips nuzzled across the clenched muscles of her stomach.

"This chemistry has nothing to do with skill." His fingers trailed up the back of her thighs, sending a rash of goose bumps over her skin. "And everything to do with fate."

Her pounding heart came to a perfect halt.

Fate.

Such a dangerous thing.

"What do you mean?"

Duncan pulled down her panties, a slumberous sensuality darkening his eyes as he glanced up to meet her searching gaze.

"This is more than mere lust," he murmured. "This is an obsession that goes way beyond explanation. What else could it be but fate?"

She didn't have a damn clue. It was another of those things to put on the worry-about-later list. For now her entire body was humming with an electric excitement.

"Who am I to fight against fate?" she sighed, her fingers threading through his hair in silent encouragement.

Something rippled over the starkly beautiful features before he leaned forward to place an openmouthed kiss on her inner thigh.

Callie shivered, her lashes fluttering downward as his hands skimmed up the naked curve of her butt and gripped her hips to hold her in place.

Not that she was going anywhere.

Hell, no.

She gave a small gasp as he turned his head to find the liquid heat between her legs. His tongue parted her, teasing her pleasure point with a tender urgency that soon had her entire body pulsing with an aching need.

God Almighty. It was just as wondrous as she remembered. Just as mind blowing.

Duncan had called it obsession. And perhaps that's what it was. A hot, ruthless obsession that could easily consume her.

She sucked in a strangled breath, her knees feeling weak as he laved her most sensitive nub of flesh with a growing insistence. Oh, yes. Her fingers tightened in his hair, her breath rasping loudly in the silent room. That was the exact, perfect spot.

But Duncan was in the mood to tease.

Or maybe he just enjoyed torturing her.

Over and over, he brought her to the peak of fulfillment, only to pull away at the last second.

Her eyes fluttered open as his mouth shifted to brand hot, restless kisses over the curve of her hip.

"I intended to do this all afternoon," he rasped against her skin. "But, I need to be inside you. Deep inside you."

Hovering on the brink of her climax, she shifted her hands to grasp his shoulders and urge him upward.

"Then do it," she commanded in a thick voice.

He chuckled as he straightened, lowering his head to stroke his tongue down the length of her neck. He nuzzled her pounding pulse before his head was dipping even lower and his lips covered the tip of her throbbing nipple.

Callie moaned at the dizzying sensations. Should she be worried that this man had the ability to make her melt with vulnerable longing?

Especially when they might soon be parted?

The brief moment of uncertainty was forgotten as he used his teeth to pleasure her nipple with a tender urgency that was tightening her muscles and making her legs weak. A low growl rumbled in his throat as his hands skated down her heated skin and grasped her hips. Then, without warning, he was turning her around and urging her toward the wall.

Caught off guard, she swiveled her head to regard him over her shoulder. "Duncan?"

The lean features were tight and bathed with a damp perspiration, as if he were struggling against a mighty force.

"Trust me," he husked as he wrenched off his jeans and underwear. Then, he pressed his body to her back and buried his face in the curve of her neck. "I promise you'll like this."

"But . . ."

Her words came to a choked halt as his fingers slid down the gentle swell of her stomach and then through the dampness between her legs.

"I've spent a hundred nights tossing and turning on that bed, imagining what I would do with you if I ever managed to lure you here." He gave a punishing nip on the curve of her shoulder while his finger slid inside her and began to stroke with a slow insistence. "This was number one."

Her head fell back against his shoulder. A delicious pressure was beginning to build within her. Later she would tell him a few of her own fantasies.

But that would be later, she conceded as she felt his hard cock pressing between her legs. With gentle care he removed his finger and then with one slow thrust he was buried deep inside her.

Returning to Valhalla, Fane entered his apartment for a quick shower and a change of clothing. Not that anyone could tell the difference. His wardrobe consisted of cammos, khakis, T-shirts, and shit-kickers.

The hunter Sentinels liked to prance around in expensive clothes and drive cars that made a real man wonder if they were compensating for something. But guardians . . . they knew what was important.

And it couldn't be bought in a store.

Making a brief stop by the morgue, he eventually made his way to the Mave's office to update her on the medics' examination of Leah's body. Then, stepping into the hall, he was debating whether to catch a quick lunch in the public dining room or to return to his apartment when a prickle of power raced over his skin.

Slowly turning, he already knew it was his Tagos approaching. Wolfe carried with him an electrical energy that was like a punch in the gut.

The tall man with a hawkish profile was dressed from head to toe in black. His dark hair was left free to flow down to his shoulders with the white streak next to his hard face shimmering in the sunlight that poured through the overhead skylight.

Wolfe halted a few feet away. They were both predators in their own way. Space was a necessity.

"Did the medics find anything?" the Tagos demanded.

He nodded. "The body was deteriorating at a normal rate."

"Meaning?"

"The magic that animated her only offered the pretense of life."

Wolfe grimaced. "Truly a walking corpse."

"Yes."

"Christ." They exchanged a hard glance that spoke of their mutual resolve to put an end to the necromancer's gruesome magic. That's what Sentinels did. Solved problems. "Where arc you off to next?"

"Florida."

"What's in Florida?"

"A monk who can hopefully give me information on ancient Sumerians."

Wolfe didn't probe. The connection between monks and guardians was a sacred trust that was never discussed outside the monastery.

"I heard you returned without Callie."

Fane clenched his hands. It had gone against every protective instinct he possessed to leave her behind. But he wasn't a fool. Callie was a grown woman who was going to do what she wanted to do.

Trying to stop her would only have made her dig in her heels.

Women.

"She insisted on remaining with the cop," he admitted in sour tones.

"Insisted?" Wolfe arched a brow. "That doesn't sound like Callie."

"She's infatuated with the bastard."

Wolfe studied him with a steady gaze that held curiosity without judgment. "Does that trouble you?"

"Only because I can't be sure her emotions aren't clouding her mind," he said. Callie would always hold a place in his heart. She was his to protect. But she wasn't the woman who stirred his passions to a raging fire. "Right now I think she'd risk any danger to be with him."

"I feel your pain, comrade." The dark gaze briefly flicked toward the closed door of the Mave's office. An instinctive action that Fane doubted the Tagos was even aware of. "Females can be unreasonable under the best circumstances."

Fane shrugged. "I have to trust O'Conner will protect her."

"Is he capable?"

"Not as capable as I am, but he has more skills than he realizes."

Wolfe was instantly intrigued. "A potential Sentinel?"

Fane smiled without humor. He'd recognized Duncan O'Conner's hidden talents the minute their paths had crossed. Not only his ability to read souls, but his superior strength. It was the only reason he'd allowed Callie to remain in his care.

Otherwise he'd have her locked in the dungeons so she couldn't sneak off the minute his back was turned.

"If I don't kill him first," he muttered.

Wolfe smiled in understanding, then both men froze as the smell of expensive leather and dangerous woman wafted through the air. Seconds later Serra rounded the corner, her stunning beauty a perilous weapon.

"Ah." Wolfe cleared his throat, careful to avert his gaze from Serra's lush body shown to perfection in the skintight leather pants and lacy bustier. "She looks like a woman on a mission. I think I'll leave the two of you alone."

"Traitor," Fane muttered, composing his expression to hide the familiar sense of frustration and raw, aching desire.

This woman was his greatest temptation.

And the promise of his doom.

Chapter Twenty

Duncan eventually called for the BBQ. He even allowed Callie to get dressed so they could eat like a civilized couple in the dining room with real forks and plates.

See . . . he wasn't a complete barbarian.

And astonishingly, he found amazing pleasure in sitting at the table arguing about music and movies and whether ice cream should be chocolate or vanilla while he fed her the finest brisket in the world.

This wasn't about heat and lust and fireworks.

Instead it was fun and peaceful and so damned . . . right . . . that a part of him knew he should be terrified.

Snatching the last square of corn bread, he was busy buttering it when the ring of his phone broke the easy atmosphere.

Automatically he reached to answer it, then his gaze was snared by the faceted sapphire blue of her eyes and he deliberately returned to buttering the corn bread.

The ringing stopped. For all of two seconds.

"Ignore it," he muttered as it started again. And again.

She reached to snatch the bread from his hand, a teasing grin tugging at her lips.

"I can if you can."

His libido stirred as she took a bite, the butter shimmering on her lower lip. He should turn off the phone and haul her back to bed.

Or even sweep aside the dishes and indulge in his fantasy of eating dessert off that pale, satin skin.

The delectable image began to form in his mind.

Callie's naked body stretched across the table. Her crimson hair shimmering in the late afternoon sunlight. Her legs wrapped around his waist as he . . .

His phone once again intruded.

"Dammit." Huffing out a resigned sigh, he reached to pluck the phone off the table. He was a Grade A idiot. It was no wonder Susan dumped his ass. "I'm sorry."

Before he could answer, Callie reached to lightly touch his hand. "Duncan."

He grimaced, bracing for the familiar lecture. "Yes?"

"Don't ever apologize for being good at your job."

Okay. That was the last thing he expected.

He studied her pale face, which revealed a calm acceptance that he was fairly certain he didn't deserve.

"I think I'm apologizing for letting it consume me," he muttered. "Or at least, that's what I've been told."

"By who?"

He shrugged. "My ex-wife, my mother, my sisters, the old lady next door—"

She held up a hand. "Yeah, I get it. They're worried about you. But that doesn't make your love for your job wrong."

He reached to grasp her fingers, searching the depths of her stunning eyes for the truth.

Could she actually understand?

"I don't want you to feel as if I'm putting you in second place."

"I don't." She leaned across the table to brush a light kiss over his mouth. "Of course, there's a difference between being obsessed with your career and using it as a barrier to keep people at a distance."

She did understand.

All too well.

"How did you know?" he demanded, grudgingly recalling the dates he'd broken because it was easier to stay at the station than spend a few empty hours trying to act interested. Or the Sunday family dinners he'd skipped because he didn't want to be the target of his meddling sisters' attempts to set him up with their endless parade of friends.

"Because I've used my fear of being rejected to do the same thing."

He smiled with rueful amusement. "So what you're saying is that we're a match made in heaven?"

"Or we're both so screwed up no one else could stand us."

He chuckled, pressing her fingers to his lips. "I'll go with that."

On cue, the phone started its insistent ringing. Callie smiled, giving his arm a squeeze.

"Answer," she commanded softly. "It might be important."

He pressed the phone to his ear, knowing she was right. This wasn't about burrowing himself in work so he could ignore the barrenness of his life. There was a crazed necromancer out there who had to be stopped.

"O'Conner," he growled, his brows lowering as he listened to the crisp voice of his chief. "Where? I'll be there in half an hour."

He ended the connection and met Callie's curious gaze.

"Who was it?" she demanded.

"The chief." He absently gathered the dirty plates and took them into the kitchen. "She said that a man appeared at the station claiming that he was the rightful owner of Calso's coin."

He hadn't realized Callie had followed him into the kitchen until she spoke directly behind him.

"Where are you supposed to meet him?"

He turned, frowning down at her expectant expression. "Callie, it's too dangerous—"

She reached up to pinch his lips together, effectively halting his protest.

"Don't go there," she warned. "We're in this together."

He nipped the tips of her fingers before pulling them from his mouth.

"Stubborn."

The aggravating female smiled, knowing she'd won. "Determined."

"Same thing," he muttered. "Come on."

He led her out of the apartment and to his car, silently promising himself he'd go hunting for a new apartment on his first day off. He had high hopes that he could convince Callie to spend more than one afternoon with him. She deserved better than this run-down complex that's only saving grace was that it happened to be close to the station.

Maybe he'd even look at a house, he decided, as he pulled out of the parking lot.

With a yard and dog and swing set . . .

He was just getting to the white picket fence when Callie thankfully yanked him from his ridiculous train of thoughts.

"You didn't tell me where we're going."

He cleared his throat, feeling heat crawl up the back of his neck. Christ.

"The police station."

She frowned. "Why did you say it might be dangerous?"

"Any place can be dangerous."

She snorted. "You were just trying to keep me from going with you."

It was true, but not for the reason she suspected.

The mere thought of the reception she was likely to receive at the police station was enough to make him grind his teeth.

Time for a distraction.

"Hey, the only time I got shot I was in a church."

His tone was teasing, but her sapphire eyes widened with a genuine horror. "You were shot?"

"A grazing wound from a teenager who was trying to steal the silver candlesticks from the altar." He hastily minimized the incident. His ma and sisters were still convinced he spent his days dodging bullets. "If I hadn't startled him he would never have shot."

She frowned. "Or he might have taken better aim."

"I'm always careful."

"No, you're not," she muttered, reaching into her purse to pull out her familiar reflective sunglasses. "But I suppose it's who you are."

Halting at a stoplight, he watched her slide on the glasses. The sight sent a tangle of emotion through him.

Fury that she had to hide who she was, combined with a sharp, aching need to return her to his apartment where he could protect her from the world.

"I could call Molinari back and tell her to reschedule the interview for tomorrow," he said roughly.

She tilted her head to the side, her glasses making it impossible to read her emotions.

"Tempting, but Fane will be returning in the morning," she reminded him.

"All the more reason to enjoy our rare time alone."

She paused, as if sifting through the various reasons for his sudden urgency to return to his apartment. Then, a slow, achingly sad smile curved her lips.

"We'll have tonight," she promised softly.

He gripped the wheel, ignoring the jackass behind him that was blaring his horn as the light turned green.

"You do realize I just volunteered to forget work?" he asked. "That's a first for me."

With an obvious effort she managed a teasing expression,

leaning across the seat to stroke her lips along the line of his jaw.

"I'm very proud of you."

He sucked in a deep breath, allowing the warm, apple scent of her to ease his strange sense of foreboding.

"How proud?"

"I'll show you," she whispered in his ear before settling back in her seat. "Later."

With a growl, he stomped his foot on the gas pedal.

Later couldn't get there fast enough.

Zak knew that his body was lying on the floor of the temple. In a distant part of his brain he could feel the hard pebbles that poked into his chest and the fine grains of dirt that drifted from the ceiling to land on his face.

He could even feel the blood that trickled from his wound to pool at the base of his skull.

His consciousness, however, was traveling through the darkness, heading deep beneath the ziggurat, as if lured by a siren's call.

At last he came to a halt, the shadows shifting to reveal that he hovered in front of an ornate sarcophagus.

He studied the elaborate symbols etched onto the gilded wood, knowing without a doubt that they had been created just for him.

He could sense it in his very soul.

Just as he could sense a presence that filled the barren tomb.

With no corporal body, he could only use his thoughts to try and communicate.

"Who are you?"

"We are the beginning."

The words vibrated in the air, the sound of a thousand voices seeming to pierce straight through him.

Beginning?

That told him nothing.

Was it supposed to be some sort of riddle, like those of the Sphinx?

He tried a new approach. "Where am I?"

"At the mouth of the underworld."

Ah. That would explain why he'd been drawn to this place. The dead had always spoken to him.

But it didn't explain why he was lying unconscious in the main temple with a gaping wound that was even now bleeding out.

"Why have you brought me here?"

"There is a story to be told."

The glyphs on the sarcophagus began to shimmer. "Your story?"

"Our story." The scent of death swirled through the air. "Watch."

Even without his body, Zak felt a stab of wary fury as the glyphs began to pulse, as if they were coming alive.

"Magic," he hissed.

"Do not interrupt."

There was an impression of pain. Zak couldn't be sure if he actually felt it or not, but he wasn't willing to risk that there was serious damage being done to his physical body.

Smothering his gut-deep hatred of being given commands, he focused on the glyphs that continued to pulse, the shimmering beneath them throwing strange shapes on the smooth walls of the tomb.

Zak watched the flickering shapes for a confused minute, at last realizing they were beginning to solidify to form a three-dimensional image of an ancient village.

He continued to watch the unfolding pictures, realizing that the village was built around this temple. There was no mistaking the vivid indigo glaze on the brick facade or the particular pattern to the window lattices.

"Who are those people?" he asked, frowning as he watched a group of robed figures descend the long staircase from the ziggurat to mingle among a gathered crowd.

"Your ancestors," the multitude of voices answered.

"Necromancers?"

"High-bloods."

He considered the unfolding drama in silence, intrigued by the strange images even as his clinical brain warned this all could be nothing more than a result of his head trauma.

Or more likely, a trick.

For now he was willing to play the game.

"Is this where high-bloods came from?"

"Yes," the voices confirmed. "We were blessed by the gods. Their powers gave us the right to rule this world."

The images shifted. Suddenly the crowd wasn't bowing in awe of the robed figures, but they were surrounding the temple, weapons held in their hands as they battled their way past the high-bloods trying to block the stairways.

"Not for long," he murmured.

The air filled with an anger that would have crushed him if he'd been in his physical form.

"The people grew jealous of our blessings."

Hmm. He didn't doubt that humans could be fickle and jealous and ready to destroy what they didn't understand. Even in these supposedly enlightened ages they remained petty little cowards.

But he was a master of manipulating the emotions of others. He easily recognized when he was being finessed.

Lies wrapped in truths.

"They attacked?"

Flames engulfed the images, the distant sound of screams filling the tomb.

"The oracles were the first destroyed, burned in their own temple. Next were the witches." The flames lowered to reveal the inner temple where the robed figures were being led into underground tunnels by armed warriors. "The Sentinels realized we were on the brink of extinction so they collected as many of our people as they could save and scattered them around the world." The images began to shift, flickering from one isolated abbey to another. "We remained in hiding for centuries."

"They created the monasteries," Zak murmured.

"Yes, as well as the pathways so our people could remain connected."

Ah. That made sense. No one spoke of the origins of the high-bloods, or the mysterious connection between the monks.

Not that he thought for a minute that he was getting the full story.

"What do you want from me?" he demanded.

The images abruptly returned to the earlier battle, this time revealing a robed figure standing at the top of the temple with a chalice held above his head, blood dripping down his arms from the deep wounds in his wrists.

The same image that was etched in the hieroglyphs in the upper temple, he recognized with a tiny jolt of shock.

Only he was the one holding the chalice.

"Sokar was our leader," the voices hissed.

Zak didn't need to ask if Sokar was the body in the sarcophagus.

He knew it beyond a shadow of a doubt.

"A necromancer?" he instead demanded.

"Yes." The image pulled back to reveal several robed figures standing behind him, their arms raised with the same wounds on their wrists.

"He, along with his trusted disciples, remained behind to ensure the rest could escape," the voices explained. "His sacrifice saved hundreds of high-bloods, but has left us trapped between the world of the living and the world of the dead."

The images abruptly ended, the room once again filled with shadows.

Zak contained his flare of frustration. He had a thousand questions. There was so much of the high-blood history that was hidden, or even lost in the mists of time.

But he wasn't a fool. He'd been allowed to see precisely what the strange voices wanted him to see and no more.

He couldn't fully trust anything he might be shown in this place.

"You still haven't told me why I'm here."

The answer came without hesitation. "The imprisonment of Sokar has stolen the connection to the dead that was once the birthright of the necromancers. We have long waited for one to be born who could return what was lost."

"And you believe I am the one?"

"We shall soon discover."

That wasn't precisely the assurance that Zak was hoping to hear, but he bit back his demands for a more definitive promise of ultimate glory.

"You will give me the power to raise the dead?"

"Open the gates," the voices whispered. "And the power will be yours."

Chapter Twenty-One

Without Fane's intimidating presence to scatter the gawkers, Callie was prepared for the avid stares as Duncan led her through the police station.

Some curious. Some hostile. Most wary. As if convinced she was some dangerous demon who worshipped the devil beneath the full moon and raised zombies on the weekends.

Moving past the large room filled with desks, filing cabinets, the usual office equipment, as well as suspicious cops, Callie kept her chin held high.

She wasn't going to apologize for who she was.

Muttering his opinion of cops who had bigger guns than brains, Duncan put a possessive hand on the lower curve of her back as he urged her toward the back of the room.

"Ignore the idiots," he said, loud enough for his words to be overheard.

Watching as one of the younger cops deliberately wrapped his fingers around the grip of his service revolver, she smiled wryly and murmured, "Easier said than done."

Duncan glared at the cop until the younger man flushed and turned away.

"I could shoot them if you want," he offered.

"That seems a little extreme."

His glare swept around the silent room. "Not to me."

A door was suddenly thrown open and a small, dark-haired woman appeared.

"If you all have time to stand around scratching your balls then there's a stack of cold case files in the basement I can start handing out," she announced, her hands planted on her hips as she watched the cops scurry to look busy. "No? Good." She turned her attention to Duncan and Callie. "This way."

Callie hid a smile as they were led out of the room and down a short hallway. This had to be the infamous Chief Molinari. Somehow she'd thought the woman would be six feet tall with horns and a tail.

Not that her diminutive size made her any less intimidating.

In fact, she reminded Callie of the Mave. Stern, frighteningly competent, and ruthless when necessary.

Keeping his hand on her lower back, Duncan urged her closer to his side as they followed the chief down the hall.

"You said the man asked for me?" Duncan demanded.

"Yep," the chief confirmed. "He wandered in off the street. He says his name is Hektor. No last name."

Odd.

"And he claims to be the owner of the coin?"

Molinari's heels clicked on the industrial tiled floor. "He said it belonged to his—"

Duncan and Callie exchanged a puzzled glance as her words trailed away.

"His what?" Duncan at last prompted.

"Brotherhood," the chief muttered.

"Brotherhood?" Duncan frowned. "Is he a gangbanger?"

"You have to see to believe."

The chief halted in front of a two-way mirror, nodding toward the interrogation room on the other side.

The room was deliberately barren, with white walls and a

linoleum floor that were bathed in a harsh fluorescent light. In the center of the space was a long table with a half dozen wooden chairs.

But it was the lone man seated at the table who captured Callie's attention.

"Christ, what now?" Duncan muttered.

Callie was wondering the same thing as she took in the stranger. He was a thin man in his late forties with short black hair smoothed from a narrow, ratlike face. His skin was tinted a honey brown, as if burnished from long days in the Middle Eastern deserts. An image only emphasized by the long white tunic he wore over a pair of loose pants.

Her eyes narrowed as she studied the small wooden box that he'd laid on the table in front of him. On the worn top was carved a strange symbol that resembled the bird that had been etched onto the vessel. The vessel that had held the coin stolen from Calso's safe.

Callie felt a sudden surge of hope.

This man clearly had some knowledge of the coin. Was it possible he could help them find the necromancer responsible for stealing it?

Duncan sent her an expressive glance that revealed he'd noticed the symbol as well, then, with a nod toward the chief, he led Callie into the interrogation room.

"Hektor," he murmured, heading toward the long table. "I'm Sergeant O'Conner and this—"

"High-blood," the man hissed, surging to his feet as he stared at Callie with open contempt.

Callie came to an abrupt halt, astonished by the man's reaction.

Not by his obvious hatred for high-bloods. That was all too common.

But his ability to instantly realize that she was more than human.

Most of the local cops had seen her at crime scenes. They

would easily recognize her, even if they hadn't already known she was coming to the station with Duncan.

But without Fane at her side, and her eyes hidden by her reflective glasses, it should be impossible for a stranger to know she was a high-blood.

Duncan, on the other hand, didn't seem remotely interested in how the man had known. He was stiff with a fury that made the air prickle with a sudden heat.

"This is Ms. Brown," he ground out between clenched teeth. "She's a partner in this police investigation."

Hektor's dark eyes flashed with a matching fury. "I won't speak in front of my enemies."

"Watch your mouth, you—"

"Duncan, it's okay," Callie hastily interrupted, scenting violence in the air.

"No, it's not," he growled. "The bastard can learn some manners or I can kick his ass."

"Either she leaves, or I do," Hektor muttered, unwilling to back down an inch.

A true fanatic, Callie acknowledged with a grimace.

"I'll wait outside."

Duncan jutted his chin to a stubborn angle. "That's not necessary."

She reached to lightly brush her hand down the rigid muscles of his forearm. She wouldn't allow Duncan to risk his job because of her.

"There's no use in wasting time," she said, turning toward the stranger with a cold smile. "Besides, the stench of prejudice is making me queasy."

There was a long silence as Duncan struggled to contain his urge to shove his fist into the man's face. At last, his cop training allowed him to resist his thirst for blood, although his expression warned he was just waiting for an excuse to snap.

With a muttered curse, he walked with her back into the hall, his hands clenched at his side.

"There's a private conference room next to the chief's office," he said, his voice rough. Callie understood. He'd already been infuriated by his fellow cops' reactions to her. Now he had to allow a complete stranger to insult her. For a man who was devoted to protecting others, it had to be making him nuts. "Wait for me there."

She discreetly brushed her fingers against his tight fist, her smile teasing. "I'll be fine."

His lips parted, but before he could remind her that her welcome wouldn't be any warmer among his friends, she was turning to make her way down the hall.

The sooner Duncan could question the stranger, the sooner they could get out of here. And she really, really wanted out.

Stepping back into the main room, Callie kept her gaze trained on the open door on the back wall, her pace steady. She hoped to slip past unnoticed. Hey, cops might be trained to be observant, but shouldn't they be busy doing police things?

Eating donuts, playing poker, harassing high-bloods . . .

As if to punish her for her snarky thoughts, she'd just entered the empty conference room when someone stepped in behind her, firmly closing the door.

Spinning around, she came face to face with the gray-haired coroner she'd seen at more than one crime scene.

"I need to speak with you, necro."

Her heart sank even as her chin tilted. She'd known this was coming. Duncan's friends weren't going to be any more pleased with their relationship, no matter how brief it might be, than Fane and her friends.

Still, she'd hoped it could be avoided until after they'd captured the mysterious Lord Zakhar.

As unlikely as it might seem, there was the possibility that they would need the humans.

Resisting the urge to tell him to go to hell, she instead calmly met his dark scowl. She would try not to be a total bitch, but then again, she wasn't going to be a damned wimp.

"I have a name," she pointed out in deliberately cool tones.

"Brown, right?"

"Callie."

"Callie." He shrugged, clearly not interested in becoming BFFs. "I'm Frank. I'm a friend of O'Conner."

"I know who you are."

"I think we need to have a little talk."

She nodded, her expression bland. "So talk."

The cop frowned, almost as if caught off guard by her calm reaction. Maybe he assumed all freaks were raised by wolves and incapable of common manners?

"Do you want to sit?"

"No." She had no sympathy for his sudden unease. "Say what you have to say."

He hesitated before he squared his shoulders. "Did you know O'Conner's ex-wife just got remarried?"

Ah. So that was the direction this was going to take.

"He told me," she said.

"He was gutted when his marriage ended," Frank informed her, the sincerity in his tone revealing he truly believed what he was saying. "It was even worse when he found out she was going to become another man's wife. Susan was his soul mate."

Callie might have been devastated by the stark claim if she didn't know the truth. Now she merely shrugged. "Why are you telling me this?"

His mouth thinned at her refusal to react as he expected. "A man does crazy things when he's been hurt," he pressed. "Things he later regrets."

"By crazy, I assume you mean spending time with me?"

"I'm sorry, but if he was in his right mind, he would never be with a—"

"Freak?" she helpfully supplied.

Heat crawled beneath his skin, his gaze shifting to the rows of chairs that faced the podium at the far end of the room.

"I'm not a fanatic. I don't hate high-bloods," he said in gruff tones. "I just know that you sort of people aren't meant to mix with humans."

She made a sound of disgust. How many people over the centuries had been made to feel isolated by those precise words?

"Separate but equal?" she said in a cold voice.

He hunched his shoulder. "Something like that."

Her lips twisted. Okay. Maybe not so equal.

Jerk.

"I appreciate your concern for your friend, but Duncan is a big boy," she said, hiding her disgust behind a mask of indifference. This man was Duncan's friend and colleague. If their relationship continued then she would have to at least pretend she didn't find him a total tool. "Don't you think he should be allowed to make his own decisions?"

Frank's expression hardened. Like most cops, he was used to people falling in line when he gave an order.

"Around here we take care of each other; it's the only way to survive," he growled. "If you truly care for O'Conner, you'll walk away and let him find a woman who fits into his life."

"His life or yours?"

"Think about it," he warned before turning to leave the conference room, slamming the door behind him.

Callie rolled her eyes, wryly wondering why she hadn't returned to Valhalla where she so obviously belonged.

"Welcome to the real world, Callie Brown," she muttered.

* * *

Duncan returned to the interrogation room in a mood that was on the wrong side of shitty.

Studying the smug little bastard, he wanted nothing more than to shove his foot up his ass. Or maybe he would shove a few of his too-white teeth down his throat . . .

Unable to do either, he folded his arms over his chest and met the dark gaze that was studying him with blatant suspicion.

"What the fuck are you staring at?" he snapped.

The dark eyes narrowed, his nose flaring as if he was sniffing the air. Or could he be sensing that Duncan wasn't entirely human?

"Are you—"

"You have until the count of five to tell me what you know about the coin before I throw your ass in jail for obstruction of justice," he abruptly interrupted.

As much as he wanted to beat the fool to a bloody pulp and leave him for the trash, he needed whatever information he might have about the coin. And he wasn't going to get anything out of the man if he feared Duncan was a high-blood.

Hektor bristled, but thankfully accepted that Duncan was human.

"I came here for your assistance, not to be threatened," he said stiffly.

"I don't give a shit. Tell me about the coin."

The man licked his thin lips. "It has a long history."

"Sumerian?"

Hektor hesitated, clearly not willing to give away more than he had to.

"It doesn't matter. The coin was created by the Brotherhood in the earliest days of civilization."

Necromancers. Mysterious coins. Secret brotherhoods. It sounded like a cheesy plot from *Indiana Jones*.

Unfortunately, Duncan couldn't laugh off the possibility that the man was speaking the truth.

"What does the coin do?"

Hektor grimaced. "It shields the chalice."

"Chalice?" Duncan rolled his eyes. "What chalice?"

"The one that opens a pathway to the underworld."

Duncan scowled. He hated mystic mumbo jumbo. "Does underworld mean hell?"

"Call it whatever you want."

"And this chalice . . . What?" He gave a wave of his hand. "It's a key to hell?"

Hektor nodded. "It allows the dead to walk."

The simple words made Duncan shudder with horror. Christ. Even having seen Leah walking around . . . Wait. He took a step forward, leaning down to place his palms flat on the table in front of Hektor.

"What game are you playing? The necromancer was raising the dead before he got his hands on the coin."

The stranger shook his head. "They were bokors."

"Meaning?"

"They're merely animated corpses that are able to be controlled for a short period of time by a necromancer."

Duncan grimaced. When did his life become filled with words like "animated corpses" and "pathways to the underworld"?

"So what do you mean when you say that the coin allows them to raise the dead?" he demanded. "Will they actually be alive?"

The narrow face hardened. "Not the coin. It was created to close the mouth of the underworld. It's the chalice that poses the true danger."

Duncan made a sound of impatience. "Will they be alive or not?"

"In a manner of speaking. The chalice allows the necromancer to fill the corpses with an evil that will give them the ability to walk among us as if they live." He leaned forward, clenching his hands on the table as his eyes filled with a hectic light. "They could infiltrate our society for days or weeks without us knowing. Or more likely—"

"What?"

"The necromancer will raise an army to destroy us all."

Duncan muttered a savage curse. Holy hell. This just got better and better.

"How do we find this . . . chalice before the necromancer can get his hands on it?"

"No one can enter the inner temple without the coin," he grudgingly confessed.

Duncan abruptly straightened. Of course the bastard would be filled with dire predictions with no genuine plan to avoid the looming disaster.

Pacing across the narrow room, he struggled to think clearly.

He was a cop.

And this was a case.

Okay, it was filled with creepy necromancers and a weirdo brotherhood, but preventing a potential crime was what he did.

And for that, he needed to be able to locate the coin or the necromancer before he could unleash hell.

Literally.

"Was Calso a part of your Brotherhood?" he abruptly demanded.

"Certainly not."

He turned to study Hektor's outraged expression. "Then why did he have the coin?"

"For centuries we kept the coin protected, then we began to realize it was being hunted."

"By who?"

The man shrugged. "The name is easily changed, but there was no doubt it was a necromancer. One who was dangerously powerful."

It would be easy to leap to the conclusion that it was Lord Zakhar. But he preferred to have real proof before he dismissed any other possibility.

"How could you be so certain it was a necromancer and not some crazy person who thought the coin was worth money?"

"Our brothers and sisters—"

"You allow females into your Brotherhood?" Duncan asked in surprise. Usually fanatics liked to keep their bizarre cults exclusive.

"If they're worthy," Hektor explained in a lofty voice. "Many are called, but few are chosen."

Duncan rolled his eyes. Yeesh. He'd walked right into that one.

"Yeah, whatever," he muttered. "Go on."

Hektor stiffened, as if insulted by Duncan's lack of respect at his grand achievement in being chosen for the Brotherhood.

Arrogant ass.

"Our brothers and sisters were being slaughtered and then returned from the grave," he at last explained.

"They had the coin?"

Hektor shook his head. "No, but they each knew the location of the coin. They were killed and their corpses used to try and slip past our defenses."

"Just like Leah," Duncan growled, shuddering at the memory of the young female being jerked around Kansas City as if she was a gruesome marionette.

"Who?"

Duncan ignored the question. He wasn't about to discuss poor Leah or how she'd been abused.

"How did you manage to recognize that they were . . . what's the word . . . bokors?"

The man shrugged, trying too hard to look casual. "We are trained to spot the walking dead."

Yeah, right.

"You want to know what I'm trained to do?" Duncan leaned forward, his eyes narrowed. "Smell bullshit a mile away."

Hektor muttered something beneath his breath, but he wasn't stupid enough to insult an armed cop to his face.

"All right. We received word from an anonymous source that the coin holder had been identified so we were able to move the coin before it could be stolen."

Duncan snorted. He'd worked with anonymous sources for years. Ninety-nine percent of the info he got from them was worth jack-squat, the other one percent was usually little better than a random guess that accidentally turned out to be right.

He wouldn't depend on an anonymous source to tell him the time of day, let alone to entrust the protection of the very reason for his existence.

"How did you know you could trust this source?" he demanded.

"They'd always been right before. Unfortunately—"

Hektor bit off his words, a flush of embarrassment crawling beneath his skin.

"Unfortunately?" Duncan prompted.

"When we were warned that Calso's name had been discovered it was decided it was too risky to move the coin until we'd found some place that couldn't be traced." The man's lips thinned with anger. "We put out word that the coin had been transferred to a new host, hoping the necromancer would be fooled long enough for us to find a more permanent solution."

A risky decision.

One that might destroy them all.

"How did Calso get the coin in the first place?"

"It was decided that the necromancer hunting the coin had found a way to recognize members of the Brotherhood." Hektor absently lifted his hand to trace a small tattoo that looked like a stylized arrow on the side of his neck. "It was imperative we find someone who had no formal connection to our group to hide the coin."

It made sense, but Duncan couldn't imagine how a group of self-righteous nut-bars had chosen a financial whiz who had a weakness for pretty strippers to harbor their most precious treasure.

"Why him?"

Hektor thinned his lips, as if he hadn't been entirely pleased with the choice.

"Calso was a trusted friend of our leader and since he was already a collector of art, it wouldn't be suspicious for him to invest in high-tech security measures."

Duncan resumed his pacing, making mental notes to check the various ways someone could have discovered Calso had the coin.

It could be done.

He didn't doubt that for a minute.

But tracking down leads took time.

Sometimes days, sometimes weeks.

Time he didn't have.

There had to be a faster way to find Lord Zakhar, or whoever the hell was using a dead woman as their personal puppet.

"Can you—" He gave a vague wave of his hand.

"Can I what?"

"Sense the coin?" he asked.

The man scowled. "I'm a human, not a high-blood. I have no unholy magics running through my veins."

Duncan narrowed his eyes. "And yet you seemed to know that Callie was a high-blood from the minute she entered the room."

"The ability to sniff out the enemy is a gift from my god," Hektor said with a sneer.

Duncan curled his lips. Hypocrite. Any powers he and his so-called Brotherhood had came from the same place as high-bloods, not from some mysterious god.

Now, however, wasn't the time for a philosophical debate.

Actually, as far as he was concerned, there was never a good time for a philosophical debate.

Instead he concentrated on the only thing that mattered.

"Fine. Can you use that god-given gift to track down the necromancer?"

The dark eyes flashed at the edge of mockery that Duncan didn't try to hide.

"If we had that power then we would have eliminated him years ago."

"Really?" Duncan asked dryly. He would bet good money the Brotherhood was very good at hiding in the shadows and very bad at actually getting off their asses and taking care of business. "Do you often eliminate people?"

The man hastily glanced toward the camera in the ceiling. "Certainly not."

Duncan was abruptly done.

He'd hoped the man could offer a way to capture the necromancer.

Instead he'd gotten fairy tales and vague threats.

"So you don't know where the coin is or how we can find

the necro who stole it," he snapped. "Why the hell are you here?"

"To warn you of the danger if the coin isn't immediately returned to our protection."

"Worthless," he muttered, heading toward the door. "Feel free to show yourself out."

Anxious to track down Callie and make sure she wasn't being hassled by his supposed friends, he hissed in frustration when Hektor was demanding his attention.

"Sergeant?"

He glared over his shoulder. "What?"

The man rose to his feet, his expression hard with warning.

"High-bloods once tried to make themselves into gods," he said in fierce tones. "Don't for a minute doubt that they won't try again."

Chapter Twenty-Two

Zak opened his eyes, briefly confused by the realization he was lying face first on a stone floor with blood dripping down his neck.

Since being burned at the stake by his rabid serfs, he'd learned to take excessive precautions not to put himself in a position where he might wake up in strange places with oozing wounds.

It wasn't just paranoia.

Not when he knew he was surrounded by enemies.

Both those who openly worked against him, and those who hid in the shadows . . .

Ignoring the pain that pounded through his skull, Zak turned his head, a grim satisfaction replacing his momentary confusion.

Even in the shadows he could make out the unmistakable glint of gold.

The chalice.

Grasping his trophy, Zak awkwardly forced himself to his feet.

It hadn't been a dream. Or a trap.

He'd spoken to the ghosts of his ancestors. And he'd been found worthy.

More than worthy, he silently gloated, forcing his heavy feet to carry him out of the temple.

Unlike the previous necromancer, he had no intention of jeopardizing his life to acquire the power necessary to raise an army. The martyr routine had never appealed to him. Not when he'd been clever enough to prepare a proper sacrifice.

What was the point of power if you couldn't use it to rule the world?

Making his way down the long staircase, he paused at the bottom, gathering his strength before he walked the short distance to the waiting witch.

His head might be throbbing and his knees threatening to collapse, but he would never show weakness.

He was too close to his ultimate success to risk a knife in the back.

Halting in front of Anya, who was still on her knees, her head bent in weariness, he reached down to grasp her arm. Yanking her to her feet, he slipped the chalice into the deep pocket of his robe.

"Is the pathway still open?" he growled.

Anya blinked, her eyes unfocused as if she'd been asleep. "Yes, but—"

"Let's go."

"What happened?" she demanded, glancing around the barren desert. "Did the coin work?"

He offered a tight-lipped smile. "I have what I need."

She studied him in the fading moonlight, her brows drawn together. "Are you bleeding?"

"How very astute of you, Anya," he drawled, refusing to speak of what had happened in the temple. "Do you intend to continue this inquest? Or perhaps we can finish it when we aren't standing knee deep in sand?"

"Fine." Her chin tilted as she held out her hand. "Let's go."

His hesitation lasted less than a heartbeat before he

grasped her fingers and braced himself for the journey. He was weary, but not helpless.

And besides, being on constant guard meant that he was prepared for any trap.

Keeping the chalice hidden in his pocket, Zak clenched his teeth as the world dissolved and he was shrouded in a choking blackness.

He hated making himself vulnerable to Anya's magic, even when it was necessary.

There was a sickening lurch as they traveled through the strange fold in space, then the world abruptly reappeared and they were standing in his private study.

With a groan, Anya dropped to her knees, her brilliant curtain of hair tumbling over her shoulders to brush the Persian carpet.

Taking a step back, Zak regarded his companion with impatience.

"Go to bed, Anya. You will be of no use until you've regained your strength," he said with a brutal lack of sympathy for her fatigue.

With an obvious effort, the witch rose to her feet, her face pale with the strain to remain upright.

"I want to know what happened in the temple."

Zak paused before giving a shrug. There was no point in hiding his success.

Not when he intended to begin the final stages of his plan within the next few days.

Perhaps even hours.

"I was given what I need to take my place as the ruler of the high-bloods," he admitted, removing the chalice from his pocket and moving to place it on the desk.

Anya sucked in a sharp breath, no doubt sensing the magic that pulsed around the golden artifact.

"What does it do?"

He ran a loving finger along the rim of the chalice. "With this I can raise armies to fight my battles."

Anya swayed, her face more pale than usual as she grasped the back of a nearby chair.

"Zak, this is too dangerous."

He sent her a frown. "What?"

"The last time we tried—"

"I have no need to be reminded of my previous failures," he snapped.

"I just want you to take this slow." Anya licked her lips. "You may mock the Mave and Valhalla, but they aren't helpless."

His cold smile hid his stab of fury.

Over the centuries he'd watched from the shadows as the high-bloods had started to ban together in small, secretive groups. He understood the philosophy that it was safer to surround yourself with people who were like you. Especially when the humans began to realize that the myths and legends they'd always thought were nothing more than fairy tales were actually true.

There were monsters in the dark.

But he'd seen the hieroglyphs on the temple wall and he understood what happened when high-bloods lived in communities, their powers revealed for the world to see.

He had no intention of becoming a visible enemy for the violent humans who were always eager to destroy what they feared.

Still, it had been a constant source of annoyance to watch the Maves come and go at Valhalla, each one commanding more power than the one before.

He was the destined leader of the high-bloods.

"They've grown complacent over the years." His lips curled into a sneer. "I must strike before they can prepare for an attack."

Anya's grip on the chair tightened until her knuckles turned white.

Fear? Desperation? Some combination of the two?

"You have no guarantee that the chalice will even work."

He shrugged. "I will soon discover one way or another."

"What do you mean?"

"I think we should have a small test."

"Zak—"

"Go to your room, Anya," he interrupted.

Soon he would have to deal with the witch.

But not tonight.

Sensing the dismissal in his tone, Anya grudgingly crossed the floor and with a last wary glance, left him alone in the study.

Zak waited until he could hear her footsteps on the stairs before running his fingers beneath the edge of the desk. There was a faint click, then a secret panel on the side slid open. With a stab of satisfaction he reached to grab the chalice, tucking it into the empty compartment before sliding the secret panel shut.

It wasn't the most secure hiding place, but the chalice pulsed with a magic that was unique to diviners. The magic of death.

No one but a powerful necromancer could use it.

To anyone else it was just a battered goblet.

With his prize tucked away for the night, Zak sank into the chair behind the desk and absently reached for the remote to turn on the plasma TV over the fireplace.

He always devoted an hour or so before bed to watch the news, both global and local. He might consider humans beneath him, but he never underestimated them as an enemy. It was imperative that he study their strengths and weaknesses.

Fast-forwarding through the tedious fascination with glamorous actors behaving badly and the unpredictable stock market, Zak abruptly rose to his feet as the image of a dead girl lying on the bank of a river was flashed on the screen.

It wasn't the sight of Leah that captured his attention. He'd known her body would eventually show up. After all, Tony had disposed of her. Which meant he'd driven to the river and tossed her in at the nearest spot, not even bothering to consider she would get snagged on the bank just a few miles away if he didn't weight her down.

Idiot.

But instead, it was when the camera panned to the side to catch the image of a lean, hard-faced man who broke away from a group of cops to speak with a young woman. A woman with hair the color of fire and eyes covered by reflective glasses.

He surged to his feet, his mind racing with possibilities.

Callie Brown.

Just the woman he wanted.

Reaching down, he stabbed a button that connected him to the intercom system.

Within seconds the groggy voice of Tony floated through the air. "Yes, sir?"

"In my study."

There was a momentary pause. "Now?"

Zak hissed with impatience. "Yes, now."

Lifting the remote control, he replayed the news clip, his narrowed gaze missing nothing as he considered the various ways to take advantage of this unexpected stroke of fortune.

He was on his fourth time through the clip when Tony at last lumbered into the room, his girth covered by a too-short robe and his hair rumpled.

"You need something?" he asked, his voice gruff.

Zak pointed toward the image on the television screen. He'd paused it at the point where the blond-haired man was speaking with the female diviner.

"Do you recognize the man?"

Tony grimaced. "O'Conner. Sergeant O'Conner of the Kansas City Police Department," he said. "He busted me about six years ago. Bastard." Tony stepped toward the television, giving a low whistle. "Who's the babe?"

With a nonchalant motion, Zak backhanded his servant, sending him crashing against the far wall.

"Never speak of her again, is that clear?"

Tony climbed slowly to his feet, wiping the blood from his split lip. "Yeah, painfully clear."

"Good."

Zak pressed Play, carefully watching the possessive manner O'Conner behaved toward Callie. They were lovers. It was obvious in the way she leaned in to his intimate touch and his protective glares whenever anyone strayed too close to them.

They were emotionally entangled, which meant that they wouldn't be able to stay away from one another.

All he had to do was keep a careful watch on the cop. Eventually Callie would leave Valhalla to spend time with him. Hopefully without the constant protection of her Sentinel.

The trick would, of course, be taking them alive.

His specialty was death.

Rewinding the tape, he watched as O'Conner spoke with his fellow police officers, taking note of the private conversation he shared with a gray-haired cop who stood apart from the others.

"What about the man?" he demanded.

"Frank," Tony muttered, scratching at his unshaved cheek.

"You know him?"

Tony shrugged. "His wife is my second cousin on my mother's side."

"Of course she is," Zak said wryly. This was precisely the reason he'd hired the bumbling idiot, and why he hadn't yet disposed of him. He was connected to every family in Kansas City. "I need you to arrange a meeting."

"Me?" Tony looked horrified. "Frank hates my guts. Calls me a blight on the family."

"Understandable," Zak drawled, tossing the remote onto his desk so he could turn to frown at his companion. "Tell him that you have information regarding Leah. Information that you're willing to sell."

"I suppose that might work," Tony said slowly, reluctance etched on his pudgy face.

"Have him meet you here tomorrow morning." Zak frowned, abruptly realizing that having a cop car on the property might not be the best idea. Didn't they have some sort of . . . GPS system? "Actually, it would be better if you pick him up."

The reluctance became more pronounced as Tony began to sweat. "You want me to bring him here?"

"Isn't that what I just said?"

"But he'll be able to tell the cops where you live," Tony blurted out.

"He won't tell anyone."

Tony grimaced. "I know Frank, and trust me, you can't bribe or intimidate the man. He's a real prick about the rules."

Zak shrugged. "He won't tell anyone, because he'll be dead."

"Dead?"

"Is there a problem?"

"I . . . no." The henchman managed a sickly smile, backing toward the door. "No problem. I'll go to my rooms and give him a call first thing in the morning."

Zak let him creep away like a mouse trying to evade a stalking cat. Tony might be a bully, but he was a coward at heart.

He wouldn't have the courage to try and escape.

"Tomorrow," he whispered softly, the power that swirled deep inside him vibrating with an awareness of the chalice that was hidden only a few inches away. "It begins."

Callie was exactly where she wanted to be . . . snuggled on Duncan's bed with his arms wrapped around her and her head resting above the steady beat of his heart.

Unfortunately, while her body was sated from the passion that had exploded the minute they entered the apartment, her mind churned with a restless frustration.

She felt tense. Jumpy.

As if she was hurtling toward a car crash she couldn't avoid.

"You're quiet."

She tilted back her head to meet Duncan's steady gaze, easily reading the concern that shimmered in the hazel depths.

"I'm worried," she admitted in low tones.

"I promise, I don't snore," he teased, clearly hoping to distract her.

Her finger brushed an absent pattern on his chest, savoring the feel of his warm satin skin even as her thoughts remained dark.

"If the necromancer has the coin, we might already be too late." She spoke her fears aloud, hoping it might lessen the knot of dread lodged in the pit of her stomach.

It didn't.

Duncan brushed his lips over her furrowed brow. "We're not too late."

She smiled wryly at his confident tone. Somehow she'd assumed that no one could match a Sentinel for arrogance.

Duncan was proving how wrong she'd been.

"How can you be so sure?"

"Hektor said something about the coin being needed to unlock the door to the underworld where there's a mysterious chalice," he explained. "Whatever the hell that means. Unless the door to the underworld is hidden in Kansas City . . . god forbid . . . the necromancer will have to travel to get to it."

Ah. So not just arrogance.

She sucked in a deep breath, trying to ease her seething anxiety. "I suppose you're right," she said, wrinkling her nose at the persistent sense of danger. "Fane made sure to warn the monks to keep an eye open for a diviner with diamond eyes. If he tries to travel with a Sentinel he'll be easily spotted."

"Clever Fane," her companion muttered.

Callie blinked at the unmistakable edge in Duncan's voice. "Would you be happier if he was stupid?"

With a swift move, he rolled on top of her, his expression hard with a jealousy he made no effort to hide. "I would be happier if I was your guardian."

Her legs instinctively parted to allow him to settle against her. She swallowed a small sigh of satisfaction. It felt so right to have his heavy weight pressing against her, the scent of his maleness teasing at her nose and the feel of his warm skin branding her with pleasure.

Here, in this bed, she felt protected. Safe.

Loved . . .

Her heart slammed against her ribs as the perilous word whispered through her mind.

Oh, gods.

A part of her knew that this wasn't the time to add yet another layer of complication to their relationship. It was already a minefield of disaster that threatened to blow up in her face when she least expected it.

Hadn't her afternoon at the police station proved that?

But the L word wasn't as easy to dismiss.

Not when Duncan's hand was running an intimate path

down the line of her collarbone and his hazel eyes were shimmering with flecks of molten gold.

"Only a Sentinel can be a guardian," she reminded him, not surprised when her voice came out a breathy whisper instead of the stern warning it should have been.

"Says who?"

Hmm. Good question.

"Tradition," she at last suggested.

"Screw tradition," he growled, lowering his head to stroke his lips down the line of her jaw. "We can make new ones."

She shivered, her hands reaching up to thread through the short strands of his hair.

"I doubt the Sentinels would agree."

He slowly pulled back, studying her flushed face with an expression that was impossible to read.

"And what about you?"

"Me?"

"Would you trust me to be your guardian?"

She hesitated. This was important.

She didn't need the sudden tension in Duncan's shoulders or the way he didn't quite meet her gaze to warn her just how much her answer meant.

But she also understood that she couldn't put any pressure on him to make a commitment he might end up regretting. Duncan O'Conner was far too much like Fane. A man with his own moral code.

He would stand by his word, even if it put him through hell. Hadn't he stayed in a loveless marriage until he'd caught his wife cheating on him?

The trick was to soothe his male pride without making any demands.

Yeah, no problem.

And next she would solve cold fusion.

"That depends," she murmured, forcing a teasing smile to her lips.

His brows drew together. "On what?"

She lifted her head to give his chin a small nip. "You have to apply for the position."

His tension eased as a wicked glow chased the shadows from his eyes.

"Is that right?"

She licked his bottom lip, forgetting this was supposed to be a distraction.

Hell, she was the one distracted.

In the best possible way.

"Mmm."

He groaned deep in his throat, his swelling cock pressing against her inner thigh.

"And how would I go about that?"

"Oh, it's a very rigorous process," she breathed.

"I can be rigorous."

She chuckled, remembering the sound of the headboard slamming against the wall less than an hour ago.

"You most certainly can," she agreed, a husky edge of lingering pleasure in her voice.

It had taken a while to convince the stubborn man that she was far stronger than most women he'd known, and that she fully approved of his . . . rigorous . . . lovemaking.

He captured her lips in a deep, drugging kiss. "Or I can be slow and thorough."

The shudder of anticipation started at the tip of her toes and rippled all the way through her.

"That works."

"But first."

Lost in the sensual spell he could cast all too easily, Callie was puzzled when Duncan pulled back to study her with a narrowed gaze.

"What?"

"I want you to tell me the truth."

Was this a game? If it was, she hoped it included more of those slow, thorough kisses.

"The truth about what?" she asked, willing to play along.

"You've been quiet since we left the station. What happened?"

Oh . . . crap.

She'd convinced herself that she'd managed to hide her distress at Frank's unwelcomed confrontation. The last thing she'd wanted was to cause trouble with Duncan's friend.

But she should have known she hadn't fooled him for a second. Sergeant Duncan O'Conner missed nothing.

"If I tell you—"

"Callie?" he prompted.

"I don't want you to overreact."

His jaw instantly clenched and Callie heaved a resigned sigh. What the hell was wrong with her?

Just warning him not to overreact was a sure way to make him overreact.

"What makes you think I'll overreact?" he snarled on cue.

"You're male."

He blinked at her blunt accusation, then his lips twisted into a rueful smile. "Fair enough," he muttered, his fingers lightly stroking her cheek. "Tell me."

Despite his gentle touch, he was wearing his cop face.

He wasn't going to let this go.

"Your friend Frank was concerned that you weren't thinking clearly," she grudgingly confessed.

His fingers tightened on her cheek, but there was no surprise that Frank had been the one to approach her. The coroner had never been particularly discreet in his dislike for highbloods.

"About you?" he asked between clenched teeth.

"In part." She ran her hands down the length of his rigid back, her touch soothing. "He believes you're devastated by the marriage of your wife."

"Ex-wife."

She tried not to be pleased by his fierce correction.

But hey, she was human. Or at least, she had the usual human emotions.

Her fingers skimmed back to his shoulders. "He's convinced that she was your soul mate and that you're going to regret our relationship once you come to your senses."

The hazel eyes darkened with the threat of violence. "He said that?"

She grimaced. "Yes."

"The bastard. I'll kill him."

"No, Duncan, he's your friend," she said in urgent tones. This was exactly what she feared. "Of course he's going to be worried about you."

"He hurt you."

She shook her head. "No he didn't."

His fingers cupped her chin as he held her gaze with a somber intensity. "Callie, if this is going to work we have to be honest with each other."

He was right. The words that Frank had spoken were already festering deep inside her. Threatening to destroy the joy she felt when she was with Duncan.

The only way to deal with it was to get it out in the open.

Like lancing an infected wound.

"He didn't hurt me, but he did remind me of the cost you'll have to pay to be with me," she said, her voice so low he had to lower his head to catch her words. "It's . . . not going to be easy for you."

He stilled, as if surprised by her words. "Not just me, Callie," he finally said. "It's going to be difficult for both of us."

She reached up to touch his jaw. "Are you sure you're ready for it?"

He studied her concerned expression before he slowly dipped down to kiss her with a tenderness that brought tears to her eyes.

"I'm trying," he murmured against her lips. "Although I can't guarantee that I won't get pissed off when I think you're being insulted."

"I don't want you losing your friends."

Another kiss. Slower . . . deeper.

"If they're truly my friends then they'll understand when I tell them to fuck off." His tongue stroked a damp path along her lower lip. "And if they want to be turd-heads, then they can get the hell out of my life."

She gave a reluctant chuckle. "Turd-heads?"

"Yep, turd-heads." He trailed a line of kisses up her jaw before he lifted his head to regard her with a hint of question. "And you? Are you ready for it?"

She held his gaze. "When I'm with you I feel like I can face anything."

His expression softened, some undefinable emotion smoldering in his eyes.

"Even jackass cops?" he rasped.

"I'm more afraid of your mother."

He smiled with a sinful intent, his hand sliding over her shoulder and down to cup the swell of her breast.

"You know, I have a perfect way of taking your mind off my ma and interfering friends." His thumb rubbed the tip of her nipple into a tight peak. "Oh, and the potential end of the world."

"Hmm." Her nails scraped down his back, a honey-heat flowing through her body. "This had better be a damned good distraction," she teased, her foot stroking up the back of his calf.

He gave a soft moan, burying his face in the curve of her neck. "Oh, I think you'll like it."

"Just like it?"

His lips found the pulse that thundered at the base of her throat.

"If I'm very lucky, you'll love it," he whispered, angling his hips and sliding deep into her body with one smooth stroke.

"Duncan—"

Chapter Twenty-Three

Dawn had barely crested when Zak left his private chambers and entered the small room at the back of the house. As always, a full breakfast was waiting for him, along with a stack of the morning papers.

He ignored the sizzling sense of anticipation that filled his veins like the finest champagne as he went through his morning routine with a careful precision. The lure of the chalice had haunted him the entire night, but now wasn't the time to be bewitched by the whispers of power.

No.

He needed an orderly mind.

An utter state of calm.

And the realization that the closer he came to achieving his destiny, the more careful he had to be.

Today he put his pawns in position and prepared the last of his strategy.

And of course, cleaned up his loose ends.

On cue, Tony entered the room, looking worse than many corpses Zak had raised.

The servant had clearly not slept. Or even bathed. His dark hair was sticking up in small clumps and his cheeks were unshaved. He'd made an effort to dress in a clean pair of slacks and a white shirt, but he'd forgotten his shoes and his belt hung unfastened around his thick waist.

"Tony," Zak murmured softly. "Where's the cop?"

The servant anxiously shifted his feet. "He's in the kitchen having a cup of coffee. I told him I had to check and make sure my employers weren't up yet."

"Excellent." Zak laid aside his napkin and rose to his feet. "He doesn't suspect he's being led to a trap?"

"Nope." Tony did more shifting. "He knows I occasionally . . . barter information for cash."

Zak rounded the table, absently straightening the cuffs of his black Armani suit. Unlike Tony, he understood the importance of presenting an image of strength.

"Use the tunnels to bring him into the basement."

The man scrubbed his fingers through his hair. "He's going to be armed."

"Human weapons don't frighten me."

"They do me," Tony muttered.

Zak shrugged. "Once the cop is in my private laboratory you may leave."

"Always supposing he doesn't shoot me in the back before we get there."

Zak smiled with a cold indifference. "It's a chance I'm willing to take."

Tony lost what little color he had left. "Fantastic."

Indifferent to his servant's barely contained panic, Zak strolled out of the room and down the hall. It was still early, but he had tasks to finish before the cop arrived.

Reaching his office, his steps slowed as he caught the unmistakable scent of candle wax and blood.

Anya.

An icy smile touched his lips as he cautiously pressed open the door and scanned the room to make sure there were no unwelcome surprises.

Nothing was out of place. Not unless he counted the

slender, redheaded woman who was covertly searching through the drawers of his desk.

Stepping into the room, he closed the door and silently glided across the carpet to stand directly behind the intruder.

"I thought I might find you here, witch," he murmured.

With a gasp, Anya whirled around to face him, her eyes wide with fear.

"Zak."

Holding her wide gaze, Zak leaned to the side and released the hidden lever. With a click the panel slid open and he reached into the compartment to remove the chalice.

"Is this what you were searching for?"

She wisely shrank back as he straightened to hold the chalice between them.

"Of course not." She swallowed, then with an obvious effort, she forced a stiff smile to her lips. "I was searching for an amulet that I dropped here yesterday."

Zak clicked his tongue, carefully setting the chalice on the desk.

"You really are a terrible liar," he drawled.

"I . . . I have no reason to lie."

"True. Such days are behind us." He reached to wrap his fingers lightly around her throat. Not hard enough to hurt. Not yet. "Tell me, Anya, why did you do it?"

She went rigid, but she was smart enough not to try and break free.

"Do what?" she croaked.

"Betray me."

"I don't . . ." She gave a choked cry as his fingers tightened. "Zak, no."

"I'm not stupid, Anya." The words were edged with ice. "There's no one else who could have kept the coin out of my grasp for so long."

"The Brotherhood—"

"A band of idiots who would never have been capable of

outwitting me if they hadn't had a spy to warn them when I was about to strike," he interrupted, his narrowed gaze watching the emotions dart over her face.

Fear . . . desperation . . . cunning.

"A spy?" she finally tried to bluff.

His thumb pressed against the pulse that thundered just below her jaw.

"You."

Her laugh was laced with a barely concealed hysteria. "You can't be serious."

"Oh, I'm very, very serious," he said softly.

"But—" She struggled to recall the glib excuses she'd used for years to divert his suspicions. "If it was me, then why wouldn't I have warned Calso?"

His gaze drifted down to the unsteady line of her lips. "I admit I thought that it was a trap until I had my hands on the chalice. Now I can only assume that something went wrong." Her breath quickened, a certain sign that his guess had been a good one. "So what happened, my dear? Did they fail to heed your warning? Or did you realize I was becoming suspicious and decide it wasn't worth the risk?"

"It makes no sense, Zak," Anya stubbornly insisted. She was nothing if not tenacious. It was the only reason she'd survived over the centuries. "My fate is tied to yours."

"So I thought."

She licked her lips, growing alarmed by his refusal to accept her innocence.

"I rescued you from the flames," she reminded him. "I stood guard over your mutilated body for a century. I led you to the hidden temple. Why would I sacrifice so much only to betray you?"

He arched his brows. Surely she wasn't hoping to stir a sense of gratitude? This woman better than anyone should know he didn't indulge in human emotions.

"That's what you're going to tell me," he assured her. "So start explaining."

"I've told you—"

He heaved a mock sigh of disappointment, his fingers slowly, ruthlessly tightening around her throat.

"We have been together a very long time, Anya. I didn't want to have to hurt you." His fingers slowly, ruthlessly began to crush her throat. "But I will."

"Don't," she managed to croak, tears streaming down her ashen cheeks.

"Tell me, witch." He leaned down until they were nose to nose, the chill of his power swirling through the air. "Tell me why."

She shuddered in pain, her hands lifting to grasp his wrists.

"Because I love you," she hissed.

"Love?"

His humorless laugh echoed through the study. This woman was capable of lust, greed, and a narcissistic ambition. But love?

A barracuda had more of a heart than she did.

"Yes," she insisted, a sudden color returning to her cheeks. "You can't be surprised. Why would any woman devote her life to a man if not for love?"

"You truly must believe me to be a fool," he sneered, his fingers easing just enough to allow her to suck in a shaky breath.

He wanted this to be slow.

And painful.

Very, very painful.

"It's the truth," she pleaded.

"I don't claim to be an expert on human emotions, but I'm fairly certain that love doesn't include treachery." He met her wary gaze, his expression cold, merciless. "Not unless you happen to be a character from Shakespeare. And you know how much I detest Shakespeare."

"It didn't start off as treachery."

"No?"

"No." The amulet around her neck glowed with a faint light. No doubt a last-ditch attempt to sway him into believing her imploring words. She'd always had a talent for coercing others. Unfortunately for her, he'd never been susceptible. "When we first met I was attracted to your power. That was why I assisted you in gaining the attention of the czarina."

He made a sound of disgust. "I didn't need your assistance."

"Maybe not, but you would never have known of your destiny unless I had revealed the temple to you."

"It would have been revealed eventually. My fate has been waiting for me since the dawn of civilization." Zak lifted his shoulder in a dismissive gesture. "Besides, I promised to make you queen of the world. A fair trade for your information."

"And that's all I desired. Even after I rescued you from the flames and protected you from your enemies. It wasn't until—" She deliberately allowed her words to trail away.

"Until?"

"Until we became lovers that my feelings deepened."

"Lovers?" His lips twisted into a humorless smile. "We had sex to ensure my ultimate victory."

She swiftly disguised the fury that flared through her eyes.

"Call it whatever you want," she said, lowering her voice to a seductive invitation. "I spent night after night in your arms and it created a bond between us."

Night after night . . .

Zak snapped his teeth together, struck by her soft words.

Christ. He'd just sworn he wasn't a fool, but it was obvious that's exactly what he'd been.

This . . . female . . . had used his lack of interest in the tedious details of procreation to hold him hostage.

And the most galling part of all, was that he hadn't even suspected he was being played.

"You clever little bitch."

With each frigid word his fingers tightened, his nails digging into her skin until blood dripped down her throat.

"Zak," Anya squawked, her eyes bulging. "Stop."

"You claimed that your dark magic made it almost impossible for you to conceive," he snarled, his lips curled with disgust. "A lie, wasn't it, Anya?"

It took several tries before she could speak past the pain. "Not entirely."

"A lie."

"No." She helplessly gripped his wrists, trying to pry away his punishing hand. "It truly is more difficult."

He studied her pale face with an uncharacteristic loathing. Emotions were a waste of energy. Regrettably, there were times when they refused to be suppressed.

Like now.

"But you made certain it was impossible."

"Yes," she rasped. "I knew once you had what you wanted you would no longer invite me to your bed."

"So why—" He bit off his question, abruptly recalling the days before Anya's announcement she was at last pregnant. "Of course. I said I was weary of your lack of production. I intended to find another woman to carry my seed."

She lowered her gaze, artfully allowing her lips to quiver. Such a fine performance, he sourly acknowledged. A pity she didn't have an audience to appreciate her effort.

"I couldn't allow you to take another lover."

"Allow?"

"I was desperate," she said in tragic tones. "In the end, all I could do was give you the child you wanted and hope that you could see that we were so much more than mere partners."

He made a sound of disgust. "You were never my partner."

Her performance faltered as a surge of bitterness darkened her eyes.

"No, I was merely a means to an end," she muttered.

True enough. His fingers tightened, making her shudder in agony.

"When did you begin betraying me to the Brotherhood?" he asked.

She clutched at his arms, a panic twisting her face as the bones began to pop in her neck.

"I can't . . . breathe."

"Oh, I think you can if you really try, my dear," he drawled. Witches didn't have the healing capabilities of a Sentinel, but they did have a higher tolerance to damage than mere humans. "Now, one more time. When did you begin betraying me to the Brotherhood?"

The amulet glowed, but this time it wasn't a futile effort to glamour him. No. Anya was frantically draining the stored magic to keep herself alive.

"Not long after you realized you could sense their presence," she grated.

How many years had been wasted because of this bitch? How long had he been denied his fate?

Anya would pay for each and every day she'd cost him.

"You never intended for me to take my place as ruler."

"Of course I did," she tried to plead. "I hoped that once you were truly committed to me—"

"Ah. You wanted a puppet you could lead around by the cock," he sliced through her words, understanding at last.

Clearly Anya's definition of love was beguiling a man until he was blinded by lust.

She dug her nails into his wrists as her legs began to sag. He was keeping her on the edge of death and her body was only minutes from a total collapse.

"And what about you?"

He shrugged. "I prefer not to be the puppet of an overly ambitious bitch."

Any pretense of affection drained from the emerald eyes to reveal the bitter resentment that festered beneath the surface.

"I meant that you're no better than me," she hissed. "You had no intention of making me your queen."

His laugh was mocking. "I promised you, didn't I?"

"An empty promise." Her head fell back, her skin becoming a pasty white as her magic faltered and the full impact of her injuries took their toll. "You're willing to sacrifice anyone, including your own family, to achieve your goals. I have never doubted for a second that I would be as easily destroyed once I was no longer any use to you." She gave an agonized laugh, blood dripping from the corner of her mouth. "I could only hope to make myself indispensable."

"Ah. No one is indispensable, Anya," he taunted, his fingers tightening until her windpipe was crushed. "A pity."

With the last of her strength, she reached up to rake her nails down his cheek.

"I'll see you in hell," she promised.

Zak heard the sound of the door opening behind him, and the muttered curse as the intruder caught sight of him ruthlessly squeezing out the last of Anya's life. But his gaze never shifted from the emerald eyes, a smile touching his lips as he savored her slow death.

Yes. This was his finest talent.

And his greatest pleasure.

He heard the sound of metal scraping against leather as the man behind him drew a gun.

"What the fuck is going on here?" he growled, his voice not quite steady.

"Patience, cop," Zak commanded, the dark power stirring deep inside him. "You're next."

Duncan wasn't a sentimental kind of guy.

Or at least . . . he'd never thought of himself as sentimental. Not until Callie Brown.

Lying on his side, he studied the tiny female who was tucked next to him. He'd been awake for hours, enchanted by the sight of her sleeping in his arms.

The pale, delicate features. The fiery hair that reflected her indomitable spirit. The lush curve of her lips that hinted at her passion. And the slender body that held a strength that would have shocked most people.

He'd cared for Susan. He truly had.

But this woman . . .

She fit against him with absolute perfection. Like two puzzle pieces that had finally been assembled.

There, see?

Sentimental.

And something else. Something fiercely possessive and dangerously protective.

He grimaced, his fingers lightly stroking over her bare shoulder. Despite his assurances to Callie that he was prepared to deal with the inevitable prejudices, he was still anxious to put his fist in Frank's face.

Friend or not, the man had no right to try and intimidate Callie. If he thought Duncan was making a mistake then he should have confronted him face to face. That he could respect. Not acting like a bully behind his back.

He gave a shake of his head, unwilling to mar the peace of this moment with such ugliness. There would be plenty of time later to worry about the rest of the world. For now it was just the two of them.

On the point of waking his sleeping beauty with a kiss,

Duncan was caught off guard when she abruptly began to thrash against him, her tiny moans of distress piercing his heart.

"Callie. Sweetheart." He sat up, pulling her tight against his chest.

She struggled against him, her breath coming in panicked gasps. "No . . . no."

His hand pressed her head against his shoulder, his arms keeping her from tumbling off the bed.

"Callie, wake up."

The low command in his voice seemed to do the trick. With a low moan she lifted her lashes, the brilliant clarity of her eyes clouded with a lingering horror.

"Duncan?"

He cupped her chin, brushing a soft kiss over her trembling lips.

"You were having a nightmare."

"Yes," she said slowly, a shudder wracking her body. "God, it was horrible."

His lips moved to stroke her temple. "Do you want to share?" he asked. "Or just forget about it?"

"I was standing at the edge of Valhalla and—"

"Callie?"

"They were everywhere," she said, bravely trying to swallow a choked sob.

"It's okay." His arms tightened around her at the feel of her trembling against him. "I've got you."

"I couldn't stop them."

"Stop who?"

"The dead."

His heart squeezed at her whispered words. Dammit. Couldn't they leave her alone even in her sleep?

His hand ran a soothing path up and down her back. "Callie, it was just a dream."

"No. Not just a dream." She tilted back her head to reveal

her troubled expression, her cheeks damp with tears. "It was real. A premonition."

He ignored the cold chill that inched down his spine. No. He wasn't going to start jumping at shadows.

They were both on edge. Wasn't it more likely her dreams were a reaction to her stress rather than some omen?

He used his thumbs to brush away her tears. "Is seeing the future one of your skills?"

"No, but—"

"Then it was just a dream," he insisted.

She sucked in a quivering breath. "It was my blood."

"What?"

"It was my blood that called them from their grave."

"Ssh." He laid his cheek on top of her head, his hand reaching up to yank aside the curtain so the morning sunlight could spill over the bed. "Nothing is going to happen to you. Not as long as I have you in my arms."

Chapter Twenty-Four

Zak studied the small cut on his palm, fascinated as a drop of blood appeared only to vanish, reappearing in the chalice he'd left on the counter of his lab.

Inside he could feel the dark power that flowed through him like a river of ice. It was the same pulsing avalanche that threatened to sear the flesh from his bones . . . and yet, different.

With the chalice it was deeper, more profound.

His senses were heightened to a near unbearable acuteness, as if his every nerve had been exposed. The fluorescent lights were almost blindingly bright, the faint brush of central air made his skin prickle, and the sound of Tony's thundering heartbeat as he cowered near the door echoed through the air.

But above it all, he was aware of the shimmering strands of magic connecting him to the corpse standing in the middle of the floor.

This wasn't the familiar slipping into the mind of the dead. He wasn't controlling an empty shell that was rapidly deteriorating.

No.

A part of Frank Sanchez remained despite his death. He

was imbued with a magic that flowed from the chalice and into Zak before flowing to Frank. The cop could walk, talk, and think for himself. The magic even made him seem alive. He blinked, occasionally sucked in an unnecessary breath, and his face could show a few sluggish expressions.

The magic also disguised the gaping wound on the side of his head where Zak had crushed his skull. Almost as if it was Frank's own memory of himself that was being shrouded around his corpse.

But while he seemed alive, he was well and truly dead, and in the absolute control of Zak.

The perfect weapon.

A smile of satisfaction curled Zak's lips as he slowly circled his newest creation. "You can hear me?" he asked softly, pleased when Frank's gaze settled on his face, awareness shimmering in the dark depths.

"Yes."

"You know who you are?"

"Frank Sanchez."

"Shit," Tony muttered from the doorway, his face a pasty white.

"Be quiet," Zak snapped, his gaze never leaving Frank's face as it scrunched into a puzzled frown. "What is it?"

"Who are you?" the coroner demanded.

Ah. So he didn't remember the moments before his death. Interesting.

"I'm your master," he said with a stern simplicity.

The frown deepened. "Bullshit—"

Zak allowed his power to flow through the bond, halting the angry words and enforcing his will on the man.

"Who am I?" he demanded.

The frown smoothed away and Frank gave a bow of his head. "Master."

"Very good." Reaching into the pocket of his Armani

pants, he pulled out his phone and held the screen toward Frank. "Do you remember this man?"

There was no hesitation. "O'Conner."

"That's right." Zak skimmed his finger across the screen to pull up another image. "And what about this woman?"

"Necro."

Zak narrowed his eyes. As soon as he was in command of Valhalla things were going to change. Beginning with humans learning their proper place.

"Her name is Callie Brown," he said in a soft, icy voice. "Say it."

"Callie Brown," Frank obediently parroted.

Satisfied, Zak returned the phone to his pocket.

"I want her brought to me," he commanded. "Do you understand?"

"Yes."

With a speed that took Zak by surprise, the cop was turning to head to the door.

"Wait," he growled, grabbing the man's arm and spinning him back around. "You don't know where she is."

Some undefinable emotion briefly flared in the dark eyes. Or more likely it was just a memory of an emotion.

He doubted that the magic filling Frank could actually give him genuine feelings.

"She's with O'Conner."

Zak narrowed his gaze. "You're sure?"

"She was at the station with him yesterday."

"Was her guardian with her?"

"No."

Zak turned away, pacing toward the stainless steel counter. Was it possible?

He'd waited so long, been denied so often.

Could destiny at last have taken a hand in ensuring his ultimate success?

Yes, a voice whispered in the back of his mind.

Fate had obviously chosen this moment for him to take his rightful place. Why wouldn't the stars align so that Callie would be precisely where he needed her to be?

Slowly turning back, he resisted the urge to rush from the house and attain the female who was the last key to his glory.

Destiny or not, he'd be a fool to put himself at risk when he was so close to glory.

"I want you to find O'Conner. If Callie is still with him I want you to capture her and bring her straight here. If he's alone I want you to keep an eye on him until she shows up." He shifted his attention to the man who was trying to disappear into the shadows. "Tony will accompany you."

"Hell no," the servant barked, his eyes bulging as he shoved away from the door.

"Excuse me?"

Tony flinched at the lethal warning laced through Zak's tone.

"Our deal never included being a sidekick to a zombie," he muttered.

Zak smiled with frigid amusement. "Is your objection to being a sidekick or working with the dead?"

Unable to find the humor in the situation, Tony began backing out the door.

"I quit."

"Tony."

Zak's voice was soft, but filled with enough power to make the henchman halt in his tracks.

"What?" Tony rasped, his belligerent attitude unable to disguise his fear.

"You will be assisting Frank," Zak informed him, his tone flat. Uncompromising. "Whether you're alive or dead while you're assisting him makes no difference to me."

* * *

"Hey, sleepyhead."

Callie woke for the second time, her earlier nightmare forgotten as she felt warm, male lips tenderly stroking over her cheek and caught a delectable scent filling the air.

Oh . . . yum.

She couldn't decide which was better. The arousing sensations of Duncan's light caresses or the aroma of cinnamon and butter and warm maple.

It was the growl of her stomach that decided.

"Hmm," she murmured, lifting her lids to discover Duncan seated at the edge of the bed with a tray filled with food perched beside him. "Do I smell waffles?"

He nodded. "I made them fresh."

"You made them?" Scooting up to lean against the headboard, her eyes narrowed as she caught sight of the fluffy waffles perfectly browned and dusted with cinnamon and powdered sugar with a dollop of whip cream on top of the stack. Beside the plate was a tiny jug of maple syrup and on the other side a bowl of ripe, red strawberries. "Liar."

"Busted," he admitted with a boyish grin that tugged directly on her heart. "I did order them. Does that count?"

Callie swallowed a resigned sigh. He was unshaven, wearing a plain white tee with faded jeans, and his hair was tumbled onto his brow. He should have looked scruffy.

Instead, he was indecently, gloriously male and so beautiful she wanted to crawl into his lap and beg him to hold her for the next eternity or so.

Lost in the fantasy, it wasn't until a golden brow arched that she was jolted out of her lovesick daze.

She grimaced. Man, she had it bad, bad, bad.

"Only if there's coffee," she forced herself to tease.

His grin widened. "Your wish is my command."

He bent down to grab a cup of coffee he'd set on the

floor, waving it beneath her nose before pressing it into her outstretched hand.

Breathing deeply of the rich aroma, she took a sip, sending Duncan an appreciative glance. He'd remembered she took three sugars with a dollop of cream.

"Perfect," she murmured, setting aside the coffee to break off a corner of the top waffle to dip it in the syrup before popping it into her mouth. "Is there a reason I'm being so shamelessly spoiled?"

He shrugged. "Because I like to spoil you."

She believed him. Duncan was a tough, macho cop, but he was also a generous lover who would always seek to please his partner.

"And because you're worried about me?" she asked softly.

"That too."

She grabbed a strawberry and pressed it to his lips.

"Thank you," she whispered.

"For what?" He took a bite of the berry, his gaze never wavering from her face. "Breakfast?"

"That too."

They shared an intimate smile, both recalling the long night filled with enough passion to light the world on fire.

The gold shimmered in his hazel eyes, suggesting that Duncan would like to do more than just remember the pleasure they'd shared.

"What time will your watchdog be arriving?" he asked, his voice a husky rasp.

Leaning to the side, she grabbed her cell phone off the nightstand to read the message she knew would be waiting for her.

She wrinkled her nose. "In half an hour."

"Damn," Duncan muttered, leashing his ready desire. "Where are you supposed to meet him?"

"In the parking lot."

He frowned. "What parking lot?"

"Here." She watched his frown deepen. "Is something wrong?"

"How does he know where I . . . wait." He held up a hand, rolling his eyes. "Stupid question."

She nodded. It had been a stupid question. "Fane is nothing if not thorough."

His jaw tightened, but he made a visible effort to keep his expression bland. "Will you return to Valhalla?"

"Yes. I have to report to the Mave."

"A shame." His gaze traveled down to where the blanket barely covered the curve of her breasts. "I have a much better way to spend the day."

"Don't you have to work?"

"Yep." His smile was wicked. "But that doesn't mean I wouldn't rather spend the day with you."

Impulsively she leaned forward, pressing a lingering kiss to his lips.

"I know the feeling."

"Mmm." His hand cupped her nape as he parted her lips to stroke his tongue into her mouth, tasting her with blatant hunger before pulling back with a rueful sigh. "Eat your breakfast before I forget we don't have time for this," he commanded.

She gave his lower lip a tiny nip. "Time for this?"

"Behave yourself, woman."

Firmly settling her back against the headboard, Duncan reached for a strawberry and held it to her mouth.

Callie obediently took a bite, savoring the tart juices that exploded in her mouth. Duncan was right, it was a shame. Hell, it was more than a shame.

She'd much rather be feasting on his hard, male body, but time was slipping away too fast to indulge their need.

Neither wanted Fane coming to look for her.

With an indulgent smile, Duncan urged her to clean her

plate, then while he whisked away the tray, Callie took a quick shower.

Returning to the bedroom she discovered her clothes had been freshly laundered and laid out on the bed and her heart melted a little more.

Crap.

This man understood women far too well.

Romance wasn't about flowers or remembered birthdays, or surprise trips to Paris.

Not that all of those things weren't great.

But it was the tiny, everyday thoughtful gestures that made a woman feel appreciated.

Loved.

Pulling on her clothes, she struggled against the aching disappointment at having to leave.

Someday she would put her foot down and insist she have the freedom to explore her relationship with Duncan.

But not today.

Until the danger was past, she had to be extra careful. Her nightmare had forced her to realize that she wasn't taking Boggs's warning as seriously as she should.

The vision of herself poised in front of Valhalla while a dark tide of death rushed past her was seared into her brain, chilling her to her very soul.

She didn't know how or why her blood could call the dead, but if there was the slightest chance the rogue necromancer could use her in his sick plans then she had to stay out of his reach.

And if that meant cowering behind the protective walls of Valhalla, so be it.

Squaring her shoulders, she forced her feet to carry her out of the bedroom into the living room where Duncan was tucking his gun into his holster.

She choked back a groan.

His golden male looks might have been too pretty if it

wasn't for the dangerous edge to his features and the hard, lean body that was built for violence.

Instead he looked . . . mouthwatering.

Barely resisting the urge to cross the short distance and press herself against the sexy invitation that was Duncan O'Conner, she forced a smile to her lips.

No moping in front of the delectable cop. He was already worried enough about her.

"Thanks for the clean clothes," she murmured. "I had no idea you could not only order a breakfast that was to die for, but you can also do laundry."

"I'm multitalented."

"You most certainly are," she whispered.

He stilled as their gazes entangled, sharing all the words they couldn't say. "Callie—"

"I should go," she abruptly breathed, slipping on her reflective glasses. "Fane will be here soon."

His jaw clenched, but he moved to place an arm around her waist, leading her toward the door. He might hate the fact that Fane was her guardian, but he wouldn't jeopardize her safety.

"I'll wait with you."

There was no point in arguing, even if she'd wanted to.

Duncan wasn't going to let her out of his sight until he'd handed her over to Fane.

Which might have been insulting if she hadn't accepted that her pride had to take a backseat until the necromancer was found. In her mind she might be a kick-ass Xena warrior, but in reality . . . yeah, not so much.

Leaving the apartment, Callie felt a strange chill brush over her skin. Almost as if she'd been touched by death.

She shivered, hastily looking down the narrow hallway that ended at a heavy fire door. There wasn't much to see. A few plastic plants in dire need of dusting and a shallow alcove that led to the second apartment.

So why did she feel as if there was something lurking just out of sight?

"What is it?" Duncan demanded, his hand on his gun.

She gave a last glance down the hall before giving a shake of her head. Obviously the nightmare had affected her even more than she'd realized.

She was jumping at shadows.

She shook her head. "Nothing."

Duncan nodded, continuing to lead her out of the building, but his hand remained on his gun.

She wasn't the only jumpy one.

They stepped into the parking lot, briefly blinded by the late afternoon sunlight.

Callie blinked, scanning the lot for a sign of the heavy vehicle that Fane always preferred.

A Hummer, a truck, an armored tank.

When there was nothing beyond the expected minivans and midsize clunkers, she glanced at Duncan in surprise.

"Not here?" he demanded.

"No. Strange." She pulled her phone out, discovering she'd missed Fane's text. "Oh. He had to wait for the monks to arrange a car. He should be here any minute."

"Good." Without warning Duncan wrapped his arms around her and dropped a kiss on the tip of her nose. "We have time for a little PDA."

"PDA?" She tilted back her head with a lift of her brows. "Dare I ask?"

"Public Display of Affection," he murmured, his sexy smile suddenly freezing as he glanced over her shoulders. "That guy looks familiar and not in a good way," he said, in full cop mode as he shoved a key into her hand. "Here. Go back to the apartment and lock the door. I'll call when Fane gets here."

She glanced over her shoulder, catching sight of the barrel-chested man with dark hair slicked from his bluntly carved face. He was half hidden behind a Dumpster, peeking around the edge in a way that had been guaranteed to catch the attention of a wary cop.

Callie didn't like it.

It screamed TRAP.

"But—"

"Please, Callie," Duncan muttered, his voice tense.

Knowing her companion wasn't going to back down until he was certain there was no danger to her, Callie heaved a resigned sigh.

"Fine." She sent him a warning glare. "But if you let yourself get hurt, I'm not going to be happy."

His answer was a gentle push toward the door and Callie heaved a resigned sigh as she reentered the building and headed the short distance to Duncan's apartment.

Halting in front of the door, she fumbled trying to fit the key into the lock. She was consumed with the knowledge that Duncan might very well be walking into danger.

He was a good cop. A *great* cop. But his obsessive determination to protect her made him vulnerable.

She didn't doubt for a second he would put himself in danger if he thought it was necessary.

Barely capable of concentrating on the simple task of unlocking the door, Callie was oblivious to the shadow that slipped through the doorway at the far end of the hall.

She had no warning that the trap she'd suspected was about to snap shut.

Not until a crippling pain exploded in the back of her head and the world went dark.

Waiting until Callie disappeared into the building, Duncan walked with a commanding purpose across the parking lot, his hand deliberately on his gun. If the lurker was a run-of-the-mill drug dealer he'd take off. They always did when confronted by an authority figure. Duncan could call it in and get back to Callie.

If it wasn't . . . well, he'd dealt with scumbags before.

And the man hiding behind the Dumpster had all the earmarks of being a class A scumbag.

Halting with his back to a nearby car so no one could sneak up on him, he studied the blunt features that tugged at a distant memory.

This man had crossed his path before. Not uncommon. Duncan spent a lot of time on the streets, dealing with a lot of different people. It was rare that he didn't see someone he'd encountered before. Either a criminal or a victim or just an eyewitness.

"What's your name?" he demanded, not bothering to flash his badge. No need to make it official.

Yet.

"Tony," the man muttered, a fine sheen of sweat on his brow.

Nerves? Guilt? Something worse? Only one way to find out.

"You have a reason for lurking in my parking lot, Tony?"

Tony licked thick lips, glancing toward the apartment building. "I wasn't lurking. I was—"

"Yeah?"

"Waiting for you."

"Me?" He frowned. "Why?"

"You're a cop, right?"

"I am."

"I have information for you."

Duncan remained wary. In his experience confidential informants didn't hide in parking lots waiting for a cop to appear.

And how the hell had he known where he lived?

Duncan covertly tightened his grip on his gun. "What kind of information?"

"I heard you're looking for a necro."

Duncan sucked in a sharp breath. "How did you know that?"

The man once again glanced toward the apartment building. As if looking for something.

Or someone.

"Word gets around."

No. Word didn't get around. Not to low-level criminals.

Cold spikes of suspicion pierced his heart.

This wasn't right.

"Okay." He angled his body so he could keep watch on the apartment building as he began to back away, his inner alarms screeching a belated warning. "Meet me at the police station in half an hour and we'll talk."

"No." With an unexpected lunge, Tony grabbed Duncan's arm. "Wait."

Duncan pulled his gun, pointing it between the bastard's eyes. "Let go of me."

Tony's dark eyes widened with fear, but he tenaciously held on. "I have to tell you now."

There was a distracting flare of light as the sun reflected off the glass door of the apartment building. Turning his head, Duncan watched as it was shoved open and his heart came to a brutal halt.

Callie.

Stunned, his attention turned to the man who was carrying her limp body in the opposite direction.

Was that . . .

"Frank," he muttered in confusion, the world moving in slow motion as he watched his longtime friend carrying Callie toward a car parked next to his own.

It didn't make sense.

Okay, Frank might have said some stupid things in a misguided need to protect Duncan, but he was a man of honor.

He would never hurt an unarmed female just because he didn't like high-bloods.

Never.

So what the hell was going on?

His sluggish brain struggled for a reasonable explanation.

Had Frank found Callie collapsed and was hurrying her to the hospital?

Had he realized Callie was in danger and was trying to protect her?

Had he . . .

His eyes narrowed as Frank walked directly in front of a car entering the parking lot, his head never turning even when the driver gave a blast of his horn.

"What the hell—?" Duncan breathed, a savage fear ripping through his heart. In that minute he realized there was more wrong with his friend than just his weird behavior. His aura was distorted.

As if the spark of life that danced around him in swirls of color had been sucked dry to leave behind an empty soul.

He was . . . a walking cadaver. There was no other explanation. "Shit." Yanking his arm free from Tony's grasp, he charged across the parking lot, bellowing at the top of his lungs. "Callie."

Focused on reaching Frank before he could put Callie in the car and disappear, Duncan dismissed Tony from his thoughts. The thug had clearly been nothing more than a distraction. He would deal with him once Callie was safe.

But with a speed that was shocking for a man with his bulk, Tony bulldozed into Duncan from behind, knocking him to the ground.

"Goddammit," Duncan growled, swinging his arm backward to hit Tony in the side of his head with the butt of his gun.

The man cursed, but grimly held on, his harsh grunts filling the air.

"It's too late," he panted. "It's too late for all of us."

Struggling to dislodge the man, Duncan managed to swivel around far enough to point the gun between his eyes.

"Let me go or I'll blow your brains out."

The man laughed.

Actually laughed.

"Go ahead. It will be a relief to the fate waiting for me."

Fuck.

There was nothing worse than a perp with a death wish.

Especially when that perp had information he might need.

Hissing with frustration, he resisted the desire to squeeze the trigger and instead pulled back to whack him again with the butt of the gun.

There was a dull crack as Tony's skull fractured and a gash appeared in the middle of his forehead, but insanely he continued to hold on.

Duncan growled in frustration. Enough. He was done screwing around.

Pressing his finger on the trigger, he was a breath from shooting Tony when his dark eyes crossed and the buffoon at last slumped to the side.

With a groan Duncan heaved the dead weight off him and surged to his feet.

His gaze desperately scanned the parking lot, terror gripping his heart as he caught sight of a silver car with Frank behind the wheel hurtling in his direction.

Callie . . .

She had to be in the car.

Raising his gun, he fired directly at the windshield, holding his ground even as the car picked up speed, clearly determined to run him over.

No. Christ, no.

This couldn't be happening.

Emptying his gun, he cursed as he realized the bullets

were worthless against Frank. It was as if his corpse simply absorbed the damage and reformed.

Tossing aside the weapon, Duncan braced himself. He would jump onto the hood of the car and crawl through the shattered windshield.

Almost as if sensing Duncan's intention, Frank swerved at the last minute, taking the car out of reach.

"Shit."

With a superhuman effort, Duncan lunged toward the car, his fingertips grasping the handle of the back door. Desperately he tried to keep pace as he wrenched on the handle, his shoulder twisting out of joint when Frank whipped the car sharply to the left.

The momentum of the car yanked him off his feet and he lost his grip on the handle as he went flying backward. Still airborne, he clipped his temple on the back bumper, gouging a deep wound before he was flung to the pavement.

Roaring in pained fury, he forced himself to his knees, not even noticing the body of Tony lying just feet away. Not until a sluggish stream of blood ran down the pavement to pool directly in front of him.

Oh . . . hell.

Frank hadn't been swerving to avoid Duncan.

He'd been running over the unconscious Tony.

Leave no accomplice behind . . . That was obviously the motto of the unknown necro.

At least not one who could talk.

And this one most certainly wouldn't be talking.

With a shudder, Duncan studied the mutilated body. He didn't need a doctor to tell him that Tony was dead. Not only had the front tires crushed his chest, but the back tires had nearly decapitated him.

Any information they could have got about where Frank

was taking Callie or even the plans of the necromancer was gone.

The inane thoughts whizzed through his head even as he stumbled to his feet, running toward the curb.

Too late, too late, too late . . .

The damning words were playing through his mind as a heavy black truck screeched to a halt in front of him and Fane was shoving open the door.

"Where's Callie?" he growled.

The world was spinning in a funny way, but Duncan grimly struggled to answer. "They have her," he managed to rasp, wondering why the side of his face felt damp.

It hadn't started to rain when he wasn't paying attention, had it?

Lifting his hand, he touched the warm stickiness, pulling his fingers back to reveal them coated in red.

Not rain. Blood.

Then it came to him.

Oh yeah.

Head vs. Bumper.

Head loses.

That was his last semicoherent thought before collapsing in Fane's arms.

Chapter Twenty-Five

Callie cautiously opened her eyes and glanced around.

She wasn't sure what she expected.

A crypt? A dungeon? A spooky castle complete with Renfield?

Instead she discovered she was in a high-tech lab.

Somehow, the sight wasn't remotely reassuring.

With all the gleaming metal and clinical white it made her think of a morgue for a creepy modern day Frankenstein.

Climbing off the stainless steel gurney she'd been lying on, Callie forced herself to take slow steady breaths as her gaze skimmed around the large room.

Steel cabinets. A long counter with a sink. White tiled floor and a high ceiling with fluorescent lights. Along the far wall were a line of walk-in coolers that she had no intention of investigating.

No windows.

One door that she swiftly discovered was locked.

Which severely limited her avenues of escape.

Accepting she was stuck for now, Callie turned her search to finding a weapon.

She didn't truly believe there would be something just

lying around that could destroy a powerful necromancer. That only happened in B-rated movies.

But pulling open the cabinets and rifling through the drawers kept her from giving in to the panic that pounded through her.

What good did it do to agonize over whether Duncan had been hurt? Or worse?

Or to dwell on her hideous fate if she didn't manage to escape?

She was rummaging through the last drawer when a faint scent of perfume had her whirling around to discover a woman standing in the middle of the room.

"Holy crap," she muttered.

She hadn't heard a sound. Not the sound of a door opening or closing. Or the tap of four-inch heels on the tiled floor.

Had she just appeared from thin air?

Unnerved, Callie studied the woman. She was beautiful with her long red hair and emerald green eyes. And expensive. The designer silver Dior gown and the Christian Louboutin shoes cost more than Callie's entire wardrobe and no doubt had been purchased at the chichi dress salon on the Plaza.

Then her gaze lifted back to the delicate face and her breath was wrenched from her lungs.

The sketch of the Russian mystic she'd seen in the secret monastery vault had been faded, but there was no mistaking the resemblance to this woman.

Which meant she was Lord Zakhar's accomplice. The witch who was willing to sacrifice children for power.

The female stepped forward, her gaze trained on Callie with a strange fascination.

Not that her fascination was the only thing strange about the woman.

There was something . . . off.

Callie couldn't put her finger on it.

It wasn't anything tangible.

Just a sensation that the woman was blurred around the edges, as if she were slightly out of focus.

It was weird as hell and only intensified Callie's terror.

"Hello, Callie," the female purred, her lips curving in a smile that didn't reach her eyes.

Callie grimaced. It skeeved her out that the woman knew her name.

"Who are you?"

The woman lifted her brows, as if surprised by the question. "Do you really have to ask?"

Callie frowned, wrapping her arms around her shivering body. Why was it suddenly so cold?

"Have we met?"

"Long, long ago. I'm Anya," the woman answered, her voice laced with a faint accent. "Your mother."

Callie stumbled back, painfully smacking a shoulder on a steel cabinet as a shocked horror sliced through her heart.

It was stupid.

She was being held prisoner by a crazed necromancer, she didn't know if Duncan was alive or dead, and the future of the world might very well be going to hell.

Literally.

But in this moment, nothing was more disturbing than the thought that she might actually be the daughter of this . . . this woman.

A witch who would make humans ill just for profit. And sacrifice the innocent for power.

It made her stomach turn.

"No." Callie shook her head in repudiation. "You're lying."

"You aren't blind, Callie. You have to see the resemblance," Anya ruthlessly pressed, taking a step toward Callie to grasp her chin. "The hair. The lips." There was a pause as the emerald eyes inspected Callie's features. "The cheekbones and eyes are your father's."

Callie nearly shrieked at the feel of icy fingers against her skin.

It felt so wrong.

Evil.

"Please, don't touch me," she rasped.

Anya dropped her hand, but she remained standing way too close. "I've thought about you over the years. Wondering what you were like."

With a sense of idiotic relief, Callie pounced on the outrageous claim. "If you were truly my mother then you would know that I was abandoned in a Dumpster," she hissed. "If my mother thought about me at all over the years, it would have been with the belief I was dead."

The woman smiled.

Well, her lips stretched into what Callie assumed was supposed to be a smile.

Christ.

"You think you were intended to die?" she asked.

"That's the usual reason you toss a baby in the trash."

"If I wanted you dead, you would be dead," Anya stated, the sheer lack of apology undermining Callie's certainty that she couldn't possibly be her mother.

Wouldn't the woman be pretending regret if she was trying to convince Callie she was telling the truth?

Oh . . . god.

Her stomach heaved.

"Then why throw me away?"

"By the time you were born Valhalla had been created and the Mave had sent out word to locate all high-blood babies so they could be tested. The Master of Gifts had far too many spies spread around the world to risk drawing attention to ourselves." The woman shrugged. "It became obvious the most convenient place to hide you was at Valhalla."

Convenient?

She'd been tossed into a Dumpster because it was more convenient?

Tears pricked in the back of her eyes.

There were a thousand more important questions that had to be asked. Vital information that might make the difference in halting the necromancer if she managed to escape.

But after a lifetime of claiming she didn't give a shit who her real parents might be, she was suddenly overwhelmed with the need to know more.

"If I was so much trouble wouldn't it have made more sense not to have a child at all?"

Something darkened the emerald eyes. Not precisely an emotion. More of an echo of an emotion.

"You were necessary."

A bad, bad feeling settled in the pit of Callie's stomach.

"For what?"

The woman's lips parted, but before she could speak, the door to the lab was thrust open and Callie was face to face with the necromancer.

Her heart stuttered, missing one beat and then two, before kicking back into gear so it could race out of control.

He was just as she remembered from Leah's mind.

Tall and slender with his silver hair pulled from his bronzed, astonishingly beautiful face and his diamond eyes shimmering with a frigid amusement.

This time, however he was wearing an immaculate black suit instead of the robe. And the power that had been crushing at a distance was off the charts when he was up-close and personal.

He strolled to stand beside Anya, his fingers lifting to stroke down the woman's unnaturally pale face.

"Ah. I see that you've met your mother," he drawled, his gaze never straying from Callie. "How charming."

"You," she breathed.

"Yes . . . me." He continued to stroke Anya's cheek despite

the woman's lack of response. In fact, the minute he'd entered the room Anya had shut down like someone had flicked a switch. She was there, but no one was home. "I suppose I should introduce myself."

"There's no need." Callie shivered, her attention returning to the man who was looking her over with a cold detachment. "You're Lord Zakhar." She managed an edge of disdain. Yay, for her. "Russian aristocrat and psychopath."

"And father."

Her brief spurt of defiance was demolished by the two simple words.

Father.

A hysterical laugh lodged in her throat, threatening to choke her.

Well, hell.

Of course he was her father.

It wasn't bad enough that she'd been abandoned in a Dumpster when she was a baby? Or that Boggs had terrified her with vague threats of her future the day she graduated? Or that her mother was a cold-blooded killer?

Now her father had to be a crazed necromancer who abused the dead and was no doubt plotting some nefarious scheme.

Realizing that she was on the edge of hysteria, Callie grimly tried to concentrate on more important matters. So her parents were raving, homicidal lunatics. She could indulge in a nervous breakdown if she managed to survive.

Sucking in a deep breath, she considered the best way to discover just what her father planned.

With his power, she couldn't force him.

But there was an unmistakable arrogance chiseled into his beautiful features that suggested he would be eager to brag about his cleverness.

"So why the belated family reunion?" she demanded.

"It was time," he murmured, a cold smile touching his

lips as he glanced toward the woman at his side. "Wasn't it, dear Anya?"

The witch remained unmoving, her gaze locked on the far wall.

Callie grimaced. "What's wrong with her?"

The diamond gaze shifted back to Callie. "She recently made the transition to another plane of existence."

Callie's breath tangled in her throat. "Is she—"

"Dead? Yes," he purred. "Magnificent, isn't she?"

Magnificent?

Callie's skin crawled as she took in the woman who claimed to be her mother. She looked pale, and still oddly blurred around the edges, but otherwise . . . perfect.

There was no way to tell she was a corpse.

"You sick bastard," she breathed.

Lord Zakhar thinned his lips, as if annoyed by Callie's response. "You, of all people, should appreciate what I have accomplished," he berated in chilly tones.

She didn't have to fake her revulsion.

Everything about this was wrong.

Perverted.

"And what exactly is it you've accomplished beyond killing my mother?"

"I've opened the gates to the underworld."

She blinked in genuine confusion. "I don't understand."

He ran a tender hand down Anya's long red hair. "Her body is dead, but her soul remains."

"Oh—" Callie's gut twisted with horror. It was one thing to abuse an empty shell of a body, but to imprison a person's soul . . . it was monstrous. "God."

"Yes, I am," he smoothly claimed, a vast, all-consuming emptiness briefly flaring through the diamond eyes. "A creator who will soon have an entire army of followers who are indestructible and utterly loyal."

Her gaze jerked back to her father's arrogant face.

She tried to tell herself that he was just a blowhard.

A megalomaniac who was lost in his delusions of grandeur.

But there was nothing delusional about the dead woman standing obediently next to him. Or the pulsing power that filled the air with a suffocating chill.

She didn't know if he could raise an army, but it was obvious he could control the dead.

She had to find some way to stop him.

"How?"

She hadn't noticed he'd been hiding a hand behind his back until he held it out to reveal a battered golden goblet.

"This."

Okay. That wasn't what she'd expected.

"A cup?"

"A chalice," he corrected in chiding tones. "It was made from the magic of necromancers. True necromancers like us, not the pathetic diviners who cower behind their Sentinels."

On the point of informing him that she wasn't anything like him, Callie was distracted by the small cut on his inner wrist.

"You're bleeding."

"Power demands a sacrifice."

"Blood?"

"It's the source of my life force." He lifted his arm, revealing the bead of blood that appeared from the wound only to disappear. "The chalice opens the doorway, but it's the blood that controls my children."

Callie frowned.

Was the chalice absorbing his blood?

It seemed like the most logical explanation in a world that had gone insane.

"Each . . . child takes a part of your life force?"

"Yes." He lowered his arm, his gaze trained on her pale face. "Which is why you were created, dear Callie."

She flinched.

A part of her wanted to slap her hands over her ears. Yeah, it was childish, but there was only so much a poor girl could take. And she'd had more than her share of shocks over the past half hour, thank you very much.

Unfortunately, a larger part understood there was no more running, no more hiding from her destiny.

This was what Boggs had warned of all those years ago. She knew it in the very depths of her soul.

All she could do was hope that she was strong enough to prevent her father from using her in his quest to . . . Wait, she still didn't know what his actual quest was.

"What do you mean, why I was created?"

"To take my rightful place I must have an army, but unlike my predecessor, I have no intention of becoming a martyr." He glanced toward the small wound on his wrist before his eyes lifted to meet her wary gaze. "It will be your blood that is sacrificed."

It was exactly what she expected, but that didn't halt the black wave of dread that threatened to overwhelm her.

With an effort she forced back her despair, instinctively tucking her hands behind her back. As if that would stop the lunatic.

"And if I don't want to become your sacrifice?" she croaked.

Her father smiled with cold indifference.

"It really isn't optional, my dear."

Duncan paced the inner garden of Valhalla, his seething impatience making it impossible for him to stand still.

He'd awoken two hours ago with his head aching and his shoulder on fire, but ignoring the young healer who'd insisted he remain in bed, he'd gone in search of the Mave.

He had to get back to Kansas City.

And he didn't care who he had to piss off to get there.

Unfortunately the Mave had been impossible to track down and Fane had refused to allow him to leave, claiming they were doing everything possible to locate Callie.

It wasn't that Duncan doubted the Sentinel's word; Fane would lay down his life to rescue Callie. But being forced to pace the floor while Callie was in danger was nothing short of torture.

Trying to pass the time without doing something crazy that would get himself locked in the dungeons, Duncan had called his chief to explain to her why there was a dead body in the parking lot of his apartment building.

And, oh yeah, to warn her that her most trusted coroner was not only dead, but now under the control of Lord Zakhar.

His heart squeezed at the memory of Molinari's shocked grief, but he refused to give in to his own seething emotions. He would mourn Frank once Callie was safe.

Until then . . . he was the enemy.

Pausing long enough to slam his fist into a marble fountain, he abruptly stiffened, but not in pain.

Someone had entered the garden.

Spinning around, he watched as Fane stepped from behind a trimmed hedge, his tattooed face as hard as granite.

"It's about damned time," Duncan growled, stomping his way through the flower beds to stand in front of the Sentinel. "Where's the Mave?"

Folding his arms over his bare chest, Fane met Duncan's fierce scowl with a shuttered expression and said, "She's called together the witches."

"Why?"

"She hopes they can combine their powers to locate Callie."

Duncan narrowed his gaze. He knew jack-squat about witches and their powers. "What are the odds they can?"

"Not good enough." Fane gave a jerk of his head. "Come on."

Duncan followed the man out of the garden and into a narrow hall. Then, halting in front of a seemingly blank wall, he placed his hand flat against a small scanner that was hidden in a potted plant.

The wall slid open with a soft hiss, revealing an elevator that was lined with steel and high-tech security alarms.

"Where are we going?" Duncan muttered. "The Bat-cave?"

Fane shoved him into the elevator and pushed the one button on the control panel. "To meet with the Tagos."

"Goddammit," Duncan snapped, watching the door slide close in frustration. "We've wasted enough time. We should be out searching for Callie."

Fane leaned against the smooth wall as they headed downward at heart-stopping speed. "Where?"

Well, that was the question, wasn't it?

If Duncan had so much as a fucking hint where the necromancer was keeping Callie, there wasn't a force in nature that could keep him at Valhalla. He muttered a curse.

"Don't you have some sort of mystical bond with her?" he challenged his companion.

Fane's stony expression never altered, but there was no mistaking the heat boiling from his massive body. The Sentinel was as close to the edge as Duncan.

"I can sense she's still alive, but there's something cloaking our bond," he admitted in stark tones.

"The necromancer?"

"Yes."

The elevator came to a sudden halt, the door sliding silently open.

"Perfect," Duncan snarled as he stepped out of the small cubical. "Just perfect."

"Your frustration serves no purpose, cop," a deep male voice chided.

Belatedly realizing that he'd stepped directly into a huge office, Duncan came to an abrupt halt.

Yow.

He was accustomed to the cramped police station with outdated equipment and shitty furniture.

This . . . this was a cop's wet dream.

A long, brightly lit room with a state of the art computer system and heavy wooden furniture that was spaced far enough apart to give a person privacy. On the far wall was a line of monitors that hinted at surveillance equipment that could rival the Pentagon.

Hell, he was fairly sure that some of those monitors were connected to government satellites. Maybe the high-bloods had their own satellites.

On another wall there were several doors that were closed and monitored with motion and heat sensors, making Duncan wonder what kind of secrets were lurking just out of sight.

Military grade weapons?

Super heroes?

Elvis?

Shaking his head, Duncan turned his attention to the man standing in the center of the room.

Wolfe, the leader of the Sentinels.

There could be no doubt.

He didn't have the tattoos or bulging muscles of Fane.

He didn't even wear a symbol of his authority.

But there was an unmistakable authority stamped onto the dark, exotic features that were framed by glossy dark hair that was touched with a startling streak of silver. And a predatory power in the lean body that was covered by a pair of black jeans and white tee stretched tight over a broad chest.

His feet were encased in a pair of heavy shit-kickers and spread wide, his hands planted on his hips as he regarded Duncan with a suspicious glare.

Or as Duncan's pa would say "giving him the stink-eye."

Any other time, Duncan might have been intimidated. Wolfe was the kind of guy who could daunt anyone. But right now he was consumed by his fear for Callie and in no mood for a pissing match.

"You think I should be satisfied to sit around here with my thumb stuck up my ass?" he rasped, giving his own version of the stink-eye.

"Mind your manners, cop, or you'll have something besides your thumb stuck up your ass," a new voice growled.

Hissing in shock, Duncan turned his head to watch two men step out of the shadows. Christ. He would have sworn on his favorite Sig Sauer that they hadn't been there a second ago.

So did they use a hidden entrance?

Or could they cloak themselves?

Smiling at his shock, the speaker halted next to Wolfe, looking every inch as dangerous as his Tagos.

Oh, he made a pretense of being civilized. He had his dark hair that was threaded with hints of autumn fire cut short and his lean body was attired in a blue silk shirt and black chinos.

His lean face was perfectly constructed with a wide brow and narrow nose. And while he was too masculine to be traditionally handsome, he had the sort of "tall, dark, and broody" looks that made women swoon.

His partner, on the other hand, had the beauty of an angel.

His features were delicate with a mop of light brown hair with honey highlights. And his eyes . . . in the bright light they shimmered a perfect gold.

No doubt he liked being dismissed as a lightweight, but Duncan didn't miss the muscles honed to lean perfection beneath his casual T-shirt and faded jeans, and the ruthless willingness to kill that simmered deep in the gold eyes.

Hunter Sentinels.

Duncan resisted the urge to grab his gun as the angel-looking Sentinel gave a snort.

"I'd listen to him, cop," he warned. "That size sixteen boot does some damage."

Duncan shifted until he could glance toward Fane, who'd halted just behind him. "Friends of yours?"

Fane pointed toward the silk and chino man. "Niko." His finger turned toward the angel. "Arel." He continued on to the dark-haired bad-ass. "And Wolfe." The finger shifted toward Duncan. "This is O'Conner."

Niko narrowed his gaze, his expression one of suspicion. "I thought he was human."

Wolfe smiled without humor. "He's been fooling a lot of people."

Duncan made a sound of disgust. How the hell had he ever thought his ability to see auras was a secret? Every Sentinel in the damned world could tell he wasn't human.

"Is this meeting about Callie or just to bust my balls?" he snapped.

"This meeting is for Sentinels," Wolfe answered, his words slow and deliberate, "You've been allowed to sit in because Fane is convinced of your loyalty to Callie."

"If you're asking if I'll do anything to rescue her, the answer is yes."

"Anything?" Wolfe prodded.

Duncan scowled. "What do you want from me?"

The man studied him for a long minute, his gaze seeming to strip Duncan to his soul. And maybe he could. Sentinels were proving to have a surprising range of talents.

"You can be a human cop or you can be a Sentinel," Wolfe finally said. "You can't be both."

Ah.

Duncan had known the choice was coming.

From the minute he'd committed himself to a relationship with Callie it had been obvious that they couldn't exist in two different worlds.

Hell, he didn't *want* to exist in different worlds.

Now he didn't hesitate.

"Then I'm a Sentinel," he said, astonished at how *right* the words felt. As if a missing puzzle piece deep inside him had just fallen into place. Disturbed by the sensation, he gave a strained laugh. "I don't have to get tattooed, do I?"

Fane rolled his eyes. "You aren't special enough to get tattooed."

"Don't worry. There'll be an initiation," Arel promised. "Later."

Duncan grimaced. The mind boggled at what these men might consider an initiation. "Great."

Wolfe glanced toward Fane. "Tell me what you learned in Florida."

Duncan abruptly recalled that Fane had spent the previous night searching for information on the coin.

"It's not good," the guardian admitted. "The monk warned me that we had to keep the necromancer from opening the pathway to the underworld."

Duncan recalled Hektor's warning. Hadn't he said something about a pathway to the underworld?

"And if we're too late?" Wolfe asked.

"Only an obscure ritual will close it again."

"Did he happen to know the obscure ritual?"

"No."

Wolfe swore beneath his breath. "Of course not."

Fane didn't look any happier than his leader, but with a shrug he nodded toward the wall of monitors. "What have you done here?"

"I have hunters trying to find Callie's scent and the techs

are working on tracing her phone," Wolfe said. "I've also contacted the monasteries and halted all travel."

Without warning Fane turned his attention to Duncan. "Cop?"

Three pairs of eyes were trained on him, and Duncan sensed it was his first test.

Unconsciously he squared his shoulders, speaking directly to Wolfe. "I spoke with the chief and she has an APB out on Frank," he said, not surprised when the big, tough Sentinels shuddered. No one wanted to think about how many corpses might be wandering the streets of Kansas City. "They're also tracing the GPS on his car."

"Anything?" Wolfe asked.

Duncan shook his head. "Not yet. His car was parked at his house, but he wasn't . . ." Duncan forgot what he was going to say as he sucked in a sharp breath. "Oh, shit."

Fane stepped directly in front of him, the heat of his body a tangible force. "What?"

"Frank was driving a silver car."

"So?"

"He doesn't have a silver car," Duncan muttered, rubbing the back of his neck as he shifted through the information he'd managed to gather over the past few days. "The dress lady said the woman arrived in a silver car. And there was a silver car spotted on Calso's street just before his murder. It has to belong to the necro."

Fane scowled. "Is that supposed to make sense?"

Duncan glanced toward Wolfe, a near painful urgency pounding through his veins.

"Can your techs tap into government databases?"

The Tagos was on instant guard, his dark eyes narrowing in warning. "Why?"

Duncan waved an impatient hand. "I'm not going to tell

anyone about any . . . supplementary methods you have to protect high-bloods."

Wolfe hesitated before giving a nod. "Fine. What do you want?"

"I need to trace a license plate."

Fane made a sound of surprise. "You got the number?"

Duncan unconsciously touched the bandage that covered his healing wound on his temple. "Just the last three as I flew by," he said dryly. "But it might be enough to get a hit."

Wolfe was already spinning to head toward a distant door. "This way."

Chapter Twenty-Six

It was the sort of mansion that made Duncan shake his head in disgust.

Who needed a faux castle with twelve bedrooms, gold-plated toilets, and a helicopter pad? Hell, all that was missing was the drawbridge.

Either a man with a bloated ego, or one who had the need to hide in plain sight.

It was amazing how many top drug lords lived behind the high fences of gated communities, mixing with the neighbors as if he was just another tax-paying citizen.

Tonight, however, Duncan didn't give a shit about the Olympic-sized pool or the outdoor bar that was bigger than his apartment. His only interest was standing poised at the narrow back gate as they waited for Niko to return from his scouting of the grounds.

"Cop—"

Duncan turned his head to glare at Wolfe, who stood with the silent Fane and Arel just a few feet away.

"Don't even start," he warned in low, fierce tones. "I'm going in."

The Tagos arched a brow. "Your chief isn't going to be happy if she finds out you did an illegal B and E."

Duncan snorted. "I've done a lot of things that wouldn't make my chief happy if she knew."

"There might be hope for him yet," Arel murmured with a cocky smile.

They all stiffened as there was a soft rush of air as Niko leaped over the high fence, landing with a silence that was terrifying.

Duncan had heard all the stories about Sentinels.

They were faster, stronger, with superior senses. And he'd even known he possessed a few of the qualities, even if he'd never wanted to admit it.

But to actually see them in action . . .

He grimaced. The humans would be far less complacent if they truly knew the sheer extent of the high-bloods' powers. Which was no doubt why the Sentinels had gone to such trouble to remain hidden in a shroud of mystery.

Straightening, Niko slid through the shadows to stand directly before them.

"There's a muting spell that makes it impossible to sense what's inside."

Fane was already moving. "I'll do a sweep."

"I'm coming with you," Duncan announced, the biting urgency thundering through him making him twitchy as hell.

"Hold on, Rambo." Wolfe grabbed his arm. "Fane's the only one who can trigger the spells without killing us all."

Duncan was forced to watch as Fane smoothly vaulted over the fence and disappeared.

He wanted to argue. Hell, he wanted to pull his gun and start shooting things. Beginning with the man holding him in a ruthless grip.

But he wasn't completely insane.

Not yet.

He didn't possess Fane's protective tattoos or his magical

ability to sense and destroy spells. He'd only be a liability if he went charging in like a bull in a china cabinet.

"Shit," he muttered in frustration.

Wolfe released his arm, but his lean face remained hard with an undefinable emotion. "Callie is special to all of us."

Duncan scowled at the Tagos. "Do you have a point?"

"Just listen."

Duncan's scowl deepened. Arrogant bastard. Unfortunately, he was an arrogant bastard that Callie needed if they were going to rescue her.

"I'm listening," he managed between gritted teeth.

"When Callie was brought to Valhalla she was just a tiny scrap of a thing with eyes like jewels and a smile that could melt the hardest heart," Wolfe said, a hint of affection softening the cruel curve of his mouth. "There wasn't one of us who didn't fall under her spell."

Duncan could easily picture Callie as a tiny baby, slaying the hearts of the most cynical warriors. Who wouldn't look into those magnificent eyes and fall in love?

"I'm not surprised."

"So you understand that we'll lay down our lives to keep her from being hurt."

A command, not a question.

Duncan narrowed his eyes. "We're not discussing the necromancer, are we?"

"I'll accept your help in rescuing Callie. Hell, I'd accept the help of Satan if I thought it was necessary," Wolfe said. "But trust is earned when it comes to Callie's fragile heart."

Duncan took a step forward, his hands clenched at his side.

Since becoming a cop he'd learned not to pick a fight he couldn't win. But this was too important to back down.

The Sentinels considered Callie theirs to protect. They weren't going to give him a place at her side.

He had to claim the right.

"I appreciate your concern, but Callie's trust is all that matters to me," he said, his expression warning he wasn't looking for a debate on the issue. "I intend to devote my life to making her happy. With or without your approval."

Arel snorted. "Either he's a man with a death wish or a man in love."

Duncan never allowed his gaze to waver from Wolfe's lean face. You never took your eye off a predator.

Then the tension was shattered by a low whistle near the gate.

"That's Fane," Wolfe said, rapidly taking charge as he moved to shove open the gate, gesturing for the auburn-haired hunter to go first.

Duncan tried to charge forward, only to be halted once again by Wolfe's hand grasping his upper arm.

The Tagos ignored Duncan's string of curses as he watched his fellow Sentinel trot across the manicured yard, heading toward the front of the house, only to circle toward the back.

At last the man came to a halt, tilting back his head as if he was sniffing the air.

"Niko?" Wolfe prompted.

"I have her trail," the man announced, heading toward the back terrace.

Wolfe released his grip and Duncan was in swift pursuit of Niko as he climbed the shallow steps and entered the house through a back door. Duncan didn't know if it had been locked or not, and he didn't care.

He wasn't here as a cop. He was here as a man desperate to find the woman he loved.

Hold on, Callie. Hold on . . . he silently urged.

They moved through a large kitchen, Niko in the lead followed by Duncan and then Wolfe. Fane and Arel brought up the rear, both turned to the side to make sure there were no surprises lurking in the dark.

Niko led them out of the kitchen and down a short hallway, halting when they came to a dead end.

What the hell?

Duncan frowned as Wolfe stepped past him, lifting his leg to smash his massive foot through the paneling.

Ah. A secret doorway.

Of course.

Every wicked villain had one, didn't he?

And now that Duncan took the time to think about it, he could actually sense the emptiness that marked the opening behind the paneling. Perhaps with training he could . . .

He gave a shake of his head at his inane thoughts, ducking as the splintered wood flew through the air.

Four more kicks and Wolfe had the hole large enough for Niko to squeeze through. Wolfe was next, but as Duncan moved to follow, he heard Fane give a low growl.

"Someone's here."

Duncan turned back, pulling his gun and clicking off the safety.

"The necro?"

"No."

A chill of warning inched down Duncan's spine as he walked to stand at Fane's side. For a minute he couldn't see a damned thing in the darkness. Then a shadow shifted forward, stepping into a small shaft of moonlight.

"Frank," Duncan breathed, more resigned than shocked. "I'll distract him. Keep looking for Callie."

Fane shifted to stand directly in front of him. "Cop."

"What?"

The tattooed face was stark with the brutal strain of knowing Callie was in danger.

"He's not your friend anymore."

Duncan grimaced, ignoring the ache in the center of his chest.

Frank was dead.

This . . . thing that was approaching was a creation of the same necromancer that had stolen the woman he loved.

He wouldn't hesitate to send it to the grave. Always assuming he could figure out how.

"I know." He jerked his head toward the opening in the wall. "Hurry."

Obviously reading the grim determination etched on his face, the Sentinel gave a sharp nod and slipped past Duncan.

Alone with his onetime friend, Duncan shifted to make sure he had plenty of room to fight.

And there was going to be a fight.

No doubt about that.

The only question was whether he was going to survive.

Halting a few feet from Duncan, the zombie regarded him with a blank expression, although there was nothing blank about the dark eyes.

They were filled with . . . awareness.

Duncan shuddered, his fingers tightening on the gun. It was pure instinct. He already knew it was a waste of bullets to shoot the bastard.

Besides, for now all he cared about was distracting Frank long enough for the Sentinels to find Callie and kill the necromancer.

"Hey, amigo," he said, a queasy sensation joining the stark fear in the pit of his stomach. Logically he understood this wasn't Frank. But shit . . . he looked like the man who'd taken him under his wing when he left the academy. The one who'd taught him to filet a catfish. And the one who'd taken him to a strip joint to get blotto the night his divorce was finalized. "Do you remember me?"

The creature smiled. "O'Conner."

Duncan flinched. Christ. Did the thing truly remember him?

"Yeah, that's right." He forced himself to keep talking. If he stopped to think, he would be overwhelmed by the sheer horror of the situation. "I'm looking for my friend Callie. Have you seen her?"

"She's gone."

Duncan sucked in a sharp breath. Gone? Could it be true?

He had no idea if Frank was lucid enough to know what was going on around him.

"Where did she go?"

"With the master."

Duncan growled at the mention of the necromancer, but he kept his attention focused on Callie.

"Okay, I got that she's with the . . . master." He forced the word past his lips. "But where did they go?"

Frank hesitated, as if it took a minute to process the question.

Was he mentally connected with Lord Zakhar?

Not that it mattered.

The necromancer had to know he was being hunted by every Sentinel in Valhalla.

At last Frank spoke. "To raise an army."

"An army?" Of zombies? Duncan shoved aside the horrifying thought. Nothing mattered but finding Callie. "In Kansas City?"

"No."

"Somewhere close by?"

A ripple of emotion sluggishly flowed over Frank's face. Anger. Frustration. Regret?

"You will soon discover."

A vague answer that told Duncan nothing. Did he mean that he didn't know? Or had he been commanded not to say?

Fine. He was trained in interrogation. If you couldn't get the answer you wanted from a direct approach, you came at it from another angle.

"How can Callie raise an army?"

Frank smiled and Duncan shuddered. It was creepy as hell.

"She is to be the sacrifice."

Sacrifice?

Duncan snapped.

Launching forward, he grabbed the front of his onetime friend's polo shirt, shoving the barrel of his gun beneath his chin.

"You bastard. Tell me where she is," he shouted.

Frank blinked, ignoring the gun.

Or maybe he just didn't care.

Dead was dead, after all.

Then, without warning, he tilted back his dark head to release a shrill burst of laughter.

Duncan made a sound of horror.

If the smile was creepy, his laughter was downright hair-raising.

"Christ," he muttered. "Why are you laughing?"

"I've been waiting for you, O'Conner," Frank explained.

"Why?"

"To kill you."

His disturbing smile remained intact even as he shoved his hands against Duncan's chest and sent him flying against the wall with enough force to rattle his teeth.

Surging back to his feet, Duncan squeezed off two shots, hitting Frank directly between the eyes. The zombie never halted as he moved forward, the bullet holes closing with magical ease.

Holy . . . shit.

Duncan shoved his gun back in his holster. No sense in wasting bullets. Not when there might be other enemies lurking in the dark. Enemies that might actually die from a gun-shot wound.

Besides, he was pissed-off, frustrated, and overwhelmed with terror for Callie.

A good old-fashioned beat down was just what he needed.

Waiting for Frank to take another step forward, Duncan

swung his fist directly at the man's chin, connecting with a satisfying crunch of bone.

Frank stumbled back, but swiftly recovering his balance, he resumed his stoic march toward Duncan.

Reaching behind him, Duncan grabbed a vase off a nearby table, tossing it at the zombie at the same time he kicked out with his foot.

The vase shattered against Frank's face and his kick caught him in the middle of his stomach. But once again he barely recoiled before he took a last step to stand directly before Duncan.

And then the fun began.

Managing to dodge the first punch, Duncan couldn't avoid the uppercut that banged his head against the wall and knocked him loopy. Next came the kick to the knee that made him stumble to the side, just in time to move in the path of the right hook.

Thankfully Duncan had spent his childhood being tortured by his older siblings, which meant he could not only take a beating, but could still get in a few good punches.

They might not do any good, but dammit, if he was going down, he was going down swinging.

He didn't know how long he played the punching bag for his old friend, but he was seeing double when he heard Fane's voice over the ringing in his ears.

"Cop."

A vicious blow to his stomach doubled him over, but jerking up, he managed to clip Frank on the chin with the top of his head.

Frank lost his footing and Duncan took the opportunity to glance over his shoulder at the tattooed warrior who shoved his head through the hole in the wall.

"Callie?" he demanded of the Sentinel.

Fane gave a bleak shake of his head. "Gone."

"Goddammit."

The word had barely left his lips when Frank was on his feet and moving back in for the kill.

The bastard was nothing if not persistent.

Duncan braced for another beating, too consumed with his rage at the knowledge they'd wasted hours on a wild goose chase to give a shit.

But just as Frank was close enough to continue the fight, three shadows appeared from behind him to drive him to the ground.

Duncan leaped out of the path of Wolfe as he went flying past, hitting the same wall that Duncan had smashed into earlier.

"We have to get him downstairs," the Tagos muttered, jumping to his feet as he absently wiped the blood from his bottom lip.

Duncan frowned, watching in horror as Frank pinned Arel to the floor, impervious to Niko's vicious kicks to his head.

"Why?"

"There's a panic room we can lock him in."

Duncan shuddered. "Do you think it will hold him?"

"Hell, I don't know," the Sentinel muttered. "But it will give us a few hours to come up with a better plan."

Duncan grimaced.

A better plan . . .

Yep, that about summed it up.

Callie had heard horror stories over the years of abandoned children who'd gone in search of their birth parents.

She knew one witch who had approached her mother only to have the hysterical woman pull out a gun and shoot her in the leg. Another psychic learned he'd been removed from the home by the police when it was discovered that his father was using him to read the minds of ATM customers to discover their PIN numbers.

Still, she was fairly certain that she took first prize in the Worse-Parents-Ever contest.

Seated in the back of the silver car, she kept her gaze firmly on the passing scenery. It didn't matter she couldn't see a damn thing in the darkness. Anything was better than having to look at her psychopathic father seated next to her in the backseat of the car.

Or worse, catching sight of her dead mother, who was driving the car with unnerving skill.

She didn't know how far they'd driven. It seemed like they'd been in the car for days, although she knew it couldn't have been more than a couple of hours.

There was a ripple in the chilled air as Lord Zakhar shifted on the seat. Callie grimaced. There was a temptation to stick her head in the sand and pretend they weren't speeding toward some gruesome destiny.

If she couldn't change the future, then why know the gory details before she had to?

But while cowardice seemed the preferable option, she couldn't ignore the stern voice in the back of her head that reminded her that she had a duty.

She might not know what had happened to Duncan or Fane or any of her friends, but she grimly held on to the belief that they were unharmed and searching for her.

If they managed to contact her, she needed to be able to warn them what her crazy relatives were plotting.

And how they could be stopped.

"Are you ever going to tell me where we're going?" She forced the question past her stiff lips, her gaze remaining trained on the window.

"And spoil the surprise?" her father taunted.

Callie rolled her eyes. "I thought evil geniuses liked to boast about their clever plots."

"It's true I am a genius, but I refute the claim that I'm evil."

She jerked at the soft denial. "Are you kidding me?"

"Most people admire ambition," he purred.

"Ambition doesn't include killing your family or sacrificing your child," she said with blatant revulsion. "And it certainly doesn't include defiling the dead to make them your personal slaves."

"I see you inherited your mother's tendency for melodrama." His heavy sigh drifted through the air. "Unfortunate."

Her dead mother who was currently playing chauffeur?

She squashed the hysterical urge to laugh.

"Are you going to tell me where we're going?"

There was a tense pause before she heard the sound of his silk robe brushing the fabric of his seat, as if he were shrugging.

"You should be happy. I'm taking you home."

She jerked her head around to meet his smug expression. "Home?"

"Valhalla."

The breath was wrenched from her lungs. "Why?"

He pretended to be surprised by her question. "I would think that was obvious. To lead the world I'll need the power of the high-bloods."

Valhalla.

Dammit. He was right. She should have known this was their destination. A man with Lord Zakhar's bloated ego wouldn't be satisfied starting his coup anywhere but at the top.

"You can't believe they'll go along with your crazy plan?"

"Not without a proper incentive." His long fingers stroked the golden chalice he held in his lap. "Which is where you come in, my dear."

Callie battled back the bile that threatened to choke her.

The people she loved most were at Valhalla. To think for even a second that she could be a part in their destruction was sickening.

Still, she wasn't about to let her father see the level of her desperation.

It was a weakness he'd use against her.

"You expect me to convince them?" she managed to mock.

"Not you." His diamond eyes glowed with an eerie light. "The army that will be called by your blood."

She forced a disdainful smile to her lips. "Oh yes. An army of the dead."

"Yes." He frowned, as if disturbed by her seeming lack of concern.

Good. Maybe if she could keep him off guard she could find a way to escape.

"Where is this dead army going to come from?" she taunted. "Do you have the corpses stashed in the trunk?"

The diamond eyes glittered with a cold satisfaction. "The previous Mave was kind enough to insist that all high-bloods be buried in a communal crypt," he murmured. "A dozen indestructible Sentinels should offer sufficient destruction to force Valhalla to surrender, don't you think, my dear?"

Callie was shaken out of her momentary pretense of indifference.

By law all high-bloods were sent to Valhalla grounds to be buried. Not only to ensure that their bodies were given proper respect, but to prevent humans from sending the corpses to their scientists to be tested like lab rats.

And the Sentinels were given special burial crypts near the distant lake to honor them for their service. Which meant that they were outside the protective dome that covered Valhalla.

"You . . . bastard," she breathed.

He waved aside her insult. "You're becoming repetitive."

Callie sucked in a deep, steadying breath. *Anger was a waste of energy*, she sternly reminded herself.

"You can't believe this will work," she hissed.

Lord Zakhar regarded her with frigid arrogance. "Of course it will."

She shook her head. He was so . . . confident. It was damned unnerving.

"The high-bloods will never follow you."

"Then they'll be destroyed."

Callie grimaced at his aloof dismissal. Like genocide was just an everyday occurrence.

"And what about me?"

"What about you?"

"Will I die?"

"Once I have taken my place as ruler," he said with a shrug.

She snorted. Yeah, she really hit the lottery in the father sweepstakes.

"And then what will happen to your army?"

"Without your blood they'll no longer be under my control," he admitted, a hint of frustration rippling over his startlingly beautiful face before it was quickly banished. "A pity, but fortunately I can produce as many children as necessary in the future if I need new armies. Highly doubtful, of course. Once the world has tasted my power they'll be eager to bow before me."

Callie's heart missed a beat. A horde of magical, indestructible Sentinels out of control?

God Almighty.

"When you say they'll be out of your control—"

"They'll destroy anything that crosses their path," he helpfully supplied.

Why the coldhearted, amoral son of a bitch.

She clenched her hands into fists of frustrated rage. "You'll be stopped."

He arched a brow, his smile condescending. "No, my dear, I won't."

"How can you be so sure?"

"My destiny has been foreseen." His smile widened as Anya pulled the car onto the road that led to the lake. "Nothing can stop me now."

Chapter Twenty-Seven

Duncan was distantly aware of the muted bustle that filled the Sentinel office hidden in the bowels of Valhalla.

He was too much a cop not to notice the herd of techies who were tapping on their laptops in a frantic attempt to track Callie's cell phone. Or the warriors who lined the long table where Wolfe was sharing the latest information from his trackers who continued to scour the streets of Kansas City.

There were more Sentinels standing in front of the bank of monitors, occasionally punching in new coordinates to change the satellite angles or barking orders in their cell phones to direct the trackers.

But while he tactically approved of the grim, perfectly coordinated efforts to find Callie, he wasn't a cop tonight.

He was a man who had failed to protect the woman who had become the most important person in his world.

Pacing from one end of the room to the other, he absently rubbed his chest. At some point, Wolfe had halted him long enough to take away his gun. No doubt a wise decision considering Duncan was hovering on the edge of sanity. It wouldn't take much for him to snap.

Reaching the end of the room, he turned to continue his

mindless stride when he discovered his path was being blocked by a tattooed behemoth.

"You look like shit, cop," Fane informed him, his own face haggard with strain.

Duncan flipped him off. "Go to hell."

"Already there." Fane shoved a glass into Duncan's hand. "Drink."

Duncan lifted the glass to cautiously sniff the amber liquid. "What is it?"

"Relax," Fane commanded, folding his arms over his massive chest. "If I decide to kill you I'll rip out your heart, not ruin my finest aged whiskey with poison."

Duncan snorted. "Comforting."

The warrior waited for Duncan to toss the fiery whiskey down his throat before taking the empty glass and setting it on a nearby desk.

"We're all worried," he at last growled.

Duncan grimaced. "She's hurt."

"How do you know?"

"I feel it." He pressed a hand to his aching heart. "Here."

Fane stilled, his dark eyes flaring with fury.

Duncan had half expected the Sentinel to laugh. Or at least to tell him he was being a moron.

A man might be afraid for his lover. He could be worried that she was harmed. But he couldn't actually *feel* when she was hurting.

Could he?

Judging by Fane's reaction, he could.

Without warning a bone-deep relief surged through him.

Long ago, he might have stubbornly denied the mystic connection to Callie. He was magnificently skilled in denying what he didn't want to accept.

Now he readily clung to that fragile connection. She was hurt, but she was alive.

That's all that mattered.

Concentrating on the strange sensations that clenched at his heart, Duncan was caught off guard when the first alarm set off a shrill warning.

Instinctively reaching for his missing gun, he braced for an attack as overhead lights began to flash and the room exploded in a flurry of motion.

"Fuck," Fane muttered as he hurried toward the monitors along with the other Sentinels.

Duncan detoured to snatch his gun off the table before joining the huddle in front of the monitors.

"What's going on?"

It was Wolfe who answered. "The outside perimeter just went down."

Duncan frowned. Valhalla's security system was the stuff of legends. There wasn't a norm in the entire world who didn't realize it was impossible to try and breach the magical barriers.

Even the cops understood that their jurisdiction ended at the edge of the high-bloods' property. Anyone suicidal enough to stray beyond that point . . . well, they were on their own.

"The necro?" he demanded.

"It has to be," Fane seethed. "No one else would have the cojones."

Wolfe growled deep in his throat. "We should have suspected Valhalla was his ultimate goal. The arrogant bastard wouldn't settle for anything less."

True.

Not that Duncan gave a shit what brought him to Valhalla. If he was here, then Callie couldn't be far.

"Can you locate them?"

"I'm about to find out." Wolfe reached to press the edge of the monitor, switching it from camera to camera.

The images flickered so swiftly that Duncan couldn't

make out more than dark shadows and a silver shimmer he assumed was the magical dome that surrounded Valhalla.

Could the Sentinels see through the darkness?

His silent question was answered when Fane gave a low growl.

"Wolfe."

Freezing the image, Wolfe frowned as Fane pointed to several large figures standing at the edge of the dome.

"There."

What the hell?

Duncan leaned forward, struggling to make out more than fuzzy outlines.

He could see that they were large. Maybe as large as Fane and Wolfe. And each of them carried a different weapon. Swords, bows and arrows, even clubs with long spikes that looked like something out of a Renaissance fair.

Beyond that was hard to say.

To his eyes they seemed to be shrouded in fabric from head to toe, disguising their faces and any clothing that might have given a hint to their identity. Although . . . he leaned closer, studying the hands that were only faintly visible.

Tattoos.

He sucked in a sharp breath at the same time that Wolfe cursed.

"Sentinels?" the Tagos snarled. "Impossible."

"Obviously not impossible," Duncan muttered, desperately searching the monitors for any sign of Callie. "Why would they join with the necromancer?"

"They wouldn't," Wolfe said, his voice flat with denial. "Not if they're any of mine."

"Do you recognize any of them?" Fane demanded.

"Not without seeing their faces." Wolfe studied the monitor, his savage fury boiling through the air with enough heat to make Duncan sweat. "What are they wearing?"

A good question. They looked like shrouds to Duncan . . .

He made a choked sound, struck by a sudden suspicion. "I need to see them."

Wolfe frowned. "A different camera angle?"

"No," he rasped. "I need to physically see them."

Without hesitation, Wolfe nodded.

There were no annoying questions. No demands for explanations.

Just acceptance that Duncan was a part of the team and that he needed information to help them defeat the enemy.

And this was why hardened soldiers offered their complete loyalty to the Tagos. Trust was a two-way street. A truth too many leaders never learned.

"Niko, stay on coms," Wolfe commanded as he led the way to one of the back doors. "Arel, find the Mave." He pointed toward two guardian Sentinels who were nearly hidden beneath the layers of guns, swords, and . . . Holy shit, was that a rocket launcher? "You two, come with me."

They left the office and entered a cement tunnel that angled upward, Wolfe taking the lead with Duncan and Fane behind him with the arsenal twins bringing up the rear.

Duncan didn't have to ask where they were going.

This was clearly an emergency exit. One that was not only equipped with steel doors every ten feet that could block off pursuers or protect against bomb blasts, but unlike the elevators it didn't depend on electricity.

They moved in silence, each of them on high-alert as they headed upward.

Who the hell knew what might be hiding ahead?

Crazed necromancers. Demented witches.

Flesh-eating zombies.

Duncan sensed when they reached the surface, but Wolfe opened a door that led to a steep flight of stairs. Puzzled, Duncan climbed behind the Tagos, sensing they were several feet in the air.

It wasn't until they stepped onto a narrow ledge that he

realized they were standing on a watchtower that offered a perfect panorama of the perimeter. And more importantly, an unimpeded view of the ten—no wait, twelve—warriors who were chanting in low, rough voices as they laid their hands upon an invisible barrier.

"Well, cop?" Wolfe prompted in a low voice pitched to keep it from carrying on the light breeze. "What are you looking for?"

Duncan shifted to stand near the low stone wall that surrounded the ledge, thankful for the full moon that drenched the landscape in a silver light. Unlike his companions, he didn't have the ability to see in the dark.

"Auras," he said.

Wolfe and Fane moved to stand at his side while the other two Sentinels paced to the other side of the narrow ledge. Nothing would be allowed to sneak up from behind.

"Why?" Fane asked.

His lips twisted at the brutal pain that sliced through his heart, his gaze trained on the distant intruders.

"It was Callie who realized the dead wouldn't have auras."

"Shit," Fane breathed softly.

Duncan pointed toward the inner perimeter, cold dread lying heavy in his stomach. "Those men are like Frank."

Wolfe scowled. "Explain."

"A dead body has no aura. No . . . spark of life," he muttered, shuddering as he studied the men who moved with the same grace they must have possessed when they were alive. It was just wrong. On so many levels. "But these are surrounded by a darkness."

Fane made a tortured sound deep in his throat. "He's trapped their souls."

Duncan shuddered again. Poor Frank. Was he aware that he was being abused by the necromancer? It had to be torture to be trapped in his own body while it was being controlled by a psychotic megalomaniac.

"The son of a bitch," he rasped.

Wolfe gripped the top of the wall, the granite crumbling beneath his fingers. "A clever son of a bitch," he snarled, studying the warriors with a bleak expression.

Duncan glanced toward the Tagos. "Why do you say that?"

"Bokors are empty shells; these"—Wolfe struggled for a suitable label—"creatures have their former powers."

"Fuck," Fane swore. "That's why he chose guardian Sentinels."

Duncan wasn't as quick to follow. "Why?"

Wolfe grimaced. "They're the only ones capable of destroying the layers of magic that protect Valhalla."

Oh . . . shit.

There was a faint prickle of power before the tall, dark-haired Mave stepped onto the ledge, standing proud and strong as she met Wolfe's fierce gaze.

A dangerous warrior in her own right, Duncan inanely realized.

"Tell me what you need," she commanded, her pale face calm, although her dark hair was escaping from the once neat bun and there were shadows beneath her magnificent eyes.

In the moonlight her emerald birthmark seemed to shimmer even brighter than usual.

"I'll need the witches," he answered, his voice decisive. "If nothing else, they can slow down the warriors with new barriers."

The Mave nodded. "What about the diviners?"

"Shit." Wolfe scowled, clearly just realizing the potential disaster of the necromancer getting his hands on the diviners. They might not have the power of Callie, but they still had a connection to the dead. Who knew what he might be able to do with them. "Until we discover if they can be controlled by the necromancer we need to get them far away. Use the helicopters."

"The psychics?"

Wolfe considered a minute before shaking his head. "They might as well leave through the tunnels along with any humans. The healers—"

"Won't go," the Mave interrupted, her gaze straying toward the dead Sentinels who had managed to break through yet another layer of magic. "Not if they think there will be injuries."

Wolfe didn't argue. Instead he unfastened the AK-47 he'd strapped to his back on his way through the tunnel.

"I'll let you sort out the others," he said, no doubt referring to the numerous high-bloods who didn't fall into specific groups. Mutations didn't always follow a pattern. "You need to evacuate as many as possible."

There was a strange pause as the two powerful leaders exchanged a silent, emotion-charged glance that made Duncan glance away in embarrassment.

What the hell was going on between the two of them?

He heard the Mave speak softly to her Tagos. "Be careful."

"You as well," Wolfe answered, his voice thick.

Then, the tension snapped and with a brisk step the Mave was returning down the steep steps and Wolfe was barking into the com in his ear.

"Niko, take ten of your best trackers and start patrolling the perimeter. Send the rest to me."

"Weapons?" Niko's voice floated through the air.

Wolfe cast a grim glance toward the approaching Sentinels.

"Everything we have."

Callie knelt on the hard ground, her head lowered.

It wasn't a gesture of respect to the man who towered over her, his bronzed features set in an expression of icy anticipation.

Hell, no.

She'd swallow broken glass before she'd kneel before her psycho dad.

But after arriving at the entrance to the underground crypts, the necromancer hadn't wasted any time in dragging her from the car and producing a dagger to slice long wounds the length of her inner forearms.

The cuts hadn't been that deep, but they'd stung like a bitch. Then, before she could catch her breath, the bastard had called on some dark power that had slammed through Callie with the force of a freight train.

Black flecks had danced in front of her eyes as the frigid energy crashed through her, threatening to suck her down into some murky, endless hell. Desperately she'd fought against the relentless waves, knowing that one slip and she'd be consumed by the darkness.

She had no idea how long the battle lasted.

It could have been seconds or hours, but when her head cleared she'd found herself on her knees with the golden goblet perched against her thigh.

Even worse, she could feel a strange tug deep inside her. As if she were connected to something—or rather many things—just beyond her sight.

The sensations only intensified as a dozen warriors slowly stepped from the crypts, still wrapped in their funeral shrouds with their weapons in hand.

Callie cried out in horror, but her strength was being drained with every drip of blood that slid down her arms and vanished into the goblet. There was nothing she could do as they silently moved past her, the once proud warriors now under the compulsion of Lord Zakhar.

"So glorious," her father murmured, watching in pride as his monsters dismantled the layers of magic that protected her home.

"They were glorious when they were alive," she tried to

snarl, startled when her voice came out in a shaky whisper.
The warriors were sucking her life force at an alarming rate.
"They should be respected and honored for their service to
their people, not treated as disposable minions."

He flicked an indifferent glance in her direction. "So passionate, but my dear Callie, you are all disposable minions
to me."

Nice.

She grimaced, squashing her flare of revulsion toward the
man who'd spawned her.

Hate wasn't a productive emotion.

She needed resolve. Purpose. Stubborn, pigheaded obstinacy.

She had the last three in spades.

Sucking in a deep breath, she turned her attention inward,
concentrating on the mystical bond that ran from her father
through her and onto the warriors. At the same time, she
began to babble. She didn't know if the necromancer could
sense her trying to destroy the bond, but it seemed smart to
try and keep him distracted.

Just in case.

"Do you imagine that even if you take Valhalla you'll be
satisfied?" she asked, her brow furrowed as she opened herself to the icy power that pulsed through her.

She grimaced. Christ. It was like an evil umbilical cord
that connected them all together.

Her father arched a puzzled brow. "Of course I will not be
satisfied," he said, his chilling calm assuring her that he
didn't yet sense her attempt to destroy his connection to the
warriors. "I intend to rule the world."

Well of course he did.

"And then what?" she prompted, inwardly judging the
amount of life she was losing against the progress of the
warriors.

Even as she watched the second barrier went down.

God dammit.

Too fast.

There was only one more layer before they would have a direct shot at Valhalla.

And then . . .

She shook her head. She couldn't bear the thought.

"Then my destiny will be fulfilled," Lord Zakhar was saying, a smile on his lips as he contemplated his glorious future.

Arrogant ass.

"And you'll still be empty," she accused, turning her attention from the ruthless drain on her life to her connection to her father.

If she could snap her bond with the dead, then maybe she could cut off the power at its source.

"Empty of what?"

"Love, happiness . . . contentment."

He turned to stab her with an annoyed glare.

Ah. Hit a nerve, did she?

"I have no need for human emotions."

She held his gaze, finding it an anchor to help search along the cord that bound them together.

"If that were true you wouldn't have such a gaping hole inside you," she said, weirdly able to *feel* the howling abyss inside her father.

God. It was no wonder he was as cold and empty as Siberia. He'd been stripped of everything but a raw, unrelenting hunger for power.

She shivered, crushing her instinctive pity.

There were few people on the face of the earth less deserving of sympathy than Lord Zakhar.

Instead she concentrated on the odd darkness at the very center of his soul.

There.

The doorway to the underworld.

She didn't know how she knew it.

She just did.

"There is no hole," he mocked, his voice suspiciously bland. "Gaping or otherwise."

"Why are your hands clenched, Father? Are you afraid I might be right?" Callie mocked in return, glancing down at his tight fists while she inwardly surveyed the doorway.

Crap. It was more a smooth portal than an actual doorway. Like a black hole. So how the hell was she supposed to close it?

He sucked in a deep breath, forcing his hands to relax. "Stupid, child. I fear nothing."

He did, of course.

He feared being weak.

Or failing in his grand quest.

So how did she use it to her advantage?

"Yet another worthless human emotion?" she absently taunted.

He frowned, as if belatedly sensing she wasn't fully concentrating on their bickering.

"Precisely."

Oh hell.

A distraction was needed. Pronto.

"What a pathetic excuse for a man you are." She tossed out the first insult that came to mind, still anxiously probing for a weakness in the bond between them.

His eyes narrowed. "Do you hope to anger me?"

She blinked in confusion. "What?"

"You are deliberately provoking my temper."

"Why would I want that?"

"Perhaps you hope that I will become enraged enough to kill you."

Ah. That had certainly been her first thought.

Until he'd ruined the plan by saying the dead warriors

would plunder, pillage, and ravage their way across the country once she lost her control over them . . .

Her control over them.

Her heart slammed against her ribs as she realized she had the answer.

If she couldn't cut the connection, or close the doorway, she had no choice but to take command of the bond.

"Is that what you hope for, Callie?" her father impatiently snapped, forcing her to realize he was studying her with a growing suspicion.

She licked her lips, her mouth dry.

She had to keep him distracted a few more minutes.

Just long enough to call on her powers.

"Why would you think I want to die?"

"People burdened with morals are always eager to become martyrs," he said in obvious disgust.

Clearly he had no hopes for earning a sainthood.

"Maybe I just truly believe you're pathetic," she pointed out with a humorless smile.

"You're wasting your energy, my dear." He tilted his chin, turning back toward Valhalla. "I have waited too long for this moment to be goaded into a rash act of stupidity."

"It's my energy to waste."

"No longer. It's mine to control." He gave a sudden chuckle as a group of Sentinels appeared to stand in front of the dead warriors, Duncan's golden blond hair unmistakable in the moonlight. "Ah. Shall I demonstrate?"

Callie forced herself to her feet, her hand pressed to her lips as she watched the man she loved charging straight at the nearest warrior.

"No," she breathed, knowing there was no way he could survive for even a few minutes against an indestructible Sentinel. "Please—"

"You see?" Lord Zakhar sneered. "Emotions make you weak."

"You're wrong." Knowing it was now or never, Callie opened herself to her powers, allowing them to flow through her. "They give me a strength you never dreamed possible."

Her father continued to watch the unfolding battle, a cold smile of anticipation touching his lips as one Sentinel fell beneath the onslaught, and then another.

Callie frantically closed her eyes, knowing she'd never be able to concentrate if she knew Duncan was injured. The only way to protect him was to wrench away her father's command of the warriors.

Not bothering to try and control the natural power that flowed through her, Callie focused on the bond that spanned between herself and her father.

It is just like entering the mind of the dead, she assured herself.

Slip in, take command, and . . .

Well, she didn't know what happened after that, but she was about to find out.

Aiming directly at the bond, Callie slid into the darkness, losing her touch with her physical body.

It felt oddly familiar.

Cool, peaceful.

The temptation of death.

Then, at last through the surface of the bond, she found the darkness separating.

She didn't know what she expected.

The faces of the warriors. Or maybe her father. Or even the doorway to the underworld.

Instead it was the golden chalice that hovered directly before her eyes.

Of course.

The power didn't flow from her father.

It came from her.

Her blood.

Her life force.

She only needed to reach out and grasp it.

Not allowing herself time to consider the pertinent fact she'd never used her powers to do anything but search the memories of the dead, she focused on the blood pooled in the bottom of the goblet.

At first she felt nothing.

She could sense the power, but she had no way to know how to gain command of it.

Tentatively reaching out with her power, she brushed it over the chalice. The breath rushed from her lungs as she touched the minds of the warriors.

There was a startled curse from Lord Zakhar as he belatedly sensed her intrusion.

"What are you doing?" he snarled, grasping her shoulders in a grip that threatened to crush her bones.

Callie smiled through the pain as she opened her eyes and whispered one word.

"Stop."

Duncan didn't need to be a trained soldier to know the battle wasn't going well.

His first clue came when he'd pumped his entire clip of bullets into the nearest intruder and the warrior barely flinched.

Not good.

Not good at all.

Traditional weapons were obviously worthless against zombies.

Time to think outside the box.

Ducking to avoid the arrow that whizzed past his face, he darted to the side to grab the heavy chain that was coiled in the back of the jeep they'd taken to the edge of the large meadow.

He couldn't kill the zombies, but he might be able to slow one or two of them down long enough for Fane to track down the necromancer.

He grimaced at the memory of his short but violent argument with the guardian Sentinel.

Duncan had claimed it was his right to go in search of Callie and kill the bastard who'd kidnapped her. Fane, however, had kindly pointed out that he was by far the superior tracker, not to mention he'd been trained for over a century by the most fearsome warriors ever born.

And oh yeah, he was impervious to magic.

Duncan might have continued the argument—he was nothing if not obstinate—but Fane had simply melted into the darkness and disappeared.

Jackass.

Now Duncan was forced to hold back the encroaching zombies and pray that Fane was as good as he thought he was.

Another arrow flew past his face, and with an infuriated roar, Duncan whirled the chain like a lasso, watching it wrap around the nearest zombie's legs.

The creature fell to the ground and a slender female witch darted forward, chanting a spell that bound the creature in a shimmering dome of magic.

It wouldn't last.

But it did take one warrior out of the fight for a few minutes.

Duncan turned his attention to Wolfe, who was swinging a massive sword at a Sentinel who held a battle ax.

The Tagos was surprisingly skilled in wielding the heavy weapon, striking blow after blow before dancing away to avoid the swinging ax. But no matter how skilled he might be, there was no way to win against an opponent who couldn't be killed. With every passing second Wolfe was losing ground.

Further away the gathered Sentinels engaged in similar fights with the zombies, grimly struggling to keep the monsters at bay.

Pausing long enough to grab another chain from the jeep, Duncan sprinted forward. Behind him he could feel the witch following, clearly trained in battle tactics.

Good girl.

Halting a few feet from the zombie who fought against Wolfe, Duncan was preparing to throw the chain at the creature's legs when there was an odd sizzle in the air.

And then . . . the zombies abruptly froze.

Just like that.

One minute they were silently slicing and dicing their way through the line of Sentinels, and the next they were standing like mannequins, their gazes blank, as if they'd been switched off.

Cautiously lowering his sword, Wolfe circled the unmoving zombie who still held his ax midair.

"What the hell?" the Tagos muttered.

"Callie," Duncan breathed, dropping the chain as he pressed a hand to his heart.

Wolfe scowled, a shallow cut marring his cheek and a deeper slice dripping blood down his neck.

"She did this?"

Duncan gave a slow nod. He had no explanation, but he could catch Callie's scent mingled among the warriors. As if they were somehow connected to her.

"It has to be her," he muttered, hissing as he realized the sense of her deep in his heart was fading. "Dammit, we have to find her. Now."

On cue, there was a sharp whistle.

Fane.

Wolfe raised his hand, motioning to the Sentinels, who were staring at the frozen zombies in wary horror. "This way."

They jogged across the grass, entering a small clump of trees that circled a gray stone building that was nearly hidden beneath a layer of ivy.

It had to be the opening to the lower crypts, Duncan inanely acknowledged, and where the now frozen warriors had come from.

The thought had barely flickered along the edge of his mind when he caught sight of Fane, who had his hands wrapped around the neck of the tall man with silver hair and diamond eyes.

The necromancer.

A red haze filled Duncan's mind.

It was the same haze that had risen when he'd been fourteen and he'd seen the high-school quarterback slap his sister when she wouldn't let him stick his hand down her shirt.

At the time Duncan had barely been over five-foot-five and weighed less than a buck thirty, but he'd launched himself on the quarterback and managed to break the bastard's nose and knocked out three teeth before he was pulled off.

Now he was impervious to the biting chill in the air, or the fact that Fane was turning a dangerous shade of blue as the necromancer's eyes flared with a blinding light.

All he knew was that he at last had the chance to kill the man who'd taken away the woman he loved.

Charging forward, he was mere steps away when his rage was shaken by a faint scent of blood.

Shit.

Jerking to the side, he frantically searched the darkness. Callie was near.

And injured.

Any male need to personally get his hands on the necromancer was forgotten as he circled a tree to discover Callie curled on the ground, a golden chalice lying at her side.

Oh . . . Christ.

The entire world halted as he took in her pale, pale face and the blood dripping down her arms.

She looked like a broken, exotic flower that had been tossed aside by a careless hand.

Then, her lips parted on a soft sigh and Duncan's heart remembered how to beat.

"Callie," he groaned, preparing to drop to his knees at her side.

It was only the shout of warning from Wolfe that allowed him to jump to the side in enough time to avoid the nasty bolt of magic that slammed into the tree with enough force to split it in two.

Whirling around, he spotted the crimson-haired woman who was stalking toward him with obvious intent.

The witch.

And not just a witch, he realized, seeing her aura was a black swirl of death.

But a zombie witch.

Just fucking perfect.

The female raised her hand again, preparing to launch yet another offensive spell, but even as Duncan braced himself for the attack, Wolfe was stepping behind her, shoving his large sword through her back and out through her chest.

Duncan grimaced.

He'd seen some gory things in his time, but watching Wolfe lift the skewered witch off the ground made his stomach heave. It didn't help when the Sentinel walked forward and then, with a mighty thrust of his arm, had the woman pinned to a nearby tree.

The witch struggled, but for the moment she was effectively trapped.

Moving back to Callie, Duncan lowered himself to his knees, carefully slipping his arms beneath her limp body to pull her onto his lap.

He needed to feel her against him.

The beat of her heart against his chest, the brush of her breath against his cheek.

Then, wrapping his arms carefully around her fragile form, he lifted his head to watch Fane in action.

Oddly, he hadn't doubted for a second that the warrior would be able to kill the necromancer.

It didn't matter that Lord Zakhar had managed to live for centuries. Or that he had the skill to screw with the dead. Or even that his power was filling the air with a chill that would soon become unbearable.

Fane had prepared for this moment since he'd become Callie's guardian. And nothing, not even the hordes from the underworld, were going to stop him.

"Callie, stay with me, sweetheart," he murmured, stroking a hand down her back as he watched Fane slowly, ruthlessly squeeze the life from the necromancer. "Stay with me."

Chapter Twenty-Eight

It was supposed to be over.

The bad guy was dead.

Not only dead, but hacked into itty bitty pieces and set on fire, just in case he tried to come back.

But after Fane spread the bastard's ashes, Callie didn't so much as stir in Duncan's arms.

Whatever was wrong with her hadn't been solved by the necromancer's death.

Instead she continued to grow weaker.

Rushing her back to Valhalla, they were now in the high-tech wing that served as a hospital for high-bloods with a dozen healers doing their frantic best to keep her alive.

Duncan sat on the edge of the bed where Callie was lying beneath a thin sheet, her arms heavily bandaged and an IV attached to the back of her arm, replacing the blood that she continued to lose.

Fane paced the floor, his skin still faintly blue and his hands marred by frostbite.

Wolfe had come and gone, telling them that the zombie warriors remained in their statuelike state and that the witch had been locked in the crypts to keep her contained.

At least for a few hours.

Duncan barely heard the reassurances.

Who the hell cared about zombie warriors?

His entire focus was on the woman who clung to life by the thinnest thread.

Bowing his head, Duncan was busy praying to whatever god would listen when Fane came to an abrupt halt, his brows snapping together.

"Goddammit," he growled.

Duncan lifted his head. "What is it?"

The answer came when the beautiful Serra pushed open the door and entered the room.

Fane stepped forward, his face grim. "I thought the psychics were told to leave," he growled.

The female didn't bother to glance in his direction as she headed for the bed, her gaze locked on Callie.

"I make my own decisions."

"No shit," Fane muttered, but his expression eased as Serra stepped into the muted light near the head of the bed.

As usual, she was wearing a pair of leather pants and thigh-high boots with a tiny halter top that could stop traffic, but her face was pale and damp with tears, and the green eyes shimmering with a gut-deep fear.

"Oh, Callie, you idiot," she whispered in shaky tones, her hand gently brushing her friend's cold cheek. "What did the healers say?"

"She continues to lose blood no matter what they do to close the wounds," Duncan said, his voice a harsh croak.

He'd never understood the meaning of true torture until now. Nothing could be worse than feeling helpless while someone he loved slipped away.

Serra continued to stroke Callie's cheek. "Do you know why?"

Duncan pointed toward the blood-filled goblet on a nearby table. "We think it has something to do with the chalice."

The psychic glanced up, her expression hard with determination. "I can try to find out."

Duncan's heart gave a sudden leap even as Fane shook his head.

"No," he snapped. "She's too weak."

Serra sent him a challenging glance. "And if we do nothing?"

"What's she talking about?" Duncan demanded of the Sentinel.

It was Serra who answered. "I can speak directly into Callie's mind."

Duncan frowned. "Even though she's unconscious?"

"Yes."

He glanced toward Fane, who continued to scowl, before returning his attention to the psychic.

"What's the danger?"

"Because she's unconscious I'll have to go deeper to read her thoughts. It can be jolting for anyone who's not used to the intrusion. But Callie . . ." She sucked in a shaky breath, blinking back the tears. "I've been slamming into her mind since we were both kids."

He clenched his jaw, turning his attention to the woman lying unconscious on the bed.

She was dying.

He could feel it with every beat of his heart.

He had to do something.

Anything.

Even if it was dangerous.

Squaring his shoulders, he gave a short nod. "Do it."

Fane stepped toward the bed, his expression stark with fear. "Serra—"

The psychic sent him a sad smile. The sort of smile that sliced through a man's heart and left him bleeding.

"You know I'd die before I would hurt her," she said in soft, chiding tones.

He grimaced, dipping his head in regret. "Yes."

"I'll be careful," she gently promised. Turning back to Callie, Serra leaned down, staring intently at her unconscious friend for what seemed to be an eternity. At last she released a deep sigh. "I'm in."

Duncan swallowed the lump in his throat, his thumb stroking the inside of Callie's wrist to assure himself that her heart continued to beat.

"Does she know we're here?" he demanded.

"Yes." A smile touched her lips. "She can feel you holding her hand."

Duncan lifted her hand to press the tips of her fingers to his lips.

Fane shifted to stand beside Serra, his jaw clenched. "Does she know what the necromancer did to her?"

There was a long silence as Serra spoke directly into Callie's mind.

"He . . . oh my god."

Duncan stiffened, his free hand automatically reaching for the gun that was once again holstered at his side.

It didn't matter his gun had been worthless against the zombies. Or that bullets wouldn't stop anything capable of breaking through the spells guarding the room.

Rational or not, it was going to be a long, long time before he went anywhere unarmed.

"What's wrong?" he barked.

"The necromancer . . . he was her father," she said with a shudder. "And the witch was her mother."

The surge of disgusted shock was swiftly replaced by a startling sense of acceptance.

"Of course," he muttered, sharing a glance with Fane. "It actually makes perfect sense."

Fane shrugged, clearly not interested. "What did the necromancer do to her?"

Serra closed her eyes, silently communicating with Callie.

"He used her blood to bind her to the magic of the chalice," she at last said.

Fane leaned forward. "What magic?"

"It opens the pathway to the underworld."

Duncan squeezed Callie's fingers. She was connected to the underworld? Shit, shit, shit.

"How do we close it?"

Serra opened her eyes to meet Duncan's worried gaze. "She doesn't know, but she's afraid."

Afraid? Afraid of what?

"Tell her that Lord Zakhar is dead."

She shook her head. "That's not what's bothering her."

"Then what is?"

"If she dies, the Sentinels that are bound to her will be released."

Duncan parted his lips—about to snarl that there was no way Callie was going to die—only to be interrupted by Fane.

"Back to their graves?" the Sentinel demanded.

"No." Serra's expression was troubled. "They'll kill anything in their path and nothing will be able to stop them."

"God dammit," Fane snarled.

Duncan made a sound of impatience. "Look, I don't want a crazed band of indestructible zombies rampaging through Valhalla—"

Fane glared at him. "It won't stop at Valhalla."

"I get it," Duncan snapped, refusing to consider the damage the zombie warriors could cause. "But right now all I care about is Callie." He glanced back at Serra. "How do we destroy the chalice?"

She did her psychic thing, her face managing to lose even more color.

"It can't be destroyed," she whispered.

"No." Duncan was abruptly on his feet. "I don't accept that."

Fane folded his arms over his bare chest, equally determined.

"If the chalice can't be destroyed then the doorway must be closed some other way," he announced, his flat tone shaking Duncan out of his brief flare of panic. "The monk mentioned a ritual. I'll return to Russia. There has to be some mention of the chalice in the texts."

Duncan forced himself to take a deep, calming breath. Becoming hysterical wasn't going to do Callie any good. He had to think clearly. Starting with how they could close the doorway.

Pacing toward the window that offered a view of the still dark countryside, he shuffled through his memories.

There had been something nagging at him since he'd had his meeting with Hektor from the Brotherhood.

Something . . .

It hit him with enough force to make him gasp.

Fane sent him a searching glance. "You okay, cop?"

"I think we can find someone who knows the ritual much closer," he said.

"Who?"

"The Brotherhood."

Fane frowned. "You know how to contact them?"

"No, but I'm betting I know someone who does." Duncan turned his attention to Serra. "Can you stay with Callie?"

She settled on the edge of the bed, her chin jutted to a dangerous angle. Only a fool would try to pry her away from her friend.

"I won't leave her side."

Moving back to the bed, Duncan leaned down to press a lingering kiss to Callie's forehead, breathing deeply of her apple scent.

"Hang on, baby," he whispered, willing her to stay strong.

"I'm coming back with the cavalry." Straightening, he snatched the chalice off the table and met Fane's steady gaze. "Can you take me to Kansas City?"

"Let's go."

They made their way through Valhalla and into the small chapel where they stood before the familiar copper post. Fane was never chatty. Tonight he was downright mute as he gathered his powers and sent them spinning through . . . well, whatever they spun through to get to Kansas City in the blink of an eye.

It was only as they left the monastery and climbed into the waiting Hummer that he at last spoke.

"How are you going to contact the Brotherhood?" he asked, driving out of the garage and onto the nearby path. "Any personal info they gave will be bogus."

"No shit," Duncan snorted. He was a trained cop. He didn't need help smelling bullshit.

"Then how?"

"It bothered me that Hektor asked for me when he came to the station," he said.

"Why?"

Duncan shrugged, pointing for Fane to turn onto the road that led to the nearest interstate.

"No one in the public should have known the coin was missing, let alone that I was looking for it."

Fane arched a brow. "True."

"So there was either a leak at Valhalla—"

"No way," the Sentinel snapped.

"Or the police station." Duncan ignored the interruption. "Or, more likely, from the one civilian I asked to identify the vessel that held the coin."

Fane hissed out a breath. "Where is he?"

Duncan leaned forward to punch the directions into the GPS. "Drive fast."

The words had barely left his lips when Fane had stomped

on the gas pedal and they were hurtling along the road at a teeth-rattling speed.

Holy hell.

Duncan hastily buckled his seat belt, tucking the chalice into the glove compartment so he could brace himself.

Inwardly he made a mental note never to tell a Sentinel to drive fast unless he was prepared to risk his life, and the lives of every citizen in Kansas City.

Thankfully the late hour meant there was little traffic and they managed to reach the south side of town without ramming cars off the road or taking out a hapless pedestrian.

Screeching to a halt in front of the steel and glass building, Fane had barely put the vehicle in park when Duncan was jumping out and heading to the back alley.

Girard lived in a small apartment at the rear of the art gallery. Not surprising. When you stored illegal art that could be worth over a million dollars in your basement, you wanted to keep a personal eye on it.

Lifting his arm, Duncan slammed his fist against the heavy door, bellowing at the top of his lungs. "Girard."

There was a long pause before the door was at last cracked open, and a bleary eyed Girard peered into the alley.

"You had better be a fucking naked woman or I'll—"

His words were bit off as Duncan leaned forward. "Sorry to disappoint."

"O'Conner?" The con man frowned, his peppered gray hair tousled around his face and his slender body covered by a terry cloth robe. "Do you know what time it is?"

In answer, Duncan shoved the door wider, stepping into the narrow foyer and flipping on the overhead light.

"We need to talk and you can skip the faux French accent," he warned.

Girard stumbled backward, tugging at the belt of his robe as he glared at Duncan. He didn't even bother trying to summon his image of a sophisticated art dealer.

Why bother? It was four in the morning and they both knew he'd started as a common street thug.

"This is private property, you know," he groused. "Unless you have a warrant you can get your ass out of here."

Duncan jerked his thumb toward the silent Sentinel standing at his side. "This is my warrant."

Anger tightened Girard's narrow face, but he wasn't stupid enough to argue.

"If you're here about the vessel—"

"That's exactly why I'm here," Duncan interrupted. He wasn't going to play games. Not tonight. "I need to contact the Brotherhood."

"Brotherhood?" Girard gave a faux frown, his hand lifting to covertly tug the edge of his robe higher on his neck. "Is that some sort of code?"

"Shit."

Duncan lunged forward, ripping aside the robe to reveal the arrow-shaped tattoo the man had been trying to hide. He'd never spotted it before because Girard always wore a collared shirt and tie.

Fane frowned in confusion. "What?"

"Hektor had that same tattoo on his neck," Duncan said.

Without warning the Sentinel had reached out, grabbed Girard by the throat and lifted him three inches off the ground.

"We don't have time to screw around, so let me make this simple," Fane growled, squeezing until the man's eyes bulged. "Tell me how to contact the Brotherhood or I'll snap your neck."

Duncan had to give Girard credit. Despite the sweat dripping down his face, he tried to protect his brothers.

"I don't know what you're talking about."

Duncan grabbed his chin, hoping that honesty would loosen his tongue. They didn't have time for Fane to beat it out of him.

"The pathway to the underworld was opened."

Girard stopped struggling against Fane's iron grip, a genuine fear flashing through his eyes.

"You're certain?"

"Yes."

The man licked his lips. "It's too late."

"No," Duncan snapped. "The necromancer is dead and we have the chalice. We need the Brotherhood to perform the ceremony."

Girard visibly weighed his options. If he revealed the location of the secret society and discovered Duncan had been lying, he would be toast.

But then again, if he didn't contact the Brotherhood and Duncan wasn't lying, he would be toast.

Duncan knew the second he'd conceded defeat.

"Let me go," he choked out, glaring when Fane continued to hold him off the ground. "Do you want me to contact them or not?"

Fane leaned forward, until they were nose to nose, holding Girard's weight with obnoxious ease.

The Sentinel could no doubt bench press the Hummer.

"You make one wrong twitch and you're dead," he promised in lethal tones, waiting for the man to give a jerky nod before he set him on his feet and stepped back.

"I hate high-bloods," Girard muttered, pulling a cell phone from his pocket.

Chapter Twenty-Nine

Callie woke to discover Duncan lying on the narrow bed next to her, his arm gently tucked around her waist.

His hair was rumpled, his face was lined with weariness, and his golden beard was at least three days old, but he was still the most beautiful thing she'd ever seen.

"Hey, sleepyhead," he murmured, the hazel eyes filling with relief as he realized she was awake.

She frowned. She had a vague recollection of Duncan carrying her back to Valhalla. Then Serra had come and she was able to warn them of the goblet.

After that it all became fuzzy.

"The chalice?"

He grimaced. "Fane took it along with the Brotherhood to some temple in the Middle East. That's the only place they could close the doorway to the underworld."

She blinked. Brotherhood? Temple? Middle East?

"Are you drunk?" she asked.

"I feel like it." With a choked groan, he pressed his face into the curve of her neck. "God, Callie, you scared the hell out of me."

She rubbed her cheek over the top of his head, savoring

the heat of his body, which drove away the last of her father's frigid power.

She was safe.

And in the arms of the man she loved.

"I was scared too," she husked. Understatement of the year. She was going to have nightmares for decades.

He planted a kiss just below her ear. "I know you were, sweetheart, but you saved us all."

She stiffened. She was fairly certain she'd shared the reason Lord Zakhar had chosen her as his sacrifice when Serra had been rummaging around in her brain, but she had to be sure he understood the blood that ran through her veins.

"Duncan."

He concentrated on nuzzling a heated path down the line of her jaw.

"Mmm?"

"The necromancer . . ." She was forced to halt and clear her throat. "He was my—"

"He's dead." He abruptly cut her words short, pulling back to send her a warning frown. "Along with the witch."

"But they—"

"It doesn't matter." He pressed a swift, possessive kiss to her lips. "They're dead and the zombies have been returned to their graves. It's over."

Callie hesitated before heaving a sigh.

Someday they would discuss the gory details. Not only of her father's sick plot to rule the world and her desperate gamble to take control of the dead Sentinels, but what it meant to be the daughter of Lord Zakhar and his pet witch.

She also had a thousand questions about what had happened after she'd been kidnapped by her psycho father.

But that could wait until the wounds had healed and her emotions weren't still raw.

"Really and truly over?" she murmured.

"Really and truly over." Another lingering kiss. "I promise."

"Thank god."

He chuckled softly. "Shouldn't you be thanking me as well?"

She snuggled against him, her heart skipping a beat as his lips found a sensitive pulse just below her jaw.

"Did you want a medal?" she teased.

"Hmm." He nibbled down the curve of her neck. "I was thinking of a more personal thank you."

"Perhaps that could be arranged," she husked, already picturing Duncan spread naked across her bed while her tongue traced his washboard abs.

The things she intended to do to that hard, male body . . .

Her delicious thoughts were abruptly interrupted by an unwelcomed realization.

Oh . . . hell.

As Duncan had just said, it was over.

Her father was dead, the chalice had been returned to wherever it came from, and she was no longer in danger.

With an uncanny intuition, Duncan pulled back, his eyes narrowed as he sensed her distress.

"Callie, what's wrong?" he asked, giving her a warning glare as her lips parted to dismiss his concern. "And don't you dare try to tell me it's nothing."

She wrinkled her nose. "Bossy."

"It's part of my charm. Tell me what's bothering you."

She might as well. He would nag her to death if she didn't.

"Now that the necromancer is dead, you'll be returning to your old life," she said, her voice deliberately stripped of emotion.

She wouldn't pressure him into staying.

Or beg to be taken with him.

Only he could decide what he needed to make him happy.

Surprisingly, his expression eased, a tiny smile tugging at his lips. "Will I?"

"Of course." She plucked at the sheet that covered her, belatedly realizing she must look like hell with her hair sticking up like a porcupine and her body wrapped like a mummy in her hospital gown. Not that it would make Duncan stay even if she was dressed like a movie star. He wasn't that kind of guy. Still, she did have her pride. "You have your family. Your job—"

"Actually, I've taken a new job," he smoothly interrupted.

She widened her eyes in shock. "A new job? But . . . you love being a cop."

He shrugged. "I love carrying a gun and telling people what to do."

She shook her head, not about to be fooled by his light tone. This man had devoted his life to his career. He wouldn't just toss it aside as if it meant nothing.

"Duncan."

"Ssh." He pressed a finger to her lips, something that might have been contentment shimmering in his hazel eyes. "Wolfe has made me a Sentinel. Or at least I'll be one once I'm done with my training."

"A Sentinel?"

"It's perfect," he assured her. "I still get to use my skills as a cop, and from now on I won't have to hide my ability to read auras. It's my best asset." He smiled with wicked promise. "Well, one of my best assets," he corrected, his finger stroking the lush softness of her bottom lip. "And more importantly, no one will be your guardian but me."

She studied his face for any hint of hesitation. As desperately as she longed to have him become a part of her world, she would never forgive herself if he came to regret his decision.

"And this is what you want?" she pressed. "What you truly want?"

He framed her face in his hands, regarding her with a tender devotion that chased away any lingering doubts.

"You are what I want, Callie Brown."

"Oh, Duncan," she sniffed, feeling as silly and emotional as one of those girly girls she'd always mocked.

He kissed the tip of her nose. "There is one downside, I'm afraid."

His teasing tone kept her from freaking out.

"What's that?"

"The Mave mentioned something about me being a liaison between Valhalla and the civil authorities."

"I think that's a brilliant idea."

He lifted his head with a grimace. "Liaisons are supposed to be diplomatic. I have as much diplomacy as a rabid badger."

"True." She reached up to push a strand of golden hair off his forehead. Her touch sheer possession. This man was hers. Hers, all hers. Joy exploded in the center of her heart. "I can give you lessons."

The wicked smile became downright sinful. "Really?"

"Yep."

The hazel gaze slowly meandered downward, lingering on the neckline of her oversized gown that revealed the top of her breasts.

"It's going to take the proper incentive."

Breathe, Callie, breathe.

"And what incentive would that be?"

He brushed a gentle hand through her hair. "First I'm going to need a place to stay while we work on my lessons."

"I do have an apartment I would be willing to share," she offered.

"Perfect," he breathed, gold beginning to shimmer in his eyes. A sure sign of his arousal. As if the hard thrust of his erection pressing into her hip wasn't enough of a hint. "And we'll need a private getaway," he continued. "Maybe a small cabin in the woods where we can be completely alone."

Completely alone with this man? Yes, please.

"That can be arranged." She wiggled until she was lying

on her side, her hand slipping beneath his T-shirt to stroke over the hard muscles of his stomach. "Anything else?"

He peered deep into her eyes. "Just one thing."

"What?"

"Love me."

She melted into a puddle of goo, wondering how the hell she'd ever survived without this man in her life.

"With all my heart," she vowed, tears glistening in her eyes.

"Callie. My beautiful Callie."

With a groan he kissed her with a stark hunger even as his hands stroked her with a gentle restraint, as if she were a fragile object that might shatter at his touch.

On the point of assuring him that she wasn't an invalid, she was halted when he gave a sudden chuckle, speaking against her lips.

"Oh, I almost forgot."

She plunged her fingers into his hair, not particularly interested in talking.

"Forgot what?"

"We're having dinner with my family on Sunday."

Her shriek could be heard throughout Valhalla.

"Duncan!"

Please turn the page for an exciting sneak peek
of the next novel in
Alexandra Ivy's
Guardians of Eternity series,
HUNT THE DARKNESS,
coming in June 2014!

Prologue

Styx's lair
Chicago, IL

Styx was fairly certain that hell had frozen over.

Nothing else could explain the fact that in the past year he'd become the Anasso (King of All Vampires), moved from his dank caves into a behemoth of a mansion that contained acres of marble, crystal, and gilt—gilt for Christ's sake—and mated with a pure-blooded Were who also happened to be a vegetarian.

Then, as if fate hadn't had enough laughs at his expense, he'd been in an epic battle against the Dark Lord, which meant he'd been forced to make allies out of former enemies.

Including the King of Weres, Salvatore, who was currently drinking Styx's finest brandy as he smoothed a hand down his impeccable Gucci suit.

He pacified his battered pride by believing he would never have allowed the bastard over his doorstep if it wasn't for the fact that their mates happened to be sisters. His own mate, Darcy, was very . . . insistent that she be allowed to spend time with Harley, who was growing heavy with her first pregnancy.

Or was it litter?

Either way, Styx and Salvatore were forced to play nice.

Not an easy task for two über-alphas who'd been opponents for centuries.

Settling his six-foot-plus frame in a chair that had a view of the moon-drenched gardens, Styx waited for his companion to finish his drink.

As always, Salvatore looked more like a sophisticated mob boss than the King of Weres. His dark hair was pulled to a tail at his nape and his elegant features cleanly shaved. Only the feral heat that glowed in the dark eyes revealed the truth of the beast that lived inside him.

Styx on the other hand, didn't even try to appear civilized.

An Aztec warrior, he was wearing a pair of leather pants, heavy shit-kickers, and a white silk shirt that was stretched to the limit to cover his broad chest. His long black hair was braided to hang down to his waist and threaded with tiny turquoise amulets. And to complete the image, he had a huge sword strapped to his back.

What was the point in being a bad-ass if you couldn't look like one?

Setting aside his empty glass, Salvatore flashed a dazzling white smile. A sure sign he was about to be annoying.

"Let me see if I have this right," the wolf drawled.

Yep. Annoying.

Styx narrowed his dark eyes, his features that were too stark for true beauty tight with warning.

"Do you have to?"

"Oh, yes." The smile widened. "You asked the clan chief of Nevada to babysit a witch you had locked in your dungeons?"

Styx silently swore to have a chat with his mate once their guests were gone.

He hadn't intended Salvatore to know that one of his most powerful vampires had been magically forced into a mating.

Hell, he'd had a hard enough time divulging the info with

Jagr, his most trusted Raven. It was only because he needed the vampire to do research that he'd revealed the secret.

A mating was the rarest, most sacred, most intimate connection a demon could experience.

To think for a second that it could be inflicted on a vampire against his will was nothing less than . . . rape.

You didn't reveal that kind of weakness to your enemies. Even if you did have a peace treaty.

Darcy, however, was a genuine optimist who blithely assumed that Salvatore would never abuse privileged information.

Now Styx was stuck revealing the truth to the mangy mutt.

"Sally Grace was not only a powerful witch who was capable of black magic, but she worshipped the Dark Lord," he grudgingly explained, not about to admit that it had been more habit than fear that had led him to lock the female in his dungeons. Sally Grace was barely over five foot and weighed less than a hundred pounds. She hadn't looked like a threat. And she probably wouldn't have been if she hadn't been so scared. "Of course I wasn't going to take any chances."

"Why, Roke?"

Styx shrugged. "I was busy dealing with the ancient spirit that was trying to turn vampires into crazed killers."

Naturally Salvatore wasn't satisfied.

"And?" he prodded.

"And the prophet had warned that Roke would be important to the future," he muttered. He'd truly thought keeping Roke in his lair would protect him. Ah, the best laid plans of mice and vampires . . . "How the hell was I supposed to know Sally Grace was half-demon?"

Salvatore grimaced. "It must have been quite a shock to poor Roke to discover himself mated to a witch."

Styx's humorless laugh echoed through the library at the memory of Roke's fury.

"Shock isn't the word I'd use."

"She's lucky he didn't kill her on the spot."

Frustration simmered deep inside Styx. Roke might be an arrogant pain in the ass, but he was a brother. And more importantly, he was a clan chief who had a duty to his people. They had to find a way to break the mating.

And how to make damned sure it never happened again.

"He might have killed her if the magic she used didn't feel as real as any true mating."

Salvatore's amusement faded. "That bad?"

"Worse." Styx surged to his feet. "Without her knowing who or what fathered her, the witch doesn't even know how to reverse the damage."

"You're certain this isn't some trick?"

"I'm not certain of anything beyond the need to find a way to break the bond."

Salvatore poured another shot of brandy. "Do you have a plan?"

Plan? Styx grimaced. The closest they'd had to a plan the past year had been to charge from one disaster to another.

Why would this be any different?

"Sally left almost three weeks ago to search for any clues that would reveal who her father might be," he said.

"And Roke?"

"He's trying to catch her."

Salvatore arched a brow. "You let him go alone?"

"Of course not." A slow smile curved Styx's lips. "I allowed Levet to go with him."

Salvatore choked on his brandy at the mention of the tiny gargoyle who'd attached himself to both Darcy and Harley. Like a freaking barnacle that couldn't be scraped off.

A three-foot pest with delicate fairy wings in shades of blue and crimson and gold, Levet could drive a sane man to gargoyle-cide in three seconds flat.

"You are a bad, bad vampire," Salvatore murmured.

"I try."

Chapter One

Northern Canada

Roke hadn't yet given in to his overwhelming desire to commit gargoyle-cide.

But it was a near thing.

Roke was antisocial by nature, and having to endure the endless chatter from a stunted gargoyle for the past three weeks had been nothing short of torture.

It was only the fact that Levet could sense Yannah, the demon who'd helped Sally flee from Chicago, that kept him from sending the annoying twit back to Styx.

His mating connection to Sally allowed him to sense her, but Yannah's ability to teleport from one place to another in the blink of an eye meant by the time he could locate her, she was already gone.

Levet seemed to have a more direct connection to Yannah, although they still spent their nights chasing from one place to another, always one step behind them.

Until tonight.

With a small smile he came to a halt, allowing his senses to flow outward.

The sturdy cottage tucked on the eastern coast of British

Columbia was perched to overlook the churning waves of the North Pacific Ocean. Built from the gray stones that lined the craggy cliffs, it had a steep, metal roof to shed the heavy snowfalls and windows that were already shuttered against the late autumn breeze. A handful of outhouses surrounded the bleak property, but it was far enough away from civilization to avoid prying eyes.

Not that prying eyes could have detected him.

Leaving his custom-built turbine-powered motorcycle hidden in the trees, Roke moved in lethal silence in a pair of knee-high moccasins. He was dressed in black jeans, black tee, and black leather jacket. With his bronzed skin and dark hair that brushed his broad shoulders, he blended in to the darkness with ease. Only his eyes were visible. Although silver in color, they were so pale they appeared white in the moonlight, and rimmed by a circle of pure black.

Over the centuries those eyes had unnerved the most savage demons. No one liked the sensation that their soul was being laid bare.

On the other hand, his lean, beautiful features, which were clearly from Native American origins, had been luring women to his bed since he'd awoken as a vampire.

They sighed beneath the touch of his full, sensual lips and eagerly pressed against the lean, chiseled perfection of his body. Their fingers traced the proud line of his nose, the wide brow, and his high cheekbones.

It didn't matter that most considered him as cold and unfeeling as a rattlesnake. Or that he would sacrifice anything or anyone to protect his clan.

They found his ruthless edge . . . exciting.

All except one notable exception.

A damned shame that exception happened to be his mate.

Roke grimaced.

No. Not mate.

Or at least, not in the traditional sense.

Three weeks ago he'd been in Chicago when the demon-world had battled against the Dark Lord. They'd managed to turn back the hordes of hell, but instead of allowing him to return to his clan in Nevada, Styx, the Anasso, had insisted that he remain to babysit Sally Grace, a witch who'd fought with the Dark Lord.

Roke had been furious.

Not only was he desperate to return to his people, but he hated witches.

All vampires did.

Magic was the one weapon they had no defense against.

Regrettably, when Styx gave an order, a wise vampire jumped to obey.

The alternative wasn't pretty.

Of course, at the time none of them had realized that Sally was half-demon. Or that she would panic at being placed in the dungeons beneath Styx's elegant lair.

He absently rubbed his inner forearm where the mating mark was branded into his skin.

The witch claimed that she was simply trying to enchant him long enough to convince him to help her escape. And after his initial fury at realizing her demon magic had some-how ignited the mating bond, Roke had grudgingly accepted it had been an accident.

What he hadn't accepted was her running off to search for the truth of her father.

Dammit.

It was her fault they were bound together.

She had no right to slip away like a thief in the night.

"Do you sense anyone?"

The question was spoken in a low voice that was edged with a French accent, jerking Roke out of his dark broodings. Glancing downward, he ruefully met his companion's curious gaze.

What the hell had happened to his life?

A mate that wasn't a mate. A three-foot gargoyle sidekick. And a clan that had been without their chief for far too long.

"She's there," he murmured, his gaze skimming over the creature's ugly mug. Levet had all the usual gargoyle features. Gray skin, horns, a small snout, and a tail he kept lovingly polished. It was only his delicate wings and diminutive size that marked him as different. Oh, and his appalling lack of control over his magic. Roke turned back to the cottage where he could catch the distinctive scent of peaches. A primitive heat seared through him, drawing him forward. "I have you, little witch."

Scampering to keep up with his long, silent strides, Levet tugged at the hem of his jacket.

"Umm . . . Roke?"

"Not now, gargoyle." Roke never paused as he made his way toward the back of the cottage. "I've spent the past three weeks being led around like a damned hound on the leash. I intend to savor the moment."

"While you're savoring, I hope that you will recall Sally must have a good reason for—"

"Her reason is to drive me nuts," Roke interrupted, pausing at the side of a shed. "I promised her that we would go in search of her father. Together."

"*Oui*. But when?"

Roke clenched his teeth. "In case you've forgotten, she nearly died when the—"

"Vampire-god."

Roke grimaced. The creature that they'd so recently battled might have claimed to be the first vampire, but that didn't make him a god. The bastard had nearly killed Sally in an attempt to break the magic that held him captive.

"When the ancient spirit attacked her," he snapped. "She should be grateful that I was willing to wait for her to regain her strength."

Levet cleared his throat. "And that is the only reason you tried to keep her imprisoned?"

"She wasn't imprisoned," he denied, refusing to recall his panic when Sally had lain unconscious for hours.

Or his fierce reluctance to allow Sally to leave Styx's lair.

"Non?" Levet clicked his tongue, seemingly oblivious to how close Roke was to yanking that tongue out of his mouth. "I would have sworn she was locked in the dungeons."

"Not after Gaius was destroyed."

"You mean after she saved the world from the vampire-god?" the gargoyle taunted. "Generous of you."

Oh yeah. The tongue was going to have to go.

"Don't push me, gargoyle," he muttered, allowing his senses to spread outward.

He would deal with the aggravating gargoyle later.

Testing the air, he caught the scent of salty foam as waves crashed against the rocks below, the acrid tang of smoke from the chimney, and a distant perfume of a water sprite playing among the whales.

But overriding it all was that tantalizing aroma of warm peaches.

A potent aphrodisiac that once again compelled him forward.

Levet grabbed his back pocket. "Where are you going?"

Roke didn't miss a step as he swatted the pest away. "To get my mate."

"I do not believe that is a good idea."

"Thankfully I don't give a shit what you think."

"Très bien," the gargoyle sniffed. "You are the panty boss."

"Bossy-pants, you idiot," Roke muttered, heading directly for the back door.

He'd officially run out of patience twenty-one days and several thousand miles ago.

Which would explain why he didn't even consider the fact Sally might be prepared for his arrival.

Less than a foot from the back steps he was brought to a painful halt as an invisible net of magic wrapped around him, the bands of air so tight they would have sliced straight through him if he'd been human.

"What the hell?"

Levet waddled forward, his wings twitching as he studied Roke with open curiosity.

"A magical snare. *Sacrebleu.* I've never seen one so strong."

Roke flashed his fangs, futilely struggling to escape.

Damn, but he hated magic.

"Why didn't you warn me?" he snarled.

"I did," the gargoyle huffed in outrage. "I told you it was a bad idea."

Okay, he hated magic *and* gargoyles.

"You didn't tell me there was a trap."

"You are chasing a powerful witch. What did you expect?" The damned beast dared to smile. "Besides, it's such a fine spell. It would have been a pity to spoil Sally's fun."

"I swear, gargoyle, when I get out of here—"

"Are all vampires always so bad tempered, or is it just you?" a light female voice demanded, the scent of peaches drenching the air.

Roke swallowed a groan, a complex mixture of fury, lust, and savage relief surging through him.

None of it showed on his face as he turned to study the tiny female with shoulder-length hair that was a blend of deep red tresses streaked with gold. She had pale, almost fragile features with velvet brown eyes and full lips that begged to be kissed.

"Hello, my love," he said in a low, husky voice. "Did you miss me?"

* * *

Sally Grace had been well aware that she was being hunted.

Not only hunted . . . but hunted by a first class, grade A, always-get-my-man predator.

And she should know all about predators.

She'd been prey since her mother had tried to put an end to her existence with a particularly nasty spell on her sixteenth birthday. No one understood better than she did the difference between an okay hunter and one you didn't have a hope in hell of shaking off your trail.

Still, she'd managed to elude him for the past three weeks.

Twenty-one days longer than she'd expected.

Now she intended to hold her ground.

No one was putting her back in a cell.

Planting her hands on her hips, she pretended a confidence she was far from feeling.

"Why are you following me?"

His beautiful eyes shimmered a perfect silver in the moonlight.

Of course, everything about him was perfect, she acknowledged with a renegade rush of awareness.

The exquisitely carved features. The dark hair that was silky smooth. The hard, chiseled body that should only be possible with Photoshop.

And the raw, sexual magnetism that pulsed in the air around him.

There wasn't a woman alive who wouldn't secretly wish he'd handcuff her to the nearest bed.

A pity he was a coldhearted vampire who would happily kill her if her magic hadn't tied them together as mates.

She shivered despite the heavy sweatshirt and jeans she wore to combat the cold.

"Is that a joke?"

She tilted her chin. "There's nothing funny about our situation."

"I agree."

"Then why don't you return to Chicago?" she demanded in frustration. "I'm perfectly capable of tracking down my father without you."

A dark brow arched. "Really?"

"Yes, really."

"The last time you went rogue we ended up mated." His lips twisted as he stopped struggling and instead stood there with his head held high, pride etched onto his beautiful face. As if he was above noticing her tedious spell. "Forgive me if I don't entirely trust you."

Sally flinched, her eyes narrowing. Dammit. She didn't need any reminders that she was a major screwup.

Not when she was tired and frustrated and in the mood to punch something.

Really, really hard.

"Sacrebleu," a voice rasped, drawing Sally's attention to the tiny gargoyle standing at Roke's side. "You may have a death wish, vampire, but I do not. I believe I will speak with Yannah."

Sally blinked, effectively distracted by the question.

Yannah had been a strange travel companion. The small demon had happily zapped Sally to each of her mother's properties so Sally could search for clues of her father, but she'd rarely spoken and had spent most of her time zoned out as she mentally communicated with her mother, who also happened to be an Oracle.

Sally had been almost relieved when Yannah had abruptly announced she had to go home.

She was used to being on her own.

It was . . . comfortable. Familiar.

Tragic, achingly lonely, but familiar.

"She left," she informed Levet.

"Left?" His heavy brow furrowed. "What do you mean 'left'?"

"One minute she was standing next to me complaining about the dust, and the next—" She waved a hand.

"Poof," Levet finished.

"Exactly."

Without warning the gargoyle was stomping away, his tail twitching and his tiny hands waving in the air as he muttered to himself.

"Aggravating, unpredictable, impossible female."

"I feel his pain," Roke drawled.

She turned back to stab him with a glare. "Not yet, but keep it up and you will."

The silver eyes shimmered. "Release me."

Sally wrapped her arms around her waist. She could feel his anger through their bond, but more than that she could feel a seething frustration that was echoed deep inside her.

That scared her more than his irritation.

"Why should I?" she bluffed. Yeah, look at her. All bad-ass just so long as Roke remained trapped in her spell. "You're trespassing on my property."

He glanced toward the cottage. "Yours?"

She shrugged. "It was my mother's, and since I'm her only heir, I assume her various houses are now mine."

"She had more than one?"

"What do you think I've been doing the past three weeks?"

The silver gaze returned to sear over her pale face. "Running."

She sniffed, refusing to admit that running had been a large part of what she'd been doing.

There had been a little method to her madness.

"I've been searching through my mother's belongings," she said. "I hoped that she would have left some clue to my—" She bit off the word "father." Did a donation of sperm actually earn one the title of father? "To who impregnated her."

He frowned. "I thought you said that witches had a spell so their private papers were destroyed when they died."

It was true that many witches had binding spells attached to their most sensitive possessions. It gave a whole new meaning to taking "secrets to the grave." And her mother had been more secretive than most.

Still, she had to cling to some small fragment of hope. Dammit.

"They do," she grudgingly admitted. "But she wouldn't have destroyed everything. There has to be a clue somewhere."

"Release me and I'll help you search." He studied her stubborn expression, silently compelling her to obey. "Sally."

"Don't growl at me. You locked me in a cell—"

"And I let you out."

"Only because I forced you to."

A dangerous chill blasted through the air at her foolish reminder that he'd briefly been under her complete control.

"Sally, like it or not we're stuck together," he rasped between clenched teeth.

"I don't like it."

The silver eyes narrowed. "If that were true then you would be eager for my help."

She snorted. "Nice try."

"You know that vampires are the finest hunters in the world," he continued, ignoring her interruption. "And I'm one of the best."

"And so modest."

"If you were as anxious as you claim to end our mating, you would be begging for my . . . services."

His gaze deliberately lowered to take in her slender body,

making Sally tremble in reaction. Blessed goddess. The blast of sexual arousal that jolted through her made her feel like she'd been struck by lightning.

And the worst part was, she couldn't blame the intense reaction on the faux mating.

She'd been aching for Roke from the moment she'd caught sight of those dark, male features and the astonishing silver eyes. Not to mention the tight ass that filled out a pair of jeans with oh-my-god perfection.

"Jeez, could you be any more annoying?" she muttered, reluctantly releasing the spell that bound him. The spell was draining her at a rapid rate, and the last thing she wanted was to collapse in front of this man. Better that she pretended to be bored with the game. "You're free. Now go away."

The words had barely left her lips when Roke was flowing forward at a blinding speed.

"Gotcha."

"Roke." His name was a muffled protest against his chest as he lashed his arms around her and flattened her against his body.

"Don't move," he growled, pressing his face into the curve of her neck, his fangs lightly scraping her skin.

"What are you doing?"

He shuddered, his hands running a compulsive path down her back to cup her hips.

"You feel it," he whispered against her neck.

And she did.

Not just the tidal-wave of sensual pleasure at being in his arms, but the strange sensation of something settling deep inside her.

An easing of the nagging sense of "wrongness" that had plagued her since leaving Chicago.

His lips moved to press against the thundering pulse at the base of her throat.

"Do you have any idea what you did to me when you disappeared?"

Her lashes slid downward as she absorbed the stunning pleasure of his touch.

"I thought you would be happy to be rid of me," she whispered, breathing in the scent of leather, male, and raw power.

His fingers gave her hips a small squeeze. "You wouldn't have snuck away if you believed that."

The fact he was right only pissed her off.

"Just because I didn't ask for your permission doesn't mean I snuck away."

"Sally, whether this mating is some demon magic or not, it feels real to me," he rasped. "To have you disappear . . ." He shuddered, revealing the genuine pain he'd been forced to endure. "Christ."

Sally grimaced, her anger abruptly being replaced by overwhelming regret.

The mating truly had been an accident.

At the time she'd been scared and desperate or she would never have released her inner demon.

She wasn't stupid. She knew that messing with magic she didn't understand was dangerous. And until she had discovered the truth of her ancestry, she'd usually stuck to the human spells she'd learned from her witch mother.

But accident or not, she'd physically, perhaps even spiritually, bound this proud loner to her.

It was a sin she could never erase.

"I'm sorry," she husked.

His tongue traced the line of her jaw. "Are you?"

"I know this mess is partially my fault."

He jerked his head back in disbelief. "Partially?"

She was instantly on the defensive. "If your precious Anasso hadn't thrown me in the dungeons I wouldn't have needed to use my powers to escape."

He muttered a curse, returning to nuzzle a searing path of kisses down the side of her neck.

"Let's go back to your apology," he commanded.

Somehow her hands were on his shoulders, her fingers tangled in his silken hair.

"Fine. I regret any discomfort I've caused you," she managed to say, excitement jolting through her as he allowed her to feel the tips of his fangs.

God. What was wrong with her? She'd never been one of those freaks who wanted to be dinner for a vampire.

Even if their bite was orgasmic.

Now she was shaking with the need to feel those fangs sliding through her tender flesh.

"And you promise not to disappear again?" he demanded, his hands slipping beneath her sweatshirt.

She shuddered, struggling to think through the haze of lust clouding her mind.

"Not unless I think it's absolutely necessary."

He made a sound of resignation. "Have you always been so stubborn?"

"Have you always been so arrogant?"

He pressed a hard, hungry kiss to her lips. "Yes."

Romantic Suspense from
Lisa Jackson

Absolute Fear	0-8217-7936-2	$7.99US/$9.99CAN
Afraid to Die	1-4201-1850-1	$7.99US/$9.99CAN
Almost Dead	0-8217-7579-0	$7.99US/$10.99CAN
Born to Die	1-4201-0278-8	$7.99US/$9.99CAN
Chosen to Die	1-4201-0277-X	$7.99US/$10.99CAN
Cold Blooded	1-4201-2581-8	$7.99US/$8.99CAN
Deep Freeze	0-8217-7296-1	$7.99US/$10.99CAN
Devious	1-4201-0275-3	$7.99US/$9.99CAN
Fatal Burn	0-8217-7577-4	$7.99US/$10.99CAN
Final Scream	0-8217-7712-2	$7.99US/$10.99CAN
Hot Blooded	1-4201-0678-3	$7.99US/$9.49CAN
If She Only Knew	1-4201-3241-5	$7.99US/$9.99CAN
Left to Die	1-4201-0276-1	$7.99US/$10.99CAN
Lost Souls	0-8217-7938-9	$7.99US/$10.99CAN
Malice	0-8217-7940-0	$7.99US/$10.99CAN
The Morning After	1-4201-3370-5	$7.99US/$9.99CAN
The Night Before	1-4201-3371-3	$7.99US/$9.99CAN
Ready to Die	1-4201-1851-X	$7.99US/$9.99CAN
Running Scared	1-4201-0182-X	$7.99US/$10.99CAN
See How She Dies	1-4201-2584-2	$7.99US/$8.99CAN
Shiver	0-8217-7578-2	$7.99US/$10.99CAN
Tell Me	1-4201-1854-4	$7.99US/$9.99CAN
Twice Kissed	0-8217-7944-3	$7.99US/$9.99CAN
Unspoken	1-4201-0093-9	$7.99US/$9.99CAN
Whispers	1-4201-5158-4	$7.99US/$9.99CAN
Wicked Game	1-4201-0338-5	$7.99US/$9.99CAN
Wicked Lies	1-4201-0339-3	$7.99US/$9.99CAN
Without Mercy	1-4201-0274-5	$7.99US/$10.99CAN
You Don't Want to Know	1-4201-1853-6	$7.99US/$9.99CAN

Available Wherever Books Are Sold!
Visit our website at **www.kensingtonbooks.com**

Thrilling Suspense from
Beverly Barton

Available Wherever Books Are Sold!

Visit our website at **www.kensingtonbooks.com**